Frozen Betrayal

A Detective Alec Ramsay novel

By Conrad Jones

First Published by Gerricon Books 2013-02-08

Copyright Conrad Jones 2013-02-08

Prologue

A black Volkswagen Transporter turned off the motorway and indicated left at the roundabout. Snowflakes deluged the windscreen and the wipers struggled to clear the icy confetti from the glass. A huge landfill site loomed up on the left, its slopes disguised with seed grass and saplings which were buried beneath a thick blanket of white. Tiny green fingers of grass poked through the snow at the base of the trees. To a passing visitor, the first exit looked like a lay-by bordered by woods but hidden beyond the trees was an access road, which serviced a number of farms. The second exit was the main expressway signposted Warrington, Birchwood; a large town situated between the cities of Liverpool and Manchester. A phone mast sculptured like two angels kissing, towered 91 feet above the busy dual carriageway.

"A bit over the top for a phone mast," the driver, Robert Mills, said gesturing to the angels. He was nervous and agitated. They had hardly spoken a word since leaving the station. It was warm in the cab and he was sweating beneath his body armour.

"Clever way to get planning," the passenger, Mark Samuels, replied. "The tallest sculpture erected in England since Nelson's column, something to be proud of, if you give a shit."

"I don't."

"Me neither but somebody does."

"How do you know crap like that anyway?"

"It's called reading."

"I should try it sometime."

"Might be too late for you."

"I read occasionally."

"Yes I've noticed," Samuels smiled wryly. "You left your Sunday Sport in the mess hall yesterday."

"I didn't buy that."

"No but you read it."

"No one likes a smart arse."

"That saying was made up by a Sunday Sport reader."

The Volkswagen was fitted with snow-chains to help it gain purchase in the snow and the interior was adapted with a Perspex cage to hold prisoners. The clear cage had breathing holes drilled into the top, resembling a giant hamster's home. Metal security grilles separated any prisoners from the officers in the front. The van was clearly marked with the gold 'Brigade Security' logo. Private companies had been brought in by the government as a last ditch attempt to regain control of the streets when the fuel riots began. When the fuel pumps ran dry, chaos reigned and society imploded for a while. The police and the armed forces were swamped by the riots which followed and mercenary security firms were employed to help restore control. Working alongside the police and the military, they had quelled the riots and now there was a fragile peace. Order was returning much slower than the violence had erupted.

"There are fresh tracks in the snow there, Mills." Samuels said as they turned onto the track. He could see several large track vehicles had driven the route recently but one set of tyre marks looked fresher than the others. The snow that piled up on the edge of the road was black and slushy in stark contrast to the powdery white. "What makes you think there is a deal going down here and if you are so sure, why are we the only unit here?" Mark Samuels knew his partner was bent and his behaviour that morning had been edgy. Samuels had a feeling that Mills was up to no good which was no surprise. He'd been told to expect that. The difficult part was how to react to it. If he went along with whatever he was planning without questioning it, it would look suspicious but he couldn't be too awkward and put him off either.

"How long have you been doing this job now?" Robert Mills dodged his passenger's question with a question. He didn't look at Samuels as he spoke and he bit his bottom lip nervously as he thought about his next words. Caution prevented him from blurting out what was really happening. He was under pressure to collect on a deal and the others involved were not the type of men who had patience. If he failed to deliver at the end of the day, he'd be lucky to end up in hospital. A wooden box was a more realistic final destination.

"This is my second year with Brigade," Samuels answered humouring Mills. "I joined straight from the marines, long before the riots began. But I don't see what that has to do with my question. Why are we the only unit here if there's a deal going down?" Mills's arrogance wasn't lost on Samuels. He had been partnered with him for a reason unbeknown to the driver. His nerves were as taut as a drum and despite the dual aircon, sweat trickled down his back in tiny rivulets. "If there's trouble then we need police backup."

"That's the last thing we need," Mills scoffed. "Are you making decent money so far?" Mills asked nervously. The question was loaded with cynicism. He had been sucked deeper and deeper into a quagmire of corruption. His wife had left him when his drinking and gambling addictions had reached critical levels and his basic salary didn't nearly cover their monthly outgoings. The first time he was asked to look the other way, the reward covered his mortgage payments for three months. After that, there simply was no going back. The more he took, the more he was cemented into the corruption. Taking bribes from the city's criminals gave him a buzz that fed his macho ego. He was Robert Mills; he had a gun and a badge and he had gangsters in his pocket. "I don't mean pulling a few hours overtime here and there. I mean 'decent' money."

"That's a strange question?" Samuels frowned although he knew where the conversation was going. Mills was about as subtle as a brick in the teeth. "We're all on the same pay grade. You know how much I earn."

"How much did you pull last month?"

"I'm making three times the money that the marines paid, put that together with the chances of being blown to bits being slim and it's a no-brainer." Samuels wasn't clear exactly where the questions would take them but he played along anyway. Brigade Security paid well. There had been some hairy moments but compared to a tour of Helmand Province, it was a doddle. His wife and family had been on pins during his tour, holding their breath every time the telephone rang in case it was the military calling with bad news. He spent the last night before he was deployed in Afghanistan listening to her sobbing while he felt their unborn baby kicking inside her. As the transporter plane took off the next day, he felt like his heart was being ripped out.

"If you'd have seen the look on my missus's face the day I left for Afghan, you'd understand why I left the marines." The memories cut him. Leaving the marines had been the hardest decision that he'd ever made. "I couldn't put her through that again." He looked out of the window, his eyes looking into the past. "When I came home, Brigade Security were advertising for officers. They were gagging for ex-servicemen so it was the best option."

"There's a lot of your lot on board, I'll give you that, but not all of them are grasping the opportunities in front of their faces." Mills said sarcastically. "The clever ones are though."

"When you've been where we have been, it's easy to be happy with life despite the troubles. I'm paid well and go home to my family every night."

Samuels thought Brigade security would be easy in comparison to the marines. It was at first until the fuel ran dry and the riots began. The problem was that the Brigade had hired in such a rush to inflate its numbers. They simply didn't have time to vet everyone properly. Now it was riddled with corrupt officers, which didn't matter too much when the riots were in full swing as they needed numbers on the ground. Once a fragile peace had been achieved on the streets, they were being scrutinised by the legitimate law enforcement agencies and their multi-billion pound contract was in danger of being revoked. His superiors were desperately trying to expose the corruption within their force and remove it quickly to restore the integrity of the company.

Mills looked at him for a moment, his jaw taught as he spoke. "I can guarantee I'm making ten times more than you are every month." He turned his attention back to the road. A curious motorist looked at them with concern as they passed. Their helmets and black body armour made them look intimidating but that was the idea. The public weren't comfortable with the private firms employed to enforce the peace. At first they were used to secure supermarkets, fuel stations and warehouses in order to free up traditional police officers but as society imploded, their remit widened to patrolling the streets and responding to burglaries and low level crime. They had a bad reputation for hurting suspects on the way to custody and seemed to be above the law when complaints were made. "At least ten times what you take home, probably more." He reinforced the point.

Samuels left the statement about their earnings hanging. He hardly knew the driver and he didn't like him but he knew of him. So did their employers. They needed hard evidence to identify the corrupt officers so that they could remove them from their employ, prosecute them and restore their credibility. The corruption was like a cancer spreading through the ranks and it needed to be surgically removed. Robert Mills was at the top of the list.

The van moved slowly from the main road. The track was bumpy and the driver pulled the vehicle to a halt. He looked around nervously and patted the steering wheel with shaking hands. "Look, Samuels," he sighed. "We don't usually team up together do we?"

"No, why does that matter?" Samuels could tell there was something fishy coming his way. His employers had briefed him that it probably would but they also warned him that Mills may become suspicious when the rotas were swapped around.

"Well let's just say that being partnered with you today was a little inconvenient."

"If you think I requested being paired with you, then you are way off. I prefer a quiet life."

"Don't believe everything you hear," Mills laughed sourly.

"I'll make my own mind up at the end of the shift."

"A few of the men think you're all right so we're thinking about letting you in." Mills glanced sideways to gauge his reaction. "We would have asked you sooner or later so teaming up on shift today might be a blessing in disguise."

"What's this, a dating club?" Samuels laughed sarcastically. "I'm on the other bus, mate."

"Witty," Mills said with a straight face. "Let's say that me and some of the other lads have a little sideline going." He looked Samuels up and down, sizing up his partner's reaction with more detail this time. Once he had spilled the beans, there would be no cleaning them up. If Samuels wouldn't come onside then he would become an issue and issues were dangerous.

"What kind of little 'sideline' are you talking about?" Samuels twisted in his seat. He was uncomfortable and he had an idea what was coming. His superiors had encouraged him to wear a wire but he'd refused at first. They were too easy to detect and he didn't want to be unearthed as an informant before all the rogue officers were safely behind bars. He had a wife and three children to think about. He'd seen enough complaints and internal investigations brushed under the carpet to trust the system. Two months before, one of his superiors resigned suddenly after the death of his parents in a car crash. They'd been forced off the road by another vehicle which was never traced. Rumour had it that he was about to suspend two officers suspected of planting drugs on a prisoner. He resigned and the charges went away. Mark knew what they were capable of and he didn't want their attention being turned on to his family but eventually, he caved in and agreed to the wire. His employers convinced him that it was the only way to nail Mills and they assured him that as soon as he had damning evidence on tape, Mills would be handed over to the police and his family would be relocated until he was sentenced and out of harm's way. Mark wasn't happy about it but the long term career prospects the mission would bring were too good to pass up.

"Let's say you play along for now and then I fill you in on the details later," Mills shrugged. He waited for a response but none came. "Let's hope they're already here. I need you to act as backup, that's all I need you to do." The driver turned away biting his lip again. He switched the radio off and guided the Volkswagen along the road through the trees. Sycamores and oaks were interspersed with silver beech trees, their branches bare and weighted down with snow, their twigs dangling like bony fingers with icicle fingernails. The track was pitted with deep potholes and the vehicle rocked violently as it trundled along. "All you have to do is watch my back, you'll get the gist of it as we go along."

"Stop here a minute," Samuels raised a gloved hand. "What are you talking about?" The vehicle jerked and slid slightly on the snow as it stopped. "I don't want to get involved in anything dodgy." He decided to play it coy. Going along with it without any explanation may seem suspicious. Although he had no idea what he was being asked to do, he wanted as much information as he could glean first. He had to let Mills incriminate himself on tape. "What exactly will you be doing while I watch your back?"

The driver put the handbrake on and stared out of the window. The track ran along the embankment above the M62, which linked Liverpool with the North East and the traffic was moving freely in both directions. He took a deep breath before speaking. "There's a lot of wheeling and dealing going on and the motorways are virtually un-policed at the moment. People are making the most of a bad situation, should we say." Mills shrugged again. "Smuggling is big business at the moment."

"So you're smuggling?"

"Not us."

"So what have you got to do with it?"

"Well, we're just taking a bit of a backhander to turn the other way when some of the trading is going on."

"I'm thinking that we aren't talking about plasma screen televisions or electric kettles here are we?"

"Sometimes it might be tobacco, other times its red diesel, on the odd occasion we don't know what it is and we just take a cut." Mills skirted the details and shrugged his shoulders.

"Drugs?" Samuels asked bluntly.

"Sometimes it might be, who knows?" the driver smiled but there was no warmth in his smile. It was snake like. "There's big money in it and we have nothing to do with it apart from not being in the right place at the wrong time, if you know what I mean. We turn a blind eye and ensure that there are no patrols in the area."

"I know exactly what you mean." Samuels removed his protective helmet. "I lost some good friends clearing poppy fields in Afghanistan. They were real soldiers, not wannabes like some of this bunch." He had no time for some of the Brigade men. Some of them were ex-military but some of them were idiots desperate to be soldiers but without the gumption to sign up. There had been rumours that some of the Brigade men were involved with the drug trade but turning a blind eye to it wasn't enough to convict any of them. If he was going to take evidence back to his superiors, then he needed more than that. "There were a few wide-boys over there from an Australian regiment, who thought they could make a few quid from the Taliban by not being in the right place at the right time, as you said. They ended up in a ditch with their throats cut. I don't want any part of it, understand?"

The driver nodded slowly and looked out of the window again. He sighed as he thought about his next move. "You are obviously a man of morals and I respect that." Mills paused and lowered his voice. "But that makes things difficult for me because I'm meeting some of my clients today to pick up some cash. I have to do it today. There are no drugs involved today. I'm just picking up cash."

Samuels thought about it carefully. "You are picking up money down here?" He pointed down the track. He weighed up the pros and cons of witnessing a bribe being handed over. It was damning evidence but the dangers were blindingly obvious. If something went wrong and he was found wearing a wire, he was toast.

"Yes," Mills said. "If the money was just for me and you have a problem with it then I would leave it but some of the lads need the money today. Times are hard and I don't want to piss them off. All I am doing is picking up an envelope full of money. It will take me two minutes, that's all."

"Like I said, I don't want anything to do with it," Samuels shook his head. He had to make it convincing that he didn't want to go along. "Drop me off here and pick me up when you've finished fucking about."

"It's freezing out there, you won't have anything to do with it, Samuels," Mills persuaded. "I'll put the envelope into my flack-jacket, job done. You didn't see anything and you didn't take anything. All I need you to do is sit in the van and act as backup, that's it." Mills looked distracted by something in the wing mirror. He banged his gloved hand on the dashboard. "Shit!"

Samuels checked his mirror. He could hear a diesel engine approaching from the rear and the sloshing sound of tyres in the slush. "It's a traffic patrol." He sucked in his breath.

"Bollocks!" Mills hissed. "Leave this to me, we're cool aren't we?" He asked in a panic. The patrol car pulled alongside them next to Samuels's passenger door. "Are we cool?" Samuels saw fear in Mills's eyes. He had seen fear in the eyes of young marines and in the eyes of captured insurgents. Frightened men are unpredictable and he didn't like unpredictable.

"We're cool for now," he said as he dropped the passenger window to speak to the uniformed police officers.

The driver of the patrol car did likewise and he nodded a silent greeting although there was no friendship in the gesture. He looked at Samuels suspiciously. The battle-lines were drawn months ago. The conventional police had no respect for the private companies which they nicknamed 'plastics'. "You okay?" the officer grunted.

"Yes thanks, we're fine," Samuels smiled thinly. "What are you boys up to?" He asked.

"I was going to ask you the same question?" the police officer replied sternly. "What are you doing down here?"

Samuels glanced at the officer and turned to his partner. "He thought he saw someone broken down as we came around the roundabout but it turned out to be someone heading down the farm track. We wondered what they were up to."

"Sounds like bullshit to me," the policeman grunted. "There's nothing but farms down there."

"So they were heading to one of the farms. What's the problem?" His colleague shouted across the van. "Are you worried you might miss something?"

"You are the problem," the officer shouted back. "Plastic coppers playing at being real policemen. You're amateurs. That's the problem. We stopped to see if you were lost, broken down or just skiving. It looks a bit suspect two grown men parked up in a country lane but I wouldn't put anything past you lot."

"Haven't you got any speeding tickets to issue?" Samuels retorted. Half of him wanted to tell them what was happening but the other half knew he needed more evidence. "Thanks for your concern but we can manage without any interference from a couple of retarded dinosaurs, thanks and get lost, officer." Samuels shut the window and glared through the glass at the red faced policeman. He wanted rid of them quickly. Being abusive was the easiest way to do it. He didn't need to be able to lip read to understand what was said as the police patrol reversed away. The patrol car wheel spinned as it reversed toward the roundabout. Snow, grit and mud pinged off the Volkswagen as the police car sped away.

"Thanks for that," Mills smiled, relief on his face. "You got rid of them in a hurry." He stuck out his right hand. "Call me Bobby, everyone else does."

Mark hesitated and then shook the extended hand and followed the police car in his mirror. "Listen, Mills," he squeezed his hand firmly. "Just because I fobbed the police off doesn't mean we're on first name terms or swapping spit, understand?" Samuels felt his blood pressure rising. "Whatever you have got going on, is your business. They are the reason why I do not want to know." He gestured to the traffic cops. They had parked on the tarmac verge overlooking the motorway. "But if I get out of the van now while you drive on to meet your 'clients' they will wonder what the fuck is going on so let's get this done quickly and without being mithered by the police, okay?"

"Okay," Mills nodded eagerly. "I'll sort you out, no problem. I know you don't want any part of it but a favour is a favour and I owe you one." He slid the Volkswagen into first gear and the van moved forward slowly.

Twenty yards on, the track veered left and Samuels lost sight of the patrol car and the roundabout. There was nothing in the wing-mirror but snow and trees. "You don't owe me anything, let's get this done." The track weaved on through the trees and the van rocked annoyingly as it travelled. The two men kept a tense silence between them. Mark Samuels wasn't happy with his colleagues taking bribes on principle. Being party to it was worse but if it helped to take them out of circulation, then he was willing to see it through. The loyalty that he felt to his brother soldiers in the marines wasn't here in Brigade Security. He owed Mills nothing and he wanted nothing in return. If he offered to slip him a few hundred quid after their shift, then he would refuse to take it and he could add it to his report. Mills was scum and he needed locking up. They travelled in silence for ten minutes before they spotted a vehicle.

"There." Mills pointed to a black Range Rover, which was parked off the track next to a five-bar gate. A hawthorn hedgerow had been transformed into a thick white wall by the snow. The vehicle was occupied. The windows were steamed up and the driver wiped the glass as they approached. "This is a decent pick-up, Samuels." He said nervously. "Do you have any idea how much are we asking for this time?"

"I don't want to know," Samuels said as the vehicle pulled over.

"After that patrol car pulling in to the lay-by, I'd better tell them not to leave that way." Mills laughed. "I think we're due a bonus for that don't you?"

"Don't push me too far," Samuels warned. "There is no 'we' here, I've told you that. If you're picking up a pay off here, don't mess it up but leave me out of it."

"You worry too much."

"That's because I've spent all day in this van with you."

"Do you ever stop moaning?"

"Just be careful." Samuels shifted uncomfortably in his seat. His partner didn't know the meaning of careful. He had a reputation for becoming volatile and aggressive with suspects. His briefing had warned him to be careful around Robert Mills. He was a dangerous man. "There is a driver and two passengers, one front and one back." Samuels said. Communicating the position and number of possible insurgents on his tour of Afghanistan was like second nature to him. His army training was instinct to him. Although he wanted Mills arrested and jailed, he needed this bribe to go off without any dramas. Being a stool pigeon was one thing, but getting shot in the process was not part of the gig.

"Relax." Mills turned off the engine and watched the men in the Range Rover. They looked back nervously. "We've done this plenty of times before. They hand me an envelope, we shake hands and they tell me the time and the places where they would appreciate us not being next week, easy."

"Just get it done." Samuels opened the passenger door and climbed down into the snow. The wind was biting where it touched bare flesh. He lowered the window and rested his elbows through it. The door acted as a shield both from the wind and any stray bullets, not that he was expecting any shooting. It was habit. It also hid his hands from the men in the Range Rover. The snow squeaked beneath his combat boots as he shifted his weight to a position where he could draw his weapon in a hurry. Mills smiled and walked down the track toward the black vehicle. Samuels watched the men talking amongst themselves as Mills approached them. The hairs on the back of his neck tingled as they eyed his partner. Something felt wrong. He knew it instinctively. The passenger in the back seat appeared to be reaching for something. Samuels wanted to shout a warning but it was too late. Mills was too close to the vehicle. He could be misreading the situation and a sudden shout could become a spark, which would ignite the fumes. All he had to do was get Mills on tape and witness the handover but he had a feeling that it was going to go sour. If the men in the Range Rover were gunning for Mills, they weren't likely to let any witnesses live. Instinct took over.

Samuels slipped off a glove and reached for his gun. The Heckler & Koch P30 was loaded with a fifteen 9mm round magazine. His fingers touched the cold weapon and he slid it from its holster smoothly without signalling his actions to the men. The rear passenger lowered his window and moved across the bench seat behind the driver. If Samuels drew his weapon into view, there would be a gunfight. If he didn't and the men in the Range Rover shot first, Robert Mills was a dead man. For now, he had to take that chance. He listened intently as Mills neared them.

"Officer Mills!" The man in the back seat beamed, "fancy meeting you here." He laughed sarcastically, eyeing Samuels suspiciously. A gold tooth glinted when he smiled and there was a tribal tattoo behind his right ear. Samuels couldn't see his hair beneath his white beanie hat but it looked like his head was shaven. He leaned his head and shoulder out of the back window and pointed toward the Brigade vehicle. "Who is that, Mills?" His expression changed as he eyed Samuels. "You know I don't like strangers." He coughed up phlegm and spat it into the snow.

"He's all right, Youngy." Mills answered flatly their voices kept low but the tension in them was audible. He didn't react to the comedy hello, and he wasn't reacting to him spitting in his direction either. He peered into the front of the Range Rover. "Who are they, new boys?"

"Touché, officer Mills."

"They're not the usual muppets that you bring around with you."

"Cheeky bastard."

Samuels listened to the exchange, unimpressed with his colleague's temperament. He was jousting with dangerous drug dealers. He had heard the name, 'Youngy', before. He'd heard it in briefings from the Drug Squad. Steven Young or Youngy was a key player in the city's drug supply chain and he was wanted for numerous gangland murders but there was never enough evidence against him and witnesses had a habit of disappearing.

"I guess we both choose who we work with. Have you got the money?" Mills grunted and nodded towards the back of the vehicle. "Have you got any sweeteners in there for me?"

Samuels watched intently as Mills moved closer to the vehicle. He showed no emotion on his face. "Don't show off and get all cocky in front of your new boy, Mills," Young frowned as he spoke.

Samuels was close enough to see the ice in his blue eyes. He was cold inside; cold and dangerous. There was something else there too. His eyes were darting about between the men in the front and Mills. He was nervous. Samuels decided that this was no ordinary pay off. He couldn't just be a spectator, whether he liked it or not. Robert Mills had no military training prior to joining Brigade Security. He was from the security industry in the days before the riots. Samuels's time in the Marines had educated him enough to know when a situation smelt bad, felt bad and was about to turn bad. There was something wrong with this meeting. He was ready to react.

"You're out of order, Mills." The dealer snarled. "You need to show a little respect."

"Whatever Young." Mills walked past the rear passenger window and looked into the back of the vehicle. It was empty apart from two five litre drums of petrol. The fuel drought had made people cautious and many carried spare containers in case the pumps dried up again. "Listen, there's a patrol car on the motorway exit. If I was you, I'd follow the track that way as far as it goes. It brings you out near Irlam eventually. Where's the money?"

"I have got some money but it's not as much as you wanted I'm afraid." Young feigned a disappointed smile. "From what I'm hearing, you lot won't be around much longer, which means you're not as much of an asset as you were. Sorry but business is business."

"That's disappointing." Mills returned to the passenger window. "We had a deal." The driver burst out laughing and the front passenger joined in but his expression told Samuels that he didn't think that it was funny. He looked edgy and uncomfortable. The men in the front had their hair cropped close to their scalp and there were pus-filled spots on the back of the driver's neck. "You two want to lay off the Sustanon." Mills ducked to look them in the eyes. "It gives you acne and makes your balls shrivel up." He held up his forefinger and thumb. "It will make your cock smaller than it is already. That's why you started taking steroids, right?" Mills asked seriously. "Small cock syndrome?"

Steven Young laughed as his minders turned purple with rage. He slapped his thigh with the palm of his hand. "You're a funny man, Mills lad!"

"Not as funny as you bringing a couple of meatheads to protect you." Mills looked at the minders again. "What are they going to do if it kicks off, lift me up and down like a dumbbell?"

"We've heard enough!" The passenger moaned. He reached into the glove box for something. Samuels didn't know what it was but he guessed it wasn't a sandwich. The driver shouted a command amongst the torrent of abuse but his words were lost on Samuels. He opened the door to climb out, reached inside his jacket and held something out. Samuels couldn't see what it was; his view was blocked by his colleague. He raised the P30 but he couldn't get a clean shot. He ran around the open door of the Volkswagen and zigzagged through the deep snow toward the other vehicle. He saw Mills take something from his utility belt and watched the driver grab his eyes and crumple to the floor of the foot well screaming abuse. Saliva dribbled from his chin as he rocked backwards. He banged his head painfully on the gear stick. In the confined space of the Range Rover, the CS gas was inescapable. Steven Young and the passenger writhed in their seats as Mills continued to spray the gas. When he was sure that Steven Young was neutralised, he stopped for a second to give the driver a second blast of the debilitating gas in the face.

"That's enough, Mills," Samuels shouted, as he approached. "Check the vehicle for weapons." His military training kicked in, taking control of the situation was critical. "The passenger reached for something. There is no way they have come here unarmed." The snow crunched beneath his boots as he ran. Mills opened the rear door and reached inside.

"Look at this!" He lifted a nine millimetre Uzi in the air. "Is this your machine gun? You could get five years for carrying this, now where is the money, Young?" He struck the dealer across the elbow with the machinegun. There was an audible crack as the elbow joint was splintered by the impact and Mill gave him another blast of burning gas in the face. "Where is it?"

"My arm, you twat!"

"I'll break every bone in your body if you don't hand over the cash."

"You're dead when you go down," Young wailed. His voice was thick with mucus. His words were barely understandable. "You have no idea who you're fucking with this time!"

"I'm messing with a dribbling idiot at the moment. Last chance, where's the cash?" Mills shouted. He grabbed his feet and pulled him across the seat and out of the Range Rover. Young landed heavily on the back of his neck. The snow cushioned the fall slightly but there was a sickening thud as he landed. "Where is the money that you owe me?"

"Fuck off," Young gurgled. He clutched his eyes as the burning gas stung them and his nostrils felt like they were full of acid. Mills gripped the injured arm and twisted it violently. The elbow cracked again and the dealer's body shook with spasms as the pain reached his brain. "Okay, okay!" The wailing reached a new high. The sound of his agony carried on the wind across the acres of snow covered fields.

"Where is it?"

"My back pocket, go on take it because when you do, you're fucked," Young burbled. The meaning was lost on Robert Mills. "I'm going to kill you, you bastard!" He hissed. A string of mucus hung from his nose and his face was covered in deep red blotches.

"Whatever." Mills turned him over roughly and searched the pockets of his jeans. He pulled out a thick brown envelope and ripped it open. He looked at the contents and his face darkened. "Cover him for a minute." He shouted to Samuels. "Do you think I'm an idiot, Young?"

"Ha, fuck you, arsehole." The dealer gurgled. He laughed despite the pain. "You've touched the money, game over you fucked up this time, Mills lad."

"Shut up, you prick," Mills hissed. He kicked the dealer in the stomach and saliva sprayed from his lips. "This is short. Where is the money?"

"Robert Mills, you're under arrest," the driver of the Range Rover struggled to speak. He reached up and showed them what he'd pulled from his pocket earlier. Seconds before Robert Mills deployed his gas he'd reached into his pocket and pulled out his badge.

"Ha ha ha ha!" Young howled. He rolled in the snow, laughing like a lunatic. "You're going down, sunshine and when you do, I'll be waiting."

"I've told you to shut up!" Mills looked closely at the driver's badge. It looked real enough. He snatched it from his hand. "Where did you get that?"

"Drug Squad, you're under arrest." The driver struggled to his feet, although he could hardly breathe.

"They're coppers, you prick!" Young coughed the words. "You're fucking nicked, ha ha!"

Samuels went around the vehicle and opened the passenger door, covering the injured man with his pistol. The man reached inside his coat and removed an identity card. "They're real ID cards," Samuels shouted across the vehicle. "They are Drug Squad." He felt relieved that they were police officers. It took the pressure of him. Robert Mills had been the victim of a sting operation from two sides, one from his employers and the other from the law. He grabbed the disabled officer's arm and lifted him back into his seat.

"Here use this," he gave him a tissue.

"Thanks," the Drug Squad officer slurred. "We'll have to take you in too."

"I understand," Samuels nodded and stepped back from the door to let him climb out.

Before he could say anything else, Mills aimed the Uzi into the front of the vehicle and squeezed the trigger. The machine gun kicked violently as it unleashed its deadly load of white hot nine millimetre bullets. The sound of automatic gunfire echoed across the fields frightening a flock of starlings into flight. The driver and his colleague were hit multiple times before the Uzi clicked empty. Blood and viscera splattered across the vinyl roof and grey brain matter sprayed the remaining windows and dribbled down the glass in rivulets of pinkish goo. The driver's cheekbone and top lip were ripped off completely exposing his lower teeth in a zombie smile. Leona Lewis continued to sing about her burning love and in the silence after the gunshots, it seemed apt to Samuels.

"Mills!" Samuels shouted. He dived for cover as bullets ricocheted into the air. When the firing stopped, he ran to the front of the vehicle and looked at the twitching bodies inside. "What the hell have you done?" He whispered under his breath. As he turned to the rogue officer, Robert Mills raised his pistol and fired at him. The bullet smashed into his throat, smashing his larynx and ripping his spinal cord. Samuels felt like he'd been hit by a lightning bolt. Pain flashed through his brain and he dropped like a stone. He was losing consciousness but he heard more shots fired and the drug dealer screamed in agony. He felt the cold seeping through his body as he lay mortally wounded. He thought about his wife and his children as his body became numb and the grey sky turned to the colour of dark slate. He was slipping away but he clung to the hope that the police would have backup and that they would help. He'd seen men survive horrific injuries before and he hoped that he could. His wife and children smiled at him from across the table at The Harvester, chicken nuggets and milkshakes and cookie dough pudding with ice cream. He could smell the sweet aroma of sticky ribs. Then he felt cold again, the stench of petrol choked him. He could taste the burning fuel in his mouth and it stung his eyes. He opened them and tried to blink the pain away. Mills was pouring unleaded from a can. Samuels tried to scream as Mills lit a match. As the flames engulfed him, his lungs were seared by the heat and the flesh on his face, blistered, bubbled and turned black.

 Robert Mills threw the empty Gerry can into the inferno. Sweat poured from beneath his helmet into his eyes. Cold rivulets ran down his back, his heart threatened to burst through his chest. Panic gripped him as he watched the bodies burn. He couldn't see how he could walk away from this one. All he could do was run and then pass the blame onto Mark Samuels and deny any involvement. If he said another dealer shot them and set fire to them before escaping, it would be hard to disprove his version of events. He turned and ran clumsily towards the Volkswagen. The snow made it hard going, his breath came in short bursts and his lungs burned with exertion. He was stopped in his tracks as a thunderous blow hit him in the forehead, knocking him off his feet. There was a blinding flash and then nothing.

Carol Barker looked on at the massacre, petrified by fear. Her hide in the woods gave her the perfect vantage point from which to see the sting in operation. Her camera had captured everything despite her shaking hands being frozen by shock. Had she stayed put, no one would have known that she'd witnessed the slaughter.

CHAPTER 1

42 Beech Close

"I think they're coming back, Daddy," Jodie's top lip quivered as she spoke. The little girl was terrified. "I can hear one of them coughing." She added as she clung to his leg with both arms. "What do they want, Daddy?"

"They're looking for your mummy, I think. I can hear them too, Munchkin," he ruffled her hair gently to calm her. "They can't get in here. Don't be scared, I'll keep you safe." Jodie held onto his thigh as if her life depended on it. To be fair to her, both their lives were hanging in the balance and although she was only six years old, she sensed his fear. "I need you to hide in the attic again, okay." He said peeling her from him. He lifted her up and ran up the stairs to the third floor landing of the townhouse. The folding aluminium ladder, which accessed the converted loft space, was deployed and ready to use. Ged knew they would come back. He grabbed the middle rung and carried his daughter up the steps until he could put her safely into the attic bedroom. "You wait here and don't make a sound okay. When they're gone, I'll whistle. Do not unlock the hatch for anyone else, Jodie, no matter what they say, okay?"

"Okay, hurry up please. It's cold up here, Daddy!" Tears filled her eyes and she bit her bottom lip. She nodded and stepped back from the hatch with her moth-eaten companion, who was affectionately called Monkey, dangling from her left hand. Her father forced a smile and a wink as he pushed up the hatch. His stomach tightened and fear gripped him. He wasn't sure if it was the drugs wearing off that made his hands shake. "Push the bolt, Jodie." He shouted to her through the wood.

"Okay, Daddy." He heard her muffled reply. "Hurry up please!" She whined. Jodie hated the dark but the attic was the safest place for her. He felt sick inside as he stood at the top of the stairs. If they managed to break in this time and anything happened to him, his six-year old daughter was in the attic alone in the dark, with no food and hardly anything to drink. Losing this battle was not an option. He sprinted down the staircase to the second floor landing and grabbed the Mossberg. He had cleaned the barrels earlier that morning. Despite the fact that he knew the shotgun was loaded, he checked it anyway. He was not sure whether it was fear, nerves or a strong will to survive and protect Jodie that made him triple check everything, whatever it was, it had kept them alive so far. He picked up his rucksack and pulled it on to his back. It was crammed full of twelve-gauge cartridges, about thirty in total and the weight of the lead shot was multiplied by the muscle wastage he had suffered since his habit became a real addiction.

If they broke through the shutters and he needed to use more than two shells, then they were in trouble. Time was critical. He'd used two shells the night before and the sight of one of their pack with his hand blown clean off was enough to send the others running. The severed appendage was still lying in the deep snow outside the garage door, a puddle of congealed blood formed beneath it but the latest deluge of snow was already beginning to cover it up. The gunshots were deafening but no one called the police because no one dared to. The private security firms, who were charged with controlling the curfew, were less than useless. The public realised it was better to be a silent witness than become a target for the animals that prowled the inner cities during the dark hours. Nobody wanted to draw attention to their home, turning from witness to victim overnight.

He took the lower stairs two at a time. When he reached the first floor landing, he ran into the front bedroom and peered through the curtains at the deserted Cul-de-sac below. Jodie was right, they were coming back. They'd parked their black Chrysler at the end of the close. This time, there were more of them. He counted five. There was no way of telling their age or gender because of the thick clothing that they were wearing. The daytime temperature hadn't climbed above minus five for nearly a week and at night time, it plummeted much lower. They looked like scavengers from a post apocalypse movie, wrapped up in thick clothing, gloves, hats and balaclavas. They could have been the teenage children of people he once knew. They might be the offspring of neighbours or friends. Who knows? It really didn't matter any more. He owed them money and they wanted it. They also wanted to know where his wife Carol and their daughter were, badly enough to kill him if he wouldn't cooperate.

He had been trying to keep a diary to document what was happening to them but his entries were sporadic at best and the drugs made him ramble sometimes. Carol was adamant that he documented each day in detail. He persevered with it because he thought that one day it may make sense to someone who remembered these dark times. The heroin made the days blur into one. He wasn't sure where or when it all started. He didn't think anyone did know the truth. Not the real truth. If they did, surely they would have done something about it. When the riots began, civilisation collapsed. The gangs were in control for months and now that the government had reorganised, the criminals clung to the anarchy tenaciously. Things in the city centres were returning to some kind of normality but they had control of the suburban streets after dark and their numbers were growing week by week. Their grip was insidious and their poison was seeping through the remnants of society from the hardcore addicts on park benches up to the boardrooms of the world's richest businessmen. The troubles had made it worse; society had crumbled for a while. In comparison to the speed at which anarchy descended, the restoration of order was a slow process.

Ged wasn't sure what normal was any more. He didn't remember his life before drugs. It was like they had always been there. He remembered his first puff on a joint, which was years ago when he was at school. It seemed so harmless. How could smoking a bit of weed with the older kids have become such a big deal? Could he have stopped then? If he had known then where it would lead him, would he have chosen a different path in life? He thought he would. He liked to think that he would have but would he actually have had the strength of character to break away from the friends, whose social life revolved around drugs? Back then, he was Ged Barker, one of the boys. Could he have been Ged Barker the career man without the drugs, who knows? If he had, he would never have met Jodie's mother, Carol.

They met when she was researching the casual use of heroin for an article, which she was writing. The mutual attraction was instant and something inside her made her think that she could rescue him from his habit. She convinced him that it was just a habit, not an addiction. Carol was the one shining light in his dark life and he had to keep her whereabouts secret. He couldn't let them know where she was, no matter what happened. She wouldn't tell him why she went into hiding; she said she couldn't but she couldn't take Jodie either. She said she would explain everything soon and they could all go away together. That was three months ago. Since then, his habit was consuming him. Ged justified it to himself by blaming the drugs on the stress he was under. If he had given up the drugs when he was young, he wouldn't have met her and Jodie would never have been born. He wouldn't change that for the world. She was his world. After Carol's vanishing act, Jodie became his only focus in life, apart from drugs of course.

It was all such a mess and he wasn't sure when it all went wrong. What he did know for a fact, was that in the space of three months, the world he knew disappeared to be replaced by an unrecognisable nightmare. The weather men banged on about climate change and global warming all the time. The last few summers were dull and the last few winters were severe. Last Christmas it got worse all of a sudden, and after the summer when the rains started, they never stopped. Floods blighted the country and then the rain turned into bitter winter weather, suited more to the Antarctic than Europe. To compound the freak conditions, tension between Israel and Iran increased and as the world imposed tighter sanctions, Iran slowed its oil production and refused to sell it to the West. America flexed its military muscles but no one was prepared to endure yet another invasion of Muslim land. All its exports went to China and India. Oil stopped flowing to Europe and so prices soared.

Limited supplies caused panic buying and before the petrol stations ran dry, transportation almost stopped completely. He remembered seeing a clip on the six o'clock news where a man was beaten to death at an Esso garage because he filled up four plastic containers as well as his petrol tank, his greed infuriating the desperate drivers behind him to the point of violence. The same day a woman in Waitrose was stabbed over the last few bottles of mineral water that had been left on the shelf. It was just the start. Armed police escorted deliveries of food to supermarkets, their contents worth more than gold.

Petrol was rationed, the emergency services came first and then the supermarkets were given priority for deliveries but their shelves were nearly empty and small businesses shut down overnight. Riots and looting began in London and within days, they spread across the entire country, mirrored by the same unrest in Germany and France. The Spanish economy crashed along with the Italian and the Greek banks. The European community was in disarray as rioting spread rapidly across the Western World. There was a domino effect as the crashing money markets engulfed the American and Japanese financial institutions.

Despite their own oilfields, the Americans suffered the same discontent; their gun culture intensified the violence on the streets. Depleted police forces couldn't contain the riots as they lost hundreds of officers to the violence. The armed forces were mobilised but their numbers dwindled as desertion took a hold. Young soldiers picked returning home to protect their families from the rioters as their priority. International trade ground to a halt. Society as he knew it disintegrated for a while. It felt like years but in reality it was less than three months before the fighting calmed down. Twelve months on, things were stabilising internationally but life on the streets of the suburbs was anarchic. The electricity supply had returned but it still went off sporadically for a few hours at a time. In the midst of all the chaos, Carol carried on reporting the news to the masses, until she disappeared.

Their voices snapped him back from his thoughts. Ged looked through the curtains and watched them approaching the house. They made no attempt to hide or keep quiet. He could hear them laughing as they walked across the snow covered lawn. One of them had a bad cough. It was his coughing which alerted Jodie to their return. He stopped and kicked at the severed hand with his boot. Someone made a joke of it and the gang laughed raucously. The cougher picked up the hand and bent the fingers so that the middle digit was raised and he flicked it to his friends. Enjoying the reaction from his posse, he manipulated the fingers into a V-sign and repeated the abusive gesture. They loved it when he stuck the index finger up his nose and twisted the hand around to remove a thick green bogey. He licked the gooey lump off the dead finger and chewed it while his friends feigned disgust behind their laughter. The fact that the hand was once attached to one of their friends seemed unimportant to them. As he watched them, Ged couldn't fathom what was important any more. Tired of the clowning around, one of them pointed to the window from where he watched them. The gang stopped laughing and five sets of eyes glared at the house.

He pulled the curtain across as if the thin fabric would make him invisible but they had seen him. They knew he was in there. The ground floor windows were protected with metal security blinds, which could concertina when the occupier needed to open the window. Ged bought them from B&Q, fitting them before the troubles started and the shuttering had worked to keep them out so far. Ged's nerves were on a knife edge as the effects of the heroin waned. The receptors in his brain were beginning to prick him. He needed a hit. Shivers ran through him and he pulled his black fleece hoody tightly around him as his thoughts drifted to the previous day.

"What are you doing, Dad?" Jodie had called to him. Things were confusing enough for him but for a six year old girl, it was incomprehensible. Her face looked urchin like, covered in dirt and dust. Ged had been sparked out on the couch. The heroin and a lack of proper sleep left him weak and disorientated. She had been playing in the cellar because it was freezing outside and Carol made him promise that Jodie's presence at the house was kept secret. Her blond hair looked lank and greasy but he couldn't let her wash it until the power came back on. It had been off for three hours already.

"Hey, gorgeous," he ruffled Jodie's hair. "Come here and give me a kiss." His voice was thick with sleep and phlegm. When he moved his arms, he could smell his own body odour. He'd collected a stash of various deodorants and aftershaves from nearby shops when they were available but they were just masking the smell of his sweat. He needed to move and keep Jodie safe but he wanted to be sure that when they travelled, they were unobserved. If he screwed up and the cold didn't kill them, the dealers would. Jodie squeezed him tightly, despite his body odour. He guessed what they say about

unconditional love from your child is true although he thought he was pushing it to the limit.

"Are you hungry, Munchkin?" He kept asking her that, even though he knew the answer only too well. Jodie was losing weight every day and he could feel her ribs sticking out. He was feeling weaker as the weeks went by. His muscle mass was shrinking and his clothes were hanging lose. They were close to running out of tinned food now, so he rationed it to one tin a day each. Their diet consisted of soups, beans, custard, rice pudding and various tinned fish. They were not about to starve to death but he needed to find a safe haven, until Carol made contact. Considering how young Jodie was, she hadn't moaned once. "Are you very hungry?"

Jodie raised her eyes to the sky in response to his stupid question. "Yes, Daddy, I'm hungry but we've already eaten today." She put her arms around his neck and squeezed tightly. "We only have a few tins left." Sometimes, he was not sure who was looking after whom.

"Well, I think we can eat again because we need to make a move in the next few days, so we'll need all our strength." He'd smiled to soften the blow. Jodie was terrified of going outside. If he was honest, he was terrified of going outside. "We need to go to the city centre which will take us about thirty minutes to drive and then we are going to stay with some friends for a few days and they might have news about mummy."

They were going to leave the day before yesterday, but Jodie was sick that morning and he thought the worst but it was just a tummy bug. Their mishmash diet had given her the trots. He gave her some Imodium in her beans earlier that day. He thought she hadn't noticed until she asked him, "What medicine have you crushed in my beans, Daddy?"

"You might be six but you have your mother's brains."

"I think you are tricking me, Daddy," Jodie wagged her finger at him.

"Tricking you to take medicine is a good thing."

"Not about my beans, about mummy."

"What do you mean, darling?"

"Mummy would have rung us if she was okay." Her bottom lip quivered and he could see that she was trying hard not to cry. "Lots have people have died, Daddy. The man on the news said so."

He'd held her tightly and her sobbing broke. She hadn't cried for weeks. He guessed it was going to break sometime. He felt her warm tears on his neck and the lump in his throat told him that he wasn't far away from breaking himself. Not in front of her, no way. He had to be strong for his daughter. "Now listen to me." He whispered. "Mummy rang before the phones went off didn't she?"

"Yes," Jodie sobbed and wiped her snotty nose with the back of her hand. "But she hasn't called for a long time."

"That is because the telephones aren't working, Munchkin." He peeled her away from his neck to look into her eyes. "Daddy's mobile hasn't worked for weeks. Mummy will have called my mobile and realised that it is not connected." He'd wondered why she hadn't called or text, despite the fact that she said she couldn't.

"But what about the other telephone?" Jodie sobbed. "Why hasn't she called that one?"

"That is the landline, darling." He smiled and tried to keep his voice calm. Inside, he was struggling to explain anything. "Our landline is broken, baby." He couldn't explain that it had been cut off because he spent what little money they had on his drugs. The utility companies were reeling from the price of oil and their tolerance of late payments was zero.

"I know but when will they fix it?" She cried freely. "Mummy won't know where we are, daddy." She buried her head into his neck and sobs wracked her body. "She'll be all alone."

"No, Jodie," he told her. He tried to be as solid in his conviction as he could be under the circumstances. "She is safe in the hospital. She told us not to go there, remember?"

"Why though, Daddy?" Jodie wiped dribble from her chin. "Why did she make you promise not to go there?" Her tears were making clean streaks on her face.

"Mummy was having treatment, you know that." He lied and kissed her forehead. "She loves you and she misses you, and she doesn't want us to get sick. That's why she said we couldn't go there. Do you understand?" He felt his eyes filling with tears and he couldn't fight them any more. They spilled over and ran down his cheeks, mingling with Jodie's. She pulled away and looked at him.

"Don't cry, Daddy." She kissed his cheek and it made him worse. He tried hard not to break down. She wiped a tear from his cheek and looked at the wetness on her fingers curiously. "When can we see mummy?"

"Well," he swallowed hard, fighting the tears back, "I think that we should go to the city centre and see what the soldiers say. If they say things are getting better, we'll take the car and drive to the hospital, okay?"

"Is that where Mummy is?" Jodie's eyes lit up and her smile broke his heart. "Are you sure she won't come home to look for us?" Jodie sniffed and used her sleeve to stem the snot that accompanied her tears. "Will they have quorn in the hospital for mummy to eat?"

"They will have tons of it, Munchkin," he lied. Carol was a vegetarian. She lived on quorn even though Jodie and Ged loathed the stuff.

That was when they had come knocking for the first time. Fear shook him from his memories of the previous day as loud banging echoed up the stairs for the second time in two days. This time it wasn't a memory, it was real knocking, urgent, violent knocking. He gripped the shotgun and headed down the stairs. He thought about his daughter in the attic bedroom and tears formed in his eyes, blurring his vision. He felt weak and his hands were trembling. This time, he didn't know if he would be able to fight them off.

CHAPTER 2

Silver Lane

Kathy stared at the gruesome scene in front of her. The vehicle was almost unrecognisable as a Range Rover. The fire had destroyed the tyres, lowering the vehicle drastically and the interior was nothing more than charred cinders. The charcoaled remains of three bodies lay at peculiar angles inside the vehicle. Smoke tinged with hues of blue and grey drifted from the blackened bodies into the cold air. A fourth body smouldered in the deep snow a few metres away; too far away to have been consumed by the same fire which had engulfed the four by four and its occupants. A fifth body lay face down in the snow fifty yards away untouched by fire, shot through the helmet by what looked like a high velocity bullet. The smell of burnt rubber mixed with the sweeter smell of burnt human flesh. It reminded her of the smell of a pork roast left in the oven too long. There were many questions to answer about the position of the dead and the causes of their violent demise but she was an expert in deciphering such conundrums. This was no road traffic accident. The vehicle was parked in an isolated spot on a farm access road, miles from the main arterial routes which surrounded the nearby town. As she analysed the scene for the first time, she knew that it was going to be a long, cold day.

"First impressions?" the familiar voice of a senior officer interrupted her thoughts. She worked for three forces which meant that she had several taskmasters at once. Merseyside, Cheshire and Greater Manchester Police were all reliant on her department. Bishop was a man that took some getting used to. His voice reminded her of a teacher she studied with at university. His words crisp and sharp and his accent gave away nothing of where he was from but it indicated a generic public school education. His boots squeaked in the snow as he approached her. Detective Superintendent Bishop was a stern faced man with an abrupt, sometimes arrogant manner. He looked like he was about to climb Everest in his winter gear. He banged his Gortex gloves together as he surveyed the carnage.

"Do you want me to give you my best guess?" she shrugged without taking her eyes from the scene. "You know that I won't speculate."

"I'd just like your first impressions, that's all," his breath made plumes in the icy air as he spoke.

"I think we are looking at a multiple murder scene where the killer or killers have tried to destroy any evidence by torching the bodies. All except that one," she smiled thinly. A police cadet could have assumed as much. Kathy had been investigating crime scenes long enough to know that anything she speculated on could be twisted and thrown in her face later on. It was the story of her life so far. No matter how hard she tried to please, people were never satisfied. Although she was an attractive, intelligent woman, her string of previous lovers never deemed it enough to stick around. Her career was demanding and nobody thus far was prepared to play second fiddle to it.

"Thanks for nothing," Bishop gritted his teeth. "I'd worked that out for myself."

"Ask a stupid question."

"I didn't think it was a stupid question."

"Who called it in?" Kathy changed the subject. The scene was chaotic and no one seemed to know who was first on the scene.

"I'm not certain yet," he mumbled. "A traffic patrol was parked near the motorway," Bishop nodded towards the direction of the junction. "They heard gunfire and drove down to investigate."

"That is a Brigade Security uniform," Kathy pointed to the only body untouched by fire. "Did they see a Brigade vehicle?"

"I haven't debriefed the officers yet," Bishop lied. "There is obviously no sign of any vehicle here now, is there?"

"Well he didn't parachute in. There are two sets of footprints leading from the bend in the road there and vehicle tracks heading towards Irlam that way?" She made her statement sound like a question and left it hanging.

"I think there is more to this than meets the eye, Kathy."

"Oh, I've got that impression already, Superintendent," she scoffed trying to keep the cynicism out of her voice but failing miserably. "Is there anything that you want to tell me before I begin my analysis?"

"I don't want to cloud your view of things but we believe that two of those bodies are undercover officers from the Drugs Squad," he lowered his voice as he spoke to prevent curious ears from hearing. Crime scene officers were milling around waiting for Kathy to allocate their roles in the search for evidence. White suits covered their winter wear. They made a path from the track to the scene using yellow tape as the borders to protect any evidence which was left in the snow.

"Why would you believe that two of your officers are here unless you know for a fact that they're missing?" She wasn't known for beating around the bush. "You don't misplace two detectives."

"Okay, we know for a fact that they're missing," he replied curtly. "Have you heard of Steven Young?"

"The dealer from Liverpool?"

"Yes, 'Youngy' to his friends."

"I've seen a few of his customers and some of his victims on the slab over the years."

"DS nailed him a month ago and he squealed like a bitch and turned evidence. The two officers assigned to escort him on a sting haven't checked in since yesterday."

"They were running a sting with two officers and no backup?"

"They had their reasons for that," he snapped. "We need to know what happened here quickly. Especially what Brigade Security were doing here. Bloody plastics are rotten to the core," he grumbled using the tag which had been given to the security company's officers, 'plastic policemen'. "We all want them out, Kathy, so find out what went on here." Bishop's face reddened. "Please." He added as an afterthought.

"Oh, I bet you do," Kathy raised an eyebrow. "It sounds like someone's job is on the line."

"There will be no cover up, Kathy," he flushed red and shook his head. "Obviously it's gone tits-up and I want to know why." His profanity sounded ridiculous tinged with his Etonian English. Swearing didn't sit with his educated aplomb. "Young was offering something big. That's why DS went along with it."

"I'd better get on before the snow starts again. It'll be dark in four hours. I've got my work cut out. I need to know exactly where your uniformed officers have trodden and where they've driven their vehicles too. There are tracks all over the place here, which give us a good indication of what happened. Keep your men back behind the tree line until we're done." She turned and walked away without ever making eye contact with him. Their professional relationship had always been tetchy at best. Bishop was an impatient man and his constant demands for the forensic results of a growing number of serious crimes drove her to distraction. The fact that she was staring at the smouldering results of someone's incompetence didn't matter. There were five dead bodies to identify. She didn't care if the findings cost a senior officer his job; she had a job to do.

"Yes, you do that and please keep me posted." Bishop called after her but his words fell on deaf ears. He muttered under his breath as he turned away from the scene. "Anything you need let me know." Kathy glanced back and nodded imperceptibly.

"Okay everyone, gather around and let's get this thing done quickly and by the numbers before the weather turns," Kathy called her team together. "Max and Tina, you take the vehicle and the bodies inside. As soon as you are finished photographing everything, I want the bodies out and the vehicle covered on the back of the flatbed. Get it to the hanger as quick as. Bishop thinks that this is an undercover operation which turned bad." The team swapped glances as she spoke. The fact that there could be police officers amongst the dead heightened their concern. "Frank, take the fourth body and mark up the tracks which lead to and from the burnt body and then check over the fifth please."

Frank, Max and Tina moved without waiting for another instruction. They knew what had to be done. "Susan, I want you to photograph and mark every tyre mark and footprint from the tree line to the hedges further down the track. Let me know what you're finding as we find it okay. Bishop is breathing down my neck on this one." Her team set about their business as she watched the uniformed police reversing their vehicles down the access road towards the trees. "Susan!" she had an afterthought.

"Yes?"

"When you're done here, take a look around inside the tree line too."

Susan followed her gaze and grimaced. "No problem," she smiled and set off placing blue plastic markers in the snow as she walked. Kathy watched her team photographing the bodies and tracks and waited until they were done before approaching. It was time to get up close and personal with the recently dead.

CHAPTER 3

The Cul-de-sac

Ged positioned himself at the top of the stairs and aimed the Mossberg at the front door. He didn't think they would be able to kick it in. There were too many locks and bolts on it. The frame would give before the door did. The knocking got louder and the door shook visibly beneath the force of the blows.

"Come on, Ged." A voice came through the letterbox. "We only want to talk to you."

"Leave us alone," Ged shouted back. He immediately regretted his choice of words.

"Us?" The voice taunted him. "Is your little girl in there with you?"

Ged bit his lip and squeezed the shotgun. The urge to release both barrels at the door was painful. He felt terribly alone. If Carol was here she would know what to do. She would call the police and Jodie would be safe. He couldn't call the police because he promised Carol he wouldn't plus he hadn't paid the bills. Heroin was more important. He made sure they had food and water and the electric bill was paid on time but something had to give for him to afford his habit and the landline was dispensable. The mobile was the only communication that he had left although the network coverage was sporadic. He still carried it everywhere in his pocket, looking at the screen every twenty minutes or so in the hope that Carol would message or call. He charged it up religiously when the battery was low. Not having the mobile in his pocket was like losing his right arm. Working or not, it had to be there. Sometimes when Jodie was sleeping, he read the last text messages Carol sent. He'd lost count of the number of times he had written long replies and pressed 'send' but nothing came back. Even when the phone wasn't connected, it was worth a try. It made him feel closer to her somehow. The voice returned and snapped him back to reality.

"Ged, we can sort this out, mate." The voice was cool and calm and almost friendly. "You owe us money. I know you haven't got it because you're a scag-head and scag-heads never have any money, do they, Ged?"

Ged moved down the staircase one step at a time. He sat down four steps from the top, never moving his aim from the door. "You haven't had any gear from us for four days now, mate." The voice coaxed him. "You must have used it all by now. I bet your gagging for a hit, aren't you?"

Ged felt his hands trembling and he felt sick in the pit of his stomach. It was like hunger but a thousand times worse. He wiped the sweat from his palms onto his jeans and then put them back on the shotgun.

"Look, Ged, we can forget the money and start again." The voice remained cool. "Tell us where Carol is and I'll drop five wraps through the letterbox as a peace offering. We'll forget the cash and call it quits. Come on, Ged, you know it makes sense."

For a moment, he considered it. Five wraps. Five wraps and the slate wiped clean. All he had to do was tell them where Carol was. He'd let her and Jodie down already. His habit was too much for her to tolerate and they moved out before the riots although she allowed him regular access. He'd nearly lost them once and he didn't want to lose them again. He loved Carol; she was the love of his life; the mother of his beautiful daughter, his soul-mate and the only person he trusted. Betraying her was out of the question even if he did know where she was and the truth was, he didn't know. Not for sure. They wouldn't let him off the hook anyway. If he told them, they would still torment him until he paid them. The wraps they were offering were probably laced with rat poison or caustic soda. It would be suicide to take anything from them now.

"I don't know where she is. She left me months ago," Ged shouted. "Fuck off and leave me alone!"

"I can't do that, Ged." The voice sounded concerned. "I need to speak to her you see. Look, tell me where she is and we'll forget the money. You can have as much scag as you need. I'm not going to hurt her. I just need a chat with her."

"I told you, I don't know where she is," Ged shouted. "I'll have your money for you next week." He looked at a framed picture on the wall. It was a photograph of Carol picking up an award for investigative journalism. He wondered how a woman with so much inner strength had ever seen anything good inside of him.

"Ged, it's not about the money, mate!" The voice was tinged with anger now. "I want to know where that slag you live with is!"

Ged stood up and bolted down the stairs. His breath felt trapped in his lungs and he could feel his heart beating against his chest. He pulled the Mossberg tightly into his shoulder and aimed at the letterbox. His nerves were jangling as he placed his finger on the trigger. The desire to squeeze the trigger was burning inside him. He could see gloved fingers holding the flap open. If he fired, the dealer may take some shot in the face but there were four more of them out there. The flap flicked closed and he heard muffled voices through the door. Then he heard laughter. The flap opened again and a wrap of heroin dropped onto the doormat. 'Keep Calm and Carry On' the doormat read. Carol loved the slogan so much she bought everything she could find with it on. 'Keep Calm and Have a Cup of Tea' was emblazoned across the tea and coffee caddies, oven gloves, tea towels and chopping board. Ged felt the pain of loss when he thought about her. The tiny wrap near the door could take the pain away for a while. It would sooth his nerves and let him drift into the world where there was no pain, no loss. He stepped towards the front door. The pine coloured, laminate flooring creaked beneath his Timberland boots. His eyes were fixed on the foil wrap. His mind was screaming at him to pick it up. He didn't have to give them anything. He could pick up the wrap and wait until they went away. When Jodie went to bed, he could chase the dragon and drift into oblivion.

"Here, Ged, It's a peace offering," the voice was calm again. "Sorry I called her a slag, I know she's not, mate but I need to talk to her. My boss needs to know where she is, you know how it goes, Ged. No one wants to hurt her, mate. We just need to talk to her."

"Why?" Ged took his eyes from the drugs and looked towards the letterbox. He didn't know the reason why she'd vanished but the voice at the door appeared to. "Why do you want to talk to her?"

"We need to know if she is going to the police, Ged."

The answer was ambiguous. Did they think that he knew something too? "Why would she go to the police?"

"Don't fuck me about, Ged." The voice sounded patronising. "We both know what I'm talking about. I am freezing out here. Where is she?"

"I don't know," he mumbled. "I haven't seen her for months."

"I wish I could believe you, mate but I don't. Enjoy the scag, I'll be back later."

The flap closed again and there was silence. Ged stared at the letterbox as if they might burst through the tiny orifice. He couldn't hear them talking or laughing or coughing. Maybe they had gone. His eyes went back to the wrap on the doormat and he lowered the shotgun and stepped tentatively toward it. The laminate groaned beneath his weight and in the silence of the dark hallway it was deafening. He froze to the spot and waited for a hail of bullets to rip through the door but none came. The letterbox remained closed and there was silence beyond the door. He took another step, watching the door intently as he did so. An acidic odour drifted to him although it didn't quite register what it was. His brain was slowed by withdrawal. Perspiration coated his limbs, his clothes felt pasted to his skin. He held the shotgun with his right hand and reached down with his left. The wood creaked as he shifted his weight. He watched the door and reached blindly for the foil. His fingers touched the coarse fibres of the mat and he glanced down to locate the wrap.

"Boo!" The voice boomed in his head and he lost his balance. The shotgun clattered across the laminate floor and he landed awkwardly on his elbow. He felt a foot on his throat and a gurgle came from his mouth as the pressure was increased. "You don't mind but we came in the back door, do you, Ged? Like I said, it's fucking freezing out there and I haven't got time to arse about."

Ged felt his eyes bulging as his windpipe was constricted by a heavy walking boot. He grabbed the foot with both hands to relieve the pressure but his attacker was much stronger than he was. "Take him into the kitchen and search the place," the voice ordered. "We need a little chat, Ged." Strong hands grabbed his ankles and he felt himself being dragged along the hallway toward the kitchen. He heard several sets of boots stomping up the stairs. His heart sank as he heard them climbing the second flight. Jodie would hear them too. He could only hope that she didn't think it was him coming for her.

CHAPTER 4

Alec Ramsay

Detective Superintendent Alec Ramsay looked out of the police station window at the city below. The offices of the Major Investigation Team were situated on the fifth floor of the fortress like Canning Place police headquarters, on the banks of the River Mersey. Metal security bars impaired the view. There were days when he wondered if they were to keep the rioters out or to keep him in. Thick snow covered the scene although the main roads and pavements were kept clear and accessible by a fleet of snowploughs that worked around the clock. Thick banks of blackened snow formed barriers between the pavements and the road.

After the riots subsided, the police and local government made a concerted effort to get life back to normal as quickly as possible. Control was restored by the army, private security companies and the police. For the first time ever, Britain's police force was armed across the ranks and private companies were contracted to help restore order. When the rioters were dispersed, the government had to get the economy moving as quickly as possible. Making sure the country's arterial routes were flowing was the number one priority and slowly, the wheels of industry started turning again. The bitter weather hampered progress though; a ferry boat was moored idle beneath the Liver Buildings. The port authorities deemed it unsafe for them to return to work until the ice disappeared from the river.

"Morning, Guv," a deep voice tinted with a thick scouse accent disturbed his thoughts, "have you got a minute?"

"Yes, Smithy, come in." He replied to the substantial head, which peered around his door. Alec ran his fingers through his tussled hair. Grey was quickly replacing the blond in a battle that only one shade would win. Only cosmetic intervention could stop the march of time but Alec was not the 'Just for Men' type. "You can come in as long as you bring a mug of coffee with two sugars in it."

"Here is one I prepared earlier," Smithy replied happily. The fat ginger detective had a constant joviality about him, which seemed to be inextinguishable. It still felt odd to Alec to see the gun holster over his detective's shirt. It reminded him of old American cop shows on a Saturday night, Starsky and Hutch, The Streets of San Francisco and the like. Alec didn't mind carrying a weapon but he wore it on his belt above his left trouser pocket instead of under his arm. "Did you want real sugar or are you still on the sweetener, Guv? I know you gave the sugar up when Gail put you on a diet." Smithy waffled but he stopped in his tracks, realising too late what he had said. "I know she's been gone a while now but it still hasn't sunk in, sorry, Guv." His voice tailed off.

"It doesn't feel that long," Alec smiled. "I use whatever is the closest to the kettle at the time." Alec shrugged and pointed to the mug, sensing his DS's discomfort. A thin smile crossed his lips as he thought about his late wife and the constant earache she doled out about his health and diet. When she was alive it felt like nagging but now she was dead, he missed her voice every minute of the day. The nights were torturously long and empty without her next to him. Functioning without his lifelong companion was a trial he faced daily. He had no idea just how much he loved her, until he watched them lower her coffin into the ground. When the tears came, he thought they would never stop, grief tore him to shreds and he was still waiting for it to subside just a little but it hadn't. He wondered if it ever would. "Gail would be turning in her grave if she heard me saying that."

"She would if she knew you were back on cigs, Guv." Smithy pretended to smoke an invisible cigarette as he put the mugs of coffee down on the black ash desk. "Live for the moment, I say. I suppose you could be hit by a bus tomorrow. My missus keeps going on about my cholesterol and my weight but I've told her not to worry because the whiskey stops the fat blocking my arteries."

"How long have you been together now?"

"Two years, Guv," Smithy winked. "A bit of a record for me they never seem to hang around very long."

"I can't imagine why," Alec laughed. "Maybe this is the one."

"I'm learning to bite my lip and switch her voice off now, Guv," Smithy chuckled. "I think I've cracked it. Don't listen and you can't argue about anything."

"Don't knock it, Smithy." Alec reached for a mug and raised it in thanks before taking a sip of the strong brew. "You would miss her if she wasn't there." Alec wasn't being morose, he was being honest.

The ginger officer blushed red, embarrassed by what he had said. "Sorry, Guv, I didn't mean to be flippant."

"Don't worry, it's just the truth." Alec took another sip of coffee and shrugged. He smiled to put his colleague at ease. "We don't realise what we have until it's gone."

"I know, Guv." Smithy raised his ginger eyebrows and grinned. "If I didn't have her voice ringing in my ears, life would be dull."

"I don't know about dull." Alec pointed to his laptop. "If we worked flat out for the next two years, we couldn't catch up with the backlog. It's chaos down there." He stood up and looked at the river. The water reflected the thick clouds above it, looking steel grey; there were large chunks of ice drifting in the current toward the Irish Sea. The view reminded him of a Christmas card or a picture from a magazine depicting a Soviet city from the cold war period where the entire scene consisted of different hues of grey. The serenity of the scene through the glass belied the lawlessness, which had spread across the city, caused by the fuel drought. He saw a cargo ship being unloaded at the huge container terminal further up the riverbank where the Mersey met the sea. The blues, greens and yellows of the containers were welcome to the eye; the only bright colours on the river. "It looks like the economy is picking up but until unemployment drops dramatically the drug dealers and scumbags are running the streets. I don't think we have to worry about life being dull."

"They should make it free, Guv." Smithy snorted. "Let the silly fuckers have as much heroin as they want, it would half the theft and burglaries over night. We could make the Drug Squad redundant or put them on traffic duty!"

"I bet you'd like to be the one to tell them too," Alec chuckled.

"Not me, Guv." Smithy feigned concern and frowned. "I couldn't see fellow officers thrown on the scrapheap, even if they are a bunch of arrogant bastards!"

"I can't see us losing our friends in the DS, sad as it seems, that's one business that won't go bust." Alec sipped his brew and watched the traffic below. It was building up now. Things really did seem to be getting back to normal. "It baffles me where the money comes from."

"Junkies will always find a way to pay for shit, Guv." Smithy slurped his brew noisily. His face hardened as he thought about his next words. "Look I wanted to have a word about this security company the brass have brought in."

"You and every detective in the building." Alec rolled his eyes toward the ceiling. "What's the problem now?"

"I've been told by one of my snouts that some of their patrols are taking backhanders to ignore the dealing that's going on," Smithy leaned forward and lowered his voice. "Some of the uniform lads are saying that they are convinced that they are actually dealing!"

Alec frowned and his wrinkles deepened. They seemed to be deeper since he had started smoking again. "I have heard the same rumours a dozen times in the last few months but where's the evidence?" He shrugged. "It's all talk. What can we do without evidence?"

"Can't you have a word with Carlton, Guv?" Smithy lowered his voice as if his words may cause offence. "They need investigating."

Alec rubbed the deep dimple on his stubbly chin with his forefinger and thumb. The bristles were almost silver in colour. "They weren't deployed on a whim. It's all coming from Westminster, Smithy. You know that I don't like it any more than you do."

"I don't understand how they thought it could ever work. They are bent, Guv."

"The sad thing is, it has worked." Alec gestured to the window. "Look down there. Six months ago we were riding around in armoured cars, now Liverpool are playing at home tomorrow and Primark is having a sale!"

"Yes, but they are bent, Guv." Smithy shook his head. "I'm hearing some bad stuff and I'm not the only one who is hearing it either. Who thought it could work, for God's sake!"

"Look at the facts." Alec turned towards him. "The Yanks used Blackwater troops to regain control after the floods in New Orleans, which worked, yes?" Alec put one finger up.

"Yes but that's America, Guv." Smithy protested weakly.

"Do you think the local police welcomed them with open arms?"

"Well, no."

"They used them in Iraq to protect the Green Zones freeing up thousands of regular soldiers to fight on the frontline, which worked." He raised a second finger.

"That was a war zone, it's different."

"What was different?" Alec raised his hands. "We had armed response officers protecting deliveries to Tesco for God's sake! You tell me what the difference is."

"It would have settled down eventually, Guv."

"Bollocks, Smithy!" Alec slapped his hand on the desk, reinforcing his point. "We lost control for three months! Three months of rioting, shootings, rapes, murders. How long could that have gone on if the government didn't do something drastic?"

"We had it contained," Smithy mumbled sulkily.

"We had jack shit contained." Alec stood up and walked to the window. He pointed to the stark landscape beyond the glass. "People were trapped in their homes and we were trapped in here doing fuck all, be real! Something had to be done."

"Okay they helped calm things down, but why are we still employing them now?"

"Nobody likes it, God only knows I don't, but once word got around that mercenaries were in control of the suburbs and they were shooting looters on the spot, the looting stopped," Alec shrugged. "Westminster knows that we are only one setback away from it erupting again and until things are back to normal, completely, they won't let it go." Alec leaned against the glass. His body seemed to sag, his rant over. "It doesn't matter what we think, it works and for the foreseeable future, we're stuck with it."

"Jesus, Alec." Smithy lowered his voice and leaned forward. "These cowboys are armed and they are on the take! They are doing more harm than good. I am being told that some of them are actually dealing, I mean come on!" His face turned purple as he spoke and tried to contain his anger. "I know you aren't in charge but you can't sit back and watch it happen."

Alec turned from the window and looked Smithy in the eyes. "As far as the government is concerned, stopping any more civil unrest is the key to getting the country off its knees. Supporting the police force with the Army and private security firms is the solution for now. Its' working in America and it's working in Europe. It's working, Smithy and for now, there's nothing we can do about it." Alec stabbed his finger towards the window. "We have control of the streets again and it doesn't matter what we think." Alec took his cigarettes from his grey suit pocket and took one from the box. He tapped the end on the box. "If you have solid evidence that anyone is dealing or taking bribes to facilitate it happening then we will take it to the Drugs Squad and have the individuals banged up." Alec was just as frustrated as his detective by the situation but he was also annoyed by the insinuation that he was compliant with the policy. He placed the unlit cigarette back in the box. He had no intentions of lighting it up. It just took the edge off the craving. "You know the score, Smithy. We can't work on hearsay or the word of a bleating grass unless it leads to something solid. If you are pissed off then go and get me some evidence but don't sit there and tell me that I'm not bothered about it because I am just as pissed off as you if there are bent officers out there!"

"Sorry, Guv," Smithy said apologetically. "I didn't mean to make out your not bothered. It's just winding me up. I feel like we're working our nuts off to get things straight and this Brigade bunch are milking the situation for their own benefit. It doesn't sit right, Guv."

"It doesn't sit right with any of us, Smithy." Alec calmed his voice. He took off his jacket and hung it on the back of his black leather chair. His eyes focused on the Glock, which was hanging from his hip. It still felt alien. Gail would have freaked if she knew he had to go to work armed. "It was never going to be a long-term solution. We cannot deny that employing them worked, can we, Detective?"

"In a fashion, I suppose."

"Now it is up to real coppers like us to restore the balance and if there are bent officers out there, then let's weed them out and lock them up."

"Every time uniform have a go at one of the plastics, they close ranks and nothing happens, Guv." Smithy whined. "It's just brushed under the carpet."

"We've got enough on our plate without chasing rumours and gossip. What exactly have you heard?" Alec sat back and decided to give his detective a chance to vent. The Glock stuck uncomfortably into his hip. Maybe a shoulder holster would be more comfortable. "I don't want to hear any bullshit, what facts have you got?"

Smithy sat forward in the chair. Alec noticed dark patches of sweat spreading beneath his arms. "You know the two undercover lads, who were shot near the motorway a few days back?" Smithy's jowls wobbled as he spoke.

"Of course I do. What about it?" Alec narrowed his eyes. "It was a stakeout gone wrong?"

"That's what Cheshire are saying but from what I'm hearing, it's bullshit. It was a sting that went bad."

"They were shot in Cheshire so what can we do? It's not under our jurisdiction." He wanted to stop the conversation now but he felt that his detective had an axe to grind and it was better to let him finish. He was also curious to hear the rumours.

"My snout on the Maple Estate reckons that they were shot by Brigade Security, not dealers, Guv." Alec was about to interrupt but Smithy held up a chubby hand to stop him. "Let me finish, Guv. Word is that it was a sting operation gone bad. He's always been reliable. He reckons there was an eyewitness to the shooting."

"He reckons or he knows for certain?"

"He knows for certain." Smithy looked Alec in the eye to confirm his feelings on the issue. "He told me that he knows the name of the witness and where they live."

"Why aren't they in protective custody?" Alec knew there was a 'but' coming.

"He wants a deal in exchange for the information, Guv." This time Smithy looked embarrassed. He knew too well how it sounded. "He's banged up on remand in Risley. He's looking at a five-stretch for carrying a firearm and going equipped to burgle." He sighed and sat back in his chair. "I know how this sounds, Guv but I believe him."

Alec's piercing blue eyes narrowed. He sighed and shook his head. "Do you have any idea how naive you sound?" He tapped his fingers irritably on the desk as he spoke. "What are we supposed to do with that?"

"I know how it sounds, Guv, but," Smithy pressed his point.

"Stop there, Smithy." Alec raised his hands and stood up. "We've got twelve murders on the go, Lord knows how many serious assaults, a bus load of missing persons to find, the phones are ringing off the wall with new crimes and you are coming in here wasting my time because some old lag wants to get out of Risley?"

"Look, Alec," Smithy appealed to his superior to listen. "He has never been wrong before. He has never let me down, not once. He was carrying a gun for the same reason we are," Smithy pointed to his pistol, "because everyone out there is carrying a weapon. He got lifted by a Brigade patrol and because he was carrying and there were tools in the boot, they nicked him. He didn't pull the weapon and he didn't resist arrest, Guv."

"So what?" Alec said sarcastically. "So what, Smithy?" He picked up his coffee and walked back to the window. Somehow the view relaxed him. "You have a snout looking at a five-stretch and he suddenly remembers that he has a key witness who can finger officers from the same unit that arrested him, for the double murder of police officers?"

"You know the score, Guv."

"No, Smithy," Alec turned and looked at him. "I'm sorry but this time I don't know the score and quite frankly I am surprised that you think you do. You're painting this snout as a poor unfortunate soul who has been hard done by and now he can help us bring the bad guys to justice. Do you want me to get the violins out?" Alec scoffed. "Fuck off, Smithy, you know better than that."

"I believe him, Guv." Smithy shrugged defeated.

"If you do," Alec pointed his index finger at the officer, "throw the ball back into his court. Tell him to spill the beans, see if it is solid and if it is, we'll tell the judge what an upstanding citizen he's been!"

"I know it sounds wrong, Guv, but I've got a feeling about this one, I really believe him."

"Go and see him then and test the water."

"I will," Smithy smiled and stood up. "Thanks, Guv."

"Don't thank me," Alec wagged the raised finger in the air, "If you want to look into this, then do it off the clock. Do it in your own time, understood?"

"Understood," Smithy agreed reluctantly. "Do you want another brew?" His face brightened as he walked toward the door.

"Yes." Alec returned the smile. It was hard not to. "Put another spoonful of sugar in it. Use the real stuff. I need the energy." As Smithy closed the door, Alec decided to make a few calls of his own. Something about the murdered police officers wasn't right. His instinct told him that internal rumours usually had a solid foundation to grow from. He would start with Kathy Brooks, head of the North West's Crime Lab.

CHAPTER 5

42 Beech Close

Ged Barker felt a freezing cold draught coming through the bottom panel of his kitchen door. He saw an aerosol can on the granite worktop; the propane canister had a nozzle fitted to it. They had used a blow torch to burn through the tough plastic and the bars which reinforced the back door. That's how they breached his defences silently. He was distracted by them at the front door whilst others were burning their way in the back. In hindsight, it was a schoolboy error on his part but defending his home against a siege wasn't his strong point. To be honest, he couldn't think what his strong point was, being a father maybe. He was good at that. Or was he? His teeth chattered loudly and his body trembled as he looked around his kitchen. The gang were helping themselves to the last of his tea bags and long-life milk. His daughter was hiding in the attic and he needed a hit of heroin to feel normal again so how could he be a good dad? His mind raced with self recrimination while he waited for them to search the house.

"You don't mind if we have a brew, do you, Ged?" One of them asked. He recognised his voice. It was the voice which he'd heard through the letterbox. "Only we're freezing on account of the fact that you're pissing me about." He took off his furry trapper's hat and placed it on the worktop next to the blowtorch. His dark hair was cropped short and his features and skin tone indicated that he was mixed race. A grey Versace scarf covered the lower part of his face and neck and he unwound it and put it into his hat. He peeled off a pair of grey ski-gloves and plonked them on the pile.

"The place is empty, Freg." A figure in a thick blue bubble-jacket walked into the kitchen. Ged felt a wave of relief wash over him. They hadn't found Jodie's hiding place and as long as she kept quiet, they wouldn't. "I've told the others to look for anything useful."

"Nice one, dickhead." Freg snapped. He unzipped his thick parka as he spoke.

"What?" Bubble-jacket sounded surprised.

"Now he knows my name is 'Freg', dickhead." Freg smiled at Ged. "He's not the brightest bulb on the tree."

"What's the problem? It's not even your real name." Bubble jacket moaned.

"Well done again." Freg grinned. "Fuck off outside and watch the front of the house."

"Can't I have a brew first?"

"No you can't."

"But it's fucking freezing."

"Move yourself before I lose my temper." Bubble Jacket bent down and crawled back through the hole in the back door on his hands and knees, mumbling abuse as he went. "The retard could have opened the door. Can you see what I mean?"

"You can't get the staff any more can you?" Ged replied sarcastically. "Bring it up on his next pay review."

"Witty, very witty, anyway, I'm Freg."

"Freg?" Ged shivered as he spoke. "How did you get that name?"

"On account of the fact my dad has a cleft pallet and can't say Fred; the kids at school used to take the piss and it stuck." Freg took a mouthful of tea. "Fucking hell, long-life milk, can't stand the stuff!"

"If I'd known you were coming I'd have got some fresh stuff in." Ged grinned nervously. Freg had something about him. He was articulate and sharp and that worried Ged.

Freg looked at him curiously. He took in the surroundings for the first time. The walls were covered with shiny white tiles fitted in a brick pattern. The units were white to match and the adjoining dining-room was tastefully furnished with a dark pine table and chairs, which contrasted the laminate flooring. Black and white photographs of the family decorated the smooth plastered walls. The chrome frames gave the room a modern feel in contrast against the wood.

"This is a nice place." Freg nodded as he looked around. He took a closer look at one of the photographs. His boots left a trail of mucky melt water wherever he stepped. "Is this your missus?" He turned toward Ged surprised.

"Yes," Ged mumbled. It was pointless denying it as they were hugging each other on a sandy beach in Jamaica. The photograph was taken before Jodie was born, before the drugs really took a hold of him and before she left him.

"She's a babe, isn't she?" Freg smiled. "You're punching above your weight there, Ged." He added. "Mind you, you look quite ripped there. Must have been a long time ago, eh?"

Ged didn't reply. He couldn't think of anything to say, witty or otherwise. Freg was right, she was a babe and there was a time when he didn't look like an addict. Time changes everything, not always for the good. Carol left him because of the drugs. She wanted him to prove that he could function without them before she would allow him back into Jodie's life.

"You seem like an intelligent man despite your nasty habit." Freg sat down at the table across from his captive. "Where did you get the shotgun?"

"I used to go clay-pigeon shooting."

"Nice gun."

"Yes, it's one of the best."

"Were you any good?"

"Not bad."

Freg pointed back to the photograph. He swigged the tea before speaking again. "She did one, didn't she?"

"Yes."

"When?"

"Before it all kicked off."

Freg raised an eyebrow. "That long ago?"

"Yes."

"The place doesn't look that bad considering you're a junkie." Freg smiled and looked around. "It's not your average crack den is it?"

"I've kept it tidy, hoping she'll come back." Ged tried to sound genuine. "They moved to the other side of the city, her and my daughter that is."

"I need to know where she is."

"Me too."

"When did you last hear from her?"

"Months ago."

"When, exactly?"

"I don't know exactly."

"What did she say?"

"When?"

"The last time you spoke."

"Just chitchat about the house, the riots, my daughter, just stuff." Ged shrugged. So far, he felt at ease with the interrogation but something told him that was Freg's doing, not his.

"Did she say anything about a gym run by a guy called Jules Lee?" Freg lifted his tea mug and stared at the logo. 'Keep Calm and Carry On' it read. He moved his eyes to look into Ged's, judging the honesty of his answer before he spoke.

"No. There was no mention of any gym." Ged kept his eyes locked into his capture's. "She said she wouldn't be in touch for a while but she didn't say why. It sounds like you know more than me. I guess that's why she left now you've asked that."

"She didn't say where she was going?"

"No."

"Did you hear anything about steroids or drug smuggling?" Freg tried a different angle.

"I've heard about lots drugs." Ged shrugged. "When the power is on, there are shootings all over the telly."

"Yes, things have got a bit on top lately," Freg laughed. He stopped laughing suddenly and leaned over the table. "Did you hear about the kids shot near Stanley Park?"

"Yes, I saw something about it on the evening news."

"What did you hear?"

"Nothing apart from that report," Ged shrugged. "They said that a neighbourhood watch group had armed themselves during the riots and a couple of them got trigger happy."

"Is that what they said?"

"Yes."

"Not the kind of thing your ex-missus would be interested in?" Freg tilted his head to one side curiously.

"I don't know what you mean, she reported on all kinds of things." It was Ged's turn to lean forward this time. "What has she got to do with a gym or drugs, what has she got involved in?"

"Did you hear about the coppers shot near the motorway?"

"A few days back?"

"Yes, like you said, it was all over the telly." Freg smiled.

"I remember it vaguely, yes but I was a bit out of it when it came on." Ged shivered again. "Any chance of my coat, I'm freezing."

"Get him a coat and give him some tea." Freg turned to a man in a black Gortex anorak. "Have the others found anything yet?"

"Not yet." Anorak looked into the teabag tin. "There's no tea left."

"Give him yours," Freg said. "Where's your coat?" He asked Ged. He was about to answer, when Freg's sidekick interrupted.

"Are you having a laugh?" Anorak scoffed. His bottom lip drooped sulkily. "I'm not giving this scag-head my tea and I'm not getting him a coat, fuck him."

"Excuse me a minute." Freg spoke quietly and nodded his head sternly. "I feel that I'm having discipline issues today. Where did you say your coat was?"

"In the cupboard under the stairs," Ged laughed. Despite the circumstances, he liked Freg, so far. He reminded him of his friends from his clubbing days, intelligent and fun but with an edge to their personality.

Freg pushed the chair backwards and walked across the dining room. Anorak was still sulking, his bottom lip curled over in a half snarl. "Boil the kettle again." Freg ordered as he walked past him into the hallway. Ged heard him open the cupboard underneath the stairs. "Which coat do you want, Ged?" He shouted.

"There's a pale blue North Face jacket hanging on the left," Ged shouted. Anorak filled the kettle full of water and switched it on. The water bubbled gently as the heat radiated through it.

"Got it." Freg walked back into the kitchen, searching the pockets of the climbing jacket as he did. "Don't be offended but don't want to be passing you a coat with a gun in the pocket."

"No offence taken." Ged took the coat and wriggled into it, fastening the zip to the top beneath his chin.

"Has the kettle boiled?" Freg turned back to the kitchenette area.

"Yes," Anorak grunted.

Freg walked up to him and took the mug from his hand without saying a word. He topped it up with boiling water and took to the table. "It might be a little bit weak but it might warm you up."

"Thanks," Ged said.

Freg walked away from him again. "If I ask you to do something," he pointed his finger into Anorak's face, "you do it first time without giving me any fucking lip."

"I've had enough of your shit," Anorak mumbled. He stepped towards the back door but he didn't get far. Freg head-butted him in the face as he neared; a sickening thud accompanied the blow and a two inch gash opened beneath his left eye. Anorak staggered against the sink, stunned by the blow. Freg grabbed the kettle and swung it over his head, bringing it down in a vicious arc. It struck Anorak on the crown, boiling water spewed across the kitchen, scalding the injured man and his knees buckled beneath him. He clung to the edge of the stainless sink with one hand, bleeding from his scalp and the gash on his cheekbone. Freg swung the kettle again, bringing it down hard onto his fingers. Anorak howled in pain. He rolled onto his back, holding his injured hand against is chest. His fingers were broken and stuck out at odd angles.

"Freg, you nutter!" Anorak writhed in agony, smearing blood across the laminate. With his good hand, he reached down to his waistband and pulled out his pistol. The Springfield-XD compact fit snugly into his jeans and he whipped it out, pointing it towards his attacker but he wasn't quick enough. Freg kicked out at the weapon and it clattered off the kitchen cupboards before skidding across the wooden floor, landing at Ged's feet. "I've had enough!" Anorak whined.

Freg seemed oblivious to where the weapon had landed. He placed his foot onto the injured man's chest, pinning him to the floor and reached for an empty milk bottle from the draining board. There was a flash of light as he smashed the glass on the worktop. The splintering sound made him feel good. He stabbed the jagged glass into the man's throat, twisting it sharply to the right. A gurgling sound escaped him as a fountain of crimson erupted from the gash. Anorak kicked his legs in a last ditched attempt to live but his struggles ceased quickly as the thick smell of blood filled the air. Freg stared at the body for long seconds after it had stopped twitching and a deadly silence fell across the house. In the chaos, Ged picked up the discarded weapon at his feet.

"Get out of my house and take him with you," Ged said quietly. He was surprised how calm he felt considering what he had just witnessed. The Springfield pistol was pointing at Freg's chest. "I don't want to shoot you but I will if you don't leave now."

"You won't shoot me," Freg turned and smiled. "Put the gun down and we'll come to some arrangement."

Ged held the pistol steady and moved around the dining table to pick up the Mossberg. "Call your boys down and leave the way you came in. Trust me, I don't need any more trouble but I will shoot you if you don't leave now."

Freg thought about it for a few seconds and then placed two fingers against his lips and whistled. They stood staring at each other as heavy footsteps stomped down the stairs. "What's up?" a voice called as the four youths piled into the kitchen. "Fucking hell what happened to Overand?" The first youth added as he looked at the dead body near Freg's feet. "How did he get a gun?" another one hissed, pointing at Ged.

"Take your friend's body and get out of my house," Ged pointed the shotgun at the intruders and slipped the pistol into his belt.

"If you don't put the gun down, we'll come back and when we do, I won't be as pleasant as I have been this time," Freg said threateningly. His face darkened. Ged could tell that the ice cold look in his eyes was the real Freg. The articulate leader had reverted to the psychopath that he really was. "Tell me where Carol is and we might forget about coming back again."

"I told you the truth," Ged shrugged. "I don't know where she is and even if I did, I wouldn't tell you. This is your last chance. Leave now."

"He can't shoot us all." One of them snarled.

"No, I can't," Ged held the shotgun tightly. "But Freg gets both barrels in the face and then you lot can take your chances on who is next. How many bullets are in this pistol? I'm guessing there are enough to take you all down. It's your choice."

71

"Drag him outside," Freg grunted towards the body. His motley crew didn't flinch. "Move it now!" he shouted and the gang rushed across the kitchen and began to heave the body towards the back door. "Open the door and drag him into the back garden." Freg ordered. "You don't mind if we leave him out there do you?" he leered at Ged. "We'll be back later anyway so we can pick him up then."

"Just get out," Ged waved the gun.

"Daddy, I'm scared," Jodie said from the kitchen doorway. "I heard all the shouting and I was scared." She looked at the body and the pool of blood smeared across the laminate and began to scream. Everyone froze for a millisecond and then Jodie turned and ran for the stairs. Her screams pierced the silence. One of the intruders moved to run after her. Ged shouldered the shotgun and squeezed the trigger.

Chapter 6

Kathy Brooks

"Hello, Alec," Kathy smiled as she approached a table near the window of the Italian restaurant. Through the double glazing she could see a tall wooden sailing ship berthed to the dock wall outside, icicles hung like diamante daggers from the rigging, the decks covered in a thick layer of snow. It reminded Kathy of a scene from a black and white disaster movie where the sailing ship had become entrapped in a polar ice flow, the sailors frozen to death below decks. "It's so nice to see you."

"And you, Kathy," Alec pecked her on the cheek. "I've been meaning to come and see you but you know how it is."

"I do," Kathy returned the kiss and smiled. "Things have been a bit surreal the last few months. There are not enough hours in the day."

"I know exactly what you mean. Please sit down."

"How have you been since…?"

"Gail died?" Alec returned her smile and tried to put her at ease. "Bloody terrible if I am honest!" He shrugged and pointed to the bench seat opposite him. "I feel like I've lost my right arm. It's funny but if it hadn't been for the riots, I think I'd have gone mad."

"Every cloud, eh Alec?" Kathy slid onto the red leather bench seat and slipped off her coat. Alec noticed how the black material of her dress accentuated the curve of her breasts. Kathy was slim, her breasts ample and perfectly shaped. She smiled as she looked around, absorbing the atmosphere. The restaurant was warm and cosy in contrast to the frozen dock beyond the glass. The ancient red bricked warehouses formed a square around the icy waters and historic boats of various shapes and sizes lined the dock. Designer shops and cafe bars once thrived along the water's edge but the riots had killed off many of the businesses. A handful of them were trading again. "Are things settling down in the city yet?" She wriggled her hips to allow the waiter to take her coat from beneath her.

"Slowly but we're getting there."

"I'll hang your coat," he spoke with a local accent. His hair was greased back to his scalp and he smelled of a musky aftershave which she couldn't recall the name of but she knew it was cheap. "May I get you some drinks, sir?"

"I'll have a glass of house red please," Kathy smiled. The waiter had dark smouldering looks and a smile which could melt a woman's resolve in a moment. The fact that his accent meant that he was from the city centre was irrelevant. She could pretend that he was Italian for an hour or so while they ate. The atmosphere was continental and she could smell the aromas of garlic and melted cheeses drifting to her. As the sun went down and the lights began to twinkle along the wharfs outside, they could have been sat in any coastal city in the world. Lights flickered into life on the ships making the scene romantic and 'normal'.

"Shall we share a bottle?" Alec fancied red wine too.

"Why not," Kathy nodded and touched his hand. They had been friends for years and although there was chemistry between them, neither wanted to spoil their relationship by jumping into an affair. Kathy would never have crossed the line while Alec was married and even now, a physical relationship with him would have felt wrong, like kissing her brother. "It's been a long week so a few glasses of wine won't go amiss."

"Shall we have Merlot?"

"A bit heavy for me."

"Shiraz?"

"I can recommend the Shiraz, Mr Ramsay," the waiter added with a knowing smile. He eyed Alec studiously, trying to make his mind up if he was, 'the Ramsay' or not. "It compliments any pasta dish perfectly."

"Perfect and three pounds cheaper too," Kathy smiled teasing him.

"I will bring your drinks immediately." The waiter eyed Alec intently. The waiter left her with a toothy grin and turned to dispose of the coats and fetch the drinks.

"He's keen," Kathy said laughing. "He doesn't think you are Gordon does he?"

"Oh, shut up," Alec blushed. It wasn't the first time he had been mistaken for the celebrity chef who shared his name. It had been useful in some restaurants when acquiring a good table and staff always fussed around him just in case. "Do you remember that restaurant in Manchester?"

"God, yes," Kathy threw her head back and laughed. "We had three waiters fussing all night and a free bottle of wine."

"It comes in handy sometimes," Alec pointed to the dimple on his chin.

"Any way I like Shiraz better even if it is cheap."

"That's why I didn't pick that one first," Alec laughed. "I didn't want you calling me a tight git!"

"Oh, why would I do that?" She sat back and frowned. "Are you paying for the meal?"

"I walked right into that one," Alec frowned. "Looks like I am now!"

"Seriously though," she lowered her voice. "How are you coping?"

"I take each day as it comes," Alec shrugged. "Work keeps me sane and red wine helps me to sleep through the night. Each day is another step. Anyway how are you?"

"I'm fine too," she sat back as the waiter arrived with the wine. He showed them the label and uncorked the bottle with a pop, offering a taste to Kathy first. "It will be fine." She said allowing him to pour it without further ceremony.

"Are you still dating Robby?"

"You mean Bobby," she laughed and sipped the wine. "That's nice." She raised her glass. "Cheers."

"Cheers," Alec saw something in her eyes. "I guess from that look in your eyes that all is not well on the dating front. Did you split up?"

"Yes, he didn't last long."

"I thought he was a high flyer with BP?"

"He was," she sipped and smiled as she swallowed. "In more ways than one."

"I don't follow," Alec took a gulp from his glass and savoured the fruity liquid.

"We were at a corporate do a few weeks back," she shrugged and avoided making eye contact. "I spent all day in town looking for a dress. He was behaving a little too giddy for my liking and then he came back from the toilet with one of his slimy colleagues with a stupid grin on his face and powder under his nose."

"Oh, I see," Alec smiled thinly. "I see what you mean. I'm sorry."

"Don't be," she looked him in the eye. "He wasn't for me anyway, Alec. He loved himself way too much for me to slot into his life. I was another accessory that's all."

The waiter returned with his pen and pad in hand and a cheesy smile which asked if they were ready to order. "Have you decided or would you like a little longer?"

They laughed and clinked glasses. "We haven't looked at the menus yet," Kathy apologised.

"We haven't seen each other for a long time, catching up and talking too much," Alec added passing her a menu.

"No problem," the waiter topped up their glasses. "I'll come back in five minutes."

Alec followed him with his eyes. He noticed for the first time that the restaurant had filled up while they'd been chatting. Things were definitely on the mend. Apart from the snow outside, it was a perfectly normal scene. "What are you having?" Kathy asked without looking up from the menu.

"Garlic mushrooms and tortellini Caruso, I think."

"What is the cheapest thing on the menu?" She joked.

"Don't you dare look at the prices," he pointed a finger.

"Have you seen the price of the steak?" she showed him the price.

"Okay, do look at the prices," he frowned. "But don't pick the cheapest thing on the menu."

"I'll have the same as you."

"That's the cheapest thing on there."

"I know."

"Well order some garlic bread too and then I won't feel so bad."

"We'll share it," she smirked. "And then I won't feel bad for spending your money."

"Shut up and order whatever you like," he scolded. "If you want garlic bread, then you shall have garlic bread."

"Deal," she nodded seriously. "As long as we can have cheese on it."

"Done." Alec stuck out his hand and Kathy shook it to seal the deal.

The waiter returned and took their order with a simple nod of the head. He flashed Kathy a quick smile but the flirtatiousness had gone. The tables were filling up and serving was taking priority.

"It's nice to see you, Alec," she raised her glass and sipped the wine.

"You too."

"But I am curious, I must say."

"What about," Alec felt the hairs on his neck stand up. Kathy was a clever lady.

"About my invite to dinner of course."

"And what makes you think I have a motive?"

"Oh let's just say it's a woman's intuition."

"Okay you've rumbled me," Alec sighed with a smile and raised his glass. "I wanted your opinion on the shootings in Warrington."

"The police officers on Silver Lane?"

"Yes."

"My initial reports are with the Cheshire DS," she frowned. "You can access them can't you?"

"Yes but I wanted to hear it from you."

"Why the interest in that; it's Cheshire's problem isn't it?"

"It could be everyone's problem if the rumours I'm hearing are true."

"And they are?"

Alec sat back as their starters arrived. The waiter presented them with pride, sprinkled black pepper and parmesan cheese on them and left in a hurry. Kathy picked up her fork and looked at him with raised eyebrows, indicating that her question was unanswered. Alec coughed and sipped his wine, choosing his words carefully.

"Some officers have heard information from their informants," Alec forked a mushroom into his mouth and chewed before continuing. "It began as snippets, little bits here and there but it is all making a picture."

"Go on, I'm listening."

"The word on the street is that the killings were a sting gone wrong and that Brigade men were the target of the sting."

"And do you think there's any substance to the rumours?"

"That's why I asked you here," Alec chewed. "Is there any possibility that the Brigade were involved in the killings?"

"You have read the preliminaries?" Kathy looked surprised at the question.

"Yes."

"And?"

"I am keeping an open mind until I hear what you think."

Kathy pushed a garlic mushroom around her plate while she thought about his question. She picked up the wine with the other hand and sipped it, looking into Alec's eyes as she swallowed.

"What I think is that you are putting me in an awkward position."

"Why?" Alec shrugged. "I have read the report but without seeing the crime scene or talking to the officers involved, I can't make an informed judgement. I need you to walk me through it."

"What are you going to do when you have made your mind up if Brigade are involved or not?"

"Well the first thing I'll have to do is apologise to one of my detectives," Alec smiled. "I bit his head off yesterday but after reading the reports, he might be right."

"Which detective?" She returned his smile.

"Smithy."

"He's a good officer," Kathy said genuinely.

"I know," Alec agreed. "That's why I'm here."

"I thought you were catching up with an old friend," she teased.

"Sorry, that sounded terrible," Alec blushed. "You know what I meant."

They sipped their wine and finished off the mushrooms without speaking further. Kathy pushed her empty plate away from her as she finished the last mouthful. She dabbed the corner of her mouth with her napkin. The waiter was on the empty dishes like a seagull swooping for bread. He looked closely at Alec still undecided if he was serving the famous chef or not. Kathy eyed Alec suspiciously too.

"What is this really about, Alec?" She finished her wine and rolled the stem of the glass between her elegant fingers. "It's not just about Smithy being right, is it?"

"Smithy believes that there was an eyewitness," Alec clasped his hands together as if in prayer and rested his chin on them. "His snout reckons that a woman witnessed the entire thing but we don't have any details. The guy wants to do a deal."

"How the hell can he know for a fact that there was a witness?" Kathy raised her eyebrows again.

"You don't seem surprised by the idea that there could have been," Alec cocked his head and dodged the question. There was no certainty about the premise but he had known Kathy long enough to know that she wasn't surprised at all. "What's the score, Kathy?"

"The truth is that I'm not sure yet, Alec," Kathy replied honestly. "I do know that Bishop is screwing the lid down so tight, that the truth might never come out until he's ready."

"What do you mean?"

"Look, Alec," Kathy pointed her index finger at him. Her face was serious and her tone stern. "We have worked together for what, fifteen years?"

"Maybe more."

"If I tell you what I really think and you go digging for evidence, the finger will point straight back at me. Bishop is not allowing all the facts to be published yet while an enquiry is conducted. Anything I tell you would seriously hurt my integrity if it comes out. He wants Brigade Security out of Cheshire and he thinks this case will help him to achieve that. If he knows that I'm talking to you.." she left the sentence unfinished.

"That won't happen," Alec shook his head to reassure her although the doubt in her eyes told him that she wasn't convinced. "All I want is your opinion. Not what the evidence points to but what you believe could have happened. If the plastics are involved in this then I want them shut down and kicked out of Merseyside too. They are rotten, Kathy but we need something solid to get Westminster to listen and this could be it."

The waiter interrupted them once more with identical plates of pasta. It was obvious that he had decided that Alec was a lookalike with the same surname and not the real 'Ramsay'. His smile was now gone as he rushed to keep up with the growing number of tables. This time the parmesan was scattered rather than sprinkled, cheese crumbs landed on the table mats and the musky aftershave now mingled with his body odour. When he left, Kathy looked blankly at her food while she thought about what Alec was asking for.

"Let me ask what you have made from reading the reports," Kathy picked up her fork and looked at Alec.

"Okay," Alec swallowed a mouthful of pasta. "There were three bodies in the vehicle, two of them undercover drugs officers and a well known dealer turned evidence, Steve Young. They were shot with a nine millimetre machinegun which you identified as an Uzi found at the scene."

Alec paused and waited for Kathy to respond but she shovelled more food into her mouth signalling that she wasn't finished listening yet.

"A fourth body was found torched near the vehicle, identified as a Brigade Security officer named Samuels. The cause of death was a bullet through the throat. From the size of the bullet wound you think it was fired from a pistol belonging to another Brigade officer named Mills. Mills's body was found untouched by fire fifty yards away with a single bullet through the skull."

"That's pretty much it in a nutshell," Kathy shrugged.

"Bollocks," Alec half laughed and the comment attracted some surprised looks from other diners in earshot. He covered his mouth with his napkin as if to silence himself and he met the shocked gazes with a stern face. They returned to their own company whispering their distaste to their companions.

"Maybe you could swear a little louder?" Kathy whispered sarcastically. "We're not in the station now, Alec!"

"I'm sorry," Alec laughed. "We both know there are so many holes missing from that report that it could have been put together by a boy scout. What has Bishop edited from the report?"

"Plenty."

"Why," Alec leaned closer, his eyes narrowed. "What is he covering up?"

"I'm not sure, Alec," Kathy sighed, "but he is covering something big, that's for sure."

"Talk to me Kathy."

"You had better order another bottle of wine," she pointed to her empty glass. "None of this came from me, Alec. I need your word on this."

"You have it," Alec reached over and touched her hand gently. "Let me in and you have my word that no one will ever know." Alec attracted the waiter's attention and ordered a second bottle. He was grateful for the extra glasses of wine if the truth be known.

"Okay, where do I begin?" Kathy raised her recharged glass. "The report doesn't clarify if the bullet which killed Samuels was fired from Mill's pistol but we know it was. We recovered the bullet using metal detectors once the vehicle had been towed. It was fired by Mills but it has been hidden from the report for now."

"Definitely by him?"

"No doubt about it," Kathy nodded. "He had two different types of gunshot residue on his right hand. They match the Uzi and the H and K P30. If it was a hit on Young, then Mills was the assassin but I don't buy that."

"So Mills lets fire with a machine gun and kills the DS officers and Young and then he draws his pistol and shoots his partner, but why?" Alec shook his head. "Cheshire isn't telling us exactly who Young was going to give evidence about so I'm inclined to go with the sting theory. If you are telling me that Mills was definitely the shooter, then I think Mills was the target of the sting."

"Maybe his partner wasn't part of the deal. Maybe he flipped when Mills killed the officers and he had to silence him," Kathy mused. "We found weapons under the seats of the Range Rover, which match the serial numbers of the officers' service weapons. Their badges were on the floor in the ashes. Mill's pepper spray had been discharged but the bodies were too badly damaged for me to say if they inhaled the gas."

"So they pulled their badges to make an arrest, not thinking that they would need their weapons and Mills hit them with the gas?"

"Maybe they didn't get the chance," Kathy answered. "A blast of that gas in a confined space would be enough to disable all three of them. The only prints on that Uzi belong to Young."

"What?"

"Exactly," Kathy reinforced the point. "If it was a sting operation to capture Brigade officers accepting bribes then fine, I can see why the officers didn't pull their weapons but not why Young was given a nine millimetre Uzi unless he grabbed it from beneath the seat in the melee. I can see no reason why he would be given a gun unless the DS officers were on the take too. And there is no explanation coming forward for why were they acting alone?"

"There are no circumstances where they would not have backup, Kathy. I don't know what happened but it stinks," Alec shook his head. "I've run some checks on the plastics and the DS officers. Mills was under discipline but Samuels was squeaky clean. He was a war hero with a wife and three kids."

"What about the DS officers?"

"Their files have been pulled but I'm on that one," Alec said with a stony face. "A contact in Cheshire's HR department owes me a favour. I'll have their files tomorrow."

"It sounds like you are calling in a lot of favours on this, Alec" Kathy warned. "Two bottles of wine and a meal for me, including cheesy garlic bread; why is this eating into you so much?" She joked but there was a serious note to it too. "Are you going out on a limb here?"

"I don't know what it is," Alec looked down at his food. "Since Gail died at Will Naylor's house. I guess the truth seems to be far more important than it did before."

"Betrayal takes its toll, Alec," Kathy smiled sympathetically. "Trusting people is hard enough without having to go through the agony you have faced."

"I don't know if it would have been easier if she'd died of cancer or been hit by a bus," Alec emptied his glass. "Do you know what hurts the most?"

"Go on."

"Not knowing."

"Explain, you've lost me."

"Not knowing how long they were sneaking around behind my back," Alec sighed. "Sometimes I lie awake and analyse everything from the day they first met. That's what happens when you're a detective you see, you can never switch off the suspicion, never." His eyes drifted back to the table. "I'm so sorry I'm rambling on here!"

"It was my fault, I think," Kathy laughed. "I don't mind you talking about Gail and Will if you want to. It was a shock for everyone, you know."

"Another time maybe," Alec smiled. "So you're convinced that Cheshire is whitewashing the investigation?"

Kathy rolled her eyes and took a gulp of her wine. "Alan Bishop is hiding something for sure but why aren't the Brigade hierarchy bouncing off the walls unless they are involved in the cover up too?" Kathy tried to return to the conversation but she could sense Alec's pain. "They lost two men bent or not, I would want to know what happened," Kathy shrugged. "Bishop had held something back from the report, which makes me wonder if Brigade is in cahoots with Bishop."

"Go on."

"Samuels was wearing a wire," Kathy said quietly. "The back of his body are intact. The flames didn't touch the underside of the body. He has a box taped to the base of his spine and wire taped to his skin."

"Jesus," Alec put his fork down and sat back. "So who was setting up who?"

"I don't know but I do know that the box was taken from evidence with Bishop's authorisation," Kathy gulped some red. "Whatever is on that chip will answer some questions."

"None of it adds up, that is why I'm looking into this, Kathy." Alec frowned and picked up the salt pot, placing it on the table next to the pepper. Moving them he explained it how he saw it. "So follow me here. Once the DS and Young were dead, Mills shot Samuels and then set fire to the vehicle and the bodies to destroy the evidence?" Alec backtracked and then pointed to the pepper, which was now Mills. "That adds up but what I don't understand is what happened to him?"

"He was killed with a single shot to head." Kathy leaned forward. "The bullet penetrated his helmet, flattened and blew the back of his head off."

"That was in the report but not in so much detail."

"That was all that was in the report, the details were edited," Kathy lowered her voice. "The size of the entry and exit wounds tells me it was a high calibre, high velocity round. The position of the body and the angle of the wound, tells me that the shot was not from the tree line. It doesn't make sense," she sipped her wine again. "If it was a hit then the shot would come from the cover of the trees or the hedgerows which means only one thing."

"Sniper."

"With talent and military training."

"Which leans more towards a hit by Young's mob trying to spring him?"

"Not in my mind, Alec."

"What do you think?"

"Ex-military with that kind of ability," Kathy turned her hands palms up. "Brigade security officers are mostly ex-military aren't they?"

"So you think that Young turned evidence, set up Mills and his buddies but Mills smelled a rat and killed all the witnesses. Then another Brigade man took him out with a sniper rifle, why?"

"Who knows, we didn't find any money at the scene. Maybe they were going to double cross Young but when the police identified themselves, they panicked. Taking Mills out silenced all the witnesses," Kathy mused. The wine was beginning to loosen her tongue and make her relax. "If a Brigade officer was charged with the murder of two police officers, what would be the result?"

"I dread to think," Alec frowned. "The brittle coalition we have with them would shatter to pieces. They would be hung out to dry in the press and their contract would be in jeopardy. The whole thing could implode."

"There you are then," Kathy shrugged. "How much is it worth?"

"Multimillions."

"If they had doubts about Mills maybe he was terminated. Perhaps the sting by DS was an unexpected inconvenience."

"I still don't know why Bishop would cover this up," Alec was stumped.

"Maybe he's covering for someone."

"Who, they're all dead."

"Apart from Smithy's eyewitness," Kathy looked through her wine glass her face distorting in the wine. "If this woman exists then she is in real danger, Alec."

"You searched the scene, could there have been an eyewitness?"

"We went as far as the tree line but there could have been some one deeper in the woods," Kathy cocked her head. "We haven't looked that far yet.

"Can you check," Alec blurted. "Is it too late?"

"Any tracks should still be there," Kathy shrugged. "It hasn't snowed heavily and the trees provide cover. I'll take my team deeper back there tomorrow."

Alec raised his glass and they clinked them together. "Deal, you can order a pudding," Alec joked.

"I will," Kathy smiled. "What is the cheapest thing on the menu?"

Chapter 7

Beech Close

Alec woke early the next morning with the thick head that red wine leaves you with. He looked at the clock and winced at the time. Four fifteen in the morning, every morning without fail he woke up. It didn't matter how tired he was or how much he'd had to drink, he awoke with a terrible feeling of loss in his guts. The cold empty space where his cheating wife once laid forced the loneliness deeper home. He missed her dreadfully despite her betrayal. The truth was he loved her, always did and always would. He had nothing but time to consider whatever mistakes he had made to drive her into a younger man's arms and sometimes the thoughts which haunted him in the small hours drove him crazy.

Her death had made him numb inside. Her betrayal with his partner and the manner of the way they were found dead and naked in each other's arms, made him sick, angry and desperately sad. They were found suffocated by smoke in an embrace strengthened by rigor. He often tormented himself about how frightened they must have been as they choked; his wife and his protégé taking their last searing breaths together. Sometimes he looked at the Glock hanging from his holster and considered pushing it beneath his chin to end it all. One quick squeeze of the trigger and all the pain and loneliness would be gone. He knew his grief and moments of intense jealousy were futile. They couldn't bring her back, wouldn't bring her back, nothing could but the cold harsh reality that she was gone and it was over in this world gripped his guts like an icy giant hand crushing his insides.

Two hours of torment had passed by when a call from the station spurred him from his grief. "There's a multiple shooting, Guv," Smithy's sleep tainted voice informed him.

"Where?" Alec was almost relieved that a major crime had happened because it took him away from the grief-riddled world of his bed.

"Halewood somewhere."

"I'm not sure that I can drive yet," Alec thought about the wine he'd consumed the night before.

"I'll pick you up on the way over there."

"Okay, do that." Alec snapped out of his self pity and Detective Superintendent Ramsay took control of his body and mind once more.

When Alec and Smithy arrived at 42 Beech Close, the scene was already being processed by the SOCO and a team of detectives from a station near to the scene. Half a dozen officers in white paper suits were whizzing about with purpose. The close was cordoned off with crime scene tape and a lone uniformed officer guarded the perimeter. Two photographers stood chatting to him smoking cigarettes. So far, the incident had not attracted a media scrum which Alec was thankful for. This part of the city was still not back to normal and the crime rate was high. The uniformed officer recognised them immediately and nodded a silent greeting as he lifted the tape.

"Who is on scene?" Alec asked ignoring a barrage of questions from the two photographers.

"Sergeant Wallace from Coppice Hill, sir," the officer replied. "The plastics security called it in, sir and Coppice Hill responded first."

"Sergeant Wallace," Smithy shook his head. "I don't know him."

"'Her', Sarge," the officer smiled. "Allison Wallace."

"Oh well, no wonder I don't know him," Smithy saluted and laughed. "Is Kathy Brooks leading the SOCO?"

"I haven't seen her, Sarge."

"I think she's busy in Cheshire," Alec mumbled. He knew where she would be working. Smithy nodded with a confused look on his face.

"Talking about Cheshire, Guv," Smithy raised a finger. "I've got a visiting order to see Vinny Walker this afternoon."

"Good," Alec nodded but kept quiet about his meeting with Kathy Brooks the night before. "I don't want to hear any bull, Smithy. He either comes up with names and addresses or he can sit and rot in there. No deals, no bullshit, understood?"

"Yes, Guv." Smithy grimaced. The ginger detective looked sheepish about delivering on his word. They trudged through the snow and approached the front garden where officers were busy looking at footprints and other residual evidence.

"Which way can we come in?" Alec shouted to one of the SOCO. The snow was still thick on the ground and he didn't want to compromise any footprint evidence which may not have been logged.

"Stay between the lines of red tape please, Guv," a man's voice came back. "The sergeant is in the kitchen and the front door is open."

"Thanks," Alec waived. As they approached the door he noticed an evidence marker next to a pinkish lump which was obviously a severed hand. "What the hell is that?"

"It's a hand, Guv," the SOCO replied matter of factly.

"Thanks for that," Alec replied sarcastically. "What I meant was, who did it belong to?"

"We don't know yet, Guv," the officer mumbled. "Plenty of bodies in there but none with a hand missing."

"Sounds grim," Smithy grunted. "The place looks well protected." Smithy noted pointing to the metal shuttering.

"Not protected enough by the look of things," Alec replied as he stepped into the porch and the smell of blood and stale excrement filled his nostrils. The house looked tidy apart from dried boot prints on the laminate flooring. At the end of the hallway, a body lay on its side, half of the skull sheared away. A puddle of congealing blood and grey matter spilled from the ruined head. His thoughts were disturbed as an ambulance screamed to halt outside, its blue lights flashing and air horns blaring.

"DS Ramsay?" A voice turned his attention back to the interior of the house. "I'm Sergeant Wallace, Coppice Hill." The sergeant approached them in her white suit. "We've found a live one, Guv but the ambulances won't turn out now unless we've got armed backup at the scene."

"Don't they know that we're all armed nowadays," Smithy tutted.

"I know," Allison agreed. "They must think we can't shoot straight."

"Smithy can't," Alec added with a deadpan expression. "Have we got any units out there?" Alec frowned. He hadn't seen any armed unit vehicles outside.

"No, Guv," she smiled thinly. "I lied. The guy is in a bad way." Alec noted that her eyes were emerald green, almost hypnotic, like a cat's. Her hair was auburn and tied up behind her head in a bun. "I'm sorry, Guv but I thought it was for the best to risk an ambulance."

"Are there armed units on the way?" Alec smiled to put her at ease.

"Yes."

"No harm done then, Sergeant. You did the right thing." Alec pointed towards the kitchen. "What have we got?"

"Come through, Guv, I'll talk you through it." She turned and walked towards the kitchen. "He's been shot in the head with a Mossberg, looks like he took both barrels." She explained as they past the body in the hallway. The stench of death grew thicker as they neared the kitchen. Alec looked inside and saw two officers bent over an injured man. He was lying on his back next to a dining table, a pool of blood spreading beneath him. "He's taken one in the left shoulder, Guv. He's lost a lot of blood but I think he'll make it now that the ambulance is here."

As she spoke, two paramedics rushed in and replaced the police officers next to the injured man. "His name is Ged Barker. He's the home owner. The Mossberg is registered to him and it was lying next to his body. He also had this pistol in his hand. He's pretty out of it, Guv but he keeps asking if we have found Jodie."

"Girlfriend?" Alec asked looking at the pictures of a couple on the wall. "We don't know he's not making any sense but we haven't found any females, Guv. One of the bedrooms belongs to a little girl, I'm sure of that, so I'm thinking daughter."

"Smithy, make sure that someone is with him at the hospital all the time. I want an armed officer next to his bed until he can tell us what happened," Alec ordered. "What do we know about him?"

"Nothing is coming up yet, Guv. He doesn't have a record."

"Okay," Alec smiled, "keep digging."

"Guv."

"There are three bodies over here, Guv," Wallace carried on her summary. "This guy and this guy were shot in the chest. Two bullets in him and three in this one."

"And the other body?" Alec frowned. It did not look like a gunshot victim.

"This is where it gets weird," she shrugged. "This poor guy has been scalded, beaten and then had his throat slashed. No gunshot wounds at all. There's blood all over the doorframe and the door here, and two blood trails lead across the path and around the front of the house to the end of the road. There are fresh tyre marks in the snow where the blood trails stop. I think one or more intruders were shot and wounded and they made off through the back door to a waiting vehicle. Once we get DNA results, we can start putting names to the bodies. None of our intruders are carrying ID."

"Intruders, Sergeant?" Alec raised his eyebrows.

Alison Wallace blushed. "The back door was burnt through with this blow torch canister and as the homeowner is shot and wounded I'm assuming it was an aggravated burglary gone wrong, Guv."

"You may be right," Alec nodded smiling. "What do we know about the hand in the front garden?"

"Nothing, Guv, except it's been there a few days. It doesn't tie in time wise with this lot in here. The SOCO reckons it's been there at least forty eight hours."

"That's a brave guess when it's been lying in the snow," Smithy grunted. He bent low and studied the melted back door panel.

"Not really, he's almost certain the hand was separated from its owner at...," she checked her notes. "8.50pm on the sixth."

"What?" Smithy scoffed trying to work out the accuracy of the doctor's theory.

"There is a watch on the wrist, Serg," she smiled. "Stopped when a shotgun pellet went through the face."

"Smart-arse," Smithy rolled his eyes to the ceiling. "The timeline might not fit but it must be connected to what we have here; Just too much of a coincidence for it not to be."

"I agree, Serg," Wallace nodded. Although she was the same rank, she respected Smithy as the more experienced detective. His reputation and that of the Major Investigation Team were known across the county. "I've already put an alert out across the hospitals. Whoever that hand belonged to, must have been admitted somewhere."

"Good thinking, any witnesses?" Smithy asked. "Have uniform knocked on any doors?"

"Yes," she turned to face him. "The street is empty apart from the end house, number 18, and they didn't hear anything. They wouldn't open the door to our officers; they just shouted through the letterbox."

"And the rest of the house?" Smithy gestured to the stairs.

"My team are searching now. There's the owner's stuff and the odd few things, which would indicate a woman lived here once but not any more," Wallace explained.

"What do you mean?"

"The face creams and make-up are empty and dried up as if someone left them here on purpose and took the new stuff with them," she shrugged. "Just a hunch but as a woman, I'd say he lives here alone with his daughter. The woman left a long time ago. It looks like it has been turned over upstairs hence my burglary theory, Guv," she turned to Alec apologetically.

"Sarge!" An urgent voice called from somewhere on the upper floors.

The detectives ran for the stairs. "What is it?" Alison shouted between the banister rails.

"We've found a child's diary in the attic, Sarge and there's some scribbling in it which says 'the bad men have come back to hurt Daddy.' The ink is smudged here, Guv. Looks like tears and they're still damp."

"It looks like you've found out who Jodie is, Sergeant." Alec bit his bottom lip. The sound of the ambulance leaving reached him as he spoke and he wondered if Ged Barker would live long enough for him to tell them what happened to his daughter. "Smithy, I want this little girl found."

"Guv, I'll call it in and start a full search operation."

"Release all the information we have on her now, starting with the press at the end of the street. No softly softly on this, tell them what we know so far. Are there any pictures of her here?" Alec turned to Wallace.

"There are some in her bedroom, Guv, but we don't know how recent they are."

"Give them all to the press, let them take photos and then get them to Canning Place," Alec spoke calmly. "I want her face all over the television within the hour, got it?"

"Guv."

CHAPTER 8

Risley Remand Centre

Risley was changed from a naval base into a remand prison in 1965. It had changed its role several times over the decades but is now a Category 'C' prison for males only. Vinny Walker had spent a number of years enjoying the hospitality at Risley but this time he was looking at a five year stretch for going equipped to burgle and carrying an illegal firearm. He'd been remanded in custody until a date at Liverpool Crown Court could be allocated for sentencing. This time around was different though. A month earlier, Vinny had been diagnosed with prostate cancer and he didn't have five years to spare. He'd pleaded guilty to the charges as he'd been caught red-handed in possession of a crowbar, some lock-picks and a Smith and Wesson and there was no point in denying it. All he could do was plead guilty with mitigating circumstances and hope for a reduced sentence from a lenient judge. In the meantime, apart from his illness, he had one bargaining chip to play.

"How did it go with your brief?" The old villain he shared his cell with asked as he walked back into his eight by four domicile. The metal door slammed closed with an echoing clang as the prison officer locked them in and the cloying stench of sweat, testosterone and flatulence filled his nostrils. He never grew accustomed to the stink of jail, no matter how long he spent there. Recreation wasn't for another three hours and he felt like climbing the walls already. His cellmate's face was criss-crossed with deep lines and wrinkles carved by the passing of time and a life of mistreating his body with drugs, cigarettes and alcohol. White stubble grew sparsely on his head and chin.

"Not too bad, Pete," Vinny winked. "He's quietly confident that I could be out of here by the end of the week if all goes to plan." A close associate had told him about the existence and whereabouts of an eyewitness to the murders of two police officers, two security guards and one of the biggest drug dealers in the city. That kind of information had value to it and he intended to use it to avoid a custodial sentence.

"Bullshit," Pete sneered. "You got caught in possession and with your previous, you're looking at a five stretch, minimum."

"Not everything is so black and white," Vinny reached under his pillow and grabbed half a roll of toilet paper. "Have you used my bog roll again you twat?"

"No," Pete exclaimed in a high pitched voice. "What do you take me for?"

"A thieving bastard like the rest of us in here."

"I'm innocent," Pete laughed. "A carriage of justice dropped me off in here."

"A miscarriage of justice, retard."

"Yes, whatever," Pete picked up his newspaper, losing interest in the conversation. "I used two pieces, that's all."

"You've used three pieces, liar."

"Okay, it was three," Pete looked around his newspaper. "How do you know that?"

"Twenty years behind bars, that's how," Vinny tapped his nose. "Three pieces of quilted bog roll equals one cig, which I'll take now." He snatched a cigarette from his cellmate's packet and held it up like a trophy before placing it behind his ear.

"Fair do, I suppose," Pete moaned. "Anyway, what's all this crap about getting out of here?"

"Now that would be telling," Vinny winked again. "Let's just say I've got something of value to offer our friends in blue."

"Oh right," Pete put the newspaper down. "Who are you grassing up this time?" Vinny had floated between being involved on the periphery of the city's crime networks and being a reliable police informer. Not because he was a grass by nature but because he was a terrible criminal who got caught more times than he could remember. Vinny was careless and his mistakes cost him dearly resulting in the loss of two decades of his freedom thus far in his miserable life.

Vinny blushed red. His reputation amongst the other cons was not good. Everyone knew that he was a grass and he had to look over his shoulder constantly. There were some dangerous men who would pay to have Vinny hurt or worse and although he should be safe in prison, he was a sitting duck. "That was all in the past," he protested. "It was a mistake. This time it's just information. No one will get banged up as a result."

"Make sure they don't, Vinny." Pete warned. "Your card is marked already in here. If they find out that you're doing another deal with the law, you won't be safe anywhere in this place even with the door locked." Pete left his last words hanging and a tense silence filled the confined space. "Have you spilled the beans to your brief or are you keeping your cards close to your chest?"

"I've told him enough," Vinny jumped on his bunk. He decided that his cellmate's warning had substance and that maybe he should keep his plans to himself.

The sound of keys being inserted into the lock disturbed the conversation. Both convicts looked expectantly towards the door as it squeaked open. "Walker," a voice boomed.

"Yes, boss," Vinny jumped off his bunk and caught the suspicious look in Pete's eyes.

"Out here now!" The voice growled.

"That bastard still thinks he's still in the army," Pete sneered. "You'd better go and see what he wants, grass." Pete hissed the word 'grass'. It could have been taken as joke but Vinny didn't think that it was meant as one.

Vinny stepped through the open door onto the landing. Two familiar faces eyed him from beneath their shiny peaked caps. One of the officers slammed the door closed behind him. They stared at him with contempt. "Twice this morning I've had to come to your cell, Walker," a screw called Price growled. Everything about him screamed ex-army. His shoes were so highly polished that they looked like glass. He walked ramrod straight and the cons said he had a brush steel up his arse. "Do you think that I'm here to nursemaid you, Walker?"

"No, boss," Vinny looked straight ahead to avoid eye contact. The last man to stare at Price ended up accidentally falling down the metal staircase which ran from the first landing to the ground. He had to eat his food through a straw for the next eight weeks. "Sorry, boss."

"Your brief has arranged for you to have an extraordinary visit from a Detective Smith of the Merseyside Major Investigation Team at four o'clock this afternoon," Price leaned forward and pressed the peak of his cap against Vinny's forehead. "A meeting with your brief this morning and now a visit from an MIT detective, now then, what the fuck are you playing at, Walker?"

"Trying to get the fuck out of here, boss," Vinny's eyes flickered towards the prison officer's for a second and then returned to the far ground.

"I wouldn't hold your breath if I was you, Walker," Price bared his teeth in a sneer. He was so close that Vinny could smell coffee and cigarettes on his breath and Old Spice aftershave. "Detective Smith will be informed about what a slimy, lying grass you are before he gets to sit down opposite you and I'll make sure of that myself. Is that clear?"

"Crystal, boss," Vinny returned the sneer with a grin.

Pete Mitchell pressed his ear to the cold metal door and listened with interest to the details of his cellmate's meeting. There were people inside who would pay handsomely for information like that. It sounded like Vinny Walker was about to turn someone 'big' in to the police and not many cons would take the chance on it being them.

CHAPTER 9

Frederick Hope

Freg winced as the doctor pierced the skin of his temple with the final stitch. He pulled the dissolving gut through the flesh and tied it off expertly. Freg could smell whisky on the old man's breath and the faint smell of urine drifted up from his trousers. As a human being he was a wreck but he was useful for patching up his associates to avoid awkward questions at the hospital. Freg grimaced at the flecks of dandruff which coated the doctor's dark suit jacket; some of them were the size of cornflakes.

Footsteps echoed off the concrete walls, sounding the alarm that someone was approaching. The derelict warehouse they used as a base was a death trap to anyone who ventured inside without knowing which floors were weight bearing and which staircases were safe. They used the floors above the third where the damp and rot were not so bad. The motley crew that were watching the triage and listening to Freg's version of what happened at Beech Close jumped into action. Weapons clicked as rounds were chambered and the gang members sprinted for the door. One of them climbed onto an ancient workbench and peered out of the window, looking for signs of any vehicles. "There's no sign of any cars."

"It's the Priest's main man," a voice came from the corridor. "He's with another two suits."

"About time," Freg moaned pushing the doctor away and pressing the new dressing to his wound. "Thanks, Doc."

"I would like to say, 'you're welcome' but I wouldn't mean it," the doctor snapped. "That kid in there is going to die unless he gets to hospital immediately. There's an infection setting into the wound."

"We'll see what the Priest says now okay, so stop whinging."

"Whinging?" the doctor replied angrily. "Every time I come here, I am putting my career at risk."

"What career?" Freg turned and laughed. "You were booted out for prescribing yourself drugs, you smackhead and we pay you well so shut it."

The footsteps grew louder and a few mumbled greetings were heard from the corridor. Then the familiar face of the Priest's enforcer appeared in the doorway accompanied by an aura of pure malevolence. His blond hair was gelled back from his face and fastened at the nape of the neck with a black braid. He wore a look of contempt on his pockmarked face as he looked around the gathering. There was a mixture of tracksuits, trainers and cheap suits and leather jackets in the room. He gathered that they were street dealers and their suppliers all linked to Frederick Hope. He placed his thumbs under the lapels of his black Crombie and glared at Freg with piercing grey eyes. The smell of Chanel aftershave drifted with him as he stepped through the door followed by two men who had to duck beneath the frame to enter the workshop.

"Mr James, nice to see you," Freg stood up and made to shake his hand but the greeting was ignored. He wasn't sure if that was his surname or first name, In fact he was positive that his name wasn't James but that's what everyone called him and he was not a man to irritate.

"Get rid of the muppets, Frederick," James smiled thinly without taking his eyes from Freg. No one waited for Freg to ask them to leave and no one questioned being called a muppet. The Priest and his henchmen were regarded as devils incarnate. They were near the top of a tree most sane people wouldn't dare to climb. "You can stay, Doc," James said as the doctor packed his stuff ready to leave. "If this conversation goes the wrong way, we may need your expertise," he added coldly. Mr James walked to the workbench and ran a finger along the firearms which were laid out, stripped and cleaned and ready to be sold. "Some quality equipment here," he said, as he looked through the glass in the window. It was thick with grime, which was decades old. The encrusted filth made the world outside look sepia in tone. He looked frozen in thought as he gazed through the grime at the city below, although the muscles in his jaw twitched as he ground his back teeth together.

"What happened?" He turned to him.

"I took a round to the side of my head," Freg nervously broke the silence. He was rarely intimidated by another man but James had an aura around him. "Just skimmed me, but I was out of it for a while." He looked at the Priest's minders who seemed to scowl in stereo. The enforcers connected to Priest and his organisation had a reputation for brutality of the type usually associated with horror fiction.

"Where is Carol Barker?" James turned and smiled. He cocked his head to the side as he waited for the answer.

"Barker flipped and the bastard had a Mossberg," Freg shrugged as he made his excuses but the look on James's face told him to get to the point. "He took three of my lads down and Moby lost his hand. He's in a bad way next door. The doc reckons he'll snuff it if we don't get him to a hospital don't you, Doc?"

"He has lost a lot of blood. He has an infection and needs specialist care," the doctor mumbled in agreement. He held his medical bag tightly waiting for the chance to leave. He had no wish to become more involved than he already was. "I can't do any more for him."

"Messy, Frederick," James smiled thinly wiping dust from his immaculate coat. "You didn't answer my question. Where is Carol Barker?"

Freg thought about his answer carefully before replying. "Barker didn't know where she was. I had a gun to his daughter's head and he still denied knowing where she was," Freg lied. "He was hysterical. If he had known, he would have told me, believe me."

James raised his eyebrows which were dark in contrast to his blond hair. "If Barker was so terrified, how the hell did he mange to shoot three of your muppets and clip you too?" His face turned to stone. "Sounds to me like he was in control, not the other way around."

"He collapsed," Freg explained with a straight face. "He was thrashing about and frothing at the mouth. I thought the guy was having a fit or a heart attack or something. I took the girl into the front room because she was screaming and one of my muppets untied him. Next thing he was up on his feet and blasting my crew like Jessie James on acid. Wesley fucked up big time untying him but he took both barrels of the Mossberg in the head for his mistake. He was a good lad but too soft."

"So you have left dead bodies behind at the scene, blood, DNA and teeth?" Priest turned over his bottom lip and frowned. "It will take them a few hours at most to identify them. The police will be all over you like shit sticks to a blanket."

"No one carried ID."

"Maybe but the police will identify them quickly and come looking for their known associates, namely you." James pointed both index fingers at Freg. "You have been sloppy and now we have the heat on us and nothing to show for it. Not good is it?"

"Do I really need to be here?" the doctor held up his hand before speaking, like a schoolboy who was scared of his teacher. He removed his black rimmed glasses and wiped sweat from his brow with the back of his hand. "I don't need to hear all this stuff. It's none of my business."

"None of your business?" James turned sharply. "I thought there was a lad in there with a hand missing, bleeding to death? Was his name Moby?"

"Yes," Freg nodded. "He's my cousin."

"There is a young man in dire straits but I can't do any more," the doctor licked his lips as his mouth went dry. He desperately needed a drink. His body was screaming with the need for whisky or methadone or better still, both. "He needs blood and surgery or he will die."

"You're right you don't need to hear this," James smiled. The doctor nodded happily and moved towards the door. "Before you go put Moby out of his misery and make the body a bit easier to dispose of."

"What?" the doctor looked horrified.

"You heard me," James glared with ice cold behind his eyes. "Kill him and dismember the body. I want him in the river feeding the fishes before tomorrow morning. There are too many loose ends already. Unless you have a problem with that, Frederick, after all he is your cousin?"

Freg held his gaze as he answered. The question had been poised as a test to see if he would endanger the network by saving his relative. "We'll do whatever we have to, Mr James. He's probably going to die anyway. Do as he says, Doc."

"I can't do that," the doctor protested. "There is no way. He needs a hospital and he will survive."

"Where is his hand?" James asked Freg politely. Too politely for comfort.

"In the front garden of Barker's gaff."

"You left that there too?"

"I planned to tidy up, honestly but Barker was blasting away. We had to leave in hurry and I was shot," Freg pointed to the stitches in his head.

"The police will have a severed hand on ice and they will be looking in every emergency room and casualty department across the country for a man who is missing a hand," James walked towards the doctor. He grabbed his wrist and pressed his thumbnail painfully hard against the pulse. The doctor buckled at the knees in agony. "Now do you think Moby will be difficult to find if we take him to hospital?"

"No, you're hurting me," the doctor gasped.

"He will slowly die in pain in that freezing cold room next door if you don't put him out of his misery," he released his grip. "Can you imagine how much pain Moby is feeling in his wrist?"

"I've given him morphine to ease the pain."

"Good, now go and give him some more. Give him all of it."

"Priest, please don't make me do this. I'm a doctor. I don't kill people when there is every chance that he will live."

"Help him, Kevin. I think our friend the doctor needs some persuasion," James nodded to one of his minders. He reached out a huge hand and grabbed the doctor by the shoulder lifting him from his feet. He scurried on tiptoes barely touching the floor as the minder carried him out of the room. His muffled protests quietened down when he realised that he was alone with the giant enforcer. Resigned to his task, he'd chosen the less painful route. "Now then, Frederick, what are we going to do about this situation?"

"We went there looking for Carol Barker but she wasn't there. Barker would have told me if he knew anything like I said, I had a gun to his daughter's head. He was hysterical. I know that he knew nothing but I made the best of a bad lot," Freg nodded seriously. "I took his daughter. We can use her to flush out Carol Barker."

James nodded slowly and gripped his broad chin between his forefinger and thumb. He glanced at the remaining minder and shrugged his shoulders. The minder rolled his eyes towards the ceiling and shook his head. "Did you hear that, Michael?"

"I did," the minder's voice sounded like he had broken glass in his throat although his accent was not local.

"What do you think about that, Michael?" James looked back at Freg and smiled. "Do you think he 'made the best of a bad lot'?"

"I think he's underestimated the impact that a missing child has on the entire community and the Priest will not be happy," Michael spoke with an educated voice which belied his appearance. "You see society sees child molesters, abusers and kidnappers, as the scum of the earth. Public opinion carries immense weight when children are involved and as such, a kidnapped child will bring the full resources of the law enforcement agencies crashing down on anyone stupid enough consider that as an option," Michael smiled and turned to Freg. "I think that Frederick here has miscalculated the consequences of taking a child hostage. He has also displayed that he is made from low moral fibre."

"What are you trying to say, Michael? Stop beating about the bush," James faked a confused expression. "Do you think that Frederick has compounded his list of catastrophic mistakes by adding child abduction and aggravated black mail to the mix?"

"I think you have summed it up perfectly." Michael grimaced at Freg. "I would be inclined to sever all ties with this individual immediately. Frederick is looking at life without parole and so are his associates."

"Michael is a clever guy. He used to be a teacher you know. What am I supposed to do now, Frederick?" James frowned. "I can't just sack you. You and your muppets are a threat to my liberty if I cut you loose and you know what that means. Threats and loose ends cannot be tolerated."

"Wait a minute," Freg stood up and wrung his hands together nervously. "We haven't hurt the girl, Mr James. We'll make sure she is okay and use her to find Carol Barker. Then I'll make sure she is dropped off at a hospital or cop-shop. Trust me this won't reflect on you."

"Where is the kid?" Michael growled.

"She's on the sixth floor, out of the way." The old tannery mill was seven storeys tall, a maze of workshops and storage barns.

"It must be minus two up there," Michael turned to James. "How old is she?"

"I don't know," Frederick babbled.

James looked angry and thoughtful at the same time. He was racing the scenarios through his mind. The sound of an electric saw disturbed his thoughts. It was followed immediately by a blood curdling scream and shouts of anguish. Footsteps clattered down the hallway and then more startled cries came from the room next door.

"What the hell is going on in there?" James snapped angrily. "Go and see, Michael." The big man slipped through the doorframe and headed towards the next room where all the commotion was coming from. "We have a got a huge problem, Frederick," James grabbed Freg's cheek painfully between finger and thumb. Instinctively Freg knew that it would be fatal to retaliate. "You dumb bastard. I should have known you were only fit for pushing smack to scumbags. Now listen to me carefully."

"I'm listening," Freg garbled. "What do you want me to do?"

"You have forty eight hours to find Carol Barker and get rid of the girl."

"What do you mean?"

"What do you think I mean?"

"Kill her?"

"I don't care what you do with her but if anyone but me and you knows she's dead or she escapes and she is found, you're going to suffer like you cannot imagine, Frederick," James hissed. "If that girl turns up then every gang in this city will know who took her because you left your name and address all over the house in Beech Close. They will know who you work for and they will know that we have a little girl hostage. If I lose face from this, then I'll cut your face off with a spoon, do you understand?"

"Yes," Freg nodded frantically. He felt sick inside. Killing the girl was not in his plan. He hadn't thought about the backlash from kidnapping her. He just saw her as a means to an end.

"You will not believe what has happened in there," Michael's gravely voice interrupted. "I've never witnessed anything like it."

"Enlighten us," James let go of Freg and smiled. His eyes gleamed now the anger gone for a moment.

"The doctor started sawing Moby up and the poor fucker came round," Michael shook his head. "He hadn't injected enough morphine. Moby sat up while the doctor was sawing off his left leg. He realised what was happening and started screaming. The doctor was so freaked he passed out."

"What's happened?" Freg asked amazed and sickened by what had happened to his cousin. They were never close but he was still a relative.

"Kevin snapped Moby's neck," Michael grabbed an invisible head with his hands and twisted it sharply to demonstrate. "The poor lad had suffered enough and there's only one person to blame for that, isn't there, Frederick?"

"How was I supposed to know Barker was armed?" Freg protested. "Youngy didn't mention shotguns."

"Youngy was a fool," James nodded sternly. "That's why he's in the morgue."

"He was unlucky," Freg protested. "They set him up didn't they?"

James swapped glances with Michael and a silent communication passed between them. "Youngy had a big mouth," James swiped his lips with an invisible zip. "Someone close to him was passing information to the police. That's how he got nicked."

"Who?" Freg looked horrified. "None of my lads would have grassed."

"That's in hand," James raised a finger, "you don't have to worry about that. It will be dealt with."

"I can cope with my area of the business now he's dead, until you put someone in his place," Freg assured him nervously but he was far from convincing. "Trust me. I'll sort this mess out."

"Like you did in Tenerife?"

"That wasn't my fault," Freg snapped. "The lad was out of order. He got what was coming to him."

"Maybe he did but he was one of your own, wasn't he?" James looked at Michael again and the minder watched Freg's reaction.

"He was on the take."

"Was he?"

"Yes, that's why I did him."

"Are you sure, Frederick because I can't trust anyone who turns on his own for nothing?" James stared at him intently. "Unstable men are a liability."

Freg flinched physically as he recalled what he'd done to Mark Overand at Beech Close. His anger issues had haunted him since his adolescent years. He had no control over is temper. When a weaker man challenged his authority or insulted him, a red mist descended and violence was his first and last instinct. He knew that he was unstable. Steven Young knew that he was unstable and kept him at arm's length for that reason. The distance he put between them hurt him badly. He looked up to Stephen. He respected him. He loved him. "I'm as stable as the next man and I won't let you down."

"You will do it once."

"I'll find Carol Barker," Freg said seriously. "Even if I have to go to the hospital and beat it out of Ged Barker myself."

"Jesus Christ, what I am I working with here?" James put his head in his hands. He looked up and walked towards the door. "Stay away from Ged Barker, you idiot," James sighed. "Forty eight hours, Frederick or I'll make sure that one of my boys uses that saw on you while you are awake. Make sure that little girl is looked after." He pointed a finger and winked at Freg as he left. He turned to his minder. "Wait with Kevin until the doctor has finished, then tidy up the loose ends, all of them. You can help, Frederick. We'll say what you're made of."

Michael nodded and waited until his boss had left the room before turning back to Freg. "He's a dangerous man," Michael gestured towards the door. "The Priest is on another level again and he'll be disappointed to say the least."

"I know that," Freg tried to gather himself. He wasn't used to being bullied, it had always been the other way around.

"You need to make sure that little girl is warm and fed properly, understand?"

"I will," Freg swallowed hard.

"I was a teacher once you know," Michael smiled thinly. "I love kids."

"Why the change of career?" Freg shrugged confused at the change of subject. It was interesting enough that this giant was once a teacher but hardly relevant.

"One of my pupils, a seven year old boy came to school with bruises all over him once too often," Michael's eyes seemed to lose focus as he remembered the boy. "I reported it of course but Social Services did nothing about it. I went around to the parents' house and had a word with the father. He was an arsehole, smackhead and he had a pop at me." Michael wandered to the window and watched the traffic below before heading for the door. "He was in intensive care for a week or so and I lost my job." Michael turned and glared at Freg as he ducked beneath the doorframe. "If any harm comes to that little girl, I'll skin you alive myself, do you hear me?"

"I hear you," Freg nodded.

"Good," Michael smiled warmly but his eyes were not smiling. "Make sure the girl is comfortable and then we'll sort out laying your cousin to rest."

"Okay, I'll sort her out now."

Michael Yates glanced at the weapons on the bench before ducking through the doorframe and heading towards the sound of the bone saw. Freg watched his huge frame disappearing down the corridor with a sick feeling rising in his throat. Mr James wanted the girl dead. His henchmen didn't know that and they would kill him if the girl died. Freg gulped silently and bile rose in his throat as the enforcer's footsteps echoed through the mill. The sound of the saw buzzing again was the final straw and he vomited all over his own shoes.

CHAPTER 10

Kathy Brooks

Kathy sat at her desk in Canning Place, trying to get her circulation moving again. She'd spent the morning trawling through the trees which bordered the crime scene on Silver Lane. The more she studied the evidence from the scene, the cloudier the picture became. She stood up and stamped her feet to get the blood flowing to her toes. The view from her window looked out over the new quarter of the city, Liverpool 1. The council had demolished an ageing bus station and some derelict office blocks and built a modern shopping area which any city in Europe would envy. It linked the city centre to the tourist hubs at the Albert Docks on the banks of the river. A few months ago, the shops were boarded up and the streets were empty but now many of the businesses were trading again and shoppers were dotted along the frozen pavements. Kathy envied them. The thought of spending an afternoon browsing amongst racks of clothes and testing the latest fragrances before sipping a large latte and reading the newspaper leisurely, made her heart sink. She was lucky to get a dinner break at the moment and the smell of the dead was the only scent she would sample for the foreseeable future. The stench never seemed to leave her and she often woke in the small hours feeling as if she was neck deep in gore. She began keeping a handkerchief doused in Aramis beneath her pillow; the musky aftershave chased the smell of decay away for a while.

A knock on the door startled her and she stepped closer to the desk, feeling a little guilty for digressing from her work even if it was just for a moment. Sometimes her conscientiousness filled her with guilt. She couldn't rest when there were people to identify and murderers to catch and despite her relentless efforts, there was a never ending stream of bodies to process. She picked up a file and pretended to study it. "Come in," she called.

"We have the preliminary results back from the victims at Beech Close, Dr Brooks," a handsome young trainee poked his head around the door. Danny Wells was witty, intelligent, gorgeous and as camp as a row of tents in a field. When he introduced himself socially, he described himself as a 'pink David Beckam' without the football talent. The women in the office loved him and the men envied him, despite his sexuality. Kathy liked him but she had to rein him in sometimes. He had the knack of being giddy and loud when the situation didn't allow for any humour. "Do you want to go through them with the team before we send them on to the MIT?"

"Who is the lead detective?"

"Alec Ramsay," Danny grimaced and shivered dramatically. "He's so stern, he frightens me!"

"He's a big pussycat," Kathy laughed. "I need to speak to him anyway. Send them to me and copy him in. We'll go through it with the team tomorrow morning."

"Okidokie, Dr Brooks," Danny pointed a well manicured index finger. "I love that perfume. It's my favourite." He beamed as he closed the door. From any other man that could have been inappropriate but from Danny, it was a compliment.

Kathy walked behind the desk and sat down in her wide leather chair. It was padded and swivelled and Kathy always said that when she retired, she was taking it home with her. Checking that the preliminary results were on her PC, she was about to call Alec when the phone rang.

"Dr Brooks," she answered abruptly. Kathy was expecting to be harassed for results which weren't ready yet but she didn't recognise the voice.

"Dr Brooks, this is Callum Gladstone speaking," the voice sounded educated and impatient. "I'm the liaison minister from the Home Office."

"I know who you are, Mr Gladstone," Kathy replied curtly. She had dealt with his office several times. Each time she was treated with minimal respect despite her professional standing. Gladstone was tasked with auditing the private security companies which the government employed to support the police. "What can I do for you?"

"I want to know what stage the investigation into the Silver Lane incident is at," he asked aloofly. "From a forensic point of view of course."

"I'm sorry but I have no brief to give you any details about any case which this lab works on," Kathy was astounded. "And you have no right to ask for any either. You need to go through the correct channels, Mr Gladstone."

"I'm a Home Office liaison minister, Dr Brooks and as such, I have access to anything that I require, whenever I require it."

"Then I suggest that you liaise with the correct channels," Kathy's blood pressure hit critical. "Do not call my direct line ever again, do you understand?" Kathy put the phone down without waiting for a reply.

"How dare you......" Gladstone was cut off mid rant.

"I can't believe the cheek of the arrogant bastard," Kathy hissed under her breath as she picked up the phone and stabbed three digits to make an internal call. She had several important issues to discuss with Alec and she needed to do it before any of the facts could be stifled by the hierarchy. The fact that he was the lead detective on the Beech Close shootings gave her a legitimate excuse to talk to him at length during working hours.

"Superintendent Ramsay," his familiar voice answered.

"Alec, its Kathy."

"Hello, you," Alec replied brightly. "I was about to call you."

"I bet you were."

"I was," he chuckled. "We've got a right mess on our plate with this missing girl. Please tell me you have the results from Beech Close."

"Is there any news on her?"

"Murmurs, but nothing solid," Alec was vague. News of the shootings at Beech Close was spreading across the city. Dead gang members were big news both to the public and to the villains. It hadn't taken long for informers to connect the dead men to associates of Steven Young. "Once we can confirm the identities of the men, we'll have a starting place to look for her, assuming they took her, obviously."

"Well, I can help you there," Kathy said briskly. Finding Jodie Barker was top of everyone's agenda. "Danny has sent the preliminary forensics to you. Have you got it?"

"I'm opening the files now," Alec said. "Brilliant work, Kathy. We've been working with a huge list of possible associates, this will narrow it down."

"You have the names of all four deceased and the identity of the man the severed hand belongs to. That should keep you going."

"I'll get this to the team immediately, thanks, Kathy," Alec was about to rush off the phone but then he remembered something. "Did you find anything more at the Silver Lane scene?"

"Yes, I did but I need half an hour of your time to go over it properly," she sounded guarded. "And I've just had a call from Callum Gladstone asking how the forensic investigation at Silver Lane is going."

"The guy's an arsehole," Alec growled. "He's supposed to police the plastics but he's so far up Adrian Salter's backside that he could brush his teeth from the inside."

"Salter is the new CEO of Brigade Security, right?"

"Don't you read your emails?"

"Only the ones which relate to my department," Kathy laughed. "What happens to the plastics and your lot is of no interest to me. Anyway you have another priority right now. Call me when you have some time to spare."

"That sounds promising."

"Don't hold your breath, Alec," Kathy warned. "It's all speculation at the moment."

"Okay, I'll call you once the team are briefed, thanks again."

"Take care, Alec," Kathy said. "Find that little girl."

"We will," Alec assured her, "talk later."

CHAPTER 11

MIT

The MIT office was an open plan area with sixty desks set out in four rows of five desks, each consisting of three work stations. The team usually ran with fifty detectives at a time, reaching sixty at full strength when their case-load demanded it. Every desk was occupied. There was a tense atmosphere amongst the gathering as the officers waited for the preliminary forensic results which could help them track Jodie Barker. A bank of digital screens displayed crime scene photographs and images of suspects and the deceased found at the scene. The room smelled of fresh coffee as several detectives wandered around, topping up the team with caffeine. Some of them chatted and gathered around computer screens as virtual searches were being carried out on internet footprints left by known suspects associated to Steve Young. Their Facebook and Twitter accounts were being trawled through in detail. Photographs and recent contacts with friends were analysed.

"Is everyone here?" Alec walked in front of the screens and clapped his hands together. His forehead creased with deep lines as he frowned at the crime scene photographs. Congealing blood looks black in digital photographs and Alec never stopped being surprised by its appearance despite his years of seeing them.

"Everyone except Smithy, Guv," Detective Sergeant Wallace answered. The reason for her presence there wasn't clear to everyone on the team. "He's left a message saying he's gone to Risley to interview someone called, Vinny Walker."

"Good," Alec smiled and loosened his tie. "This is DS Wallace, for everyone who hasn't met her yet. I've brought her in from Coppice Hill as she was the first detective on the scene at Beech Close." A murmur of greetings and half waves greeted her. "She'll be heading up one team and Smithy will be heading up the second when he gets back. Les, you take charge of Smithy's team until he gets back please."

A few disgruntled expressions were scattered amongst the attendees but Alec had no time for bruised egos. Being a team leader with MIT was a step on the way to promotion and everyone in the department had ambition as well as talent. "Alison," Alec wasted no time with pleasantries. "The four dead men at the scene are confirmed as, Raymond Carter, Wesley Naylor, Luke John and Mark Overand. The severed hand belonged to a twenty year old man called Anthony Richards or 'Moby' to his associates."

"We've got their files, Guv," Alison nodded. She looked different without her white paper suite on, extremely attractive and yet extremely professional. Her cat-like eyes were mesmerising.

"Good," Alec frowned as he glanced through their records on the screen. "They are all known to us and they are all known associates of Stephen Young, deceased. The causes of their deaths are no mystery to us, apart from Mark Overand, who wasn't shot. He was beaten and then had his throat slashed at the scene. We are sure that the homeowner shot and killed the others but Overand's death doesn't fit with the rest and there is no sign of Anthony Richards at the scene. I want your team to bring in everyone connected to these men and find Richards."

"Yes, Guv," Allison stood up and readied to get started. "We have their families, friends and associates listed already and we've applied for their mobile phone records." Some of the MIT detectives rolled their eyes at each other. Her eagerness to impress would irritate some of the cynics in the room.

"Great work," Alec encouraged her eagerness openly although he would have expected no less from any of his team. "I want to know why Ged Barker was targeted by this gang. This wasn't a robbery gone wrong, they were there for something else and if we can find that out, then we can find out why they took Jodie Barker."

"Yes, Guv."

"Les," Alec turned to the second team.

"Guv?" A fat balding detective who looked uncomfortably crammed into his grey suit and shirt answered.

"Anthony Richards was a close associate of Young's, we know that for certain but who else would run with this mob?" Alec threw the question out to the room. It needed answering if they were to get a handle on what happened. "In Young's absence, who would step up to the plate and where would they be holed up? And why would they take the girl?"

"Are we sure that they took her, Guv?" Les asked sternly.

"You don't think they did?" Alec raised his eyebrows, questioning the comment.

"I am thinking aloud, Guv," Les shrugged. "She could have run away, or she could be dead and the gang took her body to hide the fact that a kid died there too."

Alec held up one hand and looked around the room. "Does anyone else think that's a serious possibility?" There were shakes of the head and some blank faces but nobody agreed with the theory. "Good, because if the press get hold of that theory, we'll have a shit-storm raining down on us. We are working on the premise that Jodie Barker is alive and being held as a hostage for some reason, clear?"

"Guv," Les grunted.

"I'm making an appeal downstairs in twenty minutes," Alec looked at his watch. "The television will be full of it, so I don't want any cracks in our version of events, okay?" Silent faces answered him. "Jodie Barker is alive until we know any different." He reinforced the point. "We've been crucified by the press before, this time we need to be seen to be doing everything that we can positively. I want the press onside this time." The detectives remained silent as he glowered at their faces. The warning wasn't missed by anyone of them.

"Have we heard anything from the hospital about Ged Barker?" Les broke the silence. "He must have an idea what happened there."

"He's been in surgery having his spleen removed," Alec nodded. "Parsons is there now. When he comes around, we'll get some answers from him."

"I hope I'm not too late," a gruff voice tinged with a Manchester accent interrupted the brief. "Sorry to interrupt, Alec but I haven't got much time to spare."

"You're just in time," Alec shook the black detective's hand. "You all know Raymond Citrone, from the Drug Squad. He's come to brief us on Stephen Young and his associates." Alec stepped aside to let him hold the centre of the room. Raymond smiled at the gathering and slipped of his blue jacket. His shirt and tie were neat and expensive but they looked out of place beneath his short dreadlocks which protruded from his scalp like fuzzy thorns.

"What do you need to know?" Citrone shrugged. "I'm not sure how we can help."

"Whatever you can tell us about these men and their associates," Alec pointed to the screen. "And anything you can tell us which may help us to find this girl, Jodie Barker." Her image was displayed on the top right hand screen.

"Okay, let's start at the bottom and work up, Raymond Carter," Citrone grinned and his teeth looked unnaturally white. "Was a low level punk with a string of burglary convictions. We busted him for possession of cannabis last year but he walked, with a tag and a slap on the wrist. He was so far down the pecking order, I doubt he even knew who he really worked for. Wesley Naylor and David John took a fall for Young three years ago. They were caught with a kilo of crack in the boot of their car. We knew they were just delivery mules but they refused to talk and did a couple of years each. They were up to their old tricks as soon as they came out." Citrone pointed to the next screen. "Mark Overand is a new one on us. He must have joined Young's crew recently, probably after Young's arrest. Anthony

Richards, or 'Moby' to his associates, was one of Young's starlets. We think he popped a couple of dealers in Croxteth last year, which moved him up the ranks somewhat but we couldn't make anything stick." Citrone looked around at the puzzled faces before him and then turned to Alec. "You know all this already, right?"

"Pretty much," Alec nodded. "What we want to know is why there is a cloud around Young's arrest. If we knew what he was up to, then we may be able to work out what his gang was doing at Beech Close and who would step up to the mark when he was taken off the streets."

Citrone looked at his shoes for a moment before speaking. "Young was arrested by Cheshire during a sting operation. They set him up to buy twenty kilos of cocaine, or that is their story. I'm not so sure that's the actual truth but that is the official line."

"Who would take over from him?"

"This is pure speculation, okay, Anthony Richards had a cousin a few years older than he was," Citrone pointed to the screen. "His name is Frederick Hope." The sound of computer keyboards being used penetrated the silence as half a dozen Google searches were started around the room. "We don't have anything on him but we do know that he did five years of an eight year term in a Spanish jail. He was released last year during the troubles and as far as we know, he may be back here."

"What did he go down for?" Alec prompted.

"He was being followed by a joint taskforce who were investigating smuggling to and from the Canary Islands. Hope got involved in an altercation in a bar in Los Christianos and left a teenager in intensive care.

He was sent down for grievous before the taskforce could get near him for smuggling."

"Do you think he's stepped into Young's shoes?" Alec asked.

"Maybe somewhere further down the line he could but Young wasn't as big as we first thought," Citrone shook his head. "Young was a wide boy and he made a lot of money but he was never really part of the top tier of importers. He pulled off a few good deals in Tenerife and he certainly facilitated the sale of gear across the city via a network of young dealers and runners but he didn't control the importation of big consignments. Apparently the big boys tolerated him because he shifted the gear on the streets for them. He didn't control anything substantial. The top tier let us think that he did for years." There were some surprised looks around the room.

"Are you sure Young wasn't shifting the blame after his arrest?" Les piped up with a frown on his face. "Young's network has been known to us for as long as I can remember."

"That's what we thought too, Detective," Citrone nodded thoughtfully. "It turns out he was just the salesman. He was used as a front and didn't control anything."

"So why set him up?" Les pushed his point. "Why not go for the people above him?"

"Because we didn't know who they were," Citrone countered. "We needed an 'in' to the organisation and Young was the weak link."

"We?" Alec interrupted.

"What?" Citrone blushed when he realised what he had said.

"You said, 'we' didn't know who the top tier was," Alec shrugged. "Was this a combined operation with Cheshire?"

"We knew about it, obviously," Citrone backpedalled. "We gave them a lot of intelligence because we wanted them identified as much as Cheshire did but we knew nothing about the logistics of the sting. Setting up the plastics was not on our agenda. We wanted the big fish; a couple of Brigade officers on the take was way off our radar."

"We all know that the riots knocked everything out of sync including the drugs business, but was the power shift really that dramatic?" Alec asked cynically.

"The truth is that we still don't know," Citrone sighed. He paused and rubbed his chin as he thought about how much he could say without compromising his department. "Look, it is taking us all our time to catch up with the shift out there," he gestured to the window. "The fuel drought crippled the main dealers. Nothing moved for weeks, no trucks, no trains, no boats and the only people who thrived were the ones who adapted quickly. The hierarchy is unrecognisable to what it was. Getting Steven Young to turn evidence was our way of restoring the balance. His information would have given us details of the new networks."

"So, if Young was a puppet, who does pull the strings?" Alec was getting frustrated. He felt like he was being fobbed off.

Citrone smiled thinly. "All we know is that Young was going to turn evidence for Cheshire by giving them enough information to take the network apart from the top down, starting with a guy he called 'The Priest'. We know nothing about him. He's a ghost but his name keeps coming up. The rest you know already. Young was taken out before the deal was cemented and the names of the importers and the information died with him."

"So you think our best option is Frederick Hope?"

"If I was hunting Young's associates, I'd start with him and the rest won't be far away. Sorry that I can't be more help."

"Are you looking into the plastics over the coppers killed in the Young case?" Les jumped in with an embarrassing question and a murmur of support rippled through the gathering.

"It's Cheshire's case. I can't comment."

"Thanks for your input," Alec stepped forward and shook his hand. "We'll look into Hope and if we find anything of interest to you, I'll let you know." He had heard enough and wanted the detective gone.

"I doubt you will, but thanks," Citrone smiled and raised a hand in goodbye to the gathering as he grabbed his jacket and headed for the door, relief all over his face.

"Just one more question," Alec added as an afterthought, "were the joint taskforce in Tenerife investigating, drugs?" All eyes went back to their superintendent.

Citrone paused again before answering. "Partly drugs, but their main brief was to nail a firm who were moving arms and people by the container load, from Morocco into Europe via the Canaries."

"So Young was involved in arms dealing?" Alec asked gruffly. "That puts a different spin on things."

"Like I said before, we don't really know for sure but he made a lot of money in Tenerife and our sources tell us that he didn't make it importing drugs."

"Okay, thanks," Alec dismissed Citrone with a scowl. He hated the internal politics which created barriers between departments. "Thanks a bunch," he muttered beneath his breath as the detective left. "All right people, he clapped his hands together. I have to talk to the press and make this appeal. Whilst I'm gone, find Frederick Hope and anyone connected to him."

"We're on it, Guv."

"Les, I want you to dig through everything we can find about Ged Barker. There's a connection somewhere, which we haven't seen. I want to know why he was targeted and why his daughter was taken from Beech Close."

"Yes, Guv," Les stood up and began delegating to his squad of detectives. "What about the taskforce, who tracked Hope in Tenerife, maybe they'll have something we can follow up on, Guv?"

"Good thinking, Les," Alec clapped his hands. "Find out who was involved and what information they have on file. It's a long shot but it could help. The rest of you know what you need to do. Find Jodie Barker."

CHAPTER 12

HMP Risley

Detective Sergeant Smith waited patiently in the visiting room. It was a cross between a railway waiting room and a chess tournament without the pieces. The furniture was plastic and sterile, fixed to floor and in need of a good scrub. Arranged in lines, the visitors would sit facing the inmates across low coffee tables, monitored closely by CCTV and strategically placed prison officers. Today, Sergeant Smith was the only visitor. The room smelled of disinfectant mingled with the sickly sweet odour of sweat. Smithy was tired and his eyes were sore from the lack of sleep he had had the night before. Waiting around and going through the rigmarole required to enter the prison had made him wearier. He felt for his mobile phone to check his messages and panicked for a second when he realised it wasn't there; scolding himself mentally when remembered that it had been taken from him, along with his gun and his pen before he'd been allowed in.

Keys jangled and the sound of a door opening alerted him to the arrival of his snout. Vinny Walker shuffled into the room shadowed by two sour faced guards. He looked old and frightened; his skin was grey in pallor and the whites of his eyes were threaded with red veins. "Sergeant Smith. I didn't think I'd ever be pleased to see your face," Vinny sat down opposite him.

He looked a shell of the man he'd met many times over the years. "You look rough, Vinny," Smithy smiled. "How are they treating you?"

"Three hot meals a day and all the grief they can give you. The same old shit, just a different day."

"Well, you will keep getting yourself banged up," Smithy chuckled. He had a soft spot for the old villain. "How's your cancer treatment going?"

"They've done everything they can so far," Vinny shrugged. "We'll just have to wait and see if it spreads any further." His eyes showed fear despite his carefree reply. "I'd be a lot better if I could get out of here."

"I hope you're not hanging your hopes on me for that?"

"Look, my brief is working hard to get leniency because of my illness and my age but I don't have the money to buy a good barrister," Vinny said hoarsely. "You could get me out of here quickly."

"It would be quicker to dig a tunnel under the walls," Smithy teased. "It's not going to happen, Vinny, so forget it."

"You can pull some strings," Vinny leaned forward and lowered his voice. "What I've got is big. It has to be worth something." He wrung his hands as he spoke and Smithy noticed that he was shaking.

"We've got nothing to offer you, Vinny," Smithy said sternly. "If you have some information about the shootings then tell me and I'll take it back to my governor but there are no guarantees."

"You're having a laugh aren't you?" Vinny shook his head. "I can give you the name of an eyewitness to the murder of two police officers. You could get me out of here and put me in the protection program. That's the least I'll accept."

"Not a chance, Vinny, for one, you're not a witness," Smithy put his hands flat on the table. "All I have is your word for it. You can see how this looks from our point of view. Give me something solid and we might listen but right now, you're pissing in the wind."

Vinny coughed and his eyes watered. His face flushed as the strain in his chest pained him. "I need a drink of water."

"Can we get some water please?" Smithy called one of the guards. The guard grunted and frowned as he walked out of the room. "Are you alright?"

"No," Vinny took a deep breath and coughed again. "I'm not long for this world and I don't want to die in here."

"That's a bit dramatic."

"This is genuine info but I need to get out of this dump. I'm not parting with it for nothing." A coughing fit wracked his body again. The grumpy prison officer placed a paper cup filled with water on the table.

"Make sure you don't choke on that," he joked but nobody laughed.

"Fuck you very much," Smithy said with a straight face.

"What did you say to me?" The guard turned.

"You heard me quite clearly the first time." The ginger detective glared at him. The prison officer backed down, thinking better of getting into a slanging match with a senior detective from the MIT.

"Thanks," Vinny lifted the cup to his lips and drank. He leaned forward once more and whispered. "Look, you have to believe me. This is kosher."

"Maybe it is but it doesn't matter if I believe you or not," Smithy shrugged and sat back. "Without something tangible, I can't help you and we haven't got the time to waste while you arse about."

"Have I ever given you anything crap?"

"No," Smithy acknowledged, "but your credibility above me is zero. Give me something I can take to my boss and we'll see where it goes, otherwise we are finished here." Smithy looked into Vinny's red eyes and he saw his pain and desperation in them. "I can't help you unless you help yourself."

"How do I know you'll get me out of here if I tell you?"

"I never mentioned getting you out of here, Vinny." Smithy left the comment hanging.

"Come on, give me a break," Vinny whined.

"Last chance," Smithy shrugged. "I've got an investigation to get back to."

"This is like gold dust," Vinny hissed. "This is the biggest thing I've ever given to you."

"Bye, Vinny," Smithy stood up and readied to leave. "Take it easy."

The big detective turned and took two steps towards the exit. The prison guards moved from their perches. "Wait," Vinny said. "Okay, okay, sit down will you. You're killing me here. Sit down."

"You've got five minutes." Smithy slumped back down in the chair and the guards rolled their eyes and went back to their positions. "Make it quick and make it good."

Vinny sighed and wrung his hands nervously. He looked around the empty room and leaned closer. "One of the coppers murdered was trying to make money on the side," Vinny began quietly. "He knew where the meeting was going down days before it happened."

"What, he was involved in dealing?" Smithy frowned unconvinced by the theory.

"No," Vinny whispered. "Word has it he was feeding information to the press for money."

"Bullshit," Smithy jousted with the concept to draw more from him.

"Its gospel," Vinny said offended. "Word has it that he sold the location of the sting to a reporter. They witnessed the whole thing."

"Oh, of course," Smithy looked convinced. "That's why it's been all over the news. Are you taking the piss?"

"I'm telling you it's true," Vinny nodded vehemently. "The reporter told my source about the sting but she didn't tell him the details. He knows she went there for a fact and only connected the two when it hit the news."

"She?"

"Yes," Vinny looked over his shoulder as if someone was watching. "The reporter is a woman."

"Who is she?"

"Get me out of here," Vinny sat back and crossed his arms defiantly. "Put me into protection and I'll give you their names."

"Who is the source," Smithy was confused. "Where has this come from?"

"Like I said," Vinny smiled. "Get me out of here and I'll give you the lot."

"I'll tell you what is going to happen now," Smithy leaned over as if he was saying something confidential. "I'm going back to the station and I'm going to tell my governor that you have wasted my time with a bullshit story about a reporter who witnessed five people being murdered but never reported it. Thanks for nothing, Vinny."

Smithy stood up and walked towards the exit quickly. "She's disappeared, that's why it was never reported!" Vinny called after him. "It's gospel, I'm telling you!" The ginger detective heard his words but didn't turn around. Ten minutes later he was in his car driving back towards Liverpool. The investigation at Beech Close was moving at full speed and he needed to catch up. Vinny Walker went back to his cell with the feeling that he'd missed an opportunity. Fear and desperation walked alongside him.

Smithy reached over for his cigarettes with his left hand, trying to steer the Ford without weaving across the carriageway with his right. The traffic was light as he flicked radio channels and inhaled the soothing smoke. BBC Merseyside interrupted their current affairs programme to broadcast an interview with Chief Superintendent Carlton, Alec's direct superior. Smithy turned up the volume and listened to the familiar voice. As he listened, he got the feeling that the investigation was about to reach a new level.

"Since Titan was launched in April 2009, 225 criminals across the region have been sentenced to 731 years in prison," Carlton's rehearsed voice said proudly. There was nervousness to his voice which Smithy hadn't heard before. He cleared his throat and continued. "More than two million pounds of stolen goods have been recovered, 21 firearms have been taken off the streets and drugs with a street value of nearly ten million pounds have been seized." He paused to let the impressive statistics sink in. "Following our investigation into the shootings at Sliver Lane, Cheshire and the kidnapping of Jodie Barker, we are bringing the incidents under the jurisdiction of Titan." Smithy could hear the sound of cameras clicking and the chatter of Journalists in the background.

"Bollocks," Smithy swore at the news. Launching Titan would mean that Merseyside's MIT could not be in total control of the investigation. "There'll be more fucking chiefs than Indians."

"Titan is a collaboration of the six regional forces, Merseyside, Lancashire, GMP, North Wales, Cumbria and Cheshire and was formed to combat serious and organised crime that crosses the borders of our counties in the North West. The unit tackles those involved in crimes such as drug trafficking, firearms, armed robberies, cash-in-transit attacks and aggravated burglaries, the scourge of our society."

"You must have been up all night rehearsing this one," Smithy said to himself, flicking the stub out of the window. "You didn't mention anything about this, Alec, what's that all about?" He questioned aloud.

"The unit works hard with the six regional police forces, as well as partner agencies, to take criminals off our streets and to strip them of their ill-gotten gains. Titan is committed to tackling organised crime groups and their associated criminality, which has a huge impact on residents across the North West. We will not tolerate organised crime in our cities and we will continue to work pro-actively to disrupt these criminals and ultimately take them off the streets to make our communities a safer place. We are appealing to everyone to help us secure the safe return of this six year old girl. Her picture is on our website and I urge you to take a look."

CHAPTER 13

Ged Barker

Ged Barker woke up confused, thirsty and numb from the shoulders down. As his focus returned, he noticed the uniforms around the room and his memory of what had happened slowly took shape. "Where is Jodie?" He asked hoarsely. A nurse's uniform swamped his view of the room as she put water to his lips. Ged sipped the soothing liquid and swallowed. His throat felt like it was lined with razorblades. "Where is Jodie?" He repeated louder this time.

"We were hoping you could tell us that, Ged," a deep voice spoke from the side of the room. A tall man with a gaunt face and a baggy suit stepped into focus. "Can you remember what happened?" He moved closer.

"You can't talk to him until a doctor has seen him," the nurse snapped.

"Go and get a doctor then," the tall man replied curtly. The nurse tutted and left the room. "I'm DC Parsons, Ged. Your daughter is missing and we need to know what happened so that we can find her. What can you remember?"

"They broke in through the back door. They were asking me a lot of questions and then Jodie came down and one of them tried to chase her. I shot him and then I don't remember much after that," Ged said tearfully. "Jesus Christ are you sure she isn't hurt?"

"Who broke in, Ged?" Parsons avoided the question to piece things together from the beginning. "Did you know them?"

"Sort of," Ged swallowed painfully. "The water please."

"What do you mean sort of?" Parsons placed the cup to his lips and let him drink a mouthful before removing it. "It's vital that you're honest with me if we are to find Jodie."

"I owed one of them some money."

"Which one?" Parsons asked confused.

"Moby," Ged blinked and wiped his eyes with the back of his hand. "His name was Moby. I bought some gear from him occasionally."

"What are you on?" Parsons grunted. He couldn't fathom how the carnage at Beech Close was caused by a drug debt.

"Heroin," Ged replied.

"How much did you owe him?"

"Not much," Ged looked at the detective's face. "It doesn't matter anyway. That's not why they were there."

"Go on," Parsons prompted.

"He was asking me about Carol," Ged mumbled. "He kept going on about Carol and a shooting."

"Hold on a minute," Parsons interrupted. "Moby was asking about someone called Carol?"

"No," Ged snapped frustrated and confused. "Freg was asking the questions. He was in charge. He did one of them in the kitchen; that's what made Jodie kick off, she was terrified by the blood. There was blood everywhere," he rambled.

"Take another sip of water," Parsons tried to slow him down. "One thing at a time. Who is Freg?"

"He was asking all the questions," Ged swallowed and thought back. "He said his name was Fred but everyone called him Freg because his dad had a lisp or something and couldn't say his name properly." He looked at Parsons realising how silly it sounded.

"Did you get a surname?"

"No, just Freg."

"Okay, who's Carol?"

"What?"

"You said he was asking about Carol."

"She's my wife, Jodie's mother."

"Where is she?"

"I don't know," Ged snapped. "Where is my daughter? Stop hassling me and let me find my daughter." He tried to get up but the pain in his shoulder knocked him backwards. A nurse rushed in followed by a doctor and they ushered Parsons out of the way.

"This man had just had major surgery," the young doctor growled. "He's not fit to be questioned yet, Detective."

"A six year old girl is missing, Doctor," Parsons replied. "He is the only witness we have at the moment and the longer she's out there, the less chance we have of finding her alive." The doctor and the nurse exchanged concerned glances and tried to settle Ged back into a comfortable position. "Why were they asking about your wife, Ged?"

"I don't know," he began to cry. He squeezed his eyes shut and wiped the tears with the back of his hand. "It's all such a mess."

"Take your time and try to think," Parsons said calmly. "Could Jodie have run to your wife?"

"No way," Ged sobbed. "I haven't spoken to her for weeks. She left months ago and took Jodie with her but then she said she was going away for a while and couldn't contact me. She left Jodie with me. It happened sometimes when she was working on something big." His voice broke and the tears flowed freely down his cheeks.

"Detective I must insist that this man rests before you continue questioning him," the doctor stood between Parsons and his patient. "I am sorry about the girl but his welfare is my concern."

Parsons thought for a moment and then nodded resignedly. "Okay, Doctor. Let the constable know when we can talk to him." He gestured to the uniformed officer who was stood outside the room. "I think I've got the gist of it anyway." As he left the room, he dialled the number to reach Alec Ramsay.

CHAPTER 14

HMP Risley

Vinny Walker felt weak and tired when recreation time was signalled by the bell. Three short rings and then the doors on the landings were opened by the prison officers. It had been a long day and his high hopes and expectations had been dashed by his stubbornness. His desperation to die a free man had probably spoiled his chances of bargaining a deal with the police. He was so desperate not to give away his information for free, that he'd blown his chances with DS Smith. "Out of there, Walker," growled a screw as he opened the door of the cell. "I've had enough of your shit today, so move yourself!"

"I'm on my way," Vinny moaned. His joints creaked and ached as he stepped onto the metal landing. "A walk around the recreation room will do me good anyway," he said to no one.

"You're needed in the library," Officer Price boomed from behind him. "Get your arse down there quick-sharp, Walker."

"I'm not on the rota for the library today," Vinny moaned. He looked at Price and the look in his eyes told him to go to the library without any argument. "Bollocks to this." Vinny murmured.

"What was that, Walker?"

"I'm on my way to the library, Officer Price," Vinny said happily. "Look," he pointed to a wide fake smile. Working in the library was tediously boring. Sorting books into genre and alphabetical order for an hour was his idea of monotony personified. Vinny hadn't read a book since he'd left school. "I can't wait to get there."

"I would tread very carefully if I was you," Officer Price added gruffly. "I've heard whispers on the landings that you are trying to work a deal with the police," Price leaned closer to his face. Vinny lowered his gaze and looked guiltily at the floor. "You know what happens to grasses in this place, Walker, so you mark my words and tread carefully."

"I'm not grassing anyone," Vinny mumbled. "I don't know where that has come from."

"From your cellmate, you bloody idiot," Price whispered. "At your age, you should know better than to trust anyone in here." Vinny was taken aback by the concern in his voice. "I've spent longer in this shithole than you have, long enough to know that the animals in here will eat you alive."

"Honestly," Vinny answered genuinely. "I am not grassing anyone."

"I don't give a shit, Walker," Price kept his voice down. "I don't want a dead villain on my wing so you will be safer in the library for now. Move yourself." Price winked imperceptibly. Vinny thought that maybe the iron facade hid a man with some feelings and concern for the safety of the older prisoners. He turned and walked towards the wrought iron stairs, which led down to the lower landing. He noticed some of the other cons staring at him, contempt in their eyes. A few nudges and whispered comments added to his feeling of paranoia and persecution. Vinny kept his eyes fixed to the stairs, avoiding meeting the accusing stares.

As he reached the bottom of the stairs, four cons stopped their pool game and watched him intently. Vinny nodded a greeting with a thin smile but no one returned the gesture. He picked the route of least resistance and weaved his way through the prisoners cautiously making sure that he stayed out of striking range. One huge inmate stepped in front of him, blocking his path. His pitted black face scowled down at Vinny and fear gripped his stomach like a clamp in his abdomen.

"Back off, Williams," Officer Price growled from the first landing. The black prisoner looked up and stared at Price, challenging the order. "Do it now, son, or you'll be on report." Williams grinned and stepped aside. "On your way, Walker." Price barked.

"We'll see you later, grass," the big man whispered as he moved. Vinny swallowed hard and walked on quickly. He heard pool balls clatter against each other and the sound of conversations and chattering again as the cons went back to their recreation. At the end of the cellblock, Vinny stepped through an open gate and carried on down a narrow grey corridor. Two cons stood leaning against the wall menacingly. They watched him as he neared and the breath stuck in Vinny's chest, trapped by fear. He tensed as he drew level with them, waiting for a punch to strike or a shank to slash or pierce his skin but none came. He quickened his step and let out an audible sigh of relief as he reached the library door. Glancing back down the corridor, he twisted the handle and opened the door, stepping inside and closing it behind him quickly. He closed his eyes and took a deep breath, his sanctuary reached.

"Hello, Vinny," a voice made him jump. "I didn't think you were on the rota here today." Vinny put his hand to his chest and looked to his left. "What's the matter with you?" the voice chuckled. "You look frightened to death!"

"Jesus!" Vinny breathed out as he gasped. "Don't do that to me, George." He relaxed a little as he looked at the familiar figure of an ageing convict, who he had met many times inside one institution or another. "I nearly shit my pants then."

"It happens at our age," George chuckled again. "How come you're so jumpy?" He stopped laughing and looked serious for a moment. "Are you in any trouble?"

Vinny was about to answer when the lights went out and the two old villains were plunged into darkness.

CHAPTER 15

Doctor Holland

The wind which blew off the Irish Sea, cut through the doctor's winter coat like a scalpel through flesh. Sleet turned to rain, saturating his hair and face. His trousers were soaked where the water ran off his waterproof; the material clung to his legs, hampering his movement. The undulating roll of the trawler, mixed with the stench of rotting fish and diesel was making his stomach churn. He was already feeling fragile and the rocking motion added to his discomfort. The constant rattling of the float-lines against the hull was driving him insane. Every one of his senses was under attack. Withdrawal was biting him too, his nerve endings were screaming for alcohol or narcotics.

At medical school he hated working on the surgical wards. Superficial wounds and invasive surgery weren't too bad but watching amputations or crush injuries made him queasy. That's what forced him to drink in the early years of his career. Whisky calmed his nerves and took the edge off his anxiety before he arrived at work. Entering the fray of the accident and emergency department seemed easier after his self medication. As the years went by, alcohol tightened its grip on him. Mediocrity ground down any aspirations which he had left and booze drowned his disappointment. His impromptu dissection of Richards knocked him sick. Horrified by the task, he made a simple mistake with the drugs he administered. The terrible procedure hadn't started well as the young man was still alive. When Richards sat up and began screaming, he collapsed in a faint. Any hope he had of avoiding the dismemberment, was shattered when he was brought to his senses by a series of hard slaps to the face. No sooner was he back on his feet, than he was passed the bone saw to complete the gory task. He noted from the unnatural angle at which Moby's head was twisted that his neck had been snapped. Starting with the swivel joints at the shoulders and hips, the dissection hadn't taken long and it wasn't as visceral as he'd expected it to be. Removing the head was the most distressing part; Moby's eyes stared at him woefully as the saw lacerated bone and sinew with ease. When his head thudded on the floor, it rolled towards him and stopped next to his foot. The lifeless eyes still stared at him.

Despite completing the dismemberment, his torment was still not finished. The enforcers insisted that he had to see the thing through to the disposal of the body. Freg's men were charged with cleaning up the blood and splatter caused by the saw, while they carried rubble sacks full of body parts through the mill, down the stairs to the vehicle which belonged to Mr

James's transport company. The journey to the trawler port was short but blurred. The enforcers had bundled him into the back seat of the BMW, next to Frederick Hope and he could only assume by the thudding sounds from the back of the car, that the body parts had been tossed into the boot. Of course he'd tried to protest at being dragged along but his complaints went unheard.

When they reached the docks, his trauma continued. Forced to retrieve a plastic rubble sack full of remains from the car, he'd been ushered onto the trawler with his three unwanted companions. The sack was heavy and a solid lump protruded from the middle, banging against his shin as he stumbled onto the boat. His medical education and common sense told him that it was Moby's head. He shuddered as he thought about what he'd not only witnessed, but been actively involved in; the murder and disposal of a young man. Working for Steven Young was always a gamble but he had never envisaged sinking to such depths of depravity. What began as a welcome lifeline financially, had become a living nightmare. Patching up criminals had paid well and no one cared if he was drunk or high when he practised his trade but murder and the disposal of corpses was never part of the deal. A wave struck the bow of the boat and spray hit his exposed skin like tiny frozen darts. The wind added its force to the rain chilling him to the bone.

"This will do," Michael shouted from below decks. His voice was almost drowned by the wind. "The riptides here will take your cousin way out beyond the bay." He turned to Freg and pointed towards a lightship in the distance. "The undercurrent here runs all the way to The Skerries," he added with a knowing wink. "The last thing we want is him popping up somewhere in a trawler net." The sound of the engine quietened as the pilot turned the bow into the wind and the boat slowed. "Grab a bag, Doc. We need to get this done quickly while there's no shipping around."

The doctor shuffled towards the bulkhead reluctantly. The idea of taking his hands from his pockets didn't appeal. "Here wrap a piece of this around the bags, Frederick." Michael ordered, tossing large squares of wire mesh across the deck. Under normal circumstances, they were used to repair holes in the trawl net. "Bring those chains up here, Kevin." He shouted below. "Doc, once he's fastened the mesh around the sacks, thread the chains through the mesh. That'll weigh them down and ensure that he doesn't spill out in the water."

Kevin's huge bulk appeared from below and he dropped a bundle of chain onto the deck. The doctor took a length and knelt down on the saturated deck; the four men worked together. The wind and rain battered them as they worked. His fingers turned to numbed extensions of his frozen hands. The boat stopped lurching but the roll still made him nauseous. He repeated the process six times and each time he passed a weighted sack to Michael, it was tossed overboard. "This isn't right," the doctor muttered.

"Shut up, Doc," Freg hissed. "Just do as you're told."

"The splashing sound seems cruel and final."

"Shut up."

"He was a young man with all the opportunities life offers within his grasp. He chose the wrong path, but being cut into pieces and dumped like rubbish into the sea, it doesn't seem right."

"What would you have us do, Holland?" Michael towered above him. "You've been around long enough to know how these things work."

"I might have been around it too long," the doctor replied angrily. "This is my limit. You've pushed me to my limit and I'm out after this, enough is enough."

"I think you decided that a long time ago," Kevin stood menacingly behind him. "You should have got out sooner." There was something in the tone of his voice which worried the doctor.

"You're right," the doctor shouted. "I should have got out years ago. Just get me back to shore and you'll never hear from me again. You're all fucking mad." The rain eased but the wind was still biting. His nerves were prickling and his temper was taught. "Enough is enough. We're done here; turn the boat around and take me home." Freg looked between the two giants and sensed that something was amiss. They were intimidating at the best of times, but their menace had intensified since boarding the trawler.

"We're not quite done, Doc," Michael said calmly. "We need to ask you some questions."

The doctor looked at Freg for a translation but Freg was staring at Michael, equally confused. "What questions?" He asked irritably. His hands were blue with the cold. He was wet and sickened by what had happened and he was desperate for his warm living room and a bottle of whisky so that he could numb his brain. "I have nothing to answer for!" He shouted, although his heart began pounding in his chest. If he'd been found out, he was in desperate trouble.

"You were pretty close to Youngy, weren't you?" Kevin said. "Always ear wigging."

"Not really," he snapped. His heartbeat increased. "What is this all about?"

"You were feeding information to the police," Michael rubbed his hands together as he spoke. He breathed on them and clouds of vapour burst between his fingers. "That's why he was lifted."

"Bollocks," the doctor shouted. Fear made his voice sound shaky. "I did what he asked me to do and then I went home. Why would I talk to the police? I didn't know anything."

"Priest thinks you did," Kevin replied. "In fact, he has it on good authority that you did."

"He's way off the mark," the doctor scoffed but his demeanour was all wrong. "He's never met me!"

"He said to mention a copper named, Citrone to you."

Freg watched the doctor's reaction with interest, lost in the process of questioning from the enforcers. The doctor's face seemed to tense and his eyes darted around the boat looking for an escape route but they were surrounded by nothing but deep, dark, freezing cold saltwater. His face had guilt written all over it. "It was you?" Freg gasped. "Did you help stitch him up?"

"I didn't say anything to the police," the doctor babbled. "I want to speak to the Priest and I'll tell him that it's all a lie." The doctor began to shiver but it wasn't the cold which chilled him now, it was terror. "I have been loyal to Youngy for years. I can't believe you think I'm a grass."

"I am afraid the Priest has made his mind up," Michael said. He dropped a set of handcuffs on the deck next to Freg. "Cuff him, Frederick."

"Why, what's happening?" Freg mumbled unhappy with the order.

"Don't do this, Frederick," the doctor pleaded. "They killed your cousin today. Help me to talk to Priest and we can clear all this up." The enforcers moved quickly and together they grabbed him, forcing his wrists together. "Get off me!" he struggled uselessly. His feet danced in thin air like a puppet on invisible strings.

"Don't struggle, Doc," Kevin laughed coldly. "Just relax and take what comes to you. The easier you take it, the easier it will be for you."

"Get the cuffs on him now!"

"Okay, I am," Freg fumbled the manacles onto one wrist at a time. He looked into the doctor's watery eyes and saw guilt mixed with fear.

"I am telling you honestly," the doctor's voice went up an octave. "Don't do this. Priest is wrong. I haven't said anything to the police!"

The handcuffs snapped as they locked and his struggles became more urgent. "For God's sake don't do this! Let me talk to Priest at least."

"Wrap that wire around his legs," Kevin shouted. Freg reached down and grabbed a mesh square. Reaching behind the doctor, he pulled the mesh together and twisted the lose wires together in front of him. "If you don't stop struggling, I'm going to have to hurt you, Doc."

"Please don't do this," the doctor looked from one giant to the other but there was little to no sympathy on their faces. "I haven't been talking to the police. Get this Citrone guy in front of me and ask him. He's lying!" The doctor was panicking now and his voice was a scream. "It was probably him all along. The black bastard is lying!" The doctor stared at Michael for help. "He is setting me up like he set Youngy up!"

"Put those chains through the mesh and fasten them with that cord," Michael shook his head as he spoke. "Who said Citrone was a man, Doc?"

Freg worked quickly with the chains but he glanced at the doctor's face every time he spoke. Saliva was running from the corner of his mouth and running from his chin, mixed the rain and tears. "You said he was!" He shouted but Freg could see that he'd tripped up in his panic. "You said he was a bloke!" His face looked frozen by fear as any slim hope that he had vanished in the wind.

"No I didn't," Michael smiled disappointedly. Freg could see him as teacher. He had the ability to smile yet still make you feel chastised. "And I didn't say he was black either. I guess Priest was right to suspect you although I must admit, I had my doubts. Shame, Doc, I wouldn't have believed it unless I'd heard it from your own mouth."

"Michael," the doctor pleaded, "please listen to me for a moment."

"Go on, I'm listening."

"Why should we?" Kevin snapped. "Let's get this done, I'm starving."

"Please, just listen for a minute!"

"Make it quick."

"You know that I use heroin, right?" He pleaded with his eyes but there was no sympathy coming back. "Youngy used to keep me going with a bit here and a bit there. He looked after me." His voice cracked as he spoke.

"He looked after you and you stitched him up," Kevin growled. "Do we have to listen to this drivel?"

"Please, let me explain," he begged. "I got stopped by those Brigade bastards. I was on the way home from a job for Youngy. I think they followed me." He stopped and looked for a reaction from his captures. There was nothing but contempt in their eyes, so he continued. "They searched me and found my gear. They were going to take me in. I'm on licence already. If they'd charged me, I'd have gone down!" His lips quivered as he spoke. His voice was nearly a whine as he pleaded for mercy. "I couldn't go to jail. I wouldn't last five minutes in there." He left the story unfinished, buying time and fishing for empathy.

"So you did a deal with the filth?" Freg sneered.

"I had no choice, Freg," he sobbed. His body shook visibly. "They handed me over to that bastard Citrone and he offered me a way of staying out of prison. You can see that I had no choice, can't you?"

"You should have told Youngy what had happened," Michael said calmly. "He would have sorted it out. Fed false information to them or had Citrone removed. There were other options available to you, Doc."

"Throw him overboard," Kevin said lifting the doctor by the left arm. "Grab his legs, Freg."

"Gladly," he said reaching down. He gripped the old man by the ankles. "I don't believe you grassed, you bastard. You deserve everything you get."

"Please!" the doctor wailed. "Please, Michael, I'm an old man don't do this." They lifted him onto the starboard rail and he teetered above the inky black water. His words were barely coherent. "Please let me go! I'll disappear and no one will ever know. I've got money. You can have it all, please, please!"

"Sorry, Doc," Michael sighed. "One question though. What were the names of the Brigade men?"

"What?"

"What were the names of the men who took you to Citrone?"

"Barclay and Whitehouse, I think," he nodded and smiled desperately seeking a way out. "I could help you. I could tell them anything that you want me to. Please, Michael."

"Okay."

"What?" the doctor saw a lifeline. "Yes, yes, I'll tell them anything, anything at all!"

"Good," Michael nodded. "You'll be seeing them sooner than you think." He heaved the doctor up into the air and the momentum hurtled him over the rail towards the icy waves.

The doctor felt a second of weightlessness as he fell. He saw the three faces of the men on the boat, their expressions nondescript as they watched him hit the water. He felt a splash and then bitterly cold water engulfed him. The icy shock forced an involuntary sharp intake of breath which sucked the stinging salty water into his lungs. Blind panic was replaced by reluctant acceptance. Their faces blurred and disappeared as the weight of the chains dragged his trussed body down into the depths of the Irish Sea.

CHAPTER 16

Jodie Barker

Jodie pulled the massive black bubble jacket over her knees. It was ten times too big for her and it stunk of cigarettes but at least it was warm. When the men who shot her daddy, locked her in the room, she was freezing. Her pyjamas were wet when they bundled her into the big car and even though they were dry now, they still smelled of wee. When she moved inside the big coat, the whiff drifted up to her. She wished that her mummy would come and take her home. A thousand tears had soaked her cotton top and dried, only to be replaced by a thousand more. Her sleep was broken and fitful and plagued with flashbacks of the horror she'd witnessed in her kitchen. Once a happy place where her mother and father laughed while they ate dinner, it had become a dark place in her memory. A place smeared with blood and the deafening sounds of gunshots and people screaming. As she was carried through the kitchen door into the freezing wind, she saw her daddy bleeding on the floor and her screams joined the cacophony of chaos.

The men who took her had been strangely kind to her. That confused her. They shot her daddy and locked her away in a huge prison tower, yet they made sure that she was warm and they brought her sweets, chocolate and pizza. Some of them spoke to her as if she was stupid. The others didn't speak at all. She couldn't understand why they were keeping her locked away. She couldn't understand much about what had happened over the last year or so. Her concept of time was limited, yet she understood that once her family had seemed perfect, but then they left her daddy and lived in another house for a while. Then Mummy said that she had to go to work away for a while and that Daddy would look after her for a few days. Although time was still a mystery, she knew that it had been a long time since her mummy went to work. She also knew that Daddy was lying when he said she was at the hospital. He slept a lot and sometimes he was strange. His eyes looked funny and his voice changed. Sometimes he smelled bad too but she still loved him. When she thought about him being shot, the tears would start again.

Her stomach was rumbling and her throat was dry when the weak sunlight came through the dirty windows. She'd looked out of them many times and she recognised some of the buildings she could see from her lofty prison. The tower where St John lived and the big church, which her daddy said was the biggest in England or the world, she couldn't remember exactly. It was big because they had been there once and it hurt her neck when she looked up at the ceilings. She thought about using the bucket in the corner but decided to wait a bit longer. The bad men sometimes took her to the toilet in another room. It was dirty and smelly but more comfortable than the bucket. She looked around for Monkey. He didn't like being locked up either and she had to look after him. As she picked him up, the sound of footsteps coming up the stairs drifted to her. She hoped that they were bringing some food and a drink. What she really wanted was for Mummy to open the door and tell her that Daddy was okay and waiting at home for them, but she didn't think that either would happen. Tears formed in her eyes and she pulled Monkey up inside the coat and hugged him as they tumbled down her cheeks. The footsteps neared and she could tell that there was more than one bad man coming this time.

Chapter 17

Titan

Smithy stepped out of the lift into the buzz of the MIT office. A dozen voices were talking on the telephones and keyboards were being clattered on every work station. He felt a pang of guilt that he'd spent valuable time on a wild goose chase while everybody else was searching for a missing child. Explaining his meeting to his DS would be embarrassing and he didn't relish the thought. Alec Ramsay had been his superior officer for a decade and because he trusted him implicitly, he hated telling him that his instincts had been wrong. Half of him didn't like being wrong and the other half didn't want to let the team down, especially Alec.

"The governor wants to see you," a young detective called Billingham shouted from his desk.

"I bet he does," he tutted. "You got here quickly," Smithy commented. "Good to have Matrix on board," he lied.

"You know you almost sounded like you meant that, Smithy," the Matrix office laughed. Billingham was a member of a team set up specifically to disrupt the activities of organised gangs in Liverpool. "I think we're just along for the ride on this one to be honest. It's MIT's baby."

"The first I heard about it was on the radio!" Smithy walked to his desk and shook his hand. "I don't think the governor will be too happy," Smithy pretended that Alec hadn't been pre-warned although he had no idea if that was true or not. "When did you get the nod?"

"Twenty minutes ago," Billingham lowered his voice. "I don't think anyone got the heads up until Carlton spilled it on the radio."

"Some things never change," Smithy moaned. "I'd better go and face the music. Catch you later." Smithy steeled himself as he walked towards Alec's office. He thought about taking in a brew as a peace offering but decided that it might be better to make a brew after he'd taken his bollocking. He knocked on the office door, took a deep breath and twisted the handle. "You wanted to see me, Guv?"

Alec was stood next to the window talking on his mobile. He smiled and pointed to the chair mouthing, 'sit down.' "Okay, Paul. As soon as the doctors give you the nod, I want a detailed version from him," Alec frowned and Smithy could see that the DS hadn't been sleeping well again. He always looked tired these days. Alec cut off the call and walked behind the desk. "We've been put under Titan," Alec said flatly. "Every man and his dog are on their way."

"I heard Carlton on the radio."

"I heard it five minutes before he went on the radio," Alec smiled as he lied. Admitting that he'd heard the investigation was moving under Titan by e-mail and that Chief Carlton wasn't taking his calls, was not for general consumption. "On the upside, we'll have access to Cheshire's files and we can cut through the bullshit."

"The downside?"

"I haven't got time to go into the downside," Alec shook his head as if to clear his negative thoughts. "How did it go with Walker?"

"Well when I left there, I could have punched him in the nose for wasting my time," Smithy said sourly.

"Sounds like there's a 'but' coming."

"There is," Smithy paused. "Vinny reckons that one of the Drug Squad officers shot was selling information to the press. His contact told him that a female reporter knew about the sting and that she was going to watch it. He says that he knows the name of his contact and the name of the reporter," he shrugged. "It sounded like bullshit to me until he said the woman has gone missing. She hasn't been seen since the shootings. There could be something in it."

"What did he ask for in return for the names?" Alec didn't look annoyed, which surprised Smithy. He actually looked excited.

"He wants to go into witness protection," Smithy said confused. "Do you think there's something in it?"

"Parsons has spoken to Barker at the hospital," Alec stood up and paced up and down as he spoke. "Barker says that Young's gang were asking him questions about his wife, Carol Barker and guess what she does for a living?"

"Bollocks," Smithy said open mouthed. "Don't tell me she's a reporter."

"She's a reporter!" Alec slapped the desk. "We knew there was something missing and now we know what it is, Carol Barker."

"Bloody hell, Vinny was telling the truth," Smithy sighed. A pang of guilt touched his guts. "What do you want me to do, Guv?"

"Let me think," Alec paced again. He walked to the window and then stopped, gazing through the glass. "We already know the identity of the reporter so there's nothing to gain by bargaining with him for the name of his source, although we could do with knowing where the information came from." Alec turned and pointed to the phone. "Call the prison and tell him that we already have her name and that if he gives us his contact and we can find the source, we'll speak to the judge on his behalf and ask for leniency. That's the best we can do."

"Okay, Guv," Smithy said relieved. "I don't think the Drug Squad have been straight with us. Lying bastards must have known that one of theirs was on the take."

"Maybe not," Alec shook his head. "Or if they did, they didn't know until after the event. Whatever happened at Silver Lane, we don't have the full picture. Up until now it's been Cheshire's problem but now Titan has been launched, it's ours too. I want a frank discussion with Bishop. He's covering something up and I want to know why." Alec walked towards the door. "Make that call. I want the name of Walker's contact. A soon as I've spoken to Carlton, I'm going to bring everybody up to speed. We need everything we can get on Carol Barker and the two Drug Squad officers."

CHAPTER 18

Vinny Walker

Officer Price turned the lights out in the library and then locked the door from the outside, before continuing on his rounds. He had to check the kitchen, the gym, the exercise yard and the television room before doing the same again in reverse. The library door would be locked for twenty minutes before he returned, unlocked it, switched on the lights and returned to the block. What went on inside in the meantime wasn't his problem. His application to transfer to a senior position in Brigade Security was hanging in the balance. They had the contract to process prisoners in the County and Crown Courts holding cells and to transfer them to and from Britain's penal institutions. He'd applied for a supervisor's position at Chester Crown Court. It was a Monday to Friday, nine to five job with excellent pay and a pension attached. Twenty years in the prison service working shifts, weekends and bank holidays had taken its toll. He desperately wanted the job and a call from his prospective employers hinted that the position was his, if he made sure that Vinny Walker was isolated in the library for a while. They had told him that he was about to pass damaging information to the police, which would jeopardise their contract with the court system. He wasn't completely comfortable with the request but he was assured that Vinny wouldn't be hurt, just intimidated and asked to part with his information. Officer Price didn't really see it as a massive problem and he knew how prisons worked inside out and back to front. The prisoners with the most connections outside ran the institution that they were incarcerated in, simply because every prison officer had a family and friends on the outside. If they didn't comply with certain requests, their families were in peril. Most requests involved smuggling drugs, cigarettes and mobile phones into the prison. Others were preferential treatment and protecting specified inmates. It was just the natural order of things. That's the way prisons worked. Of course there were prison officers who couldn't be bought or intimidated but they were in the minority.

    Price had considered the request for less than five minutes before deciding that the financial security and increased quality of life for his family was his priority. Vinny Walker was a well known police informant and he was under constant threat from the convicted members of various crime syndicates. If he was to be roughed up a little by a couple of inmates, no one would be surprised and no one would testify to witnessing his torment anyway. It was a win-win situation. Although he was anxious about the request, the benefits outweighed the doubts.

The kitchen was busy, a cookery session in full swing under the supervision of two officers. The smell of pastry baking drifted from the door as he passed. The officers signalled that everything was fine. The yard had turned into a fourteen aside football pitch and the game was being played with as much passion and frenzy as an FA Cup final. The air was blue with expletives as the players kicked the stuffing out of each other. Three officers leaned against the wall waiting for the inevitable fist fight to begin. It happened every day and the fights were left to run for a few minutes before the guards stepped in. It was better to let these things reach their natural conclusion before interjecting. Price laughed to himself as a two footed challenge launched one inmate three feet into the air. He landed heavily on his back, winded and shaken. Price stepped inside and headed for the television room as the sound of verbal abuse reached fever pitch. The imminent exchange of blows would follow quickly. He decided that witnessing the fight could lead to unwanted paperwork and it was best to leave it to the yard guards.

The chairs in front of the screen were empty apart from one. The lone inmate turned and nodded to him as he looked in. There were a few of the usual television watchers missing, obviously employed somewhere else. Recreation time was used by the inmates for several things, some of them sanctioned and some of them not. Many of the prisoners used the time for their sexual gratification, some of it consensual, some of it not. The officers treated the time flexibly. Sometimes they sought out unsanctioned activity but usually it was overlooked. The prisoners needed their contraband, exercise and physical release as much as they needed food and water.

Depriving them completely caused trouble and unrest. Turning a blind eye sometimes was part of being a good officer, in Officer Price's opinion, anyway.

The gymnasium was busy, although some of the regular meat-heads were conspicuous by their absence. That spelt trouble, as they were the men who physically enforced the prison's code. Step out of line, default on a debt, insult another prisoner of high standing and the heavies would find you. The punishment was gauged to reflect the perceived opinion of the crime. Prison justice was harsh and swift, humiliating and brutal. Price checked his watch. Seventeen minutes had passed since he locked the library door. He checked the corridor for inmates as he approached the library door. It was empty.

Price stopped dead as he neared the door. The stainless steel handle was smeared with blood and the door was resting a few inches ajar. His heart quickened and he glanced around furtively. Licking his lips and pulling his baton, he nudged the door with his foot. The lights were on. He momentarily questioned his actions earlier. 'Had he locked the door properly?' The answer was clear and obvious in his mind. 'Yes he had.' Now he had two options, open the door and see what had happened inside or press the panic button and report the blood on the handle as the reason for sounding the alarm. He took a deep breath as he pondered his dilemma. Another officer was involved, that was without question. Someone had unlocked the door. His instinct was to sound the alarm but his involvement in the situation made him choose the other option.

Curiosity got the better of him and he pushed the door with his left hand, his weapon held tightly in his right. A chair lay upturned to the left, a stack of books scattered on the floor next to the desk. A prisoner's boot stood alone in the middle of the spilled novels. He stepped inside quickly, his weapon raised. His breath froze in his throat as he pushed the door open. Vinny Walker was lying face down on the carpet, a shank made from two toothbrushes melted together protruded from his right eye. Blood and aqueous humour dribbled from the ruined socket, forming a gooey puddle beneath his face. His tongue dangled from the corner of his grey lips which were pulled back in a sneer. In his right hand, Price could see a four inch shank made from a shard of Perspex filed into a dagger shape, the handle formed with clear tape. The blade was thick with blood. Whatever had happened, Vinny was prepared to defend himself.

Price looked up to the camera, which was housed in a protective cage in the far corner of the room. The lens was covered with square of black shiny paper. He guessed that the other side had a photograph of the library on it. The system was ancient and he'd been pushing for an upgrade for years. Civilian staff monitored the cameras on antiquated screens. Fooling the camera was child's play and didn't require a great deal of technical skill. There would be no footage of whatever had happened. He stepped closer to Vinny's body and searched the room with his eyes. Another pair of prison boots pointed to the ceiling, their occupant hidden by a bookshelf. He leaned over, craning his neck to see who it was and what condition they were in. George Richards lay on his back, his eyes wide open and lifeless. His hands were clasped over a deep wound in his chest, which Price could only assume was caused by Vinny's shank. The deaths were shocking enough but the men involved in the violence were not men known for their aggression. Vinny Walker was a bad thief and George Richards was an ageing fraudster who specialised in swindling pensioners out of their savings. Neither had ever been involved in so much as a scuffle. One of them going to the library armed with a homemade knife was beyond the realms of belief but the scenario that they had both gone there armed was in the realms of fantasy. Both men were in their sixties and in poor health.

Officer Price saw his career being flushed down the toilet. His years of service and his pension lost in the internal investigation which would follow. If he didn't play his next move very carefully. Everything he'd worked for would blow up in smoke. His throat was dry and sweat soaked his shirt beneath his armpits as he stared from one body to the next. He had no choice but to sound the alarm and pretend that he'd stumbled across the bloody scene on his rounds. There was no CCTV evidence so as long as he looked composed there was no reason to think otherwise. As his plan formed, a thick forearm gripped him across the throat. The pressure on his windpipe was incredible, crushing his larynx and closing his airways. Price was paralysed as he was lifted off his feet. His eyes nearly popped out of their sockets as the shaft of a fork was pushed into his right ear with the force of a pneumatic spike, piercing the tympanic membrane before penetrating the brain. He felt his body going into an involuntary spasm as his trousers filled with the contents of his lower bowels. His arms hung uselessly from his sides paralysed by the rupture of the brain. Pain turned to numbness as death took him.

CHAPTER 19

Matrix

DC Noonan searched through the shared files uploaded by the Serious Organised Crime Agency which was formed by the merger of the National Crime Squad and the National Criminal Intelligence Service in, 2006. Responsible for investigating international crime organisations that targeted the United Kingdom and answering directly to the Home Office, they were a powerful source of information for MIT's across the country. Although ongoing investigations were subject to security access codes, closed cases which resulted in a conviction were shared with police departments the world over. Finding the case involving Frederick Hope in Tenerife wasn't difficult. After forty minutes of research, he had enough information to take to the Superintendent and a very interesting lead which was much closer to home.

Les printed off half a dozen copies and walked to the printer to retrieve them. He hitched up his trousers and tucked in his shirt, looking around the immediate vicinity before forcing out a fart which had been brewing for ages. It came out much louder than he expected, drawing a number of disapproving glances from his colleagues. "Oops, sorry," he reddened. The smell, which followed caused further embarrassment. "Stay away from the printer for at least five minutes!" He laughed despite the reaction of those nearby. "Where is the governor?"

"In the office with Smithy." A young detective whose name escaped him pointed to the door. "Take your smelly arse with you, will you?"

"Cheers, any progress yet?" Les asked as he organised his notes into piles. "I hear Billingham from Matrix is here already."

"He is but there's nothing yet. How have you got on?"

"I might have something here but I'd better run it by the governor first," Les added as he walked through the department with a swagger. "How's teacher's pet doing?" he nodded to where Allison Wallace was working with her team. The inclusion of an officer senior to him into the team niggled him, especially a woman.

"She's doing fine, Constable, as is the rest of the 'team'," Alec's voice made him jump. The Superintendent looked annoyed by his dissent. His face glowed for the second time in a few minutes. "What have you got there?" Alec noted the papers beneath his arm. "I'm about to brief the team, so if you've got something important, let's have it first."

"You need to hear this, Guv," Les said proudly. "There's a surprise in here that I know you're going to enjoy!" He winked at the officers on the nearest desk. His cheeky scouse humour endeared him to some but not all of his colleagues. Some found him irritating, crass and arrogant. Les Noonan thought that the police force owed him a living because he was a superb detective. The police force had a different opinion of his talents. Alec tolerated him because he had a knack for turning up valuable leads from the back streets of the city although he questioned where his information came from on occasion. "Honestly, Guv, you'll be blown away by this." The chatter in the room quietened as Les spoke. His enthusiasm drew the attention of the team.

Alec shrugged and scratched his chin. "Let's get some fresh coffee on the brewer," he ordered. "I think we can do this in front of the team. Heads up for a moment, people, carry on with what you're doing but listen in."

"Guv!" Smithy's voice came from his office doorway. "I need a word." His face was ashen and his voice hinted at the fact that something was amiss. He was leaning against the frame as if he would collapse if it wasn't there.

"Over here, Smithy," Alec gestured. "Let's get this all out in the open. I don't want anyone missing out bits of what we know. Titan will be in full swing, I want everyone up to speed when they get here."

"Do you mind if I take a seat, Guv?" Billingham asked. He had a polite humble manner about him.

"Not at all, Sergeant," Alec pointed to an empty seat near the front. "You'll be able to chip in here too, I'm sure Matrix has had dealings with some of our suspects."

Smithy walked slowly to the nearest desk and sat on the edge of it next to Billingham. Alec could see from the look in his eyes that something had upset him emotionally. He thought that hearing Les's news first would give him time to compose himself before speaking in front of the team. "Okay, Les, let's hear what you've got." Alec took a cup of coffee from a tray, which was being passed around. He winced as he tasted the bitter brew. Reaching into his pocket, he took out a tube of sweeteners and popped two into the coffee. Swirling it around, he tasted it again and the bitterness was hidden.

"I've found the Hope case on the SOCA site," Les began referring to his notes. As Citrone told us, Steven Young was being shadowed by a combined taskforce." Alec noted the look in Billingham's eyes at the mention of the Drug Squad detective. It was a look of distaste.

"According to their files, they'd been following him for two years, travelling from Larache in Morocco to Spain and the Canary Islands. He'd been travelling across the Canaries buying and selling apartments and villas. It was the sums of money involved which triggered the Spanish authorities to look at him." He paused to grab a coffee and slurped at the brew loudly before continuing. "At first the Spanish authorities thought they were tracking a fraudster but when he was photographed meeting Moroccan dealers, their focus changed. It seems that they had a tip off about a cannabis shipment from Morocco but when they intercepted a Zodiac speedboat linked to the gang, they found three eastern European men and a cache of Israeli weapons, mostly handguns, Jericho 941's. The

Serbians refused to talk but it was assumed that the guns were headed for London as they had connections with some of the families there."

"That would fit in with what Citrone told us," Alec nodded in agreement. "Where does Hope fit into it?"

"Okay, this is interesting," Les held up another sheet of paper. "The taskforce chipped a container which went from Agadir to Casablanca, destined for Southampton via Santa Cruz, Tenerife." He looked up to make sure everyone was following his brief. "The container was shipped by a holding company in the Cayman Islands, registered to prolific gangster, John Palmer." Les looked at the faces around him for a reaction. Pleased by the response, he carried on excitedly. "Steven Young was on the island staying in a Villa in Los Cristianos registered to another company owned by John Palmer!"

A murmur rippled between the detectives. Palmer's name was entrenched in the annals of Spanish crime and wouldn't be erased for decades. "Is everyone familiar with the name?" Alec asked. Some of his detectives would be too young to know of him in detail. Everyone seemed happy to continue so he nodded at Les to continue.

Les had another sip of coffee, cleared his throat and focused on his information, reading on a little before speaking again. "At the time, Palmer was running a timeshare scam which offered his customers massive discounts. They paid a down payment of thousands for apartments which didn't exist, with the promise that once built, they would get their money back again, plus a guaranteed bonus of 3,000 pounds."

"Citrone said that Young made a lot on money in Tenerife, not from drugs," Allison interrupted. She blushed as eyes turned to her, their scrutinising made her realise that she'd stated the obvious.

Les looked up and tutted, "If you let me finish, you'll see the connection." He said sarcastically. His tone wasn't lost on the other detectives. "It was a simple fraud but it masked a complex web of crime behind it. Palmer was no ordinary criminal."

"Get on with it, Les," Alec prompted politely but his face showed signs of losing patience. "We have a lot to catch up with here."

"Yes, Guv," Les said realising that he'd crossed the line. "Palmer's holiday club lay on the fringe of a web of shell companies, offshore funds and protection rackets all over the Canaries," he raised a finger to indicate that this was an important point. "And at the web's centre was Lebanese Mafioso Mohamed Derbah. Between them the taskforce suspected that they were laundering up to 500 million in Tenerife for gangs from Britain, Russia and South America. They supplied weapons and money to the Amal and Hizbollah militias in Lebanon, and they were involved in the theft of 1,300 French passports on behalf of al-Qaeda. Some of that cell were linked to the Madrid bombings."

"What, Steven Young was involved with the terrorists?" Smithy scoffed.

Les held up a hand and carried on. "The taskforce was set up by a special unit from the Madrid headquarters of the Spanish equivalent of MI5, in one tapped phone call, according to Spanish police sources, Derbah discusses a delivery of 'chairs' with the Amal leader Nabih Berry. This, it is claimed, was a reference to arms. At this point, they brought in Counter Terrorist Units from all over Europe. The British operatives were tasked with following Derbah and Nabih Berry," Les paused for effect. "This is the bit you'll love," he looked at Alec and laughed dryly. "They were found shot dead in the cellar of a villa on the north of the island. No one knows who assassinated them." Les smiled and took a deep breath. "The British unit identified Young as being connected to them, via bank transfers from one of Palmer's companies." Les looked at the faces around the room. "Once they had him marked, they monitored who he travelled with. On one trip, he flew from Manchester with three other men from Liverpool. Frederick Hope was one of them. During the surveillance operation, Hope turned on one of his associates in a bar and tried to slit his throat with a bottle of Bud."

"And that's what he went down for," Alec nodded. "If he's linked to the likes of Palmer, then he was in the big league, drug importer or not."

"Correct," Les nodded. "Have a guess who the British Operative on the taskforce was?"

Alec looked at Smithy and their faces turned to stone. "Let me guess," Alec said realising why Les said that he'd love it. "John Tankersley?"

"You got it in one. Our favourite CTU operative," Les moved his hand up and down in a masturbating motion. "At least he's on hand if we want any more information; looks like we'll be making a trip to the top floor!"

"This gets better and better," Smithy sighed. "So we know how connected Young was, let's talk about how connected his killers are." He looked at Alec for permission to speak. Alec nodded silently his face creased with deep thought. "To cut a long story short, I had an informant named Vinny Walker," he smiled grimly. Alec looked up at the use of the word 'had'. "He contacted me with information that there could have been an eyewitness to the Silver Lane shootings, allegedly a female reporter tipped off by one of the Drug Squad officers who died. I didn't believe him until I spoke to the governor when I got back." Smithy nodded to Alec.

"Parsons spoke to Ged Barker when he came around," Alec jumped in. "Barker insists that the gang who broke in questioned him repeatedly about the whereabouts of his estranged wife, Carol Barker. Carol Barker's whereabouts are unknown and she's a journalist. We have to assume that the two women are the same person and it would explain why Jodie Barker was kidnapped." Murmurs became a buzz of comments and conversation as the detectives related the new information with the facts they already had. "I'm taking it that there's more to Vinny's information," Alec raised his eyebrows in a question.

"Vinny Walker was found dead in the prison library an hour ago," Smithy grimaced. "He was stabbed to death along with another inmate and a prison officer. The guy I spoke to said it looked like there had been a fight between Vinny and the other prisoner and the officer was killed during the fracas. I've known Vinny for years. He's riddled with cancer and couldn't fight his way out of a wet paper bag. It's bollocks. Someone has shut him up permanently."

There was a moment of tense silence before Billingham raised his hand slightly, "We chased some of Young's mob last year, Guv," he looked around at the team. "This guy, Frederick Hope was never mentioned. As we closed in on them, we raided a flat in Walton, found an SA80 assault rifle which had been stolen from an army barracks on Salisbury Plain, around 1,200 rounds and a large quantity of Class A substances. We posed as addicts and arrested thirteen people involved in running a twenty four hour drugs cash and carry." Billingham stood up and pointed to the picture of Anthony Richards. "This guy 'Moby' was involved in the supply line and we had him nailed. Suzie and Annie Jones, mother and daughter gave statements that Moby was their supplier. They passed the drugs onto the gang we arrested. Three days after Richards was interviewed, they disappeared." He paused again and looked away from the screen. "Young's network was connected with another gang in Manchester, fronted by a villain named Jules Lee. We were investigating him for the importation of steroids from Thailand. His customers are high profile but we couldn't pin anything on him. He's work in progress but he's definitely connected to this lot. We think one of Lee's men went to see the Jones women."

The detectives around the room listened intently. Knowing nods of the head indicated that there was no doubt about the whereabouts of the Jones witnesses. "They vanished without a trace but there were signs of a break in and a violent struggle at their flat, Richards walked." Billingham smiled grimly and sat down again.

"Citrone said that the troubles turned the supply chain on its head," Alec frowned. "What does Matrix think happened?"

"Out of chaos, opportunity arises," Billingham chuckled. "No one had any fuel, right?"

"Right," Alec prompted.

"From what we can gather, a company on the outskirts of the city, near Kirkby were already involved in the manufacture of bio diesel thanks to the Big Mac!" Confused glances were exchanged between the detectives. "McDonalds Restaurants converted all their delivery lorries to use their waste oil for fuel years ago. Once upon a time they used to sell it off but they wanted to be at the cutting edge of the 'Green' technology. You can imagine how much waste oil they have, right?"

"I'm following," Alec liked the young Matrix detective. He was sharp but had an understated way about him. "I read about it somewhere. Didn't they sell off their distribution company?"

"Yes," Billingham nodded. "They don't own it but they determine how it's run because they are their only customer. They told them that they would supply the waste oil if the company paid for the engine conversions. They had so much waste fuel that they had to farm out some of the refining to smaller companies. The company in Kirkby got a contract five years ago so when the fuel drought hit, they were already churning out thousands of gallons of bio diesel."

"How does this connect with Young?" Smithy asked confused.

"It doesn't," Billingham smiled. "Young and his associates were left high and dry but someone else tapped into the bio diesel and took control overnight. The trouble is, we don't know who it was. All we know is that the main man is known as the Priest."

"What's the name of this refinery?" Alec asked.

"Kirkby Fuels," Billingham answered. "They're on the East Lancs road."

"Les," Alec turned to Noonan. "Take one of your team and get down to Kirkby Fuels. I want to know where every gallon of fuel they've sold over the last six months went to."

"Oh come on, Guv!" Noonan moaned. Alec glared at him for a second and then turned back to Billingham, ignoring the complaint.

"There's one thing that I want to know right now," Alec made a fist with one hand and rubbed it in the palm of the other. "That refinery must have been protected through the riots. The local residents must have known that there was fuel there."

"I'm not sure what you're getting at, Guv," Smithy shook his head. "What do you mean?"

"Who provided the security during the riots?" Alec shrugged and looked around the detectives in the room. "I'll bet a month's wages that it was Brigade Security."

"Alec," a familiar voice interrupted the meeting from the doorway which led to the lifts. All eyes in the room turned to the source of the voice. Two immaculately dressed uniformed men stood next to Alec's office. "Could Superintendent Bishop and I have a word with you please?" Chief Carlton looked ruddy faced, his embarrassment disguised only by his professional appearance. He nodded a greeting to the detectives in the room but he looked uneasy and distracted.

"Take over from here, Smithy," Alec said calmly although it was not how he felt inside. The un-communicated launch of Titan needed to be explained in no uncertain terms. "I could be a while."

CHAPTER 20

The Priest

The sauna smelled of cedar wood infused with the scent of birch. Priest poured water from the wooden ladle over the coals and the steam hissed as it rose and dissipated around the enclosed space. The door opened and a blast of cold air dropped the temperature five degrees in as many seconds. Priest smiled as Colin Dean stepped onto the pine duckboards and closed the door behind him.

"Mr James," Priest greeted him with a firm handshake. His street name amused the Priest. He had thought of it himself, being a lifelong fan of the film 'Rebel without a cause'. Colin Dean had to be Mr James, it made perfect sense. "I trust your men are making sure that we have some privacy." He shifted his bloated body across the high bench seat to allow his guest to sit down. Sweat ran down his bald head in thick streams, dripping from his many chins onto his hairy chest. "There have been enough fuck ups this week."

"Michael is on the door," Dean answered meekly. "I'm sorry about our predicament but since Young was arrested, things have been a bit lackadaisical out there. We've got it in hand." Colin Dean sat down next to his employer, his body a picture of fitness in comparison. Sweat formed on his washboard stomach immediately. The large muscles in his chest twitched as he lowered himself into a comfortable position.

"It's not you that I'm concerned about," Priest said, pouring more water onto the coal. "It's the shit all over the television and newspapers which worries me. I don't want our business affected by this nonsense. There are over two hundred uniformed officers and four hundred volunteers searching for the Barker girl."

"I know," Dean wiped sweat from his eyes. "I have told Hope to make the problem go away, pronto."

"I don't want to know the details, just make it happen."

"She won't be found, full stop."

"Are you sure he's suitable to replace Young?"

"Definitely not."

"Tell me what your solution is," Priest looked at Dean's defined body and felt himself growing hard. He liked lean muscular men, although he was discreet about his sexual preference. His position was reliant upon fear and respect. The choices he made in the bedroom did nothing to bolster his authority. Many would see his homosexuality as a weakness. "I'm all ears."

"I'm going to get rid of him and slot Kevin Warren into Young's position," Dean said without looking at his boss. He could feel his eyes on him and he shuffled uncomfortably. "Michael will supervise him for a few months to allow him to settle in. It will give us more control ultimately."

"More control or more headaches?"

"The finer details are irrelevant," Dean looked at his boss. "There will always be headaches at that level, that's why we needed Young in the first place. Putting Kevin in will smooth things out. He's strong minded and loyal."

"Okay," Priest nodded slowly. "What are his credentials?"

Dean knew that the Priest would ask him detailed questions about Kevin. He always did. Being thorough was one of the reasons why he was in charge. He didn't like mistakes and he didn't tolerate failure. Researching the lower tiers of his organisation minimised employing unsuitable people and lowered the risk of allowing undercover police to penetrate their ranks. "Kevin has worked for me for a long time," Dean began. "He was one of three sons of Eira and Joe Warren, who ran the Legion in Childwall for ten years. He moved with his family to Ellesmere Port after his father was forced out of the club by the Lewis family."

"I remember the Lewis family," Priest smiled. "The oldest son, Jack wasn't it?"

"Yes."

"He was found in the boot of a Ford Granada, with his head missing?"

"That's the one," Dean smiled. "Kevin and his brother did it. His father never got over losing the club. Kevin gave his head to his father and restored their credibility."

"I like him already."

"He's solid and predictable, unlike Hope."

Priest poured more water onto the coals. "Hope was never going to be the right choice," he sat back and the cedar wood creaked as his weight shifted. "The man is unstable. Do you know his history, because I can't find anything on him?"

"Only what Young told me about him," Dean shook his head embarrassed. "Young seemed to look after him. I don't know what the attachment was but he couldn't do anything wrong in his eyes," Dean shrugged. "He was never going to step into Young's shoes. To be honest, I thought we would have Young back in place in a few months."

"So you assumed that he could handle things for a few months?"

"No, I was happy that we could handle things ourselves while Young was banged up. All he did was organise the dealers. He was a convenient front man and nothing more."

"Ah, but that is where you are wrong," Priest put his hands together as if in prayer. "It's the mistakes made at the bottom of our particular pile, which attracts the attention of the law. Watch the television, James, Jodie Barker's face is all over it and why?" He paused, "because you sent a volatile retard to carry out a complex task."

"It was hardly complex."

"Asking a man to divulge the whereabouts of his wife?" Priest said excitedly. "Come on, would you turn in your wife to a bunch of scallywags like Hope and his crew, when they had broken into your home and pointed weapons in your face?"

"He made a mess of it because Barker was armed," Dean defended him although he wasn't sure why. "They weren't expecting guns."

"This is the problem," Priest reinforced his point. "The devil is in the detail. The details are what keep us at liberty, James. Frederick Hope has no record that my investigators can find, that worries me."

"Hope will be a bad memory," Dean countered. "Leave it to me. The entire thing wouldn't have happened if Jules Lee wasn't so sloppy."

"Agreed," Priest nodded. "He's trying to retire and he's making mistakes."

"He's making too many."

"Does he have a way out?"

"None that he's going to like."

Priest sat thoughtfully for a moment, his hands still clasped together. He wiped sweat from his forehead and stole a glance at Dean's Body. Sweat glistened on his skin and the urge to touch him was overwhelming. The Priest took whatever he wanted, whenever he wanted it but Colin Dean was too important to lose. He would take out his frustrations on another, later. "There is a shipment coming in later this month, a big one," he reached for the ladle again hoping that a new cloud of steam would cool his ardour. He had to focus on business. "Are we in a position to accept it and distribute it without making the evening news?"

"We're in good shape," Dean ignored the sarcasm. "Hope and the girl aside, we couldn't be in better form, apart from the Young investigation." Dean threw a curve ball back at his boss. He was sick of his condescending attitude. Priest was quick to point out his mistakes without mentioning his own. "Do we know if Young gave anything up yet?"

"I know that when I told him to stall things, he did," Priest eyed Dean patronisingly. "He offered them Mills on a plate and that's when it went tits up."

"Kills two birds as they say," Dean grinned. "He was beginning to piss me off anyway."

"I think it's time to get rid of any lose ends we have within the Brigade," Priest said matter of factly. "The police will be all over them like a rash now, we don't want any witnesses."

"I'll take care of them," Dean agreed. "You're sure he didn't give them any names?"

"Positive," Priest lied. "If he'd given them anything, we would be having this conversation in Strangeways. However, I'm not sure where the police are up to with it all. There is a weak link in the forensic team; I'm planning on exploiting it tonight."

"At least we'll know where we stand," Dean said thoughtfully. "With all the attention at the moment, it could be prudent to delay this shipment."

"It's not an option, I'm afraid," Priest sounded adamant. "The weapons are already sold as a job lot. Jules Lee has taken them to sell onto his contacts in Moss Side. Apparently, the Somalis are about to launch a takeover bid. They need a ready-made arsenal. Easy money for us and I don't want to upset our supplier. You don't let them down more than once, if you follow."

"I follow," Dean nodded surprised. It was reassuring that the Priest realised that he wasn't bulletproof. There were organisations far bigger and more ruthless than even he was.

"Good," Priest stood up and breathed in although it didn't alter his waistline at all. His flabby breasts wobbled as he climbed onto the duckboards. "I'll bring us up to speed with the Young investigation, you tidy up our Brigade contacts. If Hope and the girl are the only problem that we have, then get rid of them and do it quickly."

CHAPTER 21

Chief Carlton

"Firstly, let me apologise for the way things have been handled, Alec," Carlton said without looking him in the eye. He rubbed his hands together nervously. "The truth is, I had no choice in the matter."

"The same applies from me, Alec," Bishop stepped forward and held out his hand. "How are you since…?"

"My wife died?" Alec completed the sentence. He was becoming accustomed to the discomfort it caused people who meant well. "I'm fine thank you, Alan." He shook his hand and gestured to the empty seats. "Now would someone like to tell me what the fuck is going on, please?"

The Chief cleared his throat and sat down, unperturbed by Alec's abruptness. He had grown a thick skin during his twenty plus years in the force. The position of Chief Superintendent allowed him to receive shit from the hierarchy above him and below him. He was three months from retiring and drawing his pension when the troubles started and the government put a block on all officers leaving the force. Every day felt like an eternity. His wife was in the early stages of dementia and her condition was deteriorating quickly. It was becoming impossible to leave her alone for any length of time. She repeatedly put on her coat, gloves and scarf adamant that she had to be at the school where she had been the headmistress for fifteen years. The fact that she'd retired five years earlier had been erased from her memory. Carlton found it traumatic watching his wife crumble before his eyes. Work had become secondary for the first time in his life. The retirement which they had planned and looked forward to all their lives, now appeared to be shattered. Instead of travelling, cruises and enjoying each others' company, he faced years of agony, caring, nursing and then grieving for his wife. He almost envied Alec. At least his loss was sudden and final. The job which he once loved had become a torment, making it difficult to get out of bed in the morning. His wife's illness and the chaos on the streets during the riots had nearly finished him. He could feel his strength waning and the pressure showed with every line on his face. "We're waiting for Adrian Salter and Callum Gladstone to arrive, Alec," he blushed as he spoke their names. "The Home Office has hinted strongly that we liaise with Brigade Security during the investigation."

"You've got to be joking!" Alec looked from one officer to the other. "Tell me he's joking."

"They're on their way down in the lift," Carlton replied.

"Down from where?" Alec asked confused. Most visitors came up to the MIT office.

"They've been talking to Kathy Brooks," Carlton explained. "Gladstone insisted that they speak to her first."

"Is she sitting in with us too?"

"I think so," Carlton nodded. "You can see why everything was done in such a rush. I am truly sorry, but I think this would have been put under Titian sooner rather than later and I absolutely guarantee that you're heading up the investigation."

Alec thought about it for a second. He rubbed the dimple in his chin. Carlton had been blindsided. It wasn't his fault. Alec had been in the force long enough to know that ultimately, Westminster pulled the strings. "I appreciate that but what the hell is Salter doing here?"

"Gladstone thinks that he should be allowed to observe the investigation," Carlton nodded but there was no conviction in his voice. "Brigade lost officers and there are important questions which need to be answered about the activity of some of their men. Salter is very concerned that some of his employees may be breaking the law and damaging the 'Brigade brand' as he puts it."

"Really, so he's worried about losing his contract?" Alec said sarcastically. "And I suppose it's got nothing to do with Westminster backpedalling on their decision to employ them in the first place." Alec snapped. "That's how I see it. How do you feel about it?"

"I feel like we'll have a spy in the camp," Bishop answered first. "If it gives us the opportunity to prove to Gladstone that Brigade Security officers are rotten, then I'm inclined to let him observe. The fact is that we don't really have much choice, Alec."

A knock on the door stopped the conversation short. Callum Gladstone stepped into the room with an air of superiority and a waft of Ralph Lauren. His navy blue pinstripe suit looked creased around the shoulders where his padded ski jacket had been. He was fifteen years younger than Alec expected, his skin tanned and his teeth perfectly straight. His dark hair was neatly cut and gelled. A sun tan was rare these days, the tourist industry creaking back into life slowly. "Good afternoon, Gentlemen," he strolled into the office and looked out of the window with a confidence that Alec didn't care for. "Very nice view, Superintendent Ramsay," he turned and offered his hand. Alec stood and reciprocated and recognised the Masonic handshake when his thumb pressed into the first joint of his forefinger. Alec was a Mason too as were most of his senior colleagues. It had its benefits career wise but he didn't buy into most of their philosophies. "We haven't met have we?" Gladstone asked knowing the answer already.

"No," Alec replied flatly.

"Please allow me to introduce Adrian Salter, CEO of Brigade Security."

"Pleasure to meet you," Salter sounded uneasy and his eyes darted from one officer to the next as he shook hands with them. He used the Mason handshake too, which explained some things to Alec. "I'm shocked at the loss of your officers and I want to say that Brigade Security will cooperate completely with your investigation. Thank you for allowing me to observe it."

He sounded genuine enough to Alec despite his objections to him being there. "We didn't 'allow' you," Alec couldn't hold his tongue. It was one of the reasons why he would never be considered for Chief Carlton's job when he finally retired but Alec wouldn't swap places for a gold clock. "I think you have Mr Gladstone to thank for that suggestion and I'm not sure that it's a foregone conclusion either."

"Of course it is most unusual for anyone to shadow this type of investigation but my job as liaison 'minister' is to make sure that we have transparency," Gladstone tried to smooth over the remark. "We have a situation never encountered before and we must adapt and evolve with the changing structure of policing as it develops. Outsourcing to companies like Brigade Security is the future and cooperation is the key, Superintendent." He delivered his rebuke as if he was talking to an audience. "I'm sure you agree that in the long term, joint policing will be about cooperation."

"Don't be too sure," Alec countered. "Until we get to the bottom of this, Brigade Security officers are high on my list of suspects. Placing a potential leak into the investigation goes against the grain, 'Minister'," Alec accentuated his rank. "As for transparency, unless all the evidence is divulged, we're running this investigation with our hands tied behind our back." A tense silence greeted the insinuation that evidence was being withheld. "As you say, cooperation is the key!" Alec cocked his head to the side slightly to provoke a response. None came.

"More chairs, Guv," Smithy opened the door without knocking. Sensing that the atmosphere in the office wasn't good, he placed two chairs down and left without another word. Before he'd closed the door, Kathy Brooks poked her head around the gap. There was an uncomfortable silence in the room as she entered and she smiled briefly at Alec and rolled her eyes to the ceiling.

"Dr Brooks," Gladstone chirped up. "Please come and join us," he stood and offered her the chair, which she was about to sit in anyway. His fake gallantry was lost on the gathering. "Sit down please, your input will be most welcome I'm sure. I can only hope that you're a little more forthcoming in this company." Gladstone smiled thinly. Alec got the impression that all had not gone well upstairs.

Kathy sat down and crossed her legs without thanking him. She smiled at the uniformed officers and nodded a greeting. Alec gathered from her demeanour that her meeting with Gladstone and Salter earlier had done nothing to endear her to the man. She looked uncomfortable in Gladstone's presence. "Well, let's get started," he clapped his hands together in a call to action. "How do these things begin?" Gladstone asked with a false smile.

"They start with the transfer of all relevant information, including the personal files on the Drug Squad officers who were shot at the scene," Alec looked at Bishop. Bishop shuffled uncomfortably in his seat. "Then I think we need an update on the details missing from the SOCR. It reads like a jigsaw with half the pieces missing." Alec saw the confused look on Salter's face, "SOCR is the scene of crime report, which Kathy's department puts together with Cheshire's detectives. At the moment, it's incomplete. Now Titian has been launched, I want everything given to my team today."

"Why?" Gladstone looked amazed and turned to Bishop. "Why on earth would it not be complete?" His tone was more suited to addressing an admin assistant than a senior police officer. "That's ridiculous, I don't understand."

"Internal politics, Minister," Alec said what everybody else was thinking but didn't want to say. "Something you'll know a lot about no doubt." Gladstone wasn't sure if he should be offended or not but Alec wasn't bothered either way. "Don't look so surprised. We see it happening on the television everyday in Westminster," Alec smiled wryly. "Someone in the government fucks up and the curtains come down while you lot decide who is to blame and who will take the fall for it. The same rules apply here except we can't walk straight into another position."

"I'm not sure that's a true picture of how government works but thank you for the insight, Superintendent," Gladstone raised his eyebrows at his bluntness. "I think we can dispense with the 'internal politics' immediately if that's the problem. Finding out what happened and restoring confidence in our experimental policing policy is the priority here."

"Bullshit," Alec put both hands on his desk and leaned forward. "That is exactly why you need to leave this investigation to us, because our 'priority' is to find a six year old girl, first and foremost," Alec looked at the other officers and they nodded in agreement.

"Absolutely," Carlton turned in his chair to face Gladstone. He straightened his spine and his expression hardened. "Finding Jodie Barker and identifying exactly who is responsible for the murder of two police officers, two Brigade officers and a high profile drug dealer is what this investigation is all about. Public confidence in Brigade Security is not on our agenda. In fact the opposite is true."

Alec sat back, reassured that Carlton was still a policeman not a politician at heart. "Could you clarify that please," Gladstone had a concerned expression on his face but it was exaggerated. Alec could see that the minister was constantly over acting. Every word he said was a monologue which had to be profound, every gesture and expression a performance for invisible cameras.

"You've read my reports," Carlton looked angry. His lips quivered and Alec could see that his fingers were twitching. "I have expressed my concerns about your policing policy from day one and I've been ordered to keep my opinions to myself. Well if its transparency that you want then let's put all the cards on the table."

Alec raised his eyebrows in surprise. Carlton must have been suffering in silence while everyone below him felt that they'd been talking to a brick wall. "Every officer, detective and constable in this building has encountered instances of Brigade Security officers bending the rules and breaking the law. We couldn't investigate the allegations thoroughly during the riots but believe me when I say that now, we will." Carlton Pointed at Alec. "I will make sure that Superintendent Ramsay and his Titan investigation gets every last thing that it needs to get to the bottom of this and if that means that Brigade Security, The Home Office and the Home Secretary are left with egg on their faces, then tough!"

"I'm disappointed by your attitude, Chief Superintendent," Gladstone was purple with rage. Alec could see the cracks in his practised performance appearing. "Perhaps you are too close to the investigation to see things in perspective. You are very close to retiring, I believe, perhaps we could expedite that process for you if you feel this investigation is too much for you." There was an implied threat in the comment and Alec felt the needles of anger pricking his mind. He was about to jump to Carlton's defence but the chief had an ace up his sleeve. Alec had underestimated his boss completely.

"You can do what you like to me, Minister," Carlton stood up. "I've authorised the launch of a Titan investigation which involves six police forces working together. Once a Titan operation is authorised, it cannot be halted until all six Chief Constables agree, nor can it be handed to any other department. All six forces agree that Superintendent Ramsay will lead the investigation and we will support that decision to its conclusion. I would suggest that you go back to Westminster and wait for us to update you, as and when we are ready to do so."

"I'm not sure that is the case and you should consider your tone, Chief Superintendent," Gladstone shook his head in disgust. He wasn't used to being on the receiving end. "The Home Office........."

"Makes and agrees police policy," Carlton talked over him. "Save your puff and wind for Westminster, because it means nothing here." Alec had to hide a smile behind his hand. He felt like a naughty schoolboy listening to one of friends giving the teacher cheek. Kathy caught his gaze and her eyes widened in surprise at Carlton's stance. Alec understood why Titan had been launched without warning. Carlton had done it on purpose to thwart Gladstone interfering in the investigation. "As for Mr Salter observing the investigation, he could end up becoming a suspect in our investigation and as such, forget it."

"The Home Secretary will be informed immediately and I can assure you that he'll be furious." Gladstone ranted. He folded his arms and sat back in his chair defiantly. "I suggest that you reconsider immediately!"

Carlton paused and looked thoughtful for a moment. Alec frowned, worried that Carlton was about to back down despite the launch of Titan. He needn't have worried. "Titan is in motion," Carlton stood bolt upright. "Now we have an investigation to run, so if you don't mind," he gestured to the door.

"I'll have your coats taken down to reception," Alec stood up and walked around the desk. Reaching for the handle he turned and smiled. "You can collect them on your way out of the building." He looked at Carlton and nodded with nothing but admiration in his eyes as Gladstone marched out of the door, followed by Salter who skulked behind him.

CHAPTER 23

SOCR

The atmosphere in the office was one of euphoric relief, although there was an underlying tension there too. Carlton looked relieved but exhausted. His tactical launch of Titan had ensured that the combined forces' investigation could not be broached by Westminster. Applying pressure to six Chief Constables simultaneously would be impossible. They sat in silence as Bishop arranged for all files to be released. Bishop looked worried as he spoke to his subordinate on the telephone. Alec tapped his fingers on the desk impatiently as he waited for the full SOCR to be sent over.

"Everything we have is being sent now," Bishop said as he ended the call and put his phone on silent. "When you read it, you'll see why we had to keep it under wraps."

"Take us through the snagging," Carlton prompted. He rubbed his eyes and sat back in his chair. "It will be quicker for you to fill in the gaps."

"God knows where to begin," Bishop looked at Kathy for support. Alec saw something flash between them. Not a personal thing but there was something that they both knew which hadn't been shared. That niggled him. He knew that most senior officers held her in high esteem and some were personal friends too. His dilemma was that it bothered him and it felt almost like jealousy.

"Tell me about the officers who were killed," Alec prioritised what he thought was the vital information. He was way off track but he didn't realise it yet. "Why were their files pulled?"

"Philip Brisco was in his third year undercover with the DS," Bishop began. His frequent glances at Kathy worried Alec. "He was a talented officer with a bright future. He had his share of blemishes of course, a few complaints of assault and one of planting evidence on a suspect. Nothing was proved. He'd worked alongside his partner Tim Baldwin for two years. They were a good team although Baldwin was a rogue from all accounts."

"Go on," Alec waited.

"Baldwin was a bad influence on Brisco. He bent the rules and took to his undercover role at little too easily sometimes. It appears that he was far more at home mixing with villains, than he was as a police officer. Last year, his DI insisted that he was tested for steroids when he piled on weight quickly. He passed the test and kept on growing. The next thing Brisco was in the gym with him every day and the pair of them turned into meat-heads in a couple of months." Bishop shrugged. "They were tested again and both passed again."

"The station gym?" Carlton asked.

"No, a place called Hard Labour, frequented by bouncers and dealers," Bishop answered quickly. "I'm sure you've heard of Jules Lee, or Coco as he's better known?"

"I've heard of him," Alec nodded. "Mixed race guy hence the nickname Coco, seems he can work for both sides without any race issues. He's connected to the Yardies in Moss Side and Young's mob here."

"That's him," Bishop nodded. "We've been trying to lift him for years. DS are certain that he's responsible for importing most of the steroids in the North West but they've never had anything on him." Bishop shook his head and looked down again. "Twice they had evidence against him and twice the witnesses vanished."

"So Brisco and Baldwin were associating with Lee and his cronies?" Carlton prompted. "That would explain the weight gain but why was their senior officer concerned about it if they were undercover?"

"Rumours were rife in the station that Baldwin was selling gear to other officers and Brigade men," Bishop frowned. "People saw how strong he'd become in a short period of time and were impressed. When they asked him what he was doing, he offered them the answer at a price, obviously."

"I've tested both bodies for steroids," Kathy backed up his story. "They're clean but their HGH count is sky high."

"Growth hormone?" Alec asked.

"Yes," Kathy agreed. "It can't be detected with standard tests for steroids and when it's used correctly, has the same effects on the body's muscle mass but it's magnified and permanent."

"They were posing as doormen before the Young arrest, working out with guys that they worked with, socialising with them and once they were in, they were key in setting Young up," Bishop paused to think. "Baldwin's bank accounts show major discrepancies. He has several large deposits paid into his accounts, always in cash, always from a different branch. The names on the paying in slips are never traceable, apart from one, paid by a man by the name of Frank Dempster."

"That rings a bell," Alec said.

"He's a local football correspondent, boxing commentator and freelance journalist," Bishop explained. Alec recognised him as soon as he mentioned boxing. He'd seen him at some of the boxing shows in town. "If there's a fight or a big match in the North West, he's there."

"Didn't he fall from grace with the BBC?" Carlton interrupted. "I'm sure he was doing very well at one time and then he made some outlandish claims that premiership coaches were buying steroids on the black market, to speed up players' recovery time?"

"I remember that," Alec said thinking back. "Nothing was proved and the scandal went away, if I remember rightly."

"He was dropped by the BBC when Sir Alex threatened to sue them. After that, he was banished to report on minor league and local events," Carlton recalled. "How much did he put into Baldwin's account?"

"Twenty grand," Bishop said quietly.

"It seems like an obvious mistake to put his real name on the payment," Kathy commented.

"Not if he wanted proof that a payment had been made," Alec explained. "If Baldwin reneged on the deal, Dempster had a hold on him."

"It's the only explanation we have as to why they went to that meeting without backup," Bishop added. "I think they were too close to Young before the arrest. They had a bond with him. They went looking for the glory stitching up Brigade officers, making the arrest, adding weight to the Young evidence and making taking ten grand each in the process."

"Has Dempster been questioned?" Carlton queried

"Not yet," Bishop blushed again. "We can't track him down.

"It would fit in with what we know," Alec sat forward. All attention turned to him. "Smithy had an informer in Risley who was certain that a journalist had a tip off about the sting on Silver Lane. He claimed that a woman, Carol Barker, witnessed the entire thing."

"Barker?" Carlton asked astounded. "As in related to Jodie Barker?"

"Mother, of said Jodie Barker," Alec looked at them individually. "The shootings at Beech Close, home of Ged Barker were as far as we can fathom, a result of a gang searching for the whereabouts of Carol. We know that the gang are the remnants of Steven Young's crew."

"How long have you known this?" Carton asked. He looked almost hurt that he didn't know.

"About an hour," Alec eyed him coolly but smiled. "I was briefing the team when you arrived. A call to you was next on my list." Carlton seemed placated by the explanation.

"So Baldwin tips off a journalist named Dempster, who may or may not, know Kathy Barker. She witnesses the shootings, then Young's gang go looking for her and kidnap her daughter?" Carlton summarised. "Why would they go looking for her and how would they know that she witnessed it?"

"And it doesn't explain why or who shot Robert Mills after the killings," Alec said confused. "Missing pieces again."

"That's not all that's missing," Bishop looked at the floor. "We are missing two vehicles and we have no explanation as to where they are."

"Two?" Alec frowned. "I guessed that you're looking for a Brigade transporter because there was no mention of one at the scene. They must have arrived in one."

"There's no trace of it and the tracker was found not far from a set of tyre tracks. Whoever drove it away, removed the device from beneath the rear wheel arch." Kathy added. Alec threw her a glance. She hadn't told him that and he had to assume that she would have done, if they'd had the time prior to the investigation being brought under Titan. "We also found tracks in the woods leading to a birdwatcher's hide. It was well hidden by the snow." She half smiled at Alec. That was what she wanted to tell him earlier. "The footsteps are normal into the hide but they are staggered and wider apart where they leave, as if she was running. There could be some substance to the witness theory."

"Did Smithy's informant reveal his source?" Carlton asked Alec. "I'm assuming he wants some kind of deal."

"He didn't get the chance," Alec answered grimly. "He was stabbed to death in Risley this afternoon. We think he was silenced."

"Jesus Christ," Carlton sucked in a deep breath. "What the hell is this all about?"

"Whatever it is, there's no doubt in my mind that it involves some heavy hitters in the drug world," Alec tapped the desk. "They are well armed, well organised and their channels of communication are equal to ours, if not better."

"Are you of the opinion that Brigade Security employees are embroiled in this organisation?" Carlton asked. "No doubt about it," Alec looked at Bishop as he answered. "I'm also convinced that police officers are involved too."

"What makes you so sure?" Bishop asked.

"The quality of the information that they're getting," Alec shrugged. "We know Baldwin was crooked but was he working alone? If he has large amounts of money in his account, then who is it from and what was he being paid for?" He looked at Carlton. "We know Brigade supplies relief officers into the prison service. If Vinny Walker was silenced, where did they get the information from?"

"This is a mess," Carlton said. "I suppose the only upside of it all is that if Jodie Barker is of value to someone, she'll still be alive."

Alec didn't answer because he wasn't so sure that he was right. Jodie Barker was only valuable as long as Carol Barker was missing. If she was found dead and Alec believed that she already was, then Jodie was a liability. "What about this second vehicle?" He looked from Kathy to Bishop, changing the subject. "I'm flummoxed by that one."

Bishop looked at Kathy again and swallowed visibly before he answered. "Initially, we thought the incident had been called in by a traffic patrol, which was parked near the M62," Bishop began, his tone subdued. "We have numerous witnesses who report seeing the vehicle parked on the verge above the exit road," he seemed to be justifying something, "turns out that it wasn't called in by them. It was called in by a farmer from down the lane who heard the gunshots and saw the smoke."

"We know there was a traffic patrol on the scene though?" Alec asked.

"The first patrol car on the scene was an armed response unit," Bishop explained. "When they arrived, the patrol car was heading down the lane in the opposite direction towards Irlam," he blushed. "The scene was ablaze, there were bodies everywhere and the armed unit parked up, called backup and secured the scene correctly. They assumed that the traffic patrol had called it in and then gone to an emergency RTA."

"I'm not following this," Carlton shook his head.

"Basically, when we checked, we didn't have any traffic patrols in the area," Bishop came clean finally. He looked at Kathy as he finished and Alec knew that she knew. Jealousy squeezed his guts again. "The camera on the armed response vehicle captured the traffic car reg-plate, it doesn't exist. The plates were bought on the net. Whoever was in that traffic car, they weren't police officers."

CHAPTER 24

Allison Wallace

Allison Wallace felt more comfortable now that the MIT investigation had been upgraded to Titan. She was no longer the only stranger in the department. New faces were appearing all the time. The resentment from

DC Noonan was blindingly obvious and she'd done well to bite her lip on a few occasions. She got the impression that the governor wasn't best pleased with him either, hence sending him on a fact finding mission which could take days. No one liked being sent on an admin job when an investigation was motoring at full pelt. She was just glad that Alec hadn't sent her. Her mobile buzzed and she checked the screen. Thirteen missed calls from her boyfriend. She pressed the busy button, taking the total to fourteen. He was a nice enough guy but insanely jealous. He wanted to get married but she knew that he wasn't the one. The week before, she had gone home with a mayonnaise stain on her coat near the collar, after rushing a sub for dinner on the way to question the witness to an armed robbery. He went quiet on her for days before he explained his suspicions as to how the stain got there. Now, every time she pulled a night shift with a male officer, Mark was convinced that she would spend the night sucking the bloke off in a car park somewhere. She knew that she was attractive but his accusations and insinuations were destroying their relationship. It was already dead in the water and she knew it. DS Ramsay had requested that she worked on an MIT investigation which had been escalated to Titan; it was her big break, her chance to be recognised as the detective that she was. Breaking up with Mark would just have to wait, simples.

She had her teeth into a theory about Frederick Hope. Allison had worked in the Child Protection Unit for a six month spell and her time there had opened her eyes on the way juvenile criminals were handled. The lack of records for Frederick Hope didn't add up and she wanted to follow a hunch. She knew that Hope was related to Richards. The family resemblance was undeniable, so she trawled through the PND searching for something which may prove her hunch was correct. Sure enough, after three hours of digging, she found what she was looking for, but the discovery did nothing to quell her anxiety for the safety of Jodie Barker. She checked the photographs one last time and convinced herself that she was right. Allison grabbed her laptop and walked to Alec's office. The door was open and he greeted her with a smile. The wrinkles at the corners of his eyes deepened but she liked that. He was ruggedly handsome for his age but she tried to push that thought from her mind. The last thing she needed on her first big case was a crush on her Superintendent.

"Sit down, Allison," Alec pointed to the chair and came around the desk. "What have you got?"

"You know that I did a spell with child protection, Guv," Allison began nervously.

"I saw it on your file, why?" Alec smiled.

"It bothered me that Hope was a ghost until he went to Tenerife," she looked up from the screen. "Someone with a criminal history like his usually starts screwing up early in life but there wasn't a mention of him anywhere, no hospital records, no dental records and no school records."

"I'm listening," Alec pulled up his chair closer. He could sense that the young sergeant was on to something.

"I searched the archives for records on the Richards family, as Citrone told us that Hope was related and they do look alike," she explained. She clicked on the screen and a newspaper cutting appeared. "Richards was arrested along with two other boys aged eleven, for a serious sexual assault on a five year old girl. Richards was placed into supervision because it was deemed that his role in the attack was as a lookout. The other two boys were unnamed at that point because the nature of the crime and their age made it sensitive for the courts. The girl's older brother testified against them too, Mark Overand"

"So they all go way back."

"Yes, Guv."

"Where was this?" Alec asked. "I don't recognise this newspaper."

"Manchester," Allison pointed to the title page. "This is the Messenger series which had local editions going out all over the borough and these are the nationals. They picked it up after sentencing. Anyway, the other two boys were convicted and sentenced to serve a minimum of fifteen years. Their identities were changed to protect them in the prison system. Obviously I can't access the probation and after care files without a warrant, but look at this."

Allison brought up two sets of pictures and Alec recognised one of them as being Frederick Hope on his arrest in Tenerife. The other was a bemused young boy in a custody suite. Alec looked from one to the other. "This is Henry Richards aged eleven, Anthony's brother," she scanned Alec's expression to see if he was picking up the likeness. "This is Frederick Hope in Tenerife."

"I can see the likeness," Alec narrowed his eyes to focus properly.

"Okay now look at this," she said excitedly. "This is Simon Young, aged eleven, allegedly the ringleader during the attack."

"Fucking hell," Alec whispered. He looked at Hope's arrest photo again and then back to the picture of Simon Young. "Simon Young is Frederick Hope."

"Simon Young also had an older brother, Steven Young, aged seventeen, at the time of his brother's arrest and already known to us by then," she tapped the screen. "Hope is Youngy's little brother."

"This is good work, Allison," Alec touched her shoulder and squeezed it gently. Allison felt a tingle down her spine. "It would explain the urgency to find Carol Barker and to take her daughter. He wants to know who killed his brother."

"He's a psycho, Guv," Allison clicked the screen again. "What he did to that little girl is beyond evil, he's sick." Another click opened up a text document. "He was released aged 26 and went straight to Tenerife with Young. This is a detailed report from the Spanish police on Frederick Hope," she pushed the laptop across the desk so that Alec could see it better and clicked off the screen saver. "He's a very bad lad, Guv."

"Let's hear it," he said looking at the screen with a concerned frown.

"Simon Young was brought up in and out of the care system where he spent several periods as a mental health patient. Classic early signs of mental problems, fire starting, violent attacks on carers and hanging his foster parent's cat with the washing line," she looked at Alec's face and the lines creased again. "He was put into Redshank correction home, aged eleven, after the assault. Six months later, he was imprisoned at Thorn Cross and soon ended up on the punishment block, after attacking two prisoners without provocation. He was transferred to the punishment block after refusing to work. He smashed up a workshop, after an altercation with a prison officer and was sent to the punishment block again two months later. He was also injected with the sedative chlorpromazine, which made him violently ill, and six months were added to his sentence. After recovering, he continued to prove a highly challenging inmate and spent many months in isolation." She paused and sat back for a moment, "Citrone didn't have any of this, because they didn't check his juvenile records, Guv. That's a huge oversight on their part isn't it?"

"Don't be naive enough to think that mistakes like that aren't made every day. They just punched his name into the PND and kept their fingers crossed. He wasn't high enough on their lists to waste any more time."

"There nothing on the PND, Guv to be fair to them," she conceded. "The rest of this is from his term in Spain, where he was locked up in Las Palmas. One week into his sentence, he attacked fellow English prisoner John Gallagher with a glass jug, and was charged with GBH, dropped to unlawful wounding, nine months were added to his sentence and he was transferred to the mainland."

"Looks like Hope has a thing about glassing people," Alec commented dryly. "Nothing like learning your lesson, is there?"

"There's a pattern, Guv," she looked pale. "They used a glass bottle on the girl when the assaulted her. You can use your imagination."

"A bullet would be my solution," Alec nodded grimly. It needed no further explanation, "people like him never change."

"He didn't, Guv," Allison continued. "He did a month in Madrid's Valdermoro jail before attacking another prison guard. By now he found that his reputation as a violent and highly dangerous inmate preceded him, and at one point he was chained to the floor of a prison van for a hearing in court. He remained in isolation, and began a fitness programme, though he continued to attack other convicts and damage prison property."

"I bet they loved him."

"He spent some time in the prison hospital and made a complaint of brutality, after recovering from a beating in solitary given to him for punching two prison officers."

"No surprise there, I'm surprised they waited that long to be honest," Alec joked dryly, "sounds like he made quite an impression."

"It gets better, Guv," she looked at him as she spoke. "He was transferred to Barcelona's La Modelo. He spent four months in isolation after he was caught trying to dig his way out of his cell!"

"Now that shows he's not too bright. Violent and stupid is not a great combination."

"After being returned to the prison's general population, he caught up with the prisoner that informed on his escape plan. He sexually assaulted the man with the neck of a bottle, before smashing it and carving 'grass' into his face, scarred him for life."

"Jesus," Alec sighed and shook his head.

"Two months later, he slashed a prisoner's throat in the kitchens."

"With a glass?" Alec raised his eyebrows.

"Jam jar, Guv," Allison smiled.

"He killed Mark Overand," Alec nodded and smiled. "At least that answers one conundrum. "He has a thing for glass and Richards was bottled in the throat."

"That's what I'm thinking too, Guv."

"Why did they release him?"

"The governor at La Modelo wished to move him on to the C unit or psycho wing. There he attacked a prisoner with a sauce bottle and was again charged with grievous bodily harm. He attempted suicide and attacked another prison officer, and was sectioned under the Mental Health Act. They were desperate to have him deported at this stage. Three months later, the riots started, their prisons reached bursting point and they kicked out all the foreign prisoners. He was put on a flight to Manchester and here he is, our problem." Allison turned to Alec and shrugged. "If he has Jodie Barker, then she's in real danger."

Alec walked back around to his chair and rubbed his forehead with his palms. "Pass that onto everyone, Allison and do me a favour will you," he opened his eyes and yawned. "See if you can find out what happened to Henry Richards and well done," he smiled. "Oh, and send Billingham in please." Allison left the office on a high. She liked working for Alec Ramsay and she felt more motivated than ever before. Going back to Coppice Hill would be a wrench. She had to make sure Alec valued her for the MIT.

"The governor wants to speak to you," she smiled as she left the office. Billingham looked worried but returned her smile. She was attractive and smart. He thought about asking her out once the case was resolved.

"Am I in trouble?" he joked.

"I don't know, are you?"

Billingham walked to the office and knocked on the doorframe. "You want to see me, Guv?"

"Shut the door and come in," Alec pointed to the chair opposite him. Billingham sat down nervously, unsure why the superintendent wanted to speak to him alone.

"How long have you been with Matrix?" Alec frowned and deep creases furrowed his forehead.

"Three years now, Guv," he replied confused. "Why?"

"I like to think that I can spot good detectives," Alec put his hands on the desk. "And bad ones too."

"Have I done something wrong?" Billingham shifted uncomfortably.

"How many of you are on the team now?" Alec ignored the question.

"Thirteen detective constables, two females and eleven male," Billingham explained, "seven are permanently undercover, the rest of us act on their information. We switch between undercover and operations every twelve months."

"Matrix has had some great results recently," Alec stood up and looked through the window. "How much contact have you had with Drug Squad?"

"We work alongside them, Guv." Billingham shrugged. "Works well sometimes, although we have our bust ups."

"Your reaction to Raymond Citrone intrigued me," Alec turned and looked at his eyes. "What's the story there?"

Billingham shuffled in his seat again and crossed his legs. He thought carefully about his answer. "I spent my first twelve months on the streets, living in a shithole bedsit at the end of Edge Lane. I worked my way into a group of dealers and addicts who supplied the students around there with their party drugs, ecstasy, cocaine and ketamine. You name it, the students wanted it," he laughed. "How they took that shit and completed university degrees at the same time was beyond me, Guv. Anyway, one of my targets got stoned off his box one night. He told me that they had a Drug Squad officer tipping them off on raids. Never told me his name but he said he was black."

Alec watched a tug boat sailing towards the docks at Bootle, towing a dredger. He needed to be careful how he broached the subject of bribery in a different department. "I suppose that narrows it down a bit."

"It did then, Guv," Billingham qualified his hunch. "There were three black officers on the DS then. One of them female, Citrone and a DC named Atkinson. Atkinson was on long term sick leave. He took a hiding when a dealer recognised him outside a club in Manchester; never returned to work."

"Which leaves Citrone," Alec nodded. "Do you think he's bent?"

"Definitely," Billingham said.

"Did you let your DI know your suspicions?"

"I did," Billingham said flatly. "His phone records were checked and his movements shadowed. As far as they could tell, he was clean."

"So, why don't you believe that?"

"There's ways and means to pass on information without doing it yourself, no one is that stupid," Billingham was adamant. "I'm not saying Citrone was tipping dealers off for his own financial gain. Maybe he had his favourite dealers, direct sources of quality information. Keep them safe, protect them from arrest and they'll give you more information on their rivals than you could glean with a hundred undercover detectives."

"Which one do you think it is?"

"Truth?" Billingham shrugged. "Both. I saw clever young girls turn from enthusiastic students to addicts in their first term. I lost count of how many ended up on the game to pay their rent and feed their habit. Citrone sanctioned it whichever way you look at it. He's a bad one, Guv."

"He'll trip up," Alec pointed his finger. "You mark my words, he'll come unstuck. Bent officers always do."

"This is between us, I hope?" Billingham stood.

"Thanks for your frankness," Alec said. "It means that we won't waste our time with anything he puts our way." Alec stored the data in his mind for use another time. Raymond Citrone was on his list of things to sort out. He would sort it one way or the other.

CHAPTER 25

Danny Wells

Danny woke up with a banging headache and a sick feeling in the pit of his stomach. His shoulders were burning as if they were on fire, the pain almost unbearable. Pins and needle racked his arms and his hands felt numb. He groaned as he opened eyes and tried to move but he still couldn't see anything. A blindfold pressed tightly around his head, allowing lamp light to leak in at the corners. A tiny slit of vision allowed him to see that the room was dimly lit and the walls were painted beige, giving it a warm cosy feeling. He could tell that he was on a double bed, tied up and naked. The bed smelled clean and fresh and from the glimpses of furniture he could see, he had to assume that he was in a Travel Inn or similar.

His memory of the club was hazy, flashes returning to him slowly. He'd been dancing and chatting with the usual faces, chasing shots of every colour under the rainbow between bottles of Magners. His friends were a mixture of queens and bisexuals who frequented the club most weekends. Some were completely out, but others were married men who walked on the wild side occasionally. Danny enjoyed their company because they all had one thing in common; they were professionals. Lawyers, doctors, financial advisors, accountants, entrepreneurs and businessmen all mingled with the peace of mind that the men they met were solvent. Danny knew some of his friends liked a bit of rough once in a while, but in the relationship game, being financially independent was high on the requirement list. Coco's was a members' only club and the annual fees were way out of reach for unemployed gay men. It was exclusive and it was safe. Cocaine and ecstasy were easily obtained, the quality and prices regulated by the establishment. If you wanted something to give you a lift and help you to dance the night away, you asked the doormen. Anyone caught buying from elsewhere selling or bringing their own drugs into the club was barred for life.

Danny was popular at the club, good looking, articulate and fun. Many of the club's members desired him but few could claim to have sampled the pleasures he could offer. He was a romantic, waiting for the right man to come along. He enjoyed sex as much as the next man but he liked to be wooed and romanced first. Love and fidelity were important to him. The few long term relationships he'd had were with older men. He found maturity and power aphrodisiacs. His preference for older men and his tendency to be submissive in the bedroom had led to his previous relationships fizzling out. His partners had pushed the boundaries too far, playful bondage becoming humiliating abuse. Once the line had been crossed, there was no going back for Danny. As his memories of the club took shape, so did his predicament. He was bound, blindfolded face down on a bed and had no recollection of how he'd got here or what he'd done.

He remembered a heavyset man at the bar, not his usual type but he'd stood out from the crowd. He was shaven headed with a nice smile and a polite way about him. His conversation was interesting and amusing. He knew some of the policemen who Danny worked for and although the man was chubby, well fat really, he towered above him and there was a physical attraction too. Danny liked to be dominated and the man was quietly imposing, almost intimidating until he smiled. The last thing he could remember was agreeing to meet for lunch the next day and exchanging numbers. Danny was secretly disappointed that he hadn't asked him to go home with him. He would have declined politely of course but being asked was good for the ego. They shared a jug of vodka and Red Bull, a line of coke and then his memory was a blank.

A toilet flushed and the sound of running water drifted from the next room. A man's voice sung a hymn tunelessly. It sounded like Jerusalem although he hummed some of it a few of the words were audible. A door opened and Danny heard heavy footsteps coming towards him.

"Are you awake, Danny?" it was the man from the club. He recognised his voice. "This will be much more fun if you are."

"Where am I," Danny mumbled. His mouth felt numb and dry. "My arms are sore, please untie me."

"Not just yet," the man answered. Danny felt him climbing onto the bed. "I need to ask you some questions and its easier if you're tied up, for now anyway, I like it this way."

"Questions about what," Danny whimpered. He was scared now. "Who are you?"

"Some people call me the Priest," the man straddled him and forced his thighs apart. He slapped his right buttock hard, his weight crushing his legs. "Now then, where shall we begin?" He sighed dramatically. "No rush, we've got all night before you'll be missed. Now say after me, 'for what I'm about to receive, may the lord make me truly grateful'."

"Are you mad?" Danny gasped. "Get off me, you freak!" A thunderous blow to the back of the head stunned him. Over the next four hours, Danny told the Priest everything that he wanted to know and then he made a phone call.

CHAPTER 26

Wayne Barclay

Wayne Barclay watched the baling machine crush a Toyota into an oblong of metal. The metal creaked and groaned like an animal in its death throes. He'd been there many times before, sometimes to lose a vehicle which they'd used to transport illicit goods and twice to lose the remains of a customer who had failed to pay, or had threatened to go to the police. Either way, the machine was invaluable for sweeping unwanted evidence away. A mountain of twisted rusting metal towered above him, a covering of thick snow made it look like a natural formation rather than manmade. The pale green steel girders of Runcorn Bridge were visible in the near distance and the rotting fish smell of the fertiliser factories dotted along the banks of the Mersey was at its most potent.

Crushing and smelting evidence had worked well for them. If there was delay between crushing and smelting, there was the obvious risk that a metal bale could be discovered, human remains compressed inside. DNA could be extracted easily but his contact at the scrapyard pushed their waste vehicles to the front of the queue for disposal. The bales were dropped into a smelter on the neighbouring site, where the metals were melted and separated from the other waste, rubber, plastics and vinyl. Human tissue was destroyed in seconds.

"Your wreckers are in next," his contact shouted. He shook his head in disgust as he approached and spat a thick globule of phlegm into the snow. "Not that they're wreckers, they're like new. Are you sure we can't come to a deal on them, fucking shame to scrap them." A hand rolled cigarette hung from the corner of his mouth. His remaining teeth looked like a broken picket fence; black stripes of grease ran from his chin to his ears on both sides of his face and his fingers were so encrusted with oil that it appeared a physical impossibility for him to ever have clean hands again. "By the time we've stripped and cleaned them, no one will be able to identify them anyway. I can make it worth your while."

"They're too hot, Nicky," Barclay shook his head. "They have to be smelted and that's why I'm waiting here until they're done, otherwise they'll be overtaking me on the M6 next week." Nicky Renton was a handy man to know but he wasn't a man to trust. His motivation was making money from anything and everything he came into contact with. Crushing new vehicles was sacrilege. He could strip a vehicle down and rebuild it with salvaged parts overnight. Chassis numbers were easily repressed and then the vehicles were sold at a premium. "Come on Wayne," Nicky slurred, his accent deeply rooted in the city. "What are you trying to say?"

"That you're bent as a nine pound note and I want to make sure they're crushed."

"Charming," Nicky laughed. He walked into the Portakabin, which acted as their office and reception. Behind it, a huge corrugated iron structure housed the garages and workshops. Nicky banged the snow from his boots and walked behind the makeshift counter which separated the customer reception, from what he jokingly described as the 'nerve centre' of his operation. He lovingly touched the bare behind of December's calendar pin-up. "Now that's one chassis I wouldn't mind bending!" He clenched his fist and waived it in a phallic gesture. He pointed to the stack of oily porn magazines on the counter. "Have a read and make yourself comfortable. I'll nip next door into the workshop and get them ready." He glanced at his watch as he stepped into the cavernous workshop area. "Vehicles like this shouldn't be crushed. I can make them disappear without a trace and we all make money." He shouted, as he disappeared.

"Crush them, Nicky, it's not up for discussion," He called after him. Barclay smiled at his persistence. The smell of fuel and brake fluid was eye-wateringly strong. He checked his mobile for the tenth time in as many minutes, no contact yet from either end. Jules Lee was becoming agitated at best and downright threatening at worst. He'd tried to placate things and broker a deal but the journalist wouldn't cooperate. Things were getting too risky and he had a bad feeling about where he was going. Through the grimy window, the Toyota thudded to the oil stained earth as a huge crane magnet released it. The baling machine was empty. Shouldn't be long now and he could get back to business. The machines stopped moving and the sound of their hydraulics faded. Long minutes ticked by while he waited for Nicky to drive the vehicles into the yard. "What's going on now?"

Silence. A radio crackled somewhere at the rear of the workshop.

"Nicky!" Barclay leaned over the counter so that his voice would carry into the garage. "Get a fucking move on will you?"

Nothing.

"Nicky!" he shouted again. "For fuck's sake!"

Nothing but the radio.

"Nicky," Barclay walked through the hatch in the counter and peered through the doorway into the workshop. Three rows of vehicles stretched towards the back of the garage in various stages of transformation. Some were being stripped ready to crush others were morphing into untraceable vehicles destined for eBay. "Nicky!"

Will Young was singing about jealousy, but that was the only sound in the workshop. Two vehicles near the doors to the yard were covered with tarpaulin. Wayne could tell from the shape and size that they were the ones he needed crushing. "Nicky!"

Silence.

Barclay checked his phone again. The screen was blank. Dempster wasn't playing ball and they couldn't keep the woman much longer. Every news flash for the last week carried pictures of the girl. Every briefing before shift was focused on finding associates of Stephen Young and searching for Jodie Barker. If they got too close, he'd top the woman. Fuck Jules Lee. He could go and whistle down the wind. There was no way he was going down for this. Mills was dead and the others were shitting their pants that they would be killed or arrested. The easiest thing to do was destroy everything connected to them and concentrate on protecting themselves. "Nicky!" he shouted at the top of the scale.

Nothing.

Barclay stepped into the workshop and squeezed between two Volvos, one the donor vehicle, the other a rebuild. He could see the entire garage was deserted. Several bonnets were up, spanners resting on the wings, mid tinker. The nerves in his spine tingled and icy fingers of fear tickled his mind. "Nicky, what the fuck is going on?"

Had the police followed him? Did they know they'd stashed the vehicles here? Had Nicky grassed, informed for a big reward? "Nicky!"

Nothing.

"Nicky!" he turned towards the office. Whatever was going on, he needed to get out of here. "Nicky, fuck this!" he tried to sound assertive but failed.

Nothing.

"I'm not playing games!"

Nothing.

"Fuck you, Nicky!"

Nothing.

"You're messing with the wrong people, you twat!"

Nothing.

"Nicky!" his voice trembled this time. Could they have gone for lunch, be on the phone, or on the toilet? Nicky and his four or five men all at the same time? Impossible. Something had happened, or was about to happen. Barclay looked out of the main garage doors; in his mind images of a dozen police interceptors roaring into the yard, lights flashing and sirens blaring. Everything was quiet. The huge crane magnet swung almost imperceptibly in the breeze, puffy snowflakes began to drift from the grey sky. He turned back into the garage. "Nicky!"

"Bollocks, Nicky!" he couldn't decide whether to walk deeper into the garage or not. Fear stopped him. Fear of what? "Nicky!"

Nothing.

"Fuck this!" he walked back towards the office. "Fuck you and fuck your money, you can forget getting paid, you fat fuck!"

Nothing.

White light flashed in his brain like a huge firework exploding. The force of the blow seemed to resonate through his body, shooting down to the tips of his toes and back again. His knees buckled and his eyes rolled to the back of his head. He felt the sensation of being carried by the arms, powerful hands digging into the soft flesh beneath his armpits. Warm fluid trickled down the nape of his neck, following the ridge of his spine. He knew it was blood. The sound of metal clanging shook him back to semi consciousness and he felt chains being wrapped around his ankles. An almighty tug tightened the metal links and he felt himself being dragged upside down, into the air. His teeth knocked together, cracking a molar and biting a chunk from his tongue. Despite the world being upside down, he focused on two huge men dressed in black. Thick leather jackets covered their suits; their shirts open at the neck. Both faces covered with balaclavas, their eyes staring.

"Who are you?" Barclay groaned. He noticed blood drops falling from his head onto the oil soaked concrete. "What do you want?"

"You brought these vehicles here to be crushed," one of them said. "Did you shoot Robert Mills?"

"I don't know what you're talking about." He panted, the blood running to his head, his face turning red as the vessels filled to bursting point.

"Let me put it another way," the voice was full of menace yet there was calm to it too. "You and your vehicles are destined for the crusher. Whether you still have all your limbs attached or you're alive or dead when the baling begins, is up to you. Now, I want to know what happened on Silver Lane." The sound of a grinder roared to life, the diamond tipped cutting wheel spinning at a thousand revolutions an minute. The whining noise made a dentist's drill sound as soothing as a lullaby.

"Nicky, you fucking grass!" he croaked. "Who are you?" He sobbed as tears began to mingle with the blood beneath him.

Nicky Renton didn't answer him, no one did, There was nothing but the sickening whine of the grinder approaching.

Wayne Barclay wasn't intact when the Volkswagen began to disintegrate around him but he was painfully aware of his body merging with the metal, his screams drowned by the screeching of the machine as the two became one.

CHAPTER 27

DC Parsons

Parsons kicked the vending machine and a bag of prawn cocktail crisps dropped into the retrieval tray. He grabbed them and opened them while he waited for the neighbouring machine to finish dispensing the brown liquid which it wrongly described as coffee. Boiling dishwater was closer to the truth. It didn't matter how bad it tasted, he'd drunk a gallon of the stuff at least. Waiting for Ged Barker to recover from his surgery had become a nightmare job. One minute he was sitting up shouting about Jodie, the next he was sleeping for hours on end. The doctors were concerned that his heartbeat wasn't as it should be. They kept him sedated and monitored him vigilantly. The vending machine stopped whirring and he took his dishwater, scalding his fingertips as he wrestled the cup from the holder. He swore beneath his breath and headed back towards the ward. The smell of floor polish and disinfectant permeated every corner of the hospital. Two nurses walked by and smiled hello, even the cleaners were letting on to him, he'd been there so long. The hospital grapevine had spread the news of who Ged Barker was, his daughter's face still dominating the local news stations.

A kerfuffle further down the corridor caught his eye and he realised that Ged Barker was in trouble. Nurses and doctors poured into the room and he could hear instructions being barked. The uniformed officer tasked with guarding Ged, was stood facing the room, watching the action from the corridor through the window. He saw Parsons approaching and gestured to him to hurry up. Parson slammed his coffee and crisps into a swing-bin and dodged a buffing machine being wielded by one of the army of cleaners and jogged the fifty yards to the ward.

"What's going on?" he asked short of breathe.

"I'm not sure but the nurse said his lips had turned blue and his breathing was laboured."

"Shit!" Parsons hissed, "How long ago?"

"About two minutes after you went for coffee."

Parsons calculated the time in his head. He'd left the room, gone out for a cigarette, used the toilets and then gone to the vending machines. "That was twenty minutes ago," Parsons said flatly. He watched the nurses switching places, applying CPR between socks from a defibrillator. "This doesn't look good."

"Shocking."

Ged's body jolted.

"Clear."

"Output?"

A shake of the head.

"Again."

"Clear."

His body twitched violently for a millisecond and then became still.

"Output?"

Another shake of the head.

"I'm going to call it," the doctor said. "It's been twenty minutes now; is everyone agreed?"

The nurses and doctors nodded sadly. Ged Barker had lost his battle.

A tall doctor with thinning blond hair looked at the time and spoke to the medical staff gathered around the bed. The expressions on their faces said it all. They were gutted Ged Barker hadn't made it. The doctor saw Parsons outside the door and he removed his rubber gloves before opening it and stepping into the corridor. "Can I have a word, Detective?" he steered Parsons away from the room gently by the arm. "I'm afraid we did our best but he wasn't responding," he shook his head and looked drained. "Nothing we tried worked. His heart just didn't respond."

"What killed him, Doctor?"

"I can't be sure but if I had to guess, pulmonary embolism," he spoke quietly. "He had a sudden onset of dyspnea, chest pain and hemoptysis."

"In English, Doc," Parsons said. "I'll have to explain this to my governor in detail."

"Sorry, he was short of breath, chest pain and coughing blood. He had cyanosis, which is blue lips and discoloured fingertips," the doctor paused. "It's all the classic signs of a blood clot in the lungs. What caused the clot, we'll never know, but it could be talc from his drug use or as a result of the surgery. Until we have the autopsy results, I can't be certain."

A television in the corridor was showing the evening news. Jodie Barker's smiling eyes looked down from the screen her fate still unknown.

CHAPTER 28

Carol Barker

As Ged Barker struggled for his last breath, Carol Barker watched their daughter's picture appearing on yet another news program. Her heart felt like it had been pierced with a white hot skewer. They had let her watch the television, well one of them had; the other was a complete bastard. The one who pulled the trigger and shot the crazy Brigade officer; he was the evil one of the two. The other was just a normal guy, being led astray by a stronger personality. He was kind to her, fed her, let her watch the television and talked to her about why they'd taken her. At least she had an idea what was going on. It didn't take away the sickening sense of helplessness she felt about Jodie. She'd begged and pleaded, offered money and her silence for him to let her go. All she wanted was to find her daughter. She knew Ged had been shot but the news said he was in hospital. He would pull through. He was tough. Jodie was a different animal. She was six years old, gentle and trusting and the gangsters who were holding her couldn't take care of her. Why would they? Carol couldn't understand why they'd taken her. For ransom maybe but surely the gang would know that Ged had no money. The guilt she felt for leaving her daughter with Ged while she chased a story which had the potential to get them all killed, crippled her. She would never leave Jodie again if the Gods ever allowed them to be reunited. She heard the key in the front door. One of them was back. She hoped it was the sheep, not the wolf.

She thought back to Silver Lane. It was supposed to be a straight forward scoop. The information was solid; it was directly from a police officer involved. What could go wrong? The hide in the woods offered a perfect filming position. There were gravel pits dotted about in the woods on Silver Lane, popular with birdwatchers and fishermen. The hide had been built from pallets of wood, painted and covered in camouflage webbing. All she had to do was film the bribe being taken and the resulting arrests would make superb TV. They would have to blur out the faces for legal reasons but for impact TV, it was a once in a career story. She'd filmed ten minutes of wading birds and ducks in the woods as her cover story, which would explain her presence in the area. The BBC would pay thousands for the footage and Dempster had a buyer lined up. It would be easy money and would raise their journalistic status to superstar level. They planned to follow it up with their undercover investigation into the sale and use of steroids in professional sport. Their two months of investigations had uncovered the entire network from the importer, Jules Lee, down to the changing rooms of a dozen high profile sporting institutions. Like most things connected to Frank Dempster, it had all turned to shit within minutes. He'd been exciting at first, successful, dynamic, romantic and a wizard between the sheets. Their affair had begun within weeks of them working together and as Ged's habit became an addiction, her infatuation grew. It had grown to the point where she was willing to leave he six year old daughter in the care of her junkie husband while she immersed herself in an adrenalin filled lifestyle. Now guilt replaced endorphins in her bloodstream and she ached to hold Jodie again.

When the shooting started, she panicked. She froze but continued filming even when he'd covered them in petrol and set fire to them. One of the men was still alive; his limbs had twitched for too long after the flames engulfed him. Carol thought she was going to vomit, until she saw the patrol car arrive. She did what her reactions told her to do. 'Run to the police.' How was she to know that they were assassins sent to kill any witnesses if the handover went wrong? They were shocked when they'd first seen her but she hadn't gauged their reactions correctly. She thought they were concerned at first. By the time she realised they weren't police officers, she was ten yards away from them staring down the barrel of a sniper rifle. The wolf wanted to shoot her there in the woods but the sheep talked him out of it, opting to handcuff her and find out who she was and what she was doing there.

Of course she told them everything. She was in fear of her life and the only way she could think of to make killing her a bad idea, was to tell them that her employers knew she was there. She told them about Frank Dempster and their evidence against Jules Lee and that the evidence had been gathered by one of the police officers shot at the scene. She had to make them believe that she was connected, valuable and would be missed. When she'd mentioned Lee, the wolf suddenly became interested in her story. It seemed that they were familiar with the name. That's when she was not just an eyewitness to the murders, she was a bargaining chip between Frank Dempster and Jules Lee. Her captors were ransoming her against the evidence which they had on Lee, in return for a life changing sum from the dealer. It all seemed to make sense, except she couldn't see how they could let her live. She could identify both of them as the killers at Silver Lane, although the final shot which killed Robert Mills was not on camera, she'd seen it. Buying time and looking for a way out was all that she could think of. Finding Jodie was everything.

She heard the door close and bolts being slammed into place. Ten seconds and then the footsteps came up the stairs, five seconds more and she would hear the key in the lock to her prison. From the fumbling noises she'd heard, there were two padlocks and one mortice lock. She didn't know where they were holding her but she knew it was a house. The room she was in was a box bedroom, a single mattress on the floor with a cheap carpet which curled up at the corners. Chocolate coloured curtains hung in tatters from the window, which was barred from the inside and shuttered outside. She was chained to a rusting radiator, handcuffed to the front with just enough leeway to reach the plastic bucket they'd left as a toilet. A single duvet and the bare mattress were her only means of keeping warm. The sheep had brought a portable TV and plugged it in close enough for her to change the channels. It was her only way of telling the time as night and day didn't penetrate her cell. The bucket stunk but she was grateful for small comforts. The men visited the house daily, sometimes three of four times a day. She had heard them carrying things in and out, their voices hushed to a whisper. On more than one occasion, she'd heard a television downstairs and the sound of plates and cups clinking. The smell of Chinese food drifted to her one night making her mouth water and intensifying the desperateness of her situation. She'd guessed it was the wolf. If it had been the sheep, he would have fed her.

The padlocks rattled and the mortice clicked. She held her breath as the door opened, praying that it was the sheep. She was starving. His face appeared in the gap first as he stepped into the room. Two things struck her immediately. His face was dark and troubled, his expression showed fear. The second was his uniform. He was a Brigade Security officer. Up to that point, she had no idea who they were or why they were involved. It answered some of her questions.

"Have you seen him today?" he asked anxiously.

"No."

"Have you heard him coming in?"

"No, nothing at all," she was curious. "Have you brought any food, I'm starving."

"Sorry," he apologised. "I put it down when I opened the door. I'll get it." He stepped out and the door opened wide. Carol saw floral wallpaper and a Picasso print hung on the wall. The door opposite was open and there was a bathroom, green porcelain furniture clashed with a burnt orange rug. The thought of soaking in a hot bath tormented her. She could smell her own body odour and her underwear was sticky and uncomfortable. The urge to wash herself and brush her teeth was unbearable.

"Here," he said placing a Tesco carrier bag in her hands. "Are you sure he's not been in?"

Carol ripped the wrapping from a cheese sandwich and bit off half of it in the first go. She shook her head as she chewed hungrily before stuffing the remaining half into her mouth. She reached into the bag and ripped the ring-pull from a diet coke, washing down the sandwich with half the tin. "He's not been here," She swallowed. "You sound worried, what's up?" She emptied the carrier bag onto the mattress, opting for a Mars Bar next. The wrapper came off in one smooth motion and she slipped the bar into her mouth, biting a chunk off. "Has something happened?"

"I don't know," he shook his head. "He didn't turn up for work today and his phone is clicking to voicemail."

"Are you both Brigade officers?" Carol gestured to the uniform. "I didn't realise." His face darkened and Carol regretted being so blunt.

"Barclay didn't want you to know," he mumbled. "This is all such a fucking mess. I should never have listened to him."

"What's your name?" she smiled still chewing on the chocolate. He paused and his eyes flickered. "You've just told me his name, so what does it matter?" She opened a packet of cheese and onion and swigged the coke again.

"Dennis," he half smiled. "Dennis Whitehouse. My mates call me Den."

"Hello, Den," she said with a mouthful of crisps. "Where do you think he's gone?"

"God knows," he shrugged. "I think we're in the shit. Didn't he bring you any food yesterday?" He pointed to the growing pile of wrappers on the floor. "I told him you'd be hungry."

"No, he never does," she smiled again trying to build on the connection they had. "I don't like him but you're a kind man, Den. I can tell that from your eyes."

"He's a prick," he relaxed a bit, leaning against the wall. "I told him from the start that we were getting in over our heads but he wouldn't listen. Wayne always knows best."

"I know the type," she patted the floor. "He's got 'arsehole' written all over him. Sit down; you're making me nervous standing there like that."

"Sorry," he blushed. "I don't suppose it can hurt now can it?"

"I don't suppose it can," she frowned. "If it has all gone wrong, you know what he's going to do don't you?"

"I never know what he's thinking."

"You won't have any choice."

"I always have a choice," he seemed offended.

"Not this time."

"He's not my boss," he said annoyed. "We're the same rank at work. We're a team."

"That's not what I see," she shrugged. She was pushing him, pressing buttons which she knew would work. He was shy but proud and she could use that. "He uses you to do his dirty work and you let him."

"I tell him when he's wrong."

"I'm sure you do, Den, but does he ever listen?"

"Sometimes."

"When?"

"Sometimes."

"Where is he now then?"

"I don't know."

"Did he ring you to discuss what he was doing?"

"No," he looked hurt. "I think he's in the shit."

"With who?" She kept her voice calm and soothing. "The police or Jules Lee?"

"I don't know but he always calls if he's not coming to work," he said looking at the empty wrappers. "The news is full of what happened and…….."

"My daughter," Carol finished his sentence. "If you find it hard to say then imagine how I'm feeling."

"I'm sorry," he said quietly. "I've asked around but no one is talking. Whoever took her, knows you were going to Silver Lane."

"You think they've got her to keep me quiet?"

"Without a doubt," he nodded. "Why else?"

"No reason," Carol felt her eyes watering. "She's a six year old girl."

"Once they know Dempster is handing over the files on Lee, they'll let her go," he smiled dumbly. "You'll see."

"They will kill Dempster and me and then my daughter," a tear ran down her cheek. "They can't let us live."

"They?" he frowned. "Who are they?" He looked into her eyes and wiped the tear from her cheek. "We're in control of our side. We decide when you're released not them."

"If you're so in control, where is Barclay?" She cried. He was melting. She could sense it. "He's either in custody or doing a deal behind your back with Jules Lee and Dempster. He'll screw you over and kill me to cover his tracks."

"He won't do any deals behind my back," he stood up angrily. "I'm no mug, you know. Where ever he is, I'm still here and I'll make sure you're okay."

"He's either messed up or he's cutting a deal."

"Don't underestimate me," he calmed and sat down. "I'm in charge here."

"Don't underestimate him," she reinforced her point. "He's a cold calculating killer and he'd do pretty much anything for money, or am I wrong?"

"He's greedy," he looked into her eyes. "I've told him so many times that we were in too deep."

"He doesn't listen to you," she wiped another tear away. "He's looking out for himself."

"We've been friends for a long time."

"Where is your friend now?"

"I don't know."

"I think he's left you to take the flack, Den," she said concerned. "If he's run, then you'll have to kill me."

"Don't be stupid," he shook his head but his eyes looked at the floor as he spoke. It was obvious that it had crossed his mind. His eyes glanced at the HK holstered on his hip. It was a subconscious action but she saw it. "It won't come to that. If Dempster had played ball, none of this would be happening."

"Really," she smiled sadly.

"Of course," he smiled back. "Barclay just wanted the money."

"And what about what he did at Silver Lane?" She cocked her head and watched his reaction. He wasn't bright, that was certain. "Do you think your friend Barclay would have let me walk away when I saw him kill that man?"

"It would be your word against ours."

"Come on, Den," she lowered her voice. "You know that if I told the police what he did, they would find evidence to back it up. He would be looking at life. So would you."

"There's no evidence," he nodded proudly. "He destroyed all the evidence."

"Could you spend twenty years in prison mixing with half the men you helped to put away?"

"It won't come to that."

"Barclay wouldn't last five minutes in there," she wept, "he couldn't let me live and neither can you."

"I can," he said assuredly. "I didn't kill anyone and if you promise not to mention my name, we could come to a deal."

"What's the deal?" she held her breath.

"You promise not go to the police or use the files on Jules Lee and I'll let you go."

Carol almost laughed. He was childlike in his perception of the world. "And you could trust me not to tell?"

"Yes," his eyes flickered again. He was lying.

"I don't believe you, Den."

"Why not," he flushed embarrassed.

"Because the police will want to talk to me," she shrugged. "They will want to know what I witnessed, who took me and why they just let me walk away unharmed. We both know what you have to do, whether Barclay turns up or not."

He eyed her but couldn't hold her gaze. Her assumption was right; she could see it on his face. Her time had run out. Whatever had happened to Barclay, she had to get out of here now before he killed her. He seemed nice enough and not too intelligent but he would kill her to save his own neck of that she was positive. "We could think of another way."

"That's a nice thought but realistically what else can we do?" she held his eyes with hers and saw something flicker in them. There was sympathy and embarrassment there but something else lurked there too. He had feelings for her, she could sense it. "You're a nice man, Den. Maybe in another life........"

"I'm not stupid," he snapped. "I know what I am."

"What's that?"

"Just an ordinary bloke," he looked at the television screen. "Women like you don't give men like me a second look."

"You'd be surprised," she chuckled. "If you'd ever met my husband, you'd see what I mean."

"What is he like?"

"He's a lot like you, kind, generous, attractive in a funny kind of way and a hopeless heroin addict."

"Really?"

"Really, as sad as it sounds."

"I'm shocked," his eyebrows raised in surprise. "That must have been hard."

"Impossible," she passed him the coke. "Do you want a sip?"

"Thanks," he took it and sipped from the tin. "You could stay here for a while until it all blows over."

"What chained to a radiator?"

"I could sort something else out, so that you can move around the house."

"I'd still be fastened to a chain, Den, waiting all hours of the day and night for you to come and feed me crisps and coke?" She looked at the floor and squeezed a tear from her eyes. Carol had always been able to turn on the waterworks at will. "What happens if one day you don't come back?"

"That won't happen."

"I bet your friend Barclay thought that this morning," she sobbed gently. "Where is he now? If I had to wait for him to feed me, I'd be dead already."

"I'm not him."

"I know you're not, you're kind," she needed more information. "What is this place anyway?"

"This house?" he looked around. "It's my grandmother's place," he shrugged. "She died years back and left it to me. I stay here sometimes; well I did before we brought you here."

"Where do you stay when you're not here?"

"With my girlfriend," he looked away again. His face darkened as he spoke about her. "She's a stupid bitch. I don't know why I bother to be honest."

"Why do you then?"

"We get on sometimes but her kids drive me mad."

"They're not yours?"

"No," he scoffed. "Wrong colour for a start, they're mixed race. Their father is a copper in the Drugs Squad, mates with Barclay. He's a prick too."

"Does he give you hassle?"

"Big time," he nodded. It was the most animated Carol had seen him. "He threatened to kill me because I gave his eldest a clip around the ear," Den frowned at the memory. "I leave her to it now and don't get involved. He gives us the run-around at work too. Do this, do that do the fucking other. He's as crooked as a pig's tail."

"Do you love her though?"

"No," he spat. "She's fat. I don't know what I saw in her."

"That's not what I asked," she smiled thinly. "Do you love her, because if you do and you have kids to look after, then you shouldn't be involved in this shit should you?"

"I don't love her," he said firmly. "She uses me for money. Times are hard and being with me takes the pressure of her. One minute I'm God's gift and the next she can't look me in the eye."

"Why don't you leave her?"

"Like I said, sometimes we get on and you know," he tilted his head coyly.

"Regular sex?" she chuckled.

"Beggars can't be choosers," he mumbled.

"I miss that the most," she said quietly.

"What?" he sounded surprised.

"Sex," she smiled thinly. "You know the closeness you get when you're with someone you like. I miss the intimacy especially when it's someone new and you're trying to find out what the other likes. You know what I mean."

"Yes," he tried to sound worldly but failed.

"It's been a long time and I miss being held," she let a tear fall again.

"Don't cry," he felt awkward and clumsy as he put his arms around her shoulder.

"Look, Den," she looked him in the eye. "Barclay could come back at any time, in which case, I'm as good as dead."

"That won't happen, I promise."

"You won't be able to stop him."

"Trust me, I will."

"I want you to do me one favour before you decide on what you're going to do," she turned on the tears again. Not too much, just enough.

"What?" He sounded concerned and he touched her hand.

"Would you let me have a hot bath and change my clothes one last time?"

CHAPTER 29

Alec Ramsay

Alec watched the kettle boil, his mind racing through the details of the case. The evidence was fractured, offering pieces of the jigsaw which he had to put together to find Jodie Barker. Ged Barker's death was a blow, not because there was overwhelming sympathy for his plight but because his six year old daughter had lost her father. His head hurt, his eyes were sore and adrenalin wouldn't let him switch off. It was always the way when an investigation started. Gail had suffered his detached company for most of their married life. Even when he was with her, his mind was somewhere else trying to solve a crime or work out where they went wrong. What had he missed, how could he have done it better, quicker, sooner, faster? The questions were always there, the answers not always forthcoming. The sun was coming up behind a blanket of grey clouds, the light dull, barely making any difference between night and day. The lights in the city twinkled yellow in the distance, the river a jet black swathe between Liverpool and the Wirral. The Anglican cathedral towered above everything. Its gargantuan towers both a warning and comfort that God was watching over the inhabitants night and day. Alec knew the truth. God had deserted this city aeons ago, long before the cathedral was built in his name. If he hadn't left and he was still around, then he was taking the piss.

Steam erupted from the kettle and it vibrated before it clicked off, the incessant bubbling subsiding gently. He looked at his empty mug vacantly, trying to coordinate his brain with his hands. Hot water, coffee, sugar and milk, but if it was so simple, why couldn't he do it in the time it took to boil the water? When he wasn't solving crimes and following decades of engrained pattern logic, he was lost. His mind was a mess. The house was so empty and quiet without Gail. Once he felt her company almost oppressive, her constant henpecking a nuisance, her conversation an irritating distraction from his thoughts about work. She was an intrusion in his thought process. Now the emptiness she'd left behind was suffocating; his loneliness a black void where he struggled to breath. Inside he was numb, cold and lost. He was constantly restless, never feeling happy or content no matter what he did or where he was. Finding something outside of work which could occupy his mind was impossible. His mind was in turmoil trying to cope with her loss. His grief seemed infinite, no beginning and no end in sight. Guilt weighed him down every minute of the day and every millisecond of the long nights. She'd betrayed him, broken her vows and turned his world upside down, but despite all the conundrums around her death, one thing was certain. It was his own fault and he couldn't get to grips with that. The truth was that he'd made her life a misery to the point where she turned to another man for love. He'd driven her to have an affair and her death in the arms of DI Will Naylor, his friend, was entirely, completely and most definitely his own fault. His eyes filled up and he looked at the tired reflection of an ageing detective, who he didn't recognise.

The ringing noise in his head became louder. He blinked and the feeling of drowning in self recrimination began to evaporate. The ringing became more acute and he snapped back to reality. He rubbed his eyes and reached for the handset, taking it from the cradle, he took a deep breath before placing it to his ear.

"DS Ramsay," he fumbled in the cupboard for the coffee.

"We've had a breakthrough, Alec," Smithy's voice sounded cautiously excited.

"What's happened?"

"You won't believe this," Smithy took a deep breath. "We had a call from Adrian Salter."

"Now you've got me worried," Alec spooned coffee into the cup and poured water on top of it.

"He called to say that Robert Mills was under investigation, hence why Kathy found a wire on Samuels," Smithy paused. "He said there several other names on their lists."

"We'd worked that one out but why not come forward with the information sooner?"

"He said Carlton was threatening to arrest Brigade officials for hampering an investigation."

"He told you that?"

"In a roundabout way, Guv." Smithy sounded coy.

"What does that mean?"

"Well, I might have sounded a bit sceptical, Guv."

"You mean you asked him to justify his information?"

"Basically, maybe not so politely."

"Go on," Alec smiled and slurped the coffee, his brain beginning to focus again.

"Brigade had a list of officers, connected to Mills," Smithy began. "One of the men under suspicion, Wayne Barclay, didn't show up for work yesterday and there's no sign of him at home. His vehicle is missing too."

"Has he done a runner?"

"They tracked his mobile, Guv," Smithy spoke slowly enjoying every word. "The signal has been stationary at a scrapyard on the dock road near Widnes. After the Silver Lane episode, Salter has bottled it. He thinks we should investigate."

"Under normal circumstances, I'd be inclined to tell him to sort it out himself but if this Barclay character worked with Mills, I'm inclined to agree with him for once."

"How do you want to handle it, Guv?"

"Get an armed response unit to secure the area until we get there," Alec swallowed half the coffee in one gulp. Take your team and Billigham and meet me there."

"ARU are already en route, Guv, thought it best to seal it off first," Smithy said proudly. "You know where it is?"

"There's only one scrapyard on that road," Alec said walking towards the bedroom. "I'll see you there in twenty minutes."

"On my way, Guv."

Alec thought about having a quick shower but parked the idea, opting for a face swill with warm water instead. His eyes looked puffy and tired but the water took some of the cobwebs away. He opened his underwear drawer and then slammed it closed angrily, knowing it had been empty all month. Organising his laundry had been impossible since Gail died. Lack of motivation on the domestic front combined with the riots meant he bought new smalls, wore them a few times and then binned them. It didn't stop him opening the drawer though, old habits die hardest. He dressed quickly in dark canvas trousers, a thermal vest beneath his open necked shirt and jacket. There was a knock on the front door as he fastened his gun to his belt and pulled on a thick black ski jacket. He checked his watch. It was too early for the postman and Smithy knew he was driving to the scrapyard.

He unclipped the leather strap on his holster and edged towards the front door with his hand on the gun. The streetlight cast a shadow through the bevelled glass. It wasn't the postman nor was it a hit man or disgruntled villain. The silhouette was the form of a woman. He opened the door and frowned in surprise. A car was parked randomly away from the kerb, the engine still running and the driver's door wide open. Thick clouds of fumes billowed from the exhaust. The interior light illuminated the inside of the empty vehicle. "Kathy?" He said to her back. She'd turned to look at the view of the city. "What the hell are you doing here?" Something was wrong, her posture, the curve of her spine and the droop in her shoulders.

"I didn't know where else to go," she turned and Alec's breath stuck in his chest. Her eyes were swollen shut, purple and black tinged with hues of blue. Her nose was distended and congealed blood hung from her nostrils. The left cheek was bloated and her jaw enlarged, her bottom lip resembled a fat slug sliced head to tail. She reached out to him as her knees folded beneath her and she collapsed on the porch.

CHAPTER 30

Jules Lee

"How long are you back for, Jules?" Murphy asked, his cockney accent defined his roots. His vest was stained with sweat patches and he dabbed his forehead with a bar towel as he spoke. "Fuck me, it's hot today!"

"Don't complain, Murph," Jules patted him on the back. "I'm over here for a few months. I had to get back to the sun, you wouldn't believe how cold it's been at home," Jules replied waving his empty glass to his wife. Her head and shoulders were just visible behind the bar making her look much younger than she was. Bee was pushing 5ft if she was lucky, vertically challenged like most of her family. "Another bottle of Leo, kaab." He smiled at her and she beamed at him like a love struck teenager. Bee missed him terribly when he went back to the UK.

"Always another bottle for you, darling," she laughed. Her English was drawn out, the vowels exaggerated as Thais do. "Always one more bottle of beer, or one more brandy, always one more for Jules!"

Her laugh was infectious, a throaty chuckle. That's why he'd chosen her to marry. Out of all the beautiful young women in Pattaya, he'd chosen Bee because of her laugh. That and the fact that she was reasonably trustworthy with the business. Most of his Thai girlfriends were thieves with smiling faces, 'snakes with tits' he called them. His last girlfriend ripped him off and broke his heart at the same time. Jules should have known better but like most middle aged men heading to Pattaya, he left his brains at Bangkok Airport. She was a brilliant actress, kind, polite and sexy. Jules believed that she genuinely loved him, a common mistake in Thailand.

At twenty years his junior, it should have been obvious. Jules had to return home on business and he offered her a way to support herself and her family without returning to selling herself in Pattaya's bars. He bought her six brand new Vespas to rent out to tourists, much to her delight. He thought she would never stop kissing him, her arms around his neck for the rest of the day. When he left for Bangkok, they were madly in love and committed to get engaged upon his return. The journey to the airport took just over two hours and upon arrival, they were turned back because the airport had been seized by 'Red Shirt' protesters. Jules spent most of the taxi ride back to Pattaya becoming increasingly concerned that he couldn't reach her on the phone. When he got back to their apartment, she was gone, no clothes, no belongings and no motorbikes. It had taken her less than four hours.

Jules became wary and the next few years he spent dating Thais casually until he met Bee. She wasn't a bar girl. He met her working in a bakery in Jontiem and was smitten on day one. They were married a month later. The bar in Thailand was a toy for Bee, a way to keep her sisters from working the bars in Walking Street when he was at home in Manchester looking after his real business. The gym and the club, Coco's, were nothing more than shop windows to sell his gear from. Steroids were his big earner. He could pick them up for peanuts in Thailand and sell them wholesale in the UK at twenty times the price. His wealth was near where he needed it to be for him to retire and live in the sun for the remainder of his days. One more deal and it was game over. The club and the gym were up for sale and he would have been away, clean as whistle until that bastard Dempster started poking his nose in. Him and the pigs who had wormed their way into the gym. Things were balanced on a pin and he could end up serving ten years, or worse, he could end up with a bullet through the back of the head for getting caught and attracting unwanted attention from the police in the UK and Thailand. The Thai police were more corrupt than any he'd encountered before but the Thai mafia were equally clinical in removing any threat to their business empire. Jules knew that if he was questioned, they would make him disappear before the Thai authorities had chance to begin an investigation.

"I've been following it on the news," Murphy took a deep swig of beer and looked at the bottle as if it was an angel before him. " Ah, that's spot on, Jules. So is it really that bad at home?"

"Worse," Jules grimaced. "The country is on its knees, it'll take years to recover."

"Glad I got out when I did."

"A couple more trips home and then that's me done too."

"Did you bring any gear back with you?" Murphy nudged him and winked. "You know what I mean." He was slurring, the Chang beer much stronger than the Leo.

"I have and I've brought some special stuff too," Jules put his finger to his lips. "Don't tell this lot or they'll all want some." He said loud enough for the line of suntanned faces at the bar to hear. Jules's bar was the hub for ex-pats in the Jontiem area of the city. Decorated in olde worlde style with wood panelling, brass ornaments, a snooker table and a jukebox, it was the nearest thing to an 'English pub' they could have. Black and white photographs of Jules in his younger years added to his Mr Fix-it reputation. Boxers, gangsters, footballers, politicians, actors and actresses all posed with the younger smiling Jules. Each photograph had a story, which changed and became more exaggerated with volume of Leo he'd drunk.

Many had made the mistake of asking him about the pictures. The locals warned holiday makers, 'unless you have a few hours to spare, don't ask Jules about the photographs.'

"What have you brought back?" a Geordie called Dave overheard him. "Come on you shady bastard, what've you got?"

The others joined in shouting and swearing, their lunchtime beer-fest becoming a teatime session. "Fuck off, you lot," Murphy shouted louder still and stood in front of the landlord protectively. "I asked him specifically to get me pork pies and black pudding."

"You greedy bastard," Geordie Dave joked. "And you were going to keep it to yourself?"

"Bastard!"

"Sneaky bastard."

"What else have you got?"

"Okay, okay, back off," Jules raised his hands in surrender. "I've brought pork pies, black pudding, smoked bacon and................" he built the suspense.

"Come on!"

"What have you got?"

The look of anticipation on their faces was priceless. Jules loved it every time he came back to Thailand. "Spam!"

"Fuck off!"

"Knob," Murphy frowned. "I didn't eat that shit when I was at home, why would I eat it now?"

"Where's the bacon?"

"I'll have black pudding, Jules."

"I'll get some from the back," he laughed off the abuse. They were good friends in a different world from the one he'd just left behind. Their idea of 'illegal substances' was buying pork pies which Jules smuggled in his luggage. Importing food was against the law but there was always a way. He didn't make any money from it but he endeared his regulars to the bar. Jules always had something good in the back, always had the latest DVD'S, the newest paperback from the UK, the cheapest Viagra and the best pint of real ale in Thailand. "Get the boys another beer, Bee darling."

"Always another beer," she chuckled, "always another beer for Jules, always just one more, darling!"

"That Stephen Leather book is there, Murph," Jules pointed to a pile of books on a bookshelf near the snooker table. "I forgot to tell you I'd got it. He posted it from Bangkok, a swap for some of Bee's cakes!" The library was his pride and joy. Four bookcases packed floor to ceiling with household names and a special cupboard which was always locked, lined the walls in the back room of the bar. The locked cupboard opened like a concertina to display his private collection of hardbacks. He loaned anything out, except his hardbacks. They were precious.

He walked through a bead fly screen which rattled as it fell back into place swinging wildly. The kitchen was warm and steamy, a huge pan of scouse simmering on the range. Home cooked food was part of the attraction of his bar. Bee was renowned for her baking. They received orders from as far away as Bangkok for her cakes and he could smell one of her creations cooking. The back door groaned as he opened it and the smell of Pattaya's storm drains hit him like a poo-bat in the face. The bar nestled beneath a five storey apartment block, along with convenience stores, a hairdressers and the obligatory massage parlour. A service corridor ran behind the retail outlets, allowing them to receive deliveries and store refuse. Jules used it to park his car. His cool boxes full of tasty contraband were in the boot. He laughed to himself at the thought of his customers arguing over the goodies he brought back from the UK. It was always entertaining to watch them outbid each other. Friendships had been pushed to breaking point over black pudding.

"Jules Lee," a voice made him jump.

"Who's asking?"

"I've got a message from the Priest."

Jules eyed the big man with suspicion. He was going to ask how the Priest knew he was in Thailand but the answer was obvious. He knew everything. The man held out an envelope and Jules took it, never taking his eyes from the messenger.

"You from Liverpool?" Jules asked as he opened the letter.

"Yes."

"Long way from home."

"So are you."

Jules read the letter and his hands began to shake, 'For what you are about to receive, may the Lord make you truly thankful.'

Three bullets from a silenced Glock smashed his sternum, lacerated his lungs and pulped his internal organs to mush. A fourth left a ragged black hole in his forehead, the back of his skull exploded in a pink mist.

CHAPTER 31

Kathy Brooks

"Stay still, Kathy," Alec said softly. "The ambulance is on its way."

He pressed an ice pack against the left side of her face. It looked like her cheekbone was depressed and the way her jaw hung off to one side, indicated that her jaw was cracked too. Her injuries looked like she'd been in a bad car crash. Alec had put her on the couch and covered her in his quilt. Blood soaked the material, blossoming into crimson patterns. He was in shock. There was no possible reason that he could think of as to why Kathy had been attacked. She slipped in and out of being lucid. How she'd driven her car was beyond him.

"Who did this to you?"

"Danny Wells," she whispered. Her voice was nothing more than a gasp.

"Danny did this to you?" Alec pictured the effeminate scientist and couldn't see him being the dealer of such violence.

"He made him call me." Her voice was horse and thick with blood and phlegm. "He hurt him so badly."

"Who did?"

"Danny," she gasped. "Danny, I think he is dead."

"Where is he, Kathy?" Alec was confused, angry and upset.

"In a hotel, in town."

"Which hotel?"

"Days Inn," her head lolled to the side and she coughed painfully. Blood splattered Alec's face and hands. Pink spray launched by each new cough. "He made him call me."

"Who made him call you, Kathy?" the sound of sirens approaching drifted to him. He prayed silently that they were coming for Kathy. She had internal injuries as well as the terrible facial damage. "Do you know who did this to you?"

"He made me pray, Alec," she croaked. "He made me pray and then he stabbed him because I refused to tell him anything!"

"Who did?"

"It was my fault," she sobbed. "I should have told him."

"What did he want to know, Kathy?"

"Silver Lane," she whispered.

"Who did this?" She was fading away, her eyes glazed.

"The Priest," she whispered. "He said he was the Priest."

CHAPTER 33

The Scrap Yard

Alec drove the eight miles to Widnes in shock. Time seemed to stand still. The road past John Lennon airport was quiet and the driving conditions were good. There had been a few flurries of snow the day before but the temperature was rising day by day. The snow was retreating slowly. He hoped that it would continue to melt slowly because if it melted quickly, the country would be under water and yet another crisis would hit the economy. Floods were the last thing the country needed. The traffic began to thicken as he neared Runcorn Bridge; the green steel looked grey in the dull daylight. The stench of rotting fish seeped into the car announcing his arrival at West Bank. Industrial units, factories and warehouses stretched out beneath the flyover in both directions. A mountain of twisted metal rose sixty feet into the air, dominating the skyline. The snow made it look like a metal volcano, extinct but broodingly dangerous. Five hundred yards down the exit ramp, he saw the first armed response vehicle. He recognised the MIT Land Rovers dotted about along the verges on both sides of the road and the presence of an ambulance indicated just how late he was to the scene. The lack of activity from the ambulance men indicated that there were no casualties at the scene, none living anyway. He'd waited until Kathy was safely on her way under the watchful eyes of the paramedics, before heading to the scene. Priorities seemed to blur into one urgent mass sometimes. Choosing the least important issue was almost impossible. The coldest heart could not have left her to the paramedics until she was stable.

Alec parked up and climbed out of the vehicle. The wind from the Mersey bit his skin where it was exposed. His mind was focused on Kathy and what the units despatched to Days Inn would discover. She said she thought Danny Wells was dead. Alec hardly knew him but he knew of him. Kathy sang his praises at every opportunity. He was a talented scientist with a bright future in law enforcement. His social life was always going to be an issue. The last gay pride festival brought thousands of tourists to the city, events and bands peppered Mathew Street and the gay quarter. Danny was key in organising the event, his picture plastered across leaflets and event guides. It didn't sit right with Alec. Being gay wasn't an issue but when it was the most important part of his persona, it was. Danny Wells was 'gay' first and then he was 'Danny Wells, Forensic Officer' second. Alec didn't think he was homophobic but he didn't approve of his openly gay and proud attitude. He'd argued with Kathy about it once, her opinion completely opposite to his. She became so hostile he changed the subject quickly and never mentioned it again. Whatever Danny Wells represented, he genuinely hoped that Kathy was wrong and that Danny was alive.

Targeting members of the police science lab was incomprehensible. The Priest and his associates appeared to think that they were untouchable, above the law and beyond the reach of justice. They had beaten Kathy to within an inch of her life and if she survived, Alec would be eternally grateful because it wasn't a given that she would. Priest had somehow lured Danny Wells to a hotel and then tricked his boss, Kathy Brooks into coming too. It was too early to know how he'd done it. If Danny had called, distressed and hurt, she would have gone to him. That's the way she was. It appeared that the man was intent on finding out something but what did he want to know so badly? How did he believe that he could escape detection? The police looked after their own and Kathy was very much one of theirs.

"Guv!" Smithy's voice called from the gates. A high concrete wall surrounded the compound, topped with three rows of razor wire. Apart from the colourful graffiti emblazoned across the grey wall, it resembled a concentration camp. The cranes and crushers loomed above the scrapyard wall. It was dismantling and recycling on an industrial scale. "I've just heard about Kathy," Smithy shook his head in disbelief. "Have you heard anything from the hospital?"

"Not yet," Alec smiled grimly. "She's in a bad way."

"I know you two are close, Guv," Smithy patted him on the back. "We'll get the bastard."

"We will," Alec was sure in his mind that if they ever cornered the Priest, he would shoot him before he would arrest him. He hoped that the man had the bottle to put up a fight at the end, because if he walked out with his hands in the air, Alec would shoot him in the face and watch him bleed. The image of Kathy's ruined features returned repeatedly to him. "What have we got here?" he said as a shiver ran down his spine.

"The owner, a small time fence by the name Nicky Renton and three of his employees were found in a staffroom at the rear of the workshop. We haven't identified all of them yet."

"Dead?"

"Yes, Guv," Smithy grimaced. "Tied up and shot through the back of the head. Looks like they were forced to kneel down and then bang bang, two shots in each." Smithy made an imaginary gun with his fingers just in case Alec didn't get the idea. "Gangland hit, very professional, Guv."

"Any sign of Barclay?"

"His car is there," Smithy pointed to a Mercedes parked inside the compound.

"Nice car for a plastic," Alec noted. "That's eighty grand's worth of motor car."

"My thoughts exactly, still, we know he was bent."

"Not on his own he wasn't," Alec said. "You don't make that kind of money on your own. Do we know who his associates are?"

"Allison is on working on it now, Guv."

"Good, have you found Barclay?"

"That's where it gets interesting," Smithy pointed to the open doors which led into the workshops. They walked across the oily ground beneath the giant crane magnet; the chains groaned as the breeze moved it gently to and fro. It had the atmosphere of a graveyard, cold, still and tinged with sadness and grief. Suddenly, the hydraulics on the baling machine kicked into life and the magnet swung away from them, towards it. They stepped inside the cavernous garage, the doors three cars wide and high enough to allow a double-decker bus inside. Vehicles were parked in neat rows for as far as he could see, merging with the gloom at the rear of the building.

"This place is massive, Guv. Traffic are going to have a field day when they start running those plates. Renton had a chop shop going in there." Smithy ignored the giant machines as they groaned into operation. Alec didn't.

"What's going on?" he watched the baling machine opening.

"Just a hunch, Guv."

"I don't like your hunches."

"You love them."

"Trust me, Smithy," Alec smiled. "I don't." The magnet hovered above the baler for a moment before dropping noisily into the machine. The sound of metal slamming into metal echoed across the yard.

A tarpaulin lay crumpled at the entrance of the garage, half inside and half outside in the snow. Another covered a vehicle just yards away. "See the chain tackle?" he pointed to a block used for lifting engines. "There's a lot of blood and viscera splattered about beneath it; looks like someone was interrogated or punished. Either way the poor bastard suffered."

Alec watched a SOCO kneeling to collect evidence. The oil stained concrete looked darker still in places, some of it glistened sticky in the overhead fluorescent lights. White globules sat next to darker pink tissue. Flesh, muscle and bone, Alec thought. He didn't need a forensic report to explain what happened there. The underworld was a lucrative place to work but careers were short and recriminations brutal. "There's a grinder on the bench covered in blood and snot," Smithy grimaced. One of the SOCO's turned and smiled at his description, shaking his head in despair. "Don't put that in your report," Smithy chuckled. "You know what I mean, Guv."

"I get the picture." Dark humour was Smithy's forte. Alec knew it was all front. Smithy was as human as the next man; he just dealt with death differently.

Alec thought the scenario over in his mind. "Even if he had associates outside of Brigade, Barclay must have been working with at least one other at work," Alec interrupted Smithy's walk through. "Have you found who he worked with at Brigade?"

"We're on it, Guv," Smithy nodded. "His partner is Dennis Whitehouse. I'm waiting for a call on him."

"Good, we need to get to him before they do."

"We do, they're not messing around," Smithy pointed to the garage. "Four men executed in the back, this one was tortured but we don't have a body." He stood next to the covered vehicle. "For my next trick," he pulled the tarpaulin off the nearest vehicle to reveal a marked Volvo, "Bishop's missing traffic interceptor."

"You think the Volkswagen is in there?" Alec pointed to the baler.

"I do, there's a vehicle in there and the engines on the balers were still hot when we arrived" Smithy nodded as the magnet swung across the compound and dropped a metal bale onto the earth with a thump. "Whoever was here before we arrived, left in a hurry." They walked over to the bale, moving around it slowly, looking for anything that could identify the mangled rectangle of metal.

"It's the right colour," Alec commented. He knelt and touched a tacky blob. "And it's bleeding."

"Guv," Smithy ignored Alec. His face was white with shock.

Alec stepped around the bale to where Smithy was stood. A single eyeball stared at them from the top of the mass, long since separated from its owner. "Wayne Barclay I presume."

CHAPTER 33

Brigade Security CEO

Adrian Salter picked up his wallet and pulled five twenties from it. He placed them on the dressing table and caught a glimpse of the girl getting dressed in the mirror. She was too skinny, her shoulders protruded too much and her breasts had inverted nipples. Still, she was enthusiastic about her work and had done her best to please him. She checked herself in the mirror, straightened her long dark hair with a brush and picked up the notes.

"Is that it," she frowned at the money. "I thought you were loaded."

"I am," Salter smiled, snakelike. "I pay what you're worth."

"Arsehole," she returned his smile, leaving without another word.

"You don't want my number then?" Salter laughed as the door slammed closed. "Everything about this city is so tacky," he moaned to himself. He took a cigarette from his packet and searched through his trousers for his lighter. "Where is the fucking thing?" He needed to go to the toilet and he needed a smoke. Failing to find his lighter, he decided that the toilet was the priority. His guts had been cramping since dinner time. Their meeting with the Chief Constable was a shambles. Gladstone was a pompous arsehole and the Chief had made him look foolish and ill prepared. On leaving the huge police headquarters, which reminded him of a concrete fortress, Gladstone dragged him to an expensive restaurant on the Albert Docks where he spent the next forty minutes ranting down the telephone, much to the annoyance of the other diners. The maitre d' was fuming but as they ordered ridiculously expensive lobster and four bottles of wine, he suffered Gladstone in silence. Gladstone was intoxicated and staggered back to his room to sulk, barely able to speak, which left Salter at a loose end. He wandered down the promenade where he was approached by the girl. She amused him for a while then an hour later the stomach cramps started. He'd had his fill of the girl anyway and the pain in his lower abdomen forced him to cut their copulation short.

    He put the unlit cigarette in his mouth and sat down on the toilet. The hotel room was plush. The docks were built from red bricks and the architects who designed the hotel had left much of them on show. The ceilings were arched, criss-crossed with metal girders. The bathroom was black marble with a walk-in shower which could wash a Ford Focus. He looked around at the luxurious fixtures and fittings and spotted his lighter next to the basin. "There it is." He half stood to reach for it and the movement squeezed the muscles around his lower intestines. What he thought was going to be trapped wind was actually a litre of diarrhoea. Involuntarily, his sphincter decided to release the offensive liquid. It squirted from his anus like a brown jet splattering the expensive porcelain, the toilet lid and a couple of metres of floor tiles. The cramps worsened and he grabbed his stomach and sat down in the mess. "Oh for fuck's sake!" he moaned as another litre or so erupted from his rear. "At least this time it's down the toilet." He gritted his teeth as yet more liquid left him. He looked at the lighter in his hand and lit the cigarette. Taking a deep suck on it, he decided to remain seated until the crisis passed. Another cramp gripped him as the room phone rang. There was a handset fitted to the wall next to the toilet. Although he'd always found that particular facility in hotels amusing, suddenly he could see the benefit.

"Adrian Salter," he tried to sound like he wasn't in pain.

"How was the girl?" the voice asked amused.

"Who is this?"

"She looked a bit skinny to me."

"I think you have the wrong room."

"How was the food this afternoon?"

"Who is this?" Curiosity stopped him from hanging up. Curiosity and something else.

"Have you got bad guts yet?"

Salter remained silent, the pain in his abdomen forgotten for a moment. The voice sounded familiar but he couldn't place it.

"What's up? A sinister chuckle filled the silence. "I just needed you to know that I can reach you anywhere."

"What do you mean?"

"A few quid placed in the right palms and anything can be achieved. You've got the shits, haven't you?"

"I don't know who this is but......"

"This is Colin Dean."

"Oh, I thought I recognised your voice, what the fuck are you playing at?" Cold sweat formed on his forehead. He wasn't sure if it was the cramps or fear. He had never met the man but they'd spoken on the telephone once. Dean was connected to a shell company who had financed a large chunk of

Brigade Security on its launch; his shareholding was the most significant individual investment, which gave him control when voting on policy change. Salter hadn't realised the man was a gangster when he took the job as CEO. By the time he did, it was too late. Salter invested his life savings into the company and now he was locked into it for the next five years.

"Language, Adrian."

"What do you want?"

"Exactly what I said, to let you know we can reach you anywhere," the voice took a different tone. "I paid a chef in the Lobster Pot to mix some special ingredients into your sauce. Laxatives are fun when used in the right manner, don't you think?"

"You are crossing the line here, Mr Dean." Salter began to get angry, his fear taking a back seat.

"Don't take it personally, Adrian. Gladstone should be pebbling the toilet by now too. We didn't just pick on you alone. Next time it will be rat poison. Do you understand?"

"What exactly do you want?"

"You need to make our investment safe. We put a lot of money into Brigade Security, provided you with fuel all through the riots, even when the police were struggling to acquire it. Your vehicles were still moving because of us."

"You were paid well over the odds."

"And you will continue to pay that price, Adrian otherwise we may have to bring in a new CEO, do you understand?"

"This is not how we do business," Salter tried to be assertive but he wasn't dealing with a regular supplier and he knew it. "We are putting the contract out to tender. You can bid on it the same way everyone else does."

"Oh dear," Dean sighed. "I don't think you're listening to me. We supply your company with bio diesel. Full stop. You need to sort out the greedy officers at the bottom of the chain because they're attracting attention and you're going to lose the contract completely. Mills and his cronies have put us directly in the spotlight and I don't like it."

"I don't have any control over corruption at officer level. We'll always have bad eggs. I'm clamping down on it already but it takes time. I have to put the fuel contract out to tender otherwise we're breaking the law."

"We don't want you to do that now do we?"

"I've given the police the name of one officer connected to Mills," Salter grimaced as the cramp hit him again. "I did it tonight."

"Wayne Barclay?"

"Yes, how did you know?"

"Did he turn up for work today?"

"No and he is on our list of monitored officers. Everything they do out of line is reported to me via their reporting officers."

"Well done, why didn't he come to work?"

"I don't know but he's obviously up to no good."

"Or dead."

"What do you mean?"

"We killed him," Dean said matter of factly. "Him and some of the thieving scumbags he was working with. He was seizing cars from people and selling them on, moving stolen goods all hours of the day and night and the police were all over him. He needed to be removed and you didn't do it."

"Jesus."

"He won't help you," Dean laughed. "Do you know how we got onto him?"

"No, of course not."

"He stashed one of your vehicles in a scrapyard near Widnes."

"What vehicle?" Salter felt dread touch him. The events at Silver Lane were still not explained. He didn't want them to be anything more than one rogue officer who went haywire.

"Why, how many are missing?"

"One."

"Which one?"

"Mills's Volkswagen."

"Right, so let's stop playing games."

"Where did it turn up?" Salter gritted his teeth and cramp crippled him again. He felt sick to the core.

"He hid them with an unscrupulous scrap dealer, who just happens to help us out occasionally. He got greedy and called us. He connected the Volkswagen to the shootings and wanted money to keep quiet."

"Where are they now?"

"We've tidied it up for now."

"The police will find out."

"Correct, now do you want that kind of attention on your company?"

"No."

"Then do as you're told and we'll tidy things up properly at our end."

"I won't be blackmailed by you or anybody else."

"Did you know that Barclay has an accomplice?"

"There are a few other names under investigation," Salter said cautiously. "I'm not certain who is involved though."

"Is one of them his partner, Whitehouse?"

"Yes, at least I think so," Salter wasn't sure. There were so many names he couldn't possibly remember them all.

"We'll erase him and tidy up any evidence they've left behind."

"You can't kill them all for God's sake!"

"'We', Adrian, the word you need to use is 'we'," Dean said sarcastically. "You're in this up to your neck. I want the list of officers under investigation. We need to make them toe the line, or disappear."

"They have families, children," Salter stopped as pain creased him. "Some of them will be innocent."

"We will investigate them before we ask questions. Nothing moves in this city unless we know about it."

"Leave it to me, things are settling down. We don't need a string of disappearances. Our tenure is in question, as it stands, you'll make things worse."

"We need to make Brigade invaluable again," Dean explained in a calm voice as if he was talking about buying a car. "We're bringing in some merchandise which will reignite the inner city power struggle," he said flatly. "People are vying for power and position everywhere and when we arm the groups loyal to us, there should be plenty of reasons for the Brigade contract to be renewed. You're either in, or out, you choose."

"I won't be bullied."

"You are not listening."

"I won't be intimidated."

"Okay, maybe Chantelle could be."

"What?"

"All alone when she walks from hockey practice at that posh boarding school you send her to," Dean chuckled again. "That school is quite remote, lots of woods and a river nearby. I wouldn't have to pay anyone to do her; she's a pretty little thing. You must be so proud."

"You bastard!" Salter struggled for words. "You go near my family and…….."

"And fuck all!" Dean shouted. "You get a grip on your men in this city and you buy your fuel from us. You make sure they are where they are told to be when we tell you to. Fuck this contract up or go to the police and I'll send your daughter home in a matchbox, understand?"

"I'll do my best," Salter whined as another litre of fluid splattered in the pan. The line went dead and his affections for Liverpool took a turn for the worse.

CHAPTER 34

Mr James

Colin Dean put the phone down and looked in the mirror. His blond hair needed washing and he felt grimy. He picked up a set of dumbbells and pumped them furiously, focusing his anger into hurting the muscles in his arms. Blue veins protruded to bursting point, his biceps looked like granite beneath his skin. His arms reached failure point and he dropped the weights with a crash on the foam mat. He used to spend two hours a day in his home made gym before allying himself with the Priest, now he was lucky to get half that time to spare. Business was taking up far too much of his time. Priest seemed to be on a mission to take on the world singlehandedly. His arrogance was wearing thin. The money was generous but he could make a decent living running the business he inherited from his father legitimately. If he did some freelancing too, he could match what Priest was paying him. His haulage company made money. It made a lot of money. When the Priest approached him, the money he offered to transport his products was impossible to refuse. When the troubles started, the value of consumer products rocketed and Colin Dean had a guaranteed supply of fuel. His vehicles created the shift in power amongst Britain's organised crime families and the Priest grew in wealth and reputation. His business ventured out into dangerous waters. Drugs, arms, people, tobacco and alcohol; there wasn't a line he wouldn't cross. Each new shipment pushed the boundaries and taunted law enforcement agencies across the globe. Dean was beginning to question his commitment to the Priest.

"Colin!" Sharon's voice shrieked up the stairs.

"What," he answered impatiently. His wife was becoming suspicious about his business activities. She was clever and she could tell by his anxiousness that he was in trouble. They'd been together a long time. His lifelong addiction to weightlifting had taken him into the world of bodybuilding, door security and the periphery of the underworld. He didn't really need the money any more but he loved the adrenalin rush of being included in a deal. That's where he met Kevin Warren and Michael Yates, brutal giants loyal to the highest bidder.

"Kevin is here!" her voice was closer now, outside the door. "I thought we were going out today," she burst into the room angrily. "You promised me!" Her face was like thunder and he knew he was pushing her love for him to the limit. Sometimes the look in her eyes betrayed her true feelings for him, contempt, disappointment and disgust. "What is he doing here again? They are trouble Colin!"

"It's just business," he swung at the punch bag which hung in the corner. His fist rattled it with a satisfying whoomp. "We can go out later, this won't take long."

"What's up, have I called at a bad time?" Kevin stood behind Sharon on the landing. "Are you having a domestic?"

"You stink," Sharon got a whiff of the big man and wrinkled her nose in disgust. "Go home and have a shower."

"Some of us have to get our hands dirty and do a bit of graft," he winked cheekily, "any chance of a brew, Sharon?"

"Shut up, Kevin," she snapped and turned angrily, taking the stairs two at a time. "I'm leaving in half an hour, Colin. You'd better be ready."

"Have you heard from Michael?"

"Yes," Kevin Warren smiled. "Jammy bastard was shacked up with a couple of hookers in Bangkok. He said he had six hours before he leaves for the airport."

"Jules Lee?"

"Silenced."

Dean nodded and looked at his notepad. His 'to do' list was increasingly becoming a hit list rather than a reminder of business transactions which needed his attention. The days of completing his tasks in the space of a few hours on the telephone, delegating to others, were gone. The networks they'd established over years were disintegrating as the power shift in the underworld continued. Now they were dealing with new faces, new threats and different challenges. All the trust was gone. Honour amongst thieves was a long forgotten myth.

"Wayne Barclay?"

"Gone but not forgotten," Kevin said nervously.

"What did he tell you?"

"He was on different shifts to Mills. He knew of him but they'd never met. They were stationed in different divisions. Barclay was making money on the side selling small time dealers and snippets of information to a nigger in the Drug Squad. Mills' operation was treading on his toes so when they got wind of the pay-off in Warrington, they decided to hit Mills and take the money," Kevin laughed sourly. "They didn't expect Mills to lose the plot."

"And the Barker woman?"

"He had her but......"

"But?" Dean interrupted. "There had better not be any 'buts'"

"He died suddenly," Kevin shrugged and blushed. "Must have had a heart attack or something, one minute he was singing like a bird then dead as a dodo a minute later!"

"Great job!" Dean shook his head. "He was our chance to find out everything."

"We know he has her somewhere."

"Will the police find his body?"

"We had to leave him in the crusher. We had a call from our asset warning us that the police were on the way to the scrapyard. We had to make a sharp exit, unfortunately, we've left bodies behind."

"As long as that's all you left," Dean raised his eyebrows.

"Both vehicles they used from Silver Lane are there," Kevin shrugged. "The police will link them and Barclay and think it's a double cross or a deal gone bad. Renton is known to them. I can't see them looking for anyone else."

"I disagree."

"Why?"

"What about his partner, Dennis Whitehouse?"

"We went to his house," he smiled. "There was no answer."

"Does he have a girlfriend, boyfriend, mother, sister, father, brother, he's somewhere, you fucking idiot," Dean snapped. "Find him and make him disappear and don't fuck this up!"

"We're on it already, calm down," Kevin said offended. "Listen if you want me to run things, then you'll have to trust me. I'll know where Whitehouse is within the hour and when I do, he's toast. The woman will be with him; she must be," Kevin's Blackberry rang as he spoke. "I need to take this," he apologised. "Go on," he smiled. "Bingo!"

"What was it?" Dean asked.

"Whitehouse uses his dead grandmother's house in Woolton Village," Kevin smiled smugly. "I'm on my way, what do you want me to do with the Barker woman?"

"She has no value now Jules Lee is out of the picture," Dean clapped his hands sharply. "Get rid of them both and I'll sort out Frederick Hope and the girl myself tonight. I want every last piece of this fucking shambles gone by tomorrow morning."

CHAPTER 35

53 Quarry St

"There's no way out," Dennis explained softly. "The windows and doors are locked and padlocked, so don't get any funny ideas." He frowned to emphasise his words. "Here's some towels and some of my Nan's old jumpers." He tossed a pile of folded clothes onto the mattress, handing the towels to her. "They're a bit old fashioned but there might be something that fits."

"Is the water hot," Carol pressed the towels to her nose. They smelled of fabric conditioner, fresh and clean. "Oh and do you have any shampoo?" she laughed cheekily.

"The water's hot," Dennis smiled. "It's a combi-boiler. I had it fitted for her a few years back, it's almost new. There's shampoo and conditioner in the bathroom although it's not the best stuff. She did all her shopping at Poundland."

"Thanks for this, Den," she blinked her eyelashes slowly, teasingly. "I really appreciate it. I know if Barclay comes back, he'll go mad won't he."

"I've told you not to worry about him," he said seriously. "I'll deal with him if he turns up."

"That's what worries me," she said with sad eyes. "Everything about this situation needs to be 'dealt' with." Her eyes filled with tears. "Including me." He looked at the floor sheepishly. "It doesn't matter what happens, I just want a shower and some clean clothes."

"Have you got everything you need?"

"Erm, this might sound rude," she paused. "Do you have any of your Nan's underwear only I've had these on for too long? You know what I mean?"

"Oh, yes, I'll take a look for you," he blushed. "I don't go in her underwear drawer, seems wrong. I can't bring myself to throw her stuff away, I keep putting it off."

"I'd be grateful."

"I'll be a minute." Carol heard him walking down the hallway. Ten steps before his footsteps changed tone, stepping from one carpet to another. It was a big house obviously. The first time they'd left her alone in the house, she'd tried to scream and make as much noise as she could by banging on the radiator but no one heard her. Barclay left her gagged but Dennis removed it whenever he came. She heard him returning. "She was only tiny," he smiled as he offered a choice of knickers. "Probably not what you'd normally choose but they're clean."

"Thanks, Den," she took them and smiled, "just one more thing then."

"What?" she looked at the handcuffs and chains and rattled them. "Oh, yes, sorry." He took a bunch of keys from his left pocket and searched for the right one. He undid each cuff with the same key, releasing her. She rubbed at the painful red welts on her wrists. "They look sore," he said surprised.

"What did you expect them to do to me, Den?"

"I'm really sorry," he shook his head in shame. "It all seems so pointless when Wayne isn't around. I don't know how I ever got involved in this shit."

"It's easily done." She looked him in the eye. Can I get undressed in the bathroom or are you going to watch me in case I try to run?" she left the question hanging with a smile. He blushed red again and nodded towards the door. Carol walked past him carrying the towels. She left the underwear and spare clothes on the mattress. He stepped back awkwardly and watched her step across the hall into the bathroom. "I'll leave the door open so you know I'm not shinning down the drainpipe." She turned and smiled coyly. The bathroom was warm and neatly organised. Her eyes darted from the window ledge to the basin, to the shelf above the bath, searching for a makeshift weapon. A nail file, scissors and a heavy vase all had potential but her eyes settled on a metal tail-comb; the tail a four-inch spike.

Carol knew this was her only chance to escape. She couldn't wait for fate to step in and help her. She placed the towels on the toilet seat and then leaned over the bath and switched on the electric shower. The sound of running water hitting the bath was so inviting that she almost put thoughts of escaping aside, almost. A hand mirror above the sink held the reflection of the bathroom door. She could see Dennis Whitehouse hovering in the hallway. He was glancing at her every now and again, waiting for the chance of a glimpse of flesh. Carol would make sure he got an eyeful just before she stuck the tail-comb into his throat.

Chapter 36

Titan

The MIT Land Rover raced through the slush, followed by three similar vehicles and two Armed Response Units. The traffic parted politely, blue flashing lights and sirens doing their job. "What's the address again?" Smithy asked. The caller replied and Alec could see Smithy's face light up. New information was coming to light quickly. "You need to get onto Noonan and tell him to send all the information over. I'll call you back."

"What's Noonan come up with?" Alec asked.

"The refinery was making a fortune during the riots. Noonan reckons their production figures don't match up with their accounts." Smithy turned in the front seat. "Seems they were supplying biodiesel to a haulage company near the docks, Dean and sons."

"Where's the connection?"

"Noonan reckons the amount of fuel they were buying doesn't add up. They were reselling, and get this," Smithy paused. "The owner, Colin Dean, has shares in a shell company who invested heavily in Brigade Security. His trucks were moving all through the riots, protected by plastics."

"I know the guy," Billingham added. "Big bloke, meat-head with long blond hair, always had it tied back. He worked on the doors in a couple of places in town a few years back mind you. His name came up several times."

"For what," Alec asked.

"If I remember rightly," Billingham thought back. "He knocked about with a couple of monsters. They were fingered for a few nasty beatings, enforcers for whoever needed someone sorting out. We knew he had lorries and vans legitimately, then a few years back, he disappeared from the scene. We thought maybe he'd realised that it was time to get out and concentrate on his business but it sounds like he allied himself and his trucks to something much bigger."

"There's the shift in power right there," Alec agreed. "If their trucks were moving and bringing in supplies, then they had control of the market. Tell Les to take whoever he needs to the haulage yard," Alec said. "We need to speak to Dean at the station."

Billingham's phone rang. He was driving with one hand and having his own conversation at the same time. He cut off the call and put the phone in his pocket. "It all seems to be adding up now, Guv."

"What have you got?"

"One of our team has been working on a dealer, called Marcus Tiffin," Billingam used the rearview mirror to look at Alec. "He's a suit working out of a business park on Rathbone Road. He has a network supplying high quality cocaine to businessmen and women who use the bars there. Looked like a small operation at first but once we looked at it in detail, they're shifting a kilo a week minimum."

"What's the link to our case?"

"He knows everyone and it's general knowledge that Carol Barker was having an affair with Frank Dempster."

"Is it solid?"

"He says it's solid," Billingham nodded. "Seems the two of them were as thick as thieves for months; they were working on some big scoop involving Jules Lee and his network."

"That makes sense," Alec said. "If Baldwin was undercover at Lee's gym, working out with the doormen, then he could have been selling information to Barker and Dempster for months. The sting on Silver Lane could have been a bonus for all of them if it had gone the way they planned it."

"If they took Jodie to apply leverage on Barker and Dempster, then she's still worth keeping alive, if they get whacked……"

"She's a liability," Alec finished off the sentence. "How long till we get to Whitehouse's place?"

"Ten minutes away," Smithy looked at his watch. "Dempster got burnt running a story on steroids in the premiership didn't he?"

"Years ago," Alec nodded. "Sounds like he couldn't let it go."

"There's an awful lot of money involved nowadays. If he could prove it, there would be sponsorship deals disappearing left, right and centre. Carol Barker should have known better than to mess about with Dempster, still, if you play with fire, Guv!"

"Full of sympathy as usual, Smithy," Alec rolled his eyes and smiled.

"Do you know where 'sympathy' is in the dictionary, Guv?"

"In between 'shit' and 'syphilis'," Alec ruined his joke. "The old ones are the best." Smithy's mobile rang again. He stuck a chubby finger into one hairy ear and placed the phone to the other.

"Smith," he shouted to the caller. "Go on." He clicked open the glove box and reached inside for a pen, tearing the top sheet from a pad of blank statement forms. "No way, pheeew!" he shook his head as he scribbled a few words. Alec couldn't see them from the back seat. The Land Rover picked up speed as the road opened up, free of traffic. "Let me speak to the governor and call you back."

"What is it?" Alec leaned around the seat. Smithy twisted his ample bulk in the seat to talk face to face. He looked concerned and confused.

"Whitehouse has two addresses," Smithy said over the blaring siren. "He owns one in Woolton, which is where we're headed but he has a girlfriend in Speke. Julie Green, thirty three, two children, Raymond and Rachel. Have a guess who's the father of her kids?"

"David Cameron?"

"Raymond Citrone."

"No surprise there," Billingham said sourly. "How else could Whitehouse and Barclay know about the set up at Silver Lane?"

"Bishop told Kathy Brooks that there was a reason why they went alone, with no back up," Alec thought aloud. "They knew there was a leak somewhere but they wouldn't have thought it was coming from Citrone. His name is beginning to irritate me," Alec thought about the significance of the news. "It could be something, could be nothing but his name keeps coming up."

"It would explain how information keeps reaching the dealers, Guv," Billingham said. "They checked his phone records. If he was making calls to his ex-girlfriend's number, no one would connect it. She could be passing information on to Whitehouse, they're tipping the dealers and creaming in the money in backhanders."

"Makes sense," Alec nodded. "What do we know about Whitehouse?"

"Not much, Guv," Smithy shouted. "Mills had a poor record but Whitehouse was clean. Should we be speaking to Citrone, once this is done?"

"For what?" Alec shrugged. "Having kids, being an estranged father? If he's dirty, we'll nail him. He's not our priority right now."

"I've never liked the guy," Smithy mumbled. He took out his Glock and checked the clip was full. "I'm not sure what to expect when we get here."

"The ARU have been briefed that there may be a hostage inside," Alec checked his weapon. "If Whitehouse has any sense, he'll give it up. If he doesn't, then we take him down. Jodie Barker has lost one parent; we're going to make sure she doesn't lose another."

CHAPTER 37

Jodie Barker

"Eat your food," Freg pointed to the bowl of beans on an upturned tea chest. "They'll go cold."

"I need the toilet," Jodie whimpered. She'd been waiting to go for ages but she didn't like using the bucket for number two's.

"Use the bucket," Freg said annoyed. "I've emptied it."

Jodie shook her head, her lips clamped tightly. She was scared, cold and hungry but she needed the proper toilet. "I want my mummy." Tears trickled from her eyes mingling with the dust and grime on her cheeks.

"Stop crying, ungrateful bitch," Freg mumbled. "Do you want me to take you to the real toilet?"

She bit her lip and nodded quickly. Freg grabbed her hand and pulled her roughly towards the door. "Take it easy, Freg," Sid stood in the corridor. "You can tell you have never been around kids," he knelt and smiled at Jodie. "Do you need number two's?" he smiled. He reached into his ski jacket and pulled out a bundle of tissues. "You'll need these, come on, I'll take you, Freg is grumpy isn't he?"

Jodie nodded without looking at Freg. She took Sid's hand and walked through the rubble to the real toilet. Decades ago, it was used by the floor manager who would have had a key to the door; his own toilet, part of his status for his position of authority. Freg waited impatiently. He was nervous around kids, especially young girls. They made him uncomfortable and reminded him of his tragic youth. He didn't want to be near Jodie because he didn't want to hurt her or cause her pain. Everything he touched turned to shit. She would be safer if he put as much distance as he could between them. Sid walked her back into the room, a natural with kids. She smiled when he held her hand and she ate her beans and drank the fruit shoot they'd brought. "Wrap this around you and keep warm," Sid smiled. "I won't be long. Read your comics for a while." He pulled the door closed, the last glimpse of Jodie's desolate expression heartbreaking.

Frederick Hope had a dilemma. Mr James had ordered him to kill the girl, so that her kidnapping couldn't be linked to him but Michael Yates had threatened to kill him if anything happened to her. The situation was hopeless. They were both nuts. He stared at the gargantuan tobacco warehouses, built on the Stanley Docks, through a clean patch on the grimy glass and tried to come up with a solution which wouldn't result in him joining the doctor at the bottom of the Irish Sea. Not that he had any sympathy for the old bastard, he was a snitch. It was his fault that his elder brother was dead. His brother was his idol, his role model and he'd missed his family desperately when he was sent down as a young boy. It wasn't his fault either.

Henry Richards was the pervert, not him. The brothers had stuck together and concocted a story which made Frederick look like the ringleader. He was far from it. The entire incident had traumatised him. All through his prison terms he was called a nonce. Every fight he was involved in was because of 'Henry fucking Richards'. They did unspeakable things to that girl and blamed him. Everyone believed them and Freg wasn't articulate enough to deny it convincingly. The entire trial and the furore of disgust which followed it seemed like a surreal nightmare; almost as if it happened to somebody else while he was watching through glass. He was found guilty. He was the abuser, the pervert, the paedophile. Word soon spread in any prison in which he was incarcerated. Inmates taunted him about using a bottle on the young girl. The thought sickened him; it haunted him day and night. Yes he was violent to other men if they targeted him and he glassed or stabbed them, bit them or slashed them to shut them up. He did whatever it took to win. Prisons were a jungle where the weak were prey for the strong. He became violent and numb to inflicting terrible injuries on adversaries in order to survive. The Richards brothers and Mark Overand took his childhood from him and he had to grow up quickly in a dangerous environment, prison. That's why he killed Mark Overand so easily at Beech Close; payback for all the years they stole from him. Henry Richards was a sick bastard and he was out there somewhere, but the authorities had made him invisible too. They changed his name and Frederick never heard of him again. He would never forget his face though, the look in his eyes while he tormented the girl. His twisted smile and evil laugh and the sick things he said to her. He could never forget the things he said and did to that little girl. Frederick hadn't had the chance to come to terms with what they did. The things they blamed him for. He hadn't settled that score yet and he doubted he ever would. The truth was, he hadn't touched that little girl and he didn't want to hurt this one either.

"What are we going to do with her?" Sid said nervously. Sid was black, of Jamaican origin and he wasn't comfortable with the situation. He had two young girls of his own at home not much older than Jodie. "I'm not happy with all this crap, Freg. This is wrong in so many ways"

"I shouldn't have taken her in the first place," Freg gazed at the huge brick monolith across the dock; black waters covered by ice and snow separated them from it. The roads at either end were linked by ancient swing bridges which crossed the canals and led on to the sea. "It was chaos in there and she was screaming so loud. I don't know what I was thinking. Mr James, or whatever his fucking name is, wants her dead."

"Fuck that," Sid sighed. "Look I don't mind dealing a bit of powder and the odd shooter but I'm not in for killing kids. I've got kids of my own."

"Have you ever been to the Sunday market over there?" Freg nodded towards the old tobacco warehouses. The ground floors had been used for hosting a market while the thirteen storeys above were left to rot.

"Of course I have, what's that got to do with anything?"

"I read there are thirty six acres of space inside those buildings, fourteen storeys of hiding places," Freg turned to look at Sid. "Mr James and the Priest are going to want the girl dead, me too probably. They'll come here."

"That guy's a freak, man," Sid said with disgust.

"Mr James?"

"He's just bad, Priest is an evil fucking freak."

"Do you know who he is?"

"No way, no one does," Sid shook his head. "But I know what he does, pervert doesn't cover it."

"What do you mean?" The hairs on Freg's neck bristled.

"Before you got out of clink, a friend of mine owed them some money," Sid lowered his voice and looked around. "I told him not to go to them but he wouldn't listen. He took half a 'k' from them and a shooter. Silly fucker didn't pay on time and Priest fucked him up badly. They blindfolded him and took him somewhere. He didn't see Priest but he heard him. He made him say prayers, man," Sid spat on the floor. "The freak made him say grace and then fucked him up the arse, man. He beat him up badly. The freak left him with a wine bottle up his arse. He took pictures and put them all over the internet, sixteen stitches and a week in hospital. The guy knew they'd come back again for their money when he got out; he ate a bullet from the gun he bought from them, blew his own fucking brains out, man."

"What did he make him say?" Freg's eyes narrowed.

"What?"

"I said what did he make him say?" Freg became agitated. "You said he made him say grace?"

"Yes, man," Sid stepped back concerned at the reaction. "'For what you are about to receive' and all that shit; he hurt him real bad."

Frederick Hope felt like he'd been punched in the stomach by The Hulk. It couldn't be a coincidence. There was no doubt in his mind who Priest was. There could be no mistake. He would remember what they made the little girl do and what he made her say. Henry Richards made her say grace. He made her say grace every time he forced himself into her, every time he used the bottle. The thoughts knocked him dizzy as if he was back there watching it all over again and he thought about the look on Jodie Barker's face every time the closed the door to her prison. He couldn't do it any longer; he was abusing Jodie mentally just as Richards had with the girl. Henry Richards had grown up to become the Priest. If he had heard his name mentioned, Richards wouldn't have realised that Frederick Hope was the same young boy they stitched up years ago. Only his brother Steven Young knew and he was dead. He wasn't sure if the revelation was a good thing or not but he did know what he had to do. "Well then, we have no choice."

"So what are we going to do?"

"If someone was to take the girl without me knowing," Freg looked out of the window. "They could hide in there for days. An army couldn't find you in there. When you know you're safe, take her to the police. Call them and say you found her there, make something up just get her away from here."

"What about you?"

"I'm going to wait here," Frederick Hope smiled. "I want to talk to Mr James and the Priest. It's time to set the record straight."

CHAPTER 38

Frank Dempster

Frank checked his mobile for text messages and emails; nothing but the usual crap. He hadn't heard anything from the men who were holding Carol Barker. At first he didn't believe them but they sent photographs of her bound, gagged and chained to a radiator. They wanted everything they had on Jules Lee, in exchange for her safe release. Eight years of research, digging and bribing would be lost. He had devoted his life to uncovering the existence of performance enhancing drugs in professional sport but no one would give him a minute. There were too many people making millions from football, rugby, cricket, boxing, cycling and athletics. No one would acknowledge that it was widespread until career cheat Lance Armstrong confessed to winning seven Tour de France titles on drugs. All of a sudden there was interest and he had all the evidence to prove that it was insidious, from the grass roots to the top flight. There was no way he was trading everything he'd worked for to keep Carol Barker alive. She was no great shakes anyway. Yes she'd been fun and they'd shared good times but she was talking about getting a divorce from her husband and setting up home together with her daughter. Fuck that. Playing happy families was not on his schedule. If he'd wanted kids, then he would have had them. His own kids, not someone else's. If they killed Carol because of his story, it would add to the depth and emotional impact of the scoop. He could see himself weeping for her loss on every television chat show for the next three years at least. Then there would be the spin-offs, books, documentaries, maybe even a film based on his exploits. Financially he would be made for life. As for Carol, there had been no contact so he had to assume she was dead. The truth was, he didn't care.

The deal was done anyway and there was no way back now. He snapped the laptop closed and slotted it into his leather satchel. His phone and car keys went into his jacket pocket. The office was the converted garage at the side of his detached house in Bowden. He stepped out into the kitchen turning off the lights and headed for the cupboard next to his huge Smeg refrigerator. He opened it to reveal neatly stacked tins of Heinz tomato soup, tuna chunks and beans. It was a cunningly simple security product. The tins looked perfectly normal except they were empty and glued in place. Lifting the entire inner shelf out, tins included, a well hidden safe was revealed. He turned the dial and punched a five digit code into the lock. The door opened with a click. Two large padded brown envelopes, six discs and three memory sticks. Eight years of work which would bring professional sport to its knees and make him a millionaire. He closed the safe and replaced the fake shelf, slamming the cupboard door before heading for the hall. A green waxed jacket hung on the banister and he pulled it over his suit, tying a grey scarf around his neck. He checked the pocket for his gloves and decided to put them on when he got to the car.

It would take him forty minutes to drive to Media City on the Salford Quays. Once there he would meet with two acquisition managers, one from the BBC, the other from ITV. When they saw the depth and quality of the evidence he had built up, they would be throwing money at him in a bidding war which would make him rich. It didn't matter to him which station took it on, although it would be good to get one over on the BBC. They dropped him years ago but now they would listen. They would have to. The BBC carried more weight abroad and would make millions from the international rights to the story. His face would become a household name, Frank Dempster, the investigator who not only uncovered the widespread use of Human Growth Hormone in sport, but had the proof that its use was rife.

He checked his appearance in the mirror on the wall, the driftwood frame reminding him of a trip to Blackpool with Carol. She'd made him carry two twisted pieces of wood a mile back to the car so that she could make a mirror from them. She was creative, that was certain. He almost felt guilty for not cooperating with the kidnappers, almost, but not quite. The whites of his eyes were threaded with red. Sleep had been hard to come by lately, ever since the disaster on Silver Lane. They could have made a fortune. He lost twenty grand but that would be peanuts when put into context with his potential gain from the HGH story. His time in the journalistic wilderness was nearly done. He licked his index finger and groomed his eyebrows, noting that they needed trimming and tinting before any imminent television appearances. There would be plenty of time for Botox and a little tweaking.

A knock on the front door made him jump nervously. He scanned the figure through the bevelled glass. It was a male, a big one at that, his bulk increased by his winter coat. Frank hid the satchel behind the meter cupboard and looked through the peephole. The man was ruddy faced and stamped his feet to keep them warm. He had a bag hanging from his shoulder. The lock clicked open almost silently as Frank twisted the handle. He peered through the gap allowed by a security chain.

"Mr Dempster?" the man frowned.

"Yes." His nerves were at snapping point, his mouth dry and his hands trembling slightly.

"Recorded delivery," he smiled. "Just need a signature please." He took a large envelope from his bag and held it up offering a rubberised gadget with a digital screen which needed signing with the other hand. "It's not as cold as yesterday."

"Oh, sorry, I haven't been out yet," Frank closed the door enough to slide the security chain off. "I was just on my way out." He added taking the envelope. He eyed the postmark and the sender details. It had been sent from Thailand. "Thanks." Frank mumbled closing the door quickly. He watched the postman's shadow shortening as he walked down the long pebble drive. The crunching footfall became quieter before it disappeared.

He ripped open the envelope and slid out a single photograph. If he hadn't been so shocked, he might have dropped it but his fingers refused to listen to his brain. He leaned against the wall for support nearly knocking the driftwood mirror from its fixings. His knees felt weak. Jules Lee lay on his back; blood soaked his chest, a dark hole drilled into his forehead. His eyes stared accusingly from the picture. Frank stared at it wide eyed not knowing what to do or how to feel. The kingpin at the centre of the importation and distribution of steroids and HGH was dead. From his wounds, Frank could tell it was a professional hit. Was the picture sent as a warning to keep his mouth shut? He checked the postal date but it was smeared and unreadable.

The enormity of what he was doing struck him in a different format. Money was no longer the measurement, consequences became the scale.

Would they try to kill him? He realised Jules Lee would probably try to silence him but who killed him? Frank was running out of options. He'd bought a gun the year before but it was stolen from his car three weeks before Silver Lane. It wasn't the type of thing one could report to the police. He wished he'd bought another one now. If he sold the story, he could ask for security and a secret location to hide. It had been done before. He had to get the story into the public eye as quickly as possible. Once the wheels began turning, he would be too high profile to assassinate. The dealers and importers would have to stay low for years. He grabbed his satchel from its hiding place and headed for the door. Looking through the peephole, his Mercedes was twenty yards away, the road was clear; the postman was walking down the neighbouring driveway. He pulled open the door and stepped out. It was warmer but he could still see his breath. He pulled the door closed behind him, keys in hand, ready to lock it when he heard steps crunching on the pebbles. His breath trapped in his chest. He didn't know whether to unlock the door and bolt back inside or turn to look at whoever was approaching. Were Lee's killers coming for him now? He couldn't turn to see his imaginary attacker. The footsteps neared and his blood pounded in his ears.

"Mr Dempster!" the voice called. "Sorry but I put this in the wrong pile," the postman was halfway up the path. "It's for you, my mistake, happens sometimes."

Frank turned slowly, terrified and confused. He saw the ruddy face he'd seen earlier; he heard his chirpy voice. There was no malice in it yet Frank was paralysed with fear. He simply couldn't speak, movement lost, his mind frozen with terror. "Are you all right, Mr Dempster?" the postman asked concerned. "You look a bit pale."

Frank felt his lip quivering. He nodded his head. "I'm just tired," he croaked. A neighbour beyond the neatly cut hedges raised his arm in hello. "All right, Frank," he called. Frank returned the greeting with a half smile. "Bit warmer today," the elderly man added.

"Yes, about time," Frank found his voice, although he was still frightened. The photograph had rattled him much more than he thought. He was in shock. Thoughts of how frightened Carol Barker must be pricked his conscience. He had never been so scared.

"Here you go, Mr Dempster," the postman handed the letter to him. "Are you sure you're okay?"

"Yes, sorry, I'm fine, thanks." He took it and looked at the writing although the details didn't register.

"You're the guy who does the boxing aren't you?" the postman pointed a finger. "It didn't register when I saw the name until I saw you earlier. Then I was thinking, where do I know that bloke from?" he laughed. "You know what that's like, right, does your head in when you can't place a face?"

"Yes," Frank managed a thin smile. "I'm a sports reporter."

"Thought so, anyway nice to meet you, I'll have to get on or I'll be in the shit for delivering late again!"

"See you," Frank lifted his hand weakly.

"Wait till I tell my lad I met you," he called from the driveway. "He loves his boxing, see you again!"

"Bye," Frank smiled and tried to pull himself together. He folded the envelope and pushed it into his pocket. He walked to the car convincing himself that he was being paranoid. All he had to do was reach Media City and he would be safe and rich. The indicators flashed and the alarm beeped as he approached. He opened the driver's door and tossed his satchel onto the passenger seat, climbing in quickly and slamming the door behind him. The key slipped into the ignition and as he turned it, the thought that they may have planted a bomb under his car flashed across his mind. The engine roared into life and he held his breath for long seconds. He looked at the dials and laughed ironically at the thought of a bomb warning light. He pushed the Mercedes into first gear and felt the wheels crunching the pebbles as he headed for the road.

CHAPTER 39

Carol Barker

The hot water soothed her aching limbs and as she lathered soap over her skin she felt more human again. It rinsed shampoo from her hair and poured down her body in rivulets of foaming bubbles. The scent of peaches drifted in the steam. For the precious minutes she showered, things felt almost normal. She glanced at the tail-comb and reality returned. As nice as it was, there was no time to waste pampering herself. She had to escape this godforsaken hole and get to the police. Jodie was her priority. There was one thing to contend with, the excuse for a man, Dennis Whitehouse. Without his gun and his sidekick, he was pathetic. He looked narrow at the shoulders, with a paunch. His hands were small and his neck was thin. He didn't look powerful. That gave her some hope. If she could wound him, it could give her time to unlock the doors and make a break for it. If she died in the process, then so be it. She was dead if she did nothing that was certain.

She rinsed her face, allowing the water to run into her eyes and mouth. Turning the water off, she pulled back the shower curtain and took a deep breath. It was time to take control of her fate. "Could you pass me a towel, Den," she called, "I've got soap in my eyes."

"Yes, hold on," he stuttered from just outside the door. He stepped into the bathroom and glanced at her naked body. Her skin was lightly tanned from a sunbed, her breasts perfectly shaped and firm. There was no fat on her stomach and the curve of her hips accentuated its flatness. She was standing side on but even from that angle he could tell her pussy was shaved. He looked at her body a second too long, mesmerised by her beauty. She hadn't noticed him ogling, her eyes were squeezed tight, covered by her hands. "Here," he placed the towel in her hand.

"Thanks," she said into the towel, wiping the imaginary soap from them eyes. "Do you have any deodorant?" She held the towel below her neck purposely allowing him to see her breasts. "It doesn't matter if you don't, just a thought."

"I've got a spare in my work bag," he tried to maintain eye contact. "It's in the car. I can get it once you're done and settled."

"You mean chained up like a dog again?"

"I don't have any other choice at the moment," he blushed. "I'll get you some women's deodorant from the shops if you like," he offered weakly.

"Oh, don't worry," she smiled and rubbed the towel over her arms and legs. Her voice sounded different, strained and tense. "I'll manage without for now. Be an angel and pass me the clothes off the bed. I've forgotten to bring them." He smiled but there was caution in his eyes. He turned and stepped across the hall. Carol reached for the metal comb and slipped it under the spare towel gripping it in her left hand. Stepping out of the bath, she turned to face the shaving mirror on the window ledge above the sink, allowing him to get a good look at her rear. She saw his reflection in the mirror as he walked back into the bathroom. He stared at her behind as he approached. It made her skin crawl but she resisted the urge to cover herself up. He was transfixed by her body but that was her plan.

"Here, I'll leave them on the bath."

"Could you rub some of this into my back," Carol asked picking up a bottle of Johnson's baby lotion. "My skin has gone so dry that it's itching all the time. You don't mind if I use some do you?" she squirted some into her hand and rubbed it into the skin of her right arm. "Here," she tipped the bottle up and he held out his right hand.

The cream felt cold as she squeezed a blob out. He rubbed it between her shoulder blades slowly at first. Shy, nervous yet excited. His breath came in short intakes; his senses tingled. He could smell her. "Is that okay?" he mumbled.

"Lower," she said watching his face in the mirror. His hand moved the cream down the small of her back following the line of her spine his excitement increasing. His eyes were fixed firmly on the curves of her hips. He was off guard, his thoughts purely on how this was going to develop. The desire to bend her over the sink and take her right there was almost irresistible. She was vulnerable and he could make the most of that. So could she. She could see the lust on his face. If he were a dog, he'd be drooling by now. His eyes were fixed on her body, his hands busy rubbing the cream into her skin. Carol was about to strike when something in his expression changed. His lips turned into a smile but it wasn't a good smile. It was more of a sneer. His eyes met hers in the mirror; realisation flashed in them.

His right hand grabbed a handful of hair at the back of her head and he twisted it violently. "Do you think I'm stupid, Carol?" he hissed. He pressed his bodyweight against her pinning her to the sink. He was stronger than she thought. "Did you think your little prick teasing act was going to work?" he twisted again, Carol gasped in pain.

"I wasn't teasing," she cried.

"You were, stupid bitch," he looked at her eyes in the mirror. "Did you think that if you let me fuck you, I'll let you walk away?" he grabbed her chin with his free hand. "Was that your plan?"

"No," Carol closed her eyes and wailed. "This was my plan!" she swung her left hand upwards in a vicious arc. The comb whizzed past her ear and pierced his left eye. There was a faint popping sound and she felt warm liquid splatter on her neck.

"You fucking bitch!" he screamed as he fell into the bathtub, thrashing around trying to pull the metal spike from the bloody socket. He ripped the shower curtain down as he tumbled. His boots clattered against the sides of the bath and his shouts became more frantic. Carol ran for the stairs, wrapping the towel around her. The stairs were wide, carpeted with beige cord, the walls dotted with family photographs. She tripped and grabbed at the banister with both hands halting her fall momentarily. Her knees scraped painfully against the coarse material, burning her skin but she managed to halt the momentum. She could hear banging in the bathroom and another chorus of screams. The stairs led to a long hallway, two doors on either side. A porch door blocked her view of the exit. Coloured panes of bevelled glass distorted the image of the front door beyond it. She froze when she realised that she'd forgotten to grab his keys from his pocket. In her panic, she'd left the most crucial part of the plan out.

"Bitch!" his voice spurred her into action. She took two stairs at a time wrapping the towel tightly around her. His footsteps stomped across the hallway towards the stairs. He was up and coming for her. Carol sprinted towards the porch. She glanced behind her and caught sight of him thudding down the stairs. Dark red blood and goo poured down his left cheek. His mouth was dangling open, a black maw fixed in a scream. He was gaining fast. Panic drove her faster and she skidded to the porch door, burning her feet on the carpet. She looked around quickly and twisted the handle. It opened and she stepped through it, slamming the door behind her. Dennis Whitehouse was only yards away. She held the handle tightly and looked at the front door. Two bolts were fitted but not locked. She twisted the Yale lock and the catch moved but the door remained still. Her heart pounded as he banged against the glass and pulled the door.

She yanked the front door but it stayed fast and didn't budge. Her eyes went to the door again and her heart sank when she saw a mortice lock fitted the middle. She felt the porch door rattle violently as his weight slammed against it. The glass vibrated threatening to shatter. He tried to twist the handle and she nearly lost her grip. "There's no way out, Carol!"

She grabbed the handle with both hands, desperately trying to resist the pressure. She couldn't keep him out for more than a few minutes. Her strength was fading and it seemed pointless. She was trapped. The door vibrated as he pulled at it. The frame rattled threatening to splinter. Carol held on for dear life, but although her life depended on it, she didn't have the hand strength to win. The handle jerked twisting her fingers and bruising her hand. She gritted her teeth and thought of her daughter but the pain was too much to bear. The pressure was too intense and she couldn't hold on any more.

Carol was about to let go when Whitehouse screamed. It was the scream of a wounded animal, hurt and surprised, terrified by something it didn't understand. Dark shadows merged into a mass which she couldn't distinguish. The pressure on the handle was released instantly and the house beyond the door fell silent for a moment. She pressed her head against the glass and knelt, her strength gone and she listened. Heavy breathing and a gurgling sound, dark liquid splattered against the glass making her fall backwards against the front door.

There was a blinding flash through the glass and then a concussion wave shook the entire building. Shards of multicoloured glass showered her. The explosion was deafening, numbing her brain for a second. Then all hell broke loose.

CHAPTER 40

Kevin Warren

Kevin Warren was a big man with a lifelong passion for weightlifting and Martial Arts. His rise through the ranks of organised crime was inevitable and he revelled in it. The assassination of Steven Young had left a gap in the hierarchy and he was ready to embrace the position. Colin Dean and the Priest had agreed to support him in his new role; all they had to do was tidy up the mess caused by Mills and his buffoons. He'd found the house used by Dennis Whitehouse easily. His contacts on the streets knew where he was. Breaking in the back door was simple.

When he looked through the kitchen door into the hallway, he'd heard the shower running upstairs He slipped into the dining room which smelled of mothballs and Brasso. The water stopped running and then there were voices, one male and one female. Then the man screamed and he heard footsteps pounding along the hall and down the stairs. He watched as a woman sprinted for the front door, her skin had the sheen of wetness. Half a minute later, Dennis Whitehouse stumbled clumsily after her. He realised that she must be Carol Barker, although what was happening, was beyond him. As Whitehouse hammered and tugged at the porch door, Kevin sneaked silently behind him. He slipped his silenced

Smith and Wesson into his belt and unclipped his stiletto from the sheath on his calf. Whitehouse was too preoccupied trying to get to the woman to notice.

Kevin wrapped his left arm across his throat, lifting and pulling simultaneously. Whitehouse shrieked as his larynx was crushed and the pressure on his spine increased. The stiletto penetrated the skin below his right ear before slicing the jugular and the windpipe with a single twist. Kevin felt his target twitch and then go limp. The woman was trapped in the porch. She couldn't go anywhere. He pulled the body down the hallway away from the porch, kicked open a door which led to a parlour and tossed him onto a floral Wilton carpet. Whitehouse landed face up, revealing the ruined eye. The woman must have inflicted that wound on him. She might be more dangerous than he thought. He wiped the blood from the blade and was about to slip it back into the sheath when movement caught his eye.

A silver canister bounced towards him, followed by another. He watched them, confused as to what they were and more to the point, who had tossed them. As his brain processed the information, a flash blinded him and the concussion wave which followed knocked him off his feet. "Armed police, get down, armed police!"

"Kitchen clear!" the voices neared, muffled by the ringing in his ears.

"Armed police!" Kevin registered four voices at least, all announcing their identity in a chorus of intimidating aggression. "Show yourself with your hands up!" they were much closer now. Kevin shook his head and rubbed his eyes. The flash had scorched the delicate tissue of his eyeballs. He pulled the gun and removed the silencer. Giving up wasn't an option. Whitehouse was slaughtered, his body on the floor next him. Life in prison didn't appeal, especially with a price on his head. The Priest couldn't allow him to live if he was locked up. The temptation to disclose information in exchange for a lighter sentence, or better conditions and privileges would always be there and the organisation couldn't risk it. He'd been on the trawler too many times. "Armed police!"

Kevin took a deep breath, stepped into the hallway and squeezed the trigger. Only one .38 calibre bullet left the gun before his head exploded like a ripe melon hit by a bus.

CHAPTER 41

Frank Dempster

Frank wished he smoked. His nerves were shattered. His focus for the last decade had been the spread of HGH in sport. When he discovered the name of one of the biggest suppliers, Jules Lee, then his life revolved around finding enough evidence to expose him and his high profile customers. Seeing the photograph of his dead body was shocking enough but it also announced the end of end of an era. His nemesis was dead. The story was still huge; maybe the biggest to hit sport for years, but something had been taken from him. Seeing Jules Lee on the television avoiding questions from a herd of reporters, eventually handcuffed and pushed into the back of a police car would never happen now. He almost felt sorry for him. If Lee was dead, maybe the threat to his own life was lessened somewhat. An hour from now it wouldn't matter. He would be safe inside the media circus.

The traffic was slow, making his journey mind numbingly boring. He hadn't got higher than third gear for the last few miles. Traffic lights and pedestrian crossings seemed to be conspiring to halt his progress. A white van pulled alongside him and the driver made eye contact. Frank looked away quickly and tried to pull forward enough to be out of his field of vision. He looked along the side of the van reading the name of the company it belonged to. It was a hire vehicle which made him breathe a sigh of relief. The lights changed to green and he nudged forward twenty yards before stopping again. He checked the rear view mirror and noticed a dark blue BMW behind him. There were two men in the front; one of them was talking on a mobile phone. A tinge of panic touched him. He thought about accelerating but the Manchester road was busy as he neared Altrincham. A high speed car chase was not on the cards, he was a terrible driver anyway. The car neared and his heartbeat increased.

Frank glanced in the mirror again for a moment too long. When he looked through the windscreen, the traffic had come to a standstill. At least the vehicle in front had. Frank noticed two things at once. There was a 'Stop Police' sign flashing in the rear window of the stationary vehicle and it was a dark blue BMW like the vehicle behind. The BMW behind him stopped millimetres from his rear bumper, blocking him in. He gripped the steering wheel and bit his lower lip nervously. He didn't know why he was being stopped but at least he would be safe with the police. Or that's what he thought until four armed officers jumped out of the vehicles, weapons raised and aimed at his head.

"Get out of the vehicle!"

"What the fuck is wrong with you?" Frank muttered as he opened the driver's door. "What's the problem?" he shouted as he climbed out.

"Put your hands on the top of the vehicle!"

"What is this all about?"

"Do it now or we will fire!"

"Bollocks," he shook his head and placed the palms of his hands on the roof. "What is this about?"

"Frank Dempster, you're under arrest for the murder of Jules Lee, you do not have to say anything but anything you do say may be used in evidence…………" the rest of their blurb was beyond his understanding. He couldn't focus on what they were saying. Rough hands patted him down searching for a weapon. His feet were kicked apart painfully, their boots bruising his ankle bone. "Do you understand your rights?"

"Are you fucking mad?" Frank laughed dryly. Pedestrians gathered to watch the action and the traffic trickled past in the remaining free lane, drivers rubbernecking the arrest. "I didn't shoot Jules Lee!"

"You know him then." A gruff voice said sarcastically.

"Yes, I know him," Frank raised his voice. "But I didn't shoot him!"

"Who said he was shot smartarse?" the cuffs clicked closed tightly on his wrists and the officer yanked his arms behind his back a little too hard.

"I found out this morning, I've seen a photograph," Frank blurted out in a panic. "Someone sent it in the post from Thailand."

"In the post?"

"Yes, in the post," Frank said angrily. "I had to sign for it. Check with this post office. This is bollocks!"

"You haven't been to Thailand recently?"

"No, I haven't been out of the house for over a week." He said adamantly.

"Can anyone verify that?"

"No," he mumbled.

"Can you explain why your passport was found in a holdall on the luggage belt at Manchester airport along with the gun used to shoot Mr Lee?"

"No, that's ridiculous," Frank babbled. "I haven't been out of the house and I don't own a gun!" he shouted this time but he remembered the gun which he had bought. The gun which was stolen; so was his passport. "I didn't shoot him!"

"Funny that, because it's got your prints all over it," the officers bundle him towards their car. "The police in Thailand want you deported immediately. Better get yourself a good lawyer."

CHAPTER 42

TITAN

Senior officers from every division in Titan and the lead detectives from Merseyside's MIT were either present, or attending virtually via video link. Chief Carlton sat bolt upright, reading his notes while everyone settled. The meeting was set up in the office space of the MIT. Every other desk was being used by a huddle of detectives as the investigation gathered pace.

"We have a lot do, ladies and gentlemen so I suggest we listen to the updates and then ask questions as you will," he looked for any objections. "Fine, if we're all in agreement, I'll hand over to Superintendent Ramsay, Alec if you could bring us up to speed please."

"What we've uncovered in the last week is a complicated web of organised crime on an international scale." He placed his hands on the desk and looked at the faces around the table. "The riots caused an imbalance in the crime families we're familiar with. Those without fuel crumbled while the others supplied the gaps in the market and became rich and took control quickly." Nods of agreement greeted his opening statement. Every police force was experiencing the shifts in power. "The difference was fuel. We've identified a bio diesel refinery in Kirkby who were stockpiling fuel years before the drought. When the pumps ran dry, they sold their surplus to a few key companies. One of them, Dean and Sons, is a large scale haulage company whose trucks travel regularly to the continent, Spain and North Africa, Morocco and everywhere in between. They made an alliance with officials from Brigade Security. Dean supplied them with fuel at a premium price and Brigade supplied security for all their shipments here and abroad. Their trucks were protected and we have to assume that some of them were loaded with contraband, drugs, tobacco, arms and people. When no one else was moving, they were, hence the shift in power."

"Who's in charge, Alec?" a voice from the video asked. The image of Cumbria's Chief Constable appeared on one of the screens. "I can't see a haulier suddenly becoming a godfather. Someone must be coordinating it all."

"All we know is the name 'The Priest'. He's a ghost. We're looking for Colin Dean, owner of Dean and Sons but he's not been seen since this morning. His wife is in custody. She's the bookkeeper so we have a lot of questions for her." He paused. "Carol Barker was recovered unhurt from a house in the Woolton area of the city. We are working on the theory that her captors were Brigade officers, involved in the Silver Lane incident. One was found dead at the scene murdered by this man, Kevin Warren." An image of Warren appeared. He looked much younger. "He was known to us, small time pusher, charged with armed robbery a few years back but he walked. His solicitor was paid by bank transfer from Dean and Sons. More recently though, we think he became an enforcer for Priest. He was shot resisting arrest this afternoon while we rescued Carol Barker. It looks like he was there to make them disappear. We found wire mesh and lengths of chain in his vehicle. They were probably headed for the river. My team are going through his mobile phone records etc now."

"And the Barker woman is connected to the reporter, Frank Dempster?"

"I'll let DS Bishop fill you in on him," Alec smiled thinly at his colleague.

"We have to be looking at a clean-up operation here, a reshuffle if you like," Bishop began. "Dempster and Barker were work mates. It appears they began an affair during an investigation into the importation of steroids, HGH and the like. Dempster had a bee in his bonnet about drugs in sport. During their investigation, they received information in exchange for money, from DC Baldwin, shot at Silver Lane. They were rattling the cage of a villain called, Jules Lee. We know Lee was an associate of Dean. Whether he was a customer using his company to import drugs, we don't know for sure but we will once their books have been analysed. We know Barker was acting on Baldwin's tip-off, filming the sting when she was discovered and taken hostage. The details we don't know yet, she's being treated for minor cuts and bruises and then she'll be interviewed."

"And the daughter?"

"Still missing but she must have been taken to silence Barker and Dempster. Jules Lee was found shot dead behind his bar in the Jontiem area of Pattaya, Thailand. Frank Dempster was arrested for his murder this afternoon."

"Is it solid?" Chief Carlton looked unsure.

"We have his passport and a gun with his prints all over it although he's protesting that he never left the country. Somebody travelled on his passport," Bishop shrugged. "We found a photograph of Lee's body at his home. Dempster claims it was sent by recorded delivery but the post office have no records of it being delivered by them. Their deliveryman didn't reach Dempster's house until late morning and he says he never saw him or spoke to him nor did he have a recorded envelope. If someone is setting Dempster up, then they're doing a bloody convincing job. The Thais want him extradited immediately. If they are successful and he gets sucked into their legal system, guilty or not, he'll be an old man before we see him on television again."

"Where are you with finding the girl?"

"We know this man has her," Alec frowned. Fredrick Hope appeared on the screen. "We now know that he was the younger brother of Steven Young. His name was changed by the probation service when he was convicted of a nasty sexual assault aged eleven. Hope and Colin Dean are our only connections to the Priest. Recovering Jodie Barker is our primary concern but I'm convinced if we find her, it will lead us to them. His gang are a new entity in the city a spin-off of his brother's organisation and we don't know where they operate from. We are trawling every source on the street which we can use. We'll find her."

"How are Kathy Brooks and Danny Wells?"

"Not good," Alec shook his head. "Danny Wells is critical. He's suffered several stab wounds and internal injuries. Kathy is out of the woods but she needs surgery to pin her jaw and cheekbone together. The bastard shattered her face."

"And she said their attacker claimed to be this 'Priest' character?"

"So he claimed," Alec nodded. "We know he picked up Danny Wells at a gay club called 'Coco's'. The owner was Jules Lee, which ties in that he had a connection to Dean and Priest. We raided the place and all CCTV for that night has been erased or so they say." Alec looked at Billingham for backup.

"I'm DC Billingham, from Matrix," he introduced himself. "We've had an officer in Coco's for a few months now. It's an exclusive members' only club and there's no tolerance of drug dealers in there. We know the place is rife with party drugs but we think they are supplied exclusively by the doormen. The membership list is impressive but some of them would rather remain in the closet, hence the security tapes are never running." He nodded to Alec.

Alec carried on. "Witnesses have described the man Wells left with and we'll have an artist's impression this afternoon. Once we have it, we'll distribute it. Witnesses say that Danny was happy and under no duress, when he left the club arm in arm with the guy." An embarrassed silence fell across the meeting. "The receptionist at the hotel said the man Danny signed in with matched the description of the man he left the club with. Again, there was no sign of anything untoward going on."

"What about evidence at the scene, Alec?" The Cumbrian officer asked.

"All the flat surfaces are wiped clean," Alec replied. "But we are waiting for the results on partial prints and other trace recovered. There was no bodily fluid found on Danny Wells; the attacker used a condom. We can't be sure who he was but the attacker identified himself as 'The Priest' to Kathy and Danny."

"There's no chance of finding the condom in the wastepipes?"

"It's a cheap hotel in the city centre," Alec shrugged. "Most of the rooms are rented by the hour. The sheets and towels are not changed in between which makes body hair, skin and prints virtually useless from a prosecution point of view, plus Danny went there of his own accord. There'll be more condoms in those wastepipes than we could analyse in a year." He shook his head and frowned. His celebrity chef face appeared. "What would it prove anyway? It couldn't prove he was in that room?"

"This might, Guv," Allison Wallace approached the meeting. "Sorry to interrupt but this has just come back from forensics."

"As I said earlier," Chief Carlton apologised. "We have a lot to do and this is very much an ongoing investigation so excuse the interruption. Go on, Sergeant."

"SOCO lifted fluid from the toilet flush in the bathroom. Looks like our attacker took off his condom to flush it and left seminal fluid on the handle. They have a partial thumbprint and DNA."

"Have we got a match?"

"Not on the PNC, Guv," she smiled at Alec. "But we have on the juvenile system. The DNA matches with Henry Richards. All we need to know now is what they changed his identity to. We have the warrant and probation is coming back to me any time now, Guv."

"Guv," Smithy's voice called from a desk nearby. His ginger hair was sweaty and plastered to his chubby head. "One of the numbers taken from Kevin Warren's mobile is switched on and we've got a lock on it."

"Where?" Alec stood up and walked over to the desk. The computer screen displayed a Google maps image. "That's the old docks."

"I can't pin it down any more than this, Guv," Smithy frowned. "But it's somewhere in between the dock road and the derelict warehouses on Stanley Road here."

"We heard there were some small time dealers operating from the old tanneries before the riots, Guv," Billingham said. "There are acres of disused buildings there. Uniform searched the place and found evidence of usage, needles, foil, empty beer cans but nothing more than that. The upper floors are a death trap so the search only extended to the lower areas. We took it of our list."

"Dispatch ARU and uniform to the warehouses," Alec ordered. "Seal off the dock road and Stanley road. I want those warehouses searched inch by inch. Frederick Hope could operate from there for years without being detected. If he is, Jodie Barker is in there somewhere."

CHAPTER 43

The Tannery

Colin Dean parked behind the tobacco warehouses on Stanley Road. The sun was fading rapidly turning day to night. Flurries of snow began to fall but never looked like halting the receding covering of white from thawing. The warehouses towered above him, fourteen storeys high, 27 million bricks and eight thousand tons of steel girders spreading nearly a kilometre to the river. At the time of construction, they were the biggest brick buildings on the planet. The interiors were cavernous spaces, arched roofs supported by monstrous steel columns which penetrated each storey. The expansive wood floors were splintered and warped in places, damp and rotten in others. Only a fool, or an extremely brave man would dare to navigate his way to the upper floors. Thirty thousand lead window frames set symmetrically around the massive buildings offered views of the river and the approach roads north and south. Much of the glass was long since smashed, the remaining panes clouded by a century of pollution. To his left were the tanneries, to the right the tobacco warehouses, Stanley Docks. Between them the frozen dock looked picturesque and the historic swing bridges at either end added to the morbid beauty of the place.

He walked towards the tanneries and the sound of Irish music drifted from the nearest building to the road. The Dublin Packet was open for business, three red nosed drinkers smoking outside on the pavement. Their Guinness glasses were clinked together in celebration of something which would be forgotten in the morning. They eyed him suspiciously as he slipped between the swing bridge and the pub. A gap in the wrought iron gates gave him access to the cobblestone roads beneath the warehouses. Frederick Hope would be on the fourth floor, the girl hidden on the sixth. Dean had decided to play it cool and trick Freg into believing he was going to take the girl to a hospital. Once he was at ease with the idea, he would shoot them both. Dropping them into the dock was too sloppy. Divers would find them in a few minutes. A big fire would destroy any evidence. He slipped his gun inside his coat and undid the buttons ready to draw it quickly when the time came. In the distance, the streetlights on the dock road twinkled into life, a string of yellow lanterns against the dark waters of the river beyond. A chill wind blew from the river cutting through his clothes and a cold shiver ran through his soul.

CHAPTER 44

Raymond Citrone

Citrone parked his Alfa on the dock road and checked his mobile. He thought about the situation he found himself in. Ten Years in the Drug Squad had been good to him. He'd reached sergeant level quickly and had a reputation for sourcing good quality information which led to regular arrests. Citrone understood the way drugs in the city worked. He felt that he understood more than most. It was an essential part of the city's personality, its economy and its importance within organised crime worldwide. It was one of the busiest ports in Europe and that geographic fact would never change. Goods of every description arrived from all over the planet. Drug smuggling was an undeniable part of life in Liverpool. Summer follows Spring; the sun rises every day and millions of pounds worth of drugs are trafficked through the planet's big ports. It was a fact of life that could not be changed. Eradicating drugs was impossible. He'd learned that in the early days on the job. Fighting a futile crusade against drugs would grind you down if you let it. What you had to do was to nurture the dealers who operated with some integrity and crush the scumbags who targeted kids. He used his ethnicity to build trust from the black community and also to strike fear into the white gangs. Sometimes he was their umbrella other times he was a 'brother' on a mission. He was a chameleon. He could blend into the city's jungle as and when he chose to. To do that, he had to mingle with the good and bad, scratch the right backs and tickle the right palms. If he made a thousand here and there in the process, then he saw that as a bonus. Genuine dealers knew the value of an open minded sergeant in the local DS and they rewarded his loyalty generously. Of course, if any of his fellow officers or superiors knew, he would be jailed for a long time. That's because they didn't understand how the city worked. They couldn't see the bigger picture. Generation after generation of officers had spent their entire careers fighting drug dealers, eventually growing old, retiring and then taking their place in one of the city's graveyards. Did any of them have 'Solved the world's drug trade' engraved on their headstone? No. The dealers were still there; the addicts were still there and they always would be. As long as you understood the way things work, then it couldn't grind you down. Citrone understood.

Things changed when the fuel drought hit. The stability he'd helped to control was gone. Supplies dried up, gangs turned on each other; his primary income vanished overnight. Then the Priest exploded onto the scene with a never ending supply of whatever the users wanted. He had transportation and suppliers, protection and brains and he cleaned up. No one could compete. Raymond Citrone did the only thing that he could do, join him. Financially, the status quo returned to his life but the rest of it turned to shit. Priest and the pricks at Brigade Security kept pushing and pushing. Things had become unmanageable. He was skating on ice so thin that it was no longer a case of if it would break but when it would. He had become Priest's lapdog but the situation wasn't sustainable.

He was investigating a different animal this time. They paid him to jump when they called but once he had learned enough about their weaknesses, order would be restored. The Titan investigation was shining a blinding spotlight onto the city's stinking underbelly and the parasites that lived there were running in all directions. When they called him this time, he was cautious about becoming involved but Colin Dean demanded that he meet him at the docks. He hinted at blowing Citrone's involvement wide open. It was the final insult. They had no respect for his value to their operation but he had to go along for a little while longer. Dean said some of Steven Young's old crew were creating waves. From what he'd heard at the station, that was an understatement. Frederick Hope was on borrowed time, so was Colin Dean. Citrone had to distance himself from them permanently. He climbed out of the Alfa and pulled his jacket tight to his neck. His Glock-17 was unholstered in his pocket; his fingers gripped the pistol. The wind blew off the river stinging his ears and the back of his neck. He put his head down and walked towards the warehouses.

CHAPTER 45

Sidney Powell held Jodie's hand as they weaved their way down the stairs from one floor to the next. He knew the building well and even the encroaching darkness didn't slow them down. The building seemed different tonight. For years it had offered them a haven but its vast spaces now hid demons in every dark corner. Its familiarity had morphed into foreboding. The ancient bricks now held contempt for those who dared to enter. Sid knew when he left this time, he would not be returning. Things had become too dangerous. Freg and the men above him were violent, unstable men with no regard for their employees, their lives outside of the business, or their families. The days of making a few hundred pounds a week, safely selling a bit of cocaine and some weed on their behalf, were gone. People were being killed left, right and centre. Kids were being kidnapped for Christ's sake. Mortgage or no mortgage, this was his last job.

"One more flight and then we're on the ground floor." Jodie looked up with frightened eyes and nodded imperceptibly. "Are you warm enough?"

"I'm okay but Monkey is cold," she said matter of factly. Her ragged companion was dangling from inside her coat. The sleeves nearly reached the floor. "Will my daddy be there?"

"I'm not sure," Sid lied. He had heard about Ged Barker on the news. Everyone had heard. "We'll get you to the police first and they can find your parents, okay?" She nodded silently again. Her eyes said she didn't believe him. She was six but she was smart. Sid knew from his own daughters that they were much smarter than their years. Jodie was no different. His relationship with them had grown tighter since Jodie was brought to the warehouse. He was a father and he recognised the desperation her parents would be feeling. If anyone took his daughters, he would kill them without a second thought. "We're nearly there, just over here and then out of that door. I bet you can't wait to go home, eh?" Jodie nodded again but her expression was one of uncertainty. "Don't look so worried."

"Where is Frederick?" a voice startled them. Jodie clung to Sid's leg, hiding behind him. "And where do you think you're taking her?"

"Mr James," Sid stuttered. "Freg said to take her for a walk while they sort out another room for her. The floorboards in the old one fell through. She was a bit frightened." He winked as if he was lying for Jodie's sake. "He said make sure that I took care of her. If you know what I mean."

Colin Dean stared at him. The story sounded credible. Maybe Hope had grown a backbone and arranged for her to be killed. "Where is he?" He repeated the question.

"I'm right here, Mr James," Freg was behind him in the shadows. "What brings you here at night?"

"I was passing," Dean turned towards him. "I said you had forty eight hours and I'm checking up to see if everything had been sorted." His blond hair reflected the yellow glow from the street lights making it look tinged with green. "Obviously, it's in hand."

"You could have phoned, Mr James," Freg tilted his head. "Why didn't you call?"

"Don't push your luck, Frederick."

"Take Jodie out, Sid," Freg said without taking is eyes from Dean's. "Do it now."

"Stay there," Dean turned and pointed at Sid and the girl. His right hand moved to his coat. "Do not move."

"Reach for that gun and I'll drop you where you stand," Freg stepped out of the shadows. A Skorpion machine pistol pointed at Dean. "Go now!" he ordered. Sid looked from one to the other and squeezed Jodie's hand. They walked quickly into the dark shadows, disappearing from sight in seconds. "Now we need a chat about your boss." Freg gestured towards the stairs with the machine gun. "Sit down." Dean tucked his coat underneath his behind and sat down. Freg neared and held out his right hand. "Pass me the gun, fingertips only or I'll spread your brains all over the wall."

The stairs creaked as Dean shifted his weight to pass him the gun. "Where is he taking the girl?" he asked as Freg stuck the pistol into his waistband.

"Somewhere safe," Freg stepped back. "I'll ask the questions."

"Fuck you."

"Fuck you, with your shit hair!" Freg snapped. "Who the fuck do you think you are?"

"You're in deep shit," Dean smiled.

"What is your real name?"

"Kenny Daglish."

"Funny," Freg smiled. "Do we have to go back to basics, you know I shoot you in the foot then you answer a question. Then you get arsey and I shoot you again, then you answer another one?"

"Colin Dean," he grunted. "Remember that well."

"Mr James?" Freg laughed. "Colin Dean goes to James Dean then Mr James, right?"

"You should try Mastermind."

"Which fucking brain box came up with that?"

"Fuck you."

"I think I prefer Mr James."

"I couldn't give a fuck what you prefer."

"Where do I find Henry Richards?" Freg crouched and kept the gun on him. He watched the expression on his face. He looked confused.

"What are you talking about?" Dean shrugged. "I don't know anyone called Henry."

"Okay, where do I find the Priest?"

"He doesn't like being bothered, Frederick," Dean smiled. "He's not a patient man. I could pass a message on for you."

"Oh, what I have to say to him needs to be said face to face," Freg grimaced. "Did you know he was born Henry Richards?"

"No but it doesn't surprise me if he's using a different name."

"Yes, but if you knew why he had to change it, then you might look at him differently," Freg tapped his nose. "He's a sick paedophile."

Dean couldn't argue. He knew Priest was sexually different to the norm. He'd heard rumours about him roughing up sexual partners. "It doesn't make any difference to me."

"Where can I find him?"

"You can't."

"I will," Freg shrugged, "with, or without you." A shuffling noise distracted Freg slightly. He was used to sharing the building with armies of rodents, some as big as cats. "Just tell me where he is and you can go."

"Put the gun down!" Citrone shouted. "I found these two at the front of the building." He pushed Sid and Jodie towards Freg. "What the fuck is going on?" He pointed his Glock at Freg. Sid and Jodie looked frightened and unsure what to do.

"Step away from him," Freg said. Sid looked nervous as he took Jodie by the hand and walked away from them.

"Where are you taking her?" Citrone didn't interfere or threaten them. "This is a mess!"

"Put your gun down, dickhead!" Freg turned the Skorpion towards him. "Get her out of here!" He shouted to Sid. "Go that way!" Sid pulled Jodie's hand and headed in the opposite direction to where they'd come from. Dean stood up and walked towards the black detective. "Quickly, Sid get her away from here!" Sid took a glance back at Freg, nodded and ran; Jodie was half pulled and half carried but she moved her legs as fast as she could. Their shapes vanished in the gloom, their footsteps fading fast.

"I'm going to reach for my badge," Citrone said calmly. "I'm a police officer. Now put the gun down slowly and no one gets hurt."

"I don't care who you are," Freg said calmly. "But if you are a police officer then you know what this is." He gestured to his weapon. "It's a Skorpion with a twenty round clip. It'll cut you both down in seconds, so put your gun down on the floor and step back."

"I can't do that."

"I want to know where I can find Henry Richards, then I'm gone. What you two do is up to you."

"How do you know that was his name?" Citrone asked surprised.

"Let's say we knew each other when we were younger."

"Okay," Citrone nodded. "What do you want to find him for?"

"I need to settle an old score," Freg grimaced. "So tell me where I can find him and we all go our separate ways."

"Shoot him," Dean snapped. "He's nothing."

"Shut up," Citrone said angrily. "Let me handle this. You've caused enough problems, idiot!" They looked at each other as the sound of sirens wailed in the distance. "The police are on their way."

"I'll find him one way or another," Freg stepped closer. "Five seconds, where is he?"

"Put the gun down!" Citrone said calmly.

"Four."

"Three seconds," Freg warned.

"The girl is getting away!" Dean shouted. "Kill him and let's get this shit cleaned up once and for all!"

"Two seconds."

"Listen to me," Citrone held up a hand to stop the imaginary clock.

"Kill him!" Dean shouted.

"One second."

"Wait!" Citrone sensed that he was going to open fire. He raised the Glock, turned to the right and fired.

Colin Dean was knocked backwards by the first shot. His face was a picture of painful surprise. The second shot hit him in the teeth before blowing an egg sized hole through the back of neck. He crumpled to the floor, dead before he landed. His blond hair turned deep red. "I'm with you, okay!" He turned to Freg. "We need to talk," Citrone held his hand up again. This time Freg nodded and listened.

"Go on."

"We haven't got long. Henry Richards was given the name David Chapel. He calls himself the Priest. This is where he stays sometimes." He held out a folded note but Freg was too cautious to take it. "There will be armed police all over the place in a minute, take it and go. I want him dead as much as you do."

"Who are you?" Freg kept the machinegun on him as he took the note and looked at it. "What's your name?"

"Detective Citrone," he nodded. "We both want Priest dead, so go."

"Citrone?"

"Yes," he nodded. "You need to get out of here."

"Did you know the doctor?" Freg's eyes narrowed.

"What doctor?"

"Doctor Holland," Freg cocked his head. "He was a junkie."

"Maybe," Citrone lied. Something in his eyes gave it away. A tick or a tiny twitch, something. "The name doesn't ring a bell."

"He told me that two Brigade officers lifted him and took him to you, remember?"

"No, I don't remember his name."

"Did you squeeze him for information?"

"We don't have time for this!"

"Did you?"

"I don't know any Doctor Holland."

"He said you were putting the squeeze on him."

"Bullshit."

"I don't think he was lying," Freg smiled sourly at the memory of the frightened old man on the trawler. "You see he was begging for his life when he told us."

"I don't know him."

"Do you know his minders?" Freg pointed to Dean's body. "They're a couple of monsters called Kevin Warren and Michael Yates?"

"I know them," Citrone nodded. "But I don't know any doctor."

"You see, they told the doctor about you. They said Priest told Mr James that he gave you information about my brother." The sirens grew louder and increased in numbers. They echoed through the warehouse seeming to come from every direction.

"What," Citrone hissed. "Who the fuck is your brother?"

"'Was'," Freg felt his blood temperature rising. "Who the fuck 'was' my brother, you mean."

"Okay, who was your brother?" Citrone asked slowly. He felt fingers of cold fear tickling his mind. His fingers tightened on the Glock.

"Steven Young."

Citrone's eyes flickered with recognition. He knew instantly that he'd been rumbled. Quick as rattlesnake he raised the gun and fired. Freg squeezed the trigger and screamed as the Skorpion kicked in his hand, "Baaasssstard!"

When the thunderous gunshots stopped, the smoking weapons lay on the ground, a growing pool of blood surrounding them slowly.

CHAPTER 46

Six Months Later

The waiter knew he'd see the couple before but she looked different somehow. There was something wrong with her face. The last time she'd looked aesthetically beautiful but the symmetry had been altered. The change was subtle but noticeable. He looked the same. His likeness to the pesky television chef was uncanny. They'd picked the same table overlooking the Albert Dock and their choice from the menu was almost the same. He remembered things like that.

"Would you like the same wine?" he smiled. "It was the Shiraz if I remember rightly."

Alec looked at Kathy for her agreement. "Yes, that would be nice," she said quietly. Her half smile was tinged with sadness. It never quite reached the corners of her lips. "If that's okay with you, Alec."

"Yes," Alec agreed. He could sense the change in her. Her demeanour had transformed. She had gone from being a confident bubbly woman to a withdrawn nervous victim. "We can start with that." He smiled but she was looking through the window, distracted by the vista. Alec followed her gaze. "A different scene, this time around."

"The difference is startling," Kathy nodded. "The sunshine certainly brings the crowds out." The docks were busy with tourists of many different ethnicities. She had heard languages which she couldn't identify as they walked to the restaurant. "I guess life goes on regardless."

"It has too, Kathy," Alec touched her hand. She withdrew it sharply. Her reaction was involuntary. "Sorry," Alec felt awkward.

"No, don't apologise," she tried a smile. "I'm still finding my feet that's all."

"It will take a while," Alec nodded. "When do you think you'll be back at work?"

"I'm not sure."

"It would do you good to get back into a routine," Alec smiled. "It worked for me after Gail died."

"Did it though, Alec?" she said flatly. "Don't you think people were walking on egg shells around you, feeling sorry for you?"

"Not that I noticed," Alec frowned. He couldn't understand why she was being so contrary. "People care about you, Kathy."

"Yes, I've noticed," she shrugged. "Sympathy is just what I need right now."

"We miss you, you know?" he laughed. "I've got no one to moan to when things aren't going to plan."

"Do they ever go to plan?" Her inner sadness was there in every word.

"Who knows what the plan is in the first place?" Alec tried to lighten the conversation. She had been quiet and distracted from the moment he'd picked her up. It had taken weeks of persuasion to get her to agree to come out for a meal. She hadn't been out of the house for months. "What doesn't kill you makes you stronger."

"Does it?" Kathy raised her eyebrows and played with her placemat. "I don't feel any stronger."

"You look fantastic, Kathy," Alec smiled. "I thought you were going to die."

"I look disfigured."

"You don't" Alec objected. "The doctors did a marvellous job."

"They did their best," Kathy said softly. "Considering what they were dealing with. There were always going to be lasting deformities."

"Come on, Kathy," Alec leaned closer. "Deformed is a strong word to use. You are still beautiful."

"Still, Alec?" she asked. "Still beautiful despite the disfigurement?"

"That's not what I meant." Alec softened his voice. "You don't see what I see when I look at you."

"Oh I do, Alec," she said irritably. "I see my new face every time I look in the mirror. I see my disfigured face every day and every night. I see how my family and friends look at me now." She looked at the crowds enjoying the shops in the sunshine. Families walking with ice creams, couples holding hands, none of it seemed to matter. "I see the reaction on their faces when they first see me. I see shock and do you know what else I see in their eyes, Alec?"

"No."

"Pity!" her eyes filled up. She sat back and bit her bottom lip as the wine arrived. The waiter sensed the atmosphere and poured the wine with a nod of his head before making a sharp exit. "They feel sorry for me, no one says it but they don't have to. I can see it in their eyes just as I can see it in yours."

"Kathy," Alec was speechless.

"Let's change the subject."

Alec sat back and thought about his next words carefully. She was fragile, very fragile. He hadn't realised just how traumatised she'd been. Priest had broken more than her face, he'd broken her spirit. "I spoke to Carol Barker last week."

"How is she?"

"Coping," Alec replied. Kathy's eyes reacted for a second and he immediately regretted using that word.

"What, you mean she's coping and I'm not?"

"It was a poor choice of words," Alec shrugged. "I just meant that she's adjusting to life with Jodie. She seems to be doing okay on her own."

"And Jodie?" Kathy tried to keep the anger out of her voice. It wasn't Alec's fault. She knew he was trying but even the slightest comment made her fly off the handle. "Has she gone back to school?"

"Yes," Alec smiled. "She's a pretty little thing. They're resilient at that age; seem to adjust better than we do."

Kathy took a mouthful of wine and stood up quickly. She walked away from the table towards the toilets without a word. Her face was red and flushed with anger. "Jesus, Alec!" he mumbled to himself. "For God's sake think about what you're saying." A couple stopped in front of the window, deciding whether to dine there or not. They laughed and held hands as they walked on. Alec couldn't help but feel the loss of his wife. He envied them. Loneliness was a terrible thing. Gail must have felt lonely despite being married. She had been alone most of their married life. He saw Kathy returning and readied himself to try to be more subtle.

"I'm sorry, Alec," she said. She sat down and sipped her wine. "I'm not myself yet. I feel so angry."

"You are bound to feel like that," Alec said. "It's only natural to be angry, bitter and pissed off with the world generally. What happened to you was horrific. You need to focus your anger in the right direction."

"You mean stop biting your head off?" she smiled but the sparkle in her eyes had gone. "I'm sorry."

"Please don't apologise," he raised his glass. "There's no need."

The waiter brought their garlic mushrooms and placed them on the table. "Any black pepper or parmesan?"

"Both for me," Alec welcomed his company however fleeting.

"Me too," Kathy didn't look at him. She didn't look at men in the eye any more. The waiter sprinkled the cheese and pepper, topped up their glasses and left to attend to other customers. The restaurant was full and several couples were waiting near the till for tables to become free.

"Danny Wells has settled back in," Alec said. He ate a mushroom and wondered if that was the best thing to talk about.

"I see him often," Kathy said. "He's been staying with me most weekends."

"I suppose his nightclubbing days had to end sometime," Alec shrugged. "He's thrown himself back into his work a little too enthusiastically," Alec raised his eyebrows. "They have to force him to go home. He's been trawling through case evidence until the early hours, unless Libby sends him home."

"It's his way of coping."

"It's obsessive," Alec corrected her. "He's a talented scientist but he needs to leave the police work to us."

"How is the investigation going?" she changed the subject subtly.

"Into Richards?"

"Yes." She looked at him strangely. "I realise you must have other cases on the go obviously but that was the one I was referring to." She sounded almost offended again.

"His network disintegrated," Alec chewed a mushroom. He swallowed it despite it being too hot. "With Colin Dean and Citrone dead, his transportation was wiped out overnight. Raymond Citrone was his feed from the force, which was another nail in the coffin," Alec sipped his wine to wash down the food. "The contract with the plastics was rescinded at last and their investors went to the wall. His company had the controlling stake."

"Did you track Hope down?" she kept her eyes on his.

"There was a lot of blood where they found Citrone, DNA belongs to Hope but we didn't find him," Alec shook his head. "Dr Libby doubts he could have survived the blood loss but we'll never know unless we find a body."

"What about Henry Richards?" her face darkened at the mention of his name.

"We're close, Kathy," he nodded. "His shell company was broke and we froze all his assets. He also upset some very dangerous suppliers abroad. We know he fled to Spain but his villa was torched a week later. He's on the run."

"Where?"

"We're not sure," Alec pushed another mushroom into his mouth to mask the lie.

"You're lying," she put her fork down.

"We know he's back in this country," Alec sipped his wine. "It's safer here for him and he doesn't have any money that we know of. Being on the run abroad costs money."

"Men like that always have money."

"We're close, Kathy, trust me," Alec said.

"Where do you think he is?"

"You're not in any danger, Kathy," Alec pushed his plate away and sat back. His appetite had gone. "You know Dr Libby has been looking after Danny while he settles back in?"

"Quick change of subject there, Alec."

"He thinks Danny has a major guilt complex about what happened to you."

"We've spoken about it," Kathy snapped. "Nobody is blaming him, especially me. We're very close since it happened."

"Does he talk about his guilt?"

"You sound like he should feel guilty, Alec." He eyes burned into his.

"I have had my moments," Alec screwed up his napkin and dumped it on the table. He sipped the wine and smiled sourly. "What happened to you shook me, Kathy."

"What do you mean 'had your moments'?"

"About blaming Danny," Alec shrugged. "I know he was being forced to call you but I have to ask myself that if I was in the same situation, would I have called you." He sat back and placed his hands on the table. "When I answer the question, the answer is no way, not a chance."

"How can you say that, Alec?" she asked incredulously. "Unless you have been in that situation, how can you possibly say that?"

"Easily," Alec said adamantly. "Nine out of ten men in that situation would not have called you, no matter what the consequences."

"He was being tortured, Alec."

"What did he think would happen to you?"

"He was terrified and in agony," Kathy's voice went up a pitch. "He thought he was going die."

"Well if the truth be known, he shouldn't have been in that situation, should he?"

Kathy spat a laugh out but there was no mirth in it. "Oh, I see," she nodded he head slowly as she spoke. "So he shouldn't have been there but he was because he's a puff?" She raised her voice and neighbouring diners glanced at them.

"It's not something that could have happened to just anyone is it?" he countered. Her aggression and contrariness were beginning to annoy him.

"Why not?" she was astounded.

"Because not everyone would have gone there in the first place for God's sake." Alec smiled sarcastically at the noisy diners nearby. "He was there because of the way he is."

"Gay?"

"No, gay and promiscuous," Alec snapped. "That lot are going to hotels in town with anything that moves. It's only a matter of time before they go off with a bad one is it?"

"There's nothing like a stereotype is there, Alec?" She wiped her hand son her napkin. "You know what?"

"What?"

"I think this was a bad idea," she shook her head.

"Oh, come on, Kathy," Alec frowned. "How could he make that call knowing what the animal was going to do?"

"He was terrified."

"Yes, for good reason too!" Alec banged his hand on the table. The diners in earshot fell silent. The conversation on Alec's table was far more interesting than their own. "He realised he could save his own skin by doing what he was told to do, calling a defenceless woman!"

"You mean it couldn't happen to a straight man, a real man, Alec?"

"Did you know he made a complaint against one of his former boyfriends for assault?" Alec leaned forward and lowered his voice.

"Yes, I did," she replied angrily. "What's that got to do with anything?"

"The case was dropped because Danny admitted that they had rough sex regularly," Alec spat the words in disgust. "How did he end up tied face down on the bed in a hotel, have you thought about that?"

"I'm leaving, Alec," she went to move. "I cannot believe what a homophobic pig you are."

"I am not homophobic!" Alec snapped way too loud. He looked around at the startled faces. The waiter had stopped, frozen in time, two plates of lasagne balanced precariously in his hands. Silence fell across the restaurant. The phone behind the reception desk pierced the silence but the receptionist ignored it and stared at the rowing couple seated in the window. "He's a pervert and that's all there is to it. He should never have been there and the spineless bastard should never have called you." He glared at the mesmerised diners as he finished speaking. He looked at the waiter and shrugged. "I think we had better have the bill please, when you can close your mouth and stop gawking at me." He loosened the collar on his shirt and felt the sheen of sweat on his skin. He cleared his throat nervously. "I'll drop you at home, Kathy." He lowered his voice.

"I'd rather walk over broken glass, in my bare feet, than get in the car with you," she stood and stormed across the restaurant for the second time. This time, she didn't come back.

CHAPTER 47

Epilogue

Alec slammed the passenger door closed. He was glad he'd left his jacket at the station; the sun's rays warmed him. The glare from the sea forced him to squint. A flock of seagulls circled overhead squawking his arrival to the world. One of the bigger birds swooped clumsily and snatched a ham sandwich from the clutches of a baffled toddler. As the realisation that his dinner had been stolen hit home, he crumpled in his buggy and cried as if his lungs would burst. His mother put her cigarette on the sea wall and handed him one of her chips, careful not to spill the can of Strongbow she held. The offering seemed to quell his tears. Alec looked at her tattoos and wondered if he belonged to the same race of human beings as the tourists on Blackpool promenade.

"DS Smith and Superintendent Ramsay, Merseyside MIT," Smithy showed his badge to a uniformed officer tasked with policing the vehicles outside the hotel. He looked harassed. A coach was double parked near the kerb, a second one behind it, engines running. The drivers were animated and angry about something. "Inspector Johnston is expecting us."

"If you swear at me once more, I'll have you nicked," the officer barked at the drivers. He turned to the detectives. "Sorry about this, it's been chaotic out here," he pointed to the coaches. "They're on the fourth floor, Sir," the officer pointed them towards the main entrance. "Could you leave me the keys in case we need to shift up?"

"No problem," Smithy handed the key over. Alec nodded a greeting to the officer as they walked though the yellow tape. "Looks like a nice place, Guv." Smithy said sarcastically. The Metropolitan had a Victorian facade, once palatial, but now cracked and dilapidated. Fluorescent cardboard in a myriad of shapes and sizes adorned the huge windows advertising a variety of doubles for a pound. The paintwork was discoloured and peeling from the frames. Alec laughed as they climbed the wide steps into the foyer. The smell of damp and stale beer hit them, making the urge to walk back into the sunshine almost irresistible. Alec thought he could easily leave a shoe behind on the sticky carpet if he wasn't careful.

"The lifts are to the left of the stairs, Guv," another uniformed officer guided them. "The inspector is waiting for you."

"Have they closed the hotel?" Alec asked.

"Yes, Guv," he nodded. "A lot of the guests are due to check out and another lot are on coaches waiting to check in. The inspector wants everyone interviewed before the guests leave."

"Good luck with that," Smithy smiled. They headed to the stairs and called the lift. Creaking noises from within the shaft announced the arrival of the car and the doors binged open. "Do you think it will make it to the fourth floor, Guv?"

"Better check the loading limit."

"I've lost some weight, Guv."

"Taking your coat off doesn't count as losing weight."

"Permission to tell you to fuck off, Guv?"

"Permission granted."

"Fuck off, Guv."

The lift rattled to the fourth floor and pinged again as the doors opened. They stepped out onto a hideously patterned carpet which was mottled with discarded chewing gum around the lift doors. The shiny black circles diminished in numbers as they moved away from the lift. "Classy," Alec commented. A gaggle of detectives and uniformed officers were gathered halfway down the corridor to their right. They stopped talking and watched the strangers curiously. "DS Ramsay?" one of them asked. His appearance was dishevelled but business like. Alec could tell at a glance he was in charge.

"DI Johnston?" he held out his hand and recognised the Masonic handshake. "Thanks for you cooperation on this."

"No problem," he said. He shook hands with Smithy without any further introductions. "It's not very pretty. My governor told me to call you when we showed him the message on the wall. He thinks it's your man."

He led them a few yards down the corridor and stepped to the side at the doorway to room 403, allowing them to enter first. The familiar smell of death reached them before they stepped inside; a mixture of copper, vomit and excrement. The faded pink carpet was splattered with blood near the bed. Arterial spray created a fan pattern from the bed, across a small cabinet and up the wall. Some of the globules had made a journey down the wall, gravity adding to the design. The heavy drapes were closed and a standard lamp illuminated the gory scene.

The victim was handcuffed face down on the bed, his arms extended as if he was diving into a swimming pool. The face was swollen and distended, bruises and contusions distorting the skin colour. A thick belt was fixed around his head acting as a gag. It had been attached so tightly that the lips were pulled back unnaturally close to the ears. Congealed blood encrusted the nose and chin and jagged stab wounds gapped on the forehead and cheek. A deep serrated gash ran from the left ear, across the windpipe and up to the right ear. The white gristle of the trachea could be clearly seen.

"He took a hell of a beating," Johnston said. "Then the killer slit his throat with that bottle before inserting it into the anus."

"Frederick Hope?" Smithy said. "Fits his MO."

Alec nodded and looked at Smithy. Above the bed scrawled in blood were the words;

paedophile bastard the priest is dead!

....

Across the promenade the Central Pier was busy. Tourists scurried between video games and side stalls. The smell of fish and chips mingled with fresh doughnuts and candy floss. Fruit machines and video games competed to make the loudest noises and the droning voice of the donkey derby commentator seemed to follow wherever he walked. He stopped and picked up a machine gun. The urge to squeeze the trigger and blow away the zombies on the screen was too much to resist. He slipped a pound coin into the slot and it slipped straight back out. "Bastard," he muttered and slipped it in again. The coin rattled through the machine and back out again. "Last chance," he warned the machine. This time the coin stuck and lights flashed indicating that one player could begin blowing the arms and legs off the army of zombies. He bit his lip as he blasted the rotting corpses, the gun vibrating in his hand as he waged war on the un-dead. It felt good. He felt good. A huge weight had been lifted from his shoulders. The wrong that had been inflicted on him and others was finally put right. The act of torturing and killing a sick pig like Richards was easy. To do it to an innocent human being would be unthinkable but he didn't regard Richards as a human. He was evil personified inside a bloated living breathing body. Not any more; the evil was dead and the natural balance restored. Anger, humiliation and guilt released in one simple act of murder.

The time ran out and the gun stopped vibrating. He placed it back into its holster and walked through the bleeping madness of machines onto the pier. The sun was shining and the sound of gulls calling soothed his being. He headed for the Ferris wheel and joined the short queue. A couple in matching shell suits took the first cradle, the safety bar barely clicking into place over their swollen bellies. Two women took the second cradle, their boots, lumberjack shirts and severe haircuts putting them squarely in the lesbian camp. He could spot them a mile away.

"You a single rider, mate?"

"Yes," he replied with a smile. He enjoyed his own company most of the time, today especially. "Just me." He smiled as he sat in the cradle. It swung gently as the wheel rotated, carrying him up a cradle at a time as more riders climbed aboard. The sky was as blue as he'd ever seen it; three wisps of cloud were lost against its vastness. As he looked around, he could see the mountains of Snowdonia in the far distance, their silhouettes resembling a herd of elephants walking trunk to tail in a line. The golden sands were dotted with holidaymakers enjoying the sun. Their numbers became sparser the closer to the sea they were. Only the most determined made it to the waves as the tide sucked the sea out, and out, threatening never to return again. Everything felt perfect. His life would start over today. What was done was done. It couldn't be changed. His mobile rang and he smiled at the name on the screen.

"What happened?"

"It's done, Kathy," Danny Wells smiled and closed his eyes, letting the sun warm his face. "He's dead. We're safe now."

Author Biography

Conrad Jones, Biography. /Conrad Jones is a 47-year-old Author, originally from a sleepy green-belt called Tarbock Green, which is situated on the outskirts of Liverpool.

His family relocated to the Welsh port, Holyhead on the Island of Anglesey the year he left school and bought a small taxi company. Conrad moved with them and worked in a number of trades including kitchen assistant, construction of children's adventure playgrounds and a spell hairdressing before branching out to run his own business as a market trader. He spent a number of years in and around North Wales before starting his career as a trainee manger with McDonalds Restaurants in 1989. He worked in management at McDonalds Restaurants Ltd from 1989-2002, working his way up to Business Consultant (area manager) working in the corporate and franchised departments.

On March 23rd 1993 he was managing the Restaurant in Warrington`s Bridge St when two Irish Republican Army bombs exploded directly outside the store, resulting in the death of two young boys and many casualties. Along with hundreds of other people there that day Conrad was deeply affected by the attack, which led to a long-term interest in the motivation and mind set of criminal gangs. He links this experience with the early desire to write books on the subject. His early novels follow the adventures of an elite counter terrorist unit, The Terrorist Task Force, and their enigmatic leader, John Tankersley, or `Tank` although his later books follow Detective Alec Ramsey and the Major Investigation Team.

His novels are set in the North West and North Wales. In 2007, he set off on an 11-week tour of the USA. The Day before he boarded the plane, Madeleine Mcann disappeared and all through the holiday he followed the American news reports which had little information about her. He didn't realise it at the time, but the terrible kidnap would inspire, The Child Taker years later. During the trip, he received news that his house had been burgled and his work van and equipment stolen. That summer was the year when York and Tewksbury were flooded by a deluge and insurance companies were swamped with claims. They informed him that they couldn't do anything for weeks and that returning home would be a wasted journey. Rendered unemployed on a beach in Clearwater, Florida, he decided to begin his first book, Soft Target. He never stopped writing after that.

He has reached over 200,000 downloads of his thriller novels and has had 7 books on the top 100 kindle charts, 3 number ones and an Amazon clicks Reader's book of the month award. Recently he has 8 stand alone novels and a horror thriller, Nine Angels and the biographies of three time world champion Russ Williams (Undisputed) and extraordinary lady, Debby Hughes (Lapping it Up).

Current Status

All of the previously published kindle thriller novels became best sellers in February 2011 because of the Kindle explosion. I now have well over 150,000 downloads so far. I am extremely excited at being published by a traditional publisher and a three book deal as the first offering is more than any author could dream of. There is a sense of excitement tinged with anxiety as many better writers have fallen flat in the paperback world. Fingers crossed that with the right marketing, word of mouth and a lot of luck, my novels will succeed. Making a living from the work that I love so much is a gift that I appreciate very much. I am a lucky man. For more information you can contact Conrad via Facebook or at jonesconrad5@aol.com

Bibliography

Soft Target

Soft Target 11 'Tank'

Soft Target 111 'Jerusalem'

18th Brigade

Blister

Alec Ramsay series

The Child Taker

Criminal Revenge

Criminally Insane

Frozen Betrayal

The Hunting Angels series

A Child for the Devil

Hunting Angels

An Angel Falls

Dark Angels

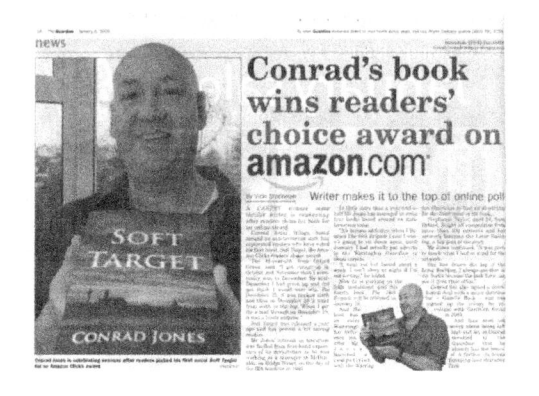

Could writer's character be cinema's new Jason Bourne?

Film producers interested in buying film rights

Conrad's book wins readers' choice award on amazon.com

Burglary gave me time to be author

Atrocity inspires novel

GOT a story or need to advertise? Call 01248 387400
E mail news@northwaleschronicle.co.uk
Distribution enquiries 01352 707033

NEWS

Author foretold Mumbai attacks

By GEOFF ABBOTT
geoff.abbott@mwn.co.uk

A HOLYHEAD author who survived an IRA bombing chillingly predicted last week's massacre in Mumbai in his first book published earlier this year.

In his thriller Soft Target, Conrad Jones tells the story of Middle Eastern terrorists who attack popular resorts and the task force sent to stop them.

The book's plot is almost a blueprint of the events leading up to the bloodbath in Mumbai's Leopold Café, Taj Mahal Palace and Oberoi Hotels where 172 victims were gunned down.

Soft Target's first chapter opens with an innocent family-outing in Florida where a suicide bomber dressed as Mickey Mouse infiltrates a crowded leisure complex and blows himself up.

The attacks escalate to a series of co-ordinated attacks at three hotels in Las vegas where terrorist snipers use residential balconies to target their victims.

"It's a bit scary really and I can't reel it in," said Conrad, whose fourth book 18th Brigade will be published this month.

Author Conrad Jones   Reader picture

"The first book Soft Target starts off at tourist destinations predominently in America and there's a chapter in Las vegas which is almost identical to what happened in Mumbai.

"To be honest it's a strange feeling to see that happening but it wasn't a surprise.

"I think it was only a matter of time when something like this would happen," he said.

In March 1993, Conrad was working as an assistant manager at MacDonald's in Bridge Street, Warrington, when the IRA exploded two bombs planted in cast iron litter bins.

The first blast outside Boots drove panicking shoppers towards the second bomb outside Argos which exploded seconds later showering the victims in shrapnel and killing Jonathan Ball, aged three, and Tim Parry,12.

Conrad said the harrowing memories of the Warrington bombings have scarred him for life but admits to using his books as a kind of "therapy" to relieve the trauma.

"It's one of those Kennedy moments because everyone remembers where they were when the bombs went off in Warrington," said Conrad referring to the assassination of American President J F Kennedy in 1963.

"When the first blast went off I knew it was a bomb and when the second one went off it was a gut-wrenching feeling," he recalls.

"When I write about these things I can put it into the pages from my own personal experience. I suppose it's my own self-therapy."

Is this a dagger I see before me? Conrad is going for gold

Printed in Great Britain
by Amazon